Praise for Sha
THE SHUDDE

"The world is coming apart at the seams in this impressive fantasy from Shinn. Once separate, the lands of the continent were bound together by the god Cordelan, so that the bounties of each would benefit the others. United, they have flourished—but they hold a dark secret. . . . Throughout, Shinn balances vivid worldbuilding, captivating characters, and a fascinating mystery. Readers won't want to put this down."

—*Publishers Weekly*

"Sharon Shinn creates a rich world balanced on the edge of disaster, with evocative, engaging characters, each with a piece of a desperately vital mystery to unravel."

—Martha Wells, author of The Murderbot Diaries

"World-altering stakes, drenched in mystery, and woven with the promise of love. Outstanding."

—Kay Kenyon
author of the forthcoming novel, *The Girl Who Fell into Myth*

"Sharon Shinn's many fans will be delighted once again by her intricate world-building, diverse characters, and complex plotting. From a beautiful noblewoman to a lost child, a mysterious priest and a fierce woman warrior, *The Shuddering City* is full of romantic and heroic figures, with enough adventure to please every fantasy reader. It's so good to have a new Shinn to lose ourselves in!"

—Louisa Morgan
author of *A Secret History of Witches* and *The Great Witch of Brittany*

"True to its title, *The Shuddering City* trembles, rumbles, shakes, and quakes. Precarious, intense, and apparently effortless, Sharon Shinn's newest novel balances between points of view and points in time like a tightrope walker dancing between two cliffs. Stakes couldn't be higher—hearts, lives, worlds—nor the rewards more plentiful. Shinn weaves a complex and human fantasy with passionate deftness, nuance, intricacy, and long-lasting warmth."

—C. S. E. Cooney, author of *Saint Death's Daughter*

"A fantastic example of a story that centers on friendship and parent-child relationships while also including important romances . . . A fast, engrossing story."

—Rachel Neumeier, author of the Tuyo series

THE SHUDDERING CITY

Also by Sharon Shinn

Uncommon Echoes
Echo in Onyx
Echo in Emerald
Echo in Amethyst

The Samaria series
Archangel
Jovah's Angel
The Alleluia Files
Angelica
Angel-Seeker

The Twelve Houses series
Mystic and Rider
The Thirteenth House
Dark Moon Defender
Reader and Raelynx
Fortune and Fate

The Elemental Blessings series
Troubled Waters
Royal Airs
Jeweled Fire
Unquiet Land

The Shifting Circle series
The Shape of Desire
Still-Life with Shape-Shifter
The Turning Season

Young adult novels
The Safe-Keeper's Secret
The Truth-Teller's Tale
The Dream-Maker's Magic
General Winston's Daughter
Gateway

Standalones and Graphic Novels
The Shape-Changer's Wife
Wrapt in Crystal
Heart of Gold
Summers at Castle Auburn
Jenna Starborn
Shattered Warrior

Collections
Quatrain
Shadows of the Past
Angels and Other Extraordinary Beings

THE SHUDDERING CITY

SHARON SHINN

FAIRWOOD PRESS
Bonney Lake, WA

THE SHUDDERING CITY

A Fairwood PressBook
November 2022

First Edition

Fairwood Press
21528 104th Street Court East
Bonney Lake, WA 98391
www.fairwoodpress.com

Cover image © 2021 by Filograph, Getty Images
Cover and book design by Patrick Swenson

ISBN: 978-1-958880-00-5
Fairwood Press Trade Edition: November 2022
Printed in the United States of America

Four quarters, four bridges,
four keys, four hearts

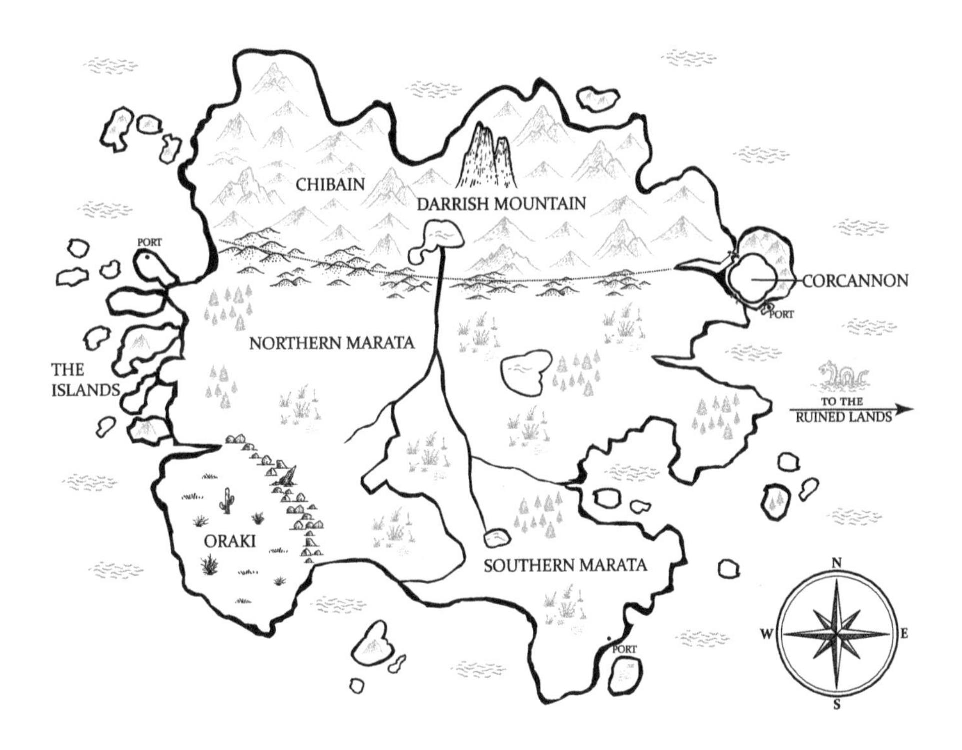

Map by Andy Holbrook

Chapter One:
Pietro

Pietro was sleeping when the world shook so hard it felt like it was coming apart. He tumbled awake and tried to roll upright, but the ground was bucking so violently that he kept being tossed back to his unyielding bed. From nearby came cries of terror and warning, and he glanced around wildly, trying to understand where he was and what was happening.

Outdoors. Apparently camping without a tent on some flat place of dancing rocks and gesticulating trees. The sky was a shredded black beginning to fray to dawn. In the faint light, Pietro could see dozens of other travelers trying to rise from their own temporary beds, shouting in confusion and alarm. As he stared, still trying to orient himself, a large tree ripped from the ground with a mighty crack and slammed onto a scrabbling mound of colorful blankets. Fresh shrieks filled the air with piercing urgency.

Someone was hurt. Maybe several someones. *Have to help,* Pietro thought, and tried again to push himself to his feet. But another tremor rolled beneath him, and he fell back to his blankets with so much force that he briefly could not think or feel. All around him were more shouts, sounds of rock hitting rock, another great *crack!* and agonizing thump as an even taller tree came down.

"The bridge!" someone was shouting, and then dozens of people were shouting. "The bridge! The bridge! *It's breaking!"*

Pietro shut his eyes tight as his memory returned in one breathless swirl. The bridge. He was at the edge of Corcannon, having made the foolhardy decision to try to seek some peace for his soul back in the very city he had abandoned because it had destroyed his peace to begin with. He had arrived last evening at dusk, just as the gatekeepers were shutting down the bridge that connected Corcannon to the rest of the continent. No one was allowed to make the journey across that canyon without full benefit of the sun. Not since a whole caravan had driven off the side fifteen years ago, plunging so far and so fast that no one on either bank had been able to hear their screams. Four bridges served the city at widely spaced intervals, and all of them closed at sunset.

A horrible metallic screeching rose above the renewed wailing of the crowd, and Pietro's eyes snapped open. The bridge was really collapsing, then, its spare, graceful lines of cable and iron wrenching themselves from their stone foundations. He wasn't sure how many other travelers had been marooned on the western bank when darkness arrived last night, but he guessed that close to two hundred souls had bedded down on this side of the gorge.

There's nowhere to go, he realized. He and his fellow travelers were camped at the northernmost bridge, which was separated from the two middle crossings by a long fissure almost as deep as the one that edged the city. It was as if a thin rocky finger reached out from the mountainous regions of Chibain to *almost*, but not quite, touch the city border. To make it to the nearest alternate crossing, travelers would lose at least a day in backtracking and another day heading to the closest bridge in Marata.

If it was still standing. If any of the bridges were still standing.

The ground seemed to have stopped moving, and Pietro cautiously pushed himself up on one elbow. All around him, he could see people on their feet, gathered in small agitated knots, hunkered down around injured companions, or working together to lift downed trees. The noise of the crowd had changed in pitch, from cries of confusion to shouts of purpose. A woman nearby was still sobbing in a low, heartbroken way, and Pietro knew a moment's cowardice. He wanted to sink into his tangled bedroll, cover his ears, wait until rescue arrived or the campers organized themselves into efficient units of aid and repair.

I'm old, he thought, dropping back to the ground. *I've put in my time succoring the sick and leading the lost. I'm old and I'm tired and I'm lost myself. Someone should stop by and look after* me.

He remained there a moment, feeling his whole body tense with the effort to lie still, and then he sighed and shoved himself upright again. When the ground stayed quiescent beneath him, he pushed himself all the way to his feet and hunted up his shoes. Then he grabbed his smaller bag, the one that held the things he couldn't afford to lose to looters, and wound his way through the debris to find the crying woman.

She looked up when he dropped to his knees beside her. He judged her to be in her middle forties, with the deep brown skin and silky black hair of someone who was purebred Cordelano. Her face was scratched and bleeding from shallow cuts, but she seemed more concerned about her left arm, which she was cradling to her chest. He automatically glanced at her bracelets to learn whatever part of her story they would tell. He couldn't get a good view of her left wrist, but her right arm was heavy with gold and silver bangles signifying her status as a married woman with many children.

"I think I broke my arm. Are you a doctor?" she asked hopefully, her eyes going to Pietro's left hand. Disappointment clouded her face as she saw only the slim ambiguous rope of twisted silver that was the least useful of all the career designations. *Sojourner,* it meant. *Seeker.* The only way to provide less information was to not bother wearing a bracelet at all.

He smiled at her reassuringly. He had never lost his ability to comfort the most distraught mourner, calm the most tortured soul. "I'm not," he said. "But I have spent much time working in infirmaries, and I can set a bone."

She held her arm out, and he began working it over carefully, cleaning one long gash before improvising a splint. He had a numbing salve that he had bought almost as a joke—*wouldn't it be marvelous if this could soothe a broken heart?*—but he spread that liberally over her arm before setting the splint in place, and she sighed in relief.

"Thank you," she said. "That's so much better."

"You might have someone check it for you as soon as you get to the city."

She glanced hopelessly toward the chasm. "I heard someone say the bridge collapsed," she said. "How will we get home?"

"I imagine that's a question that is vexing everyone this morning."

She covered her eyes with her free hand. "This one was worse, wasn't it? Worse than all the other tremors."

He was tying the last bit of ripped fabric around his makeshift splint, but now his hands stilled and he stared at her. "There have been other tremors?" he said. At her look of incredulity, he added hastily, "I haven't been in the city for ten years."

"Mostly small ones," she said. "But they've been happening for the past year or so."

Pietro tried not to show how shocked he was by the terrible news. "Well," he said, rising to his feet. "The quakes have stopped for now. Maybe they won't start up again for a good long time."

Although he knew that wasn't true.

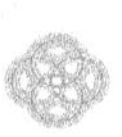

Stepping away from the Cordelano woman, Pietro strolled through the rest of the camp, trying to get a sense of what was happening. Groups of travelers gathered together, debating their options. Wait here and hope bridge repairs would be quick and reliable? Head back over toward Marata and aim for one of the middle crossings? *But what if the other bridges have also come down?* he heard someone ask. *What then?*

But suddenly the idea of traveling to Marata became a less viable option, as a few adventuresome souls returned with fresh bad news. The road behind them had cracked open during the tremor, leaving it unstable and impassable. The whole lot of them were trapped here until they could make a crossing to safer ground.

Curiosity sent Pietro to investigate the collapsed bridge and try to assess the damage for himself. He wasn't the first one to have this idea. Dozens of people were lined up a prudent distance from the edge to gaze out at the mangled mess of metal, the yawning gap, and the skyline of the city, tantalizingly out of reach. Pietro worked his way over to one side to get a better look.

The rods and cables still appeared to be solidly anchored to each bank, but the gentle metal arch had inverted and now hung in a twisted, dispirited loop over the striated gray and white walls of the canyon. The damage did not look like it would be simple to reverse. He stifled a sigh.

The crowd shifted around him and he became aware that some of the bolder souls were massed closest to the edge, shouting across the canyon to people on the other side. The city dwellers were shouting back, waving their arms in emphasis.

"What's going on?" Pietro asked, in case anyone nearby knew the answer.

A young woman glanced over. "I think they're trying to figure out how to get a pulley system across the canyon so they can send supplies over. Not much luck so far. They tried tying a rope to an arrow and shooting it over, but it fell into the canyon. Three times."

"Not promising," he admitted. She snorted.

He took a moment to give her a closer inspection. She was fair-skinned and blonde-haired, with dark brown eyes set into a serious face. A little less than medium height, lean and compactly built, possibly in her middle twenties. She wore a leather vest over a cotton shirt and leather pants, all the clothing loose enough to be comfortable without leaving floating bits that would impede her movements. Even before he glanced at the flat silver band welded around her left wrist, he knew he would see it stamped with a series of crossed swords. Her coloring marked her as being from one of the tribes that inhabited the sandy stretches of Oraki on the southern border of the continent. Her bracelet proclaimed her a professional soldier. It was not a combination often to be found in the city.

Pietro added, "But Corcannon is filled with scholars and engineers. They'll figure something out."

"Maybe," she replied. "Have you ever been here before?"

"Lived here the first sixty years of my life. I've been wandering for the last ten, but I can't imagine it's changed much."

She didn't ask him why he'd left or why he'd come back, and by that omission he judged she didn't want to answer any such questions, either. "I've never seen a place with so many buildings," she said.

He nodded and lifted his gaze so he could take in that spectacular view. Corcannon was set on a broad, flat plateau nestled against a jagged black mountain. The plateau featured just the slightest incline, so the buildings and districts rose up in ranks, one behind the other, cut through with a network of well-planned streets. From this vantage point, it seemed possible to discern every building, every door, every monument, every road. Pietro thought he could even make out the Quatrefoil, the four-petaled plaza that formed the heart of the city and held memories of all the events that had made Pietro run away in the first place.

"Many buildings," he said, "and many marvels. Technologies that exist nowhere else on this continent. Gifts brought by the god Cordelan when he brought us all our other gifts."

She shrugged so slightly it was possible to miss the motion. Outside of Corcannon, Pietro had learned, a lot of people didn't have much use for Cordelan. He was a late arrival on the scene, after people had spent centuries worshipping the mountain goddess Dar or the ocean deity Zessaya.

But Cordelan had reshaped their world, literally. Someone might choose not to worship him, but he was impossible to deny.

Pietro craned his neck to see if he could determine what kind of progress was being made. The groups on both sides of the chasm were continuing to shout at each other as they debated the best ways to get a rope across the ravine. "I'm optimistic that they will be successful in this endeavor," he said, "but it may take longer than people are prepared to wait."

Before she could answer, a teenage boy trotted up and raised his voice to the crowd. "Hey, they've set up a place to treat the wounded, and they're looking for help," he called. "They want anyone who's strong and doesn't mind the sight of blood."

The men and women standing nearby shifted and muttered, but none of them volunteered. The blonde woman next to Pietro glanced at him and shrugged again. He nodded, and they both stepped forward.

"We can help," Pietro said. "Where'd they set up an infirmary?"

"Infirmary" was too grand a word for the arrangement of bedrolls over travel trunks that had been organized in a space defined by a few confiscated crates and some canvas tarps. There were maybe a dozen people lying on the makeshift beds or seated nearby, waiting their turn to be seen by the two women who had styled themselves as doctors.

"Here to help? Good," said one, a tall, spare woman with Cordelano coloring and an abrupt manner.

"We need someone to assess who needs the most care and someone to help clean and bind wounds," added the other woman, shorter and heavier, but Cordelano like the first.

"I can bind wounds. I'm Pietro, the way," he said.

"I'm Jayla," said his companion. "I'll assess. Let's get to work."

Pietro found himself almost enjoying the next two hours of work. He liked the rhythm of moving between beds, fetching supplies, offering comfort—having a purpose, no matter how temporary or insignificant. The air grew decidedly warmer as morning arced over into afternoon, but Pietro didn't even mind the film of sweat that built up under his arms and across his face. He preferred hot to cold, sunshine to clouds. He had had enough gloom to last a lifetime.

By the time the afternoon was fairly well advanced, most of the patients had been treated and sent back to camp. Soon the only ones still waiting to be seen were two women and a small girl who hovered outside the corral of crates, as if uncertain whether they should enter. Pietro stepped over and offered his usual reassuring smile.

"Does someone need medical attention?" he asked.

One of the women came forward. She had the stocky build and all-over tan coloring often found among the people of Marata. "We think she's hurt, but we can't be sure," she said, urging the little girl in his direction.

Pietro surveyed the young patient, whom he guessed to be about seven or eight. With her wildly curly auburn hair, freckled skin, and delicate build, she looked nothing like the Maratan woman. Pietro could only assume she was from the islands, one of the small, clustered land masses that created a scalloped border on the extreme western edge of the continent. "She's Zessin," he said.

"Yes. We think she might have broken her wrist, but she doesn't speak Cordish, and neither of us understands Zessin."

"If you can't talk to her, how do you come to be traveling with her?"

The second woman spoke up. "We're not. She was in the company of an older woman who was taking her to Corcannon. *She* at least knew a few words of Cordish, so we could make a little conversation. They were supposed to be meeting some relatives somewhere, I'm not sure. But she died about a week ago. A heart attack, maybe."

The first woman took up the tale. "We couldn't leave the child on the side of the road all by herself! But we don't know what to do with her. And we can't ask her who she belongs to."

"But we think she broke her wrist," the second one repeated.

The girl glanced between the speakers as they talked, almost as if she could follow the conversation, but she made no effort to join in. Pietro struggled to remember the few Zessin phrases he had learned. What he was coming up with were *wine* and *are you interested?* And *I will.* None of them appropriate here.

"Do you know her name?" he asked.

"We think it's Aussen. Or something that sounds like that. You know the whole language just seems like a bunch of *shushing* sounds."

"Well, let's see what a doctor thinks," he said.

The shorter doctor thought the wrist was sprained, and she wrapped it accordingly once Jayla brought her the proper supplies. "You'll need to change that bandage every few days," she said as she finished up.

"But we're not going to be the ones watching her," one of the Maratan women said in an anxious voice. "She doesn't belong to us."

"Well, *someone* will have to watch out for her," the doctor said. "You can pass on our instructions to whoever it is."

Before the Maratan woman could protest again, two teenaged boys barreled into the infirmary area, trading blows and loud insults. One of them was already bleeding from a long cut on his arm, so Pietro guessed at least one of the combatants had a knife. He instinctively stepped out of their way, but the taller doctor strode forward.

"Stop it! Both of you!" she commanded. "If you've come here for help, we'll help—otherwise, go someplace else with your stupid quarrels!"

The two boys immediately broke apart and began vociferously offering their own explanations. Pietro had no interest in their tale, and he was suddenly hungry; this seemed like a good time to slip away. He glanced over at Jayla, who was watching Aussen, but he didn't bother to make excuses. He just stepped out of the small arena and into the camp.

It didn't take long to make a meal from his dwindling supplies, and Pietro spared a moment to wonder if everyone else was down to their last travel rations and canteens of water. That might make for a tense situation if the bridge wasn't repaired in a day or two. He didn't really think his fellow travelers would start raiding each other's campfires for food, but he had learned long ago that even the best people were capable of terrible things.

Hoping to discover that there had been some progress in getting a rope across the chasm, Pietro hiked back toward the fallen bridge, where a crowd was still gathered. He was encouraged to see that, while he'd been absent, workers on either side of the chasm had managed to string a thick cable across the divide, and they were even now anchoring it securely on both sides.

"Hardly does us any good," someone in the crowd grumbled. "It's not exactly a bridge."

"It's not even a pulley," someone else complained. "I thought they'd find a way to send us supplies, but that's barely better than a rope."

Suddenly there was a low murmur of awe from the front ranks of the crowd, then the middle part, and pretty soon everyone was staring. The men near Pietro shadowed their eyes to get a better look.

"I don't believe it," the first one breathed. "How can anyone do that?"

Pietro rose to the tips of his toes to get a better look. A single figure was strolling across that cable as casually and confidently as if he were walking down his own hall. He placed his feet carefully but without apparent nervousness on the support that seemed as narrow as a skein of yarn.

"What's he got in his hands?" someone called out over the low amazement of the crowd.

"Something he's using for balance, maybe," another voice replied.

By this time, the slim figure was close enough for Pietro's old eyes to make out details. He saw a young man of medium height and lithe, easy build. His skin was a deep tan that could mean a Cordelano heritage or a life spent largely outdoors, and his hair was a shaggy mass of brown curls. Pietro didn't have to look too hard to see the identifier on his left wrist—a red metal band studded with large crystals that winked cheerfully in the sunlight. This was one of the city's innumerable couriers and that bracelet was designed to catch the attention of anybody eager to flag one down. Many couriers also wore red vests, to make themselves even more visible to potential customers, though this particular individual hadn't bothered. Then again, he could hardly have hoped to attract *more* attention than he was drawing right now.

"I think he's carrying another rope," said one of the nearby men in an uncertain voice.

"He is," Pietro said, more to himself than to the onlookers nearby. "*That's* going to be the pulley."

Chapter Two: Jayla

Jayla didn't think she drew a breath from the minute she saw the young man step onto the swaying cable until the second he put his foot safely on the ground on the other side. He was a stranger, so she had no reason to care if he lost his life, but the sheer reckless audacity of his crossing filled her with admiration and envy. The canyon had to drop several thousand feet, and she couldn't imagine anyone had ever survived the fall. It was his insouciance as much as his skill that impressed her. She didn't think she had enough of either to attempt such a feat.

She hung back as a dozen men on this side of the gorge rushed forward to greet him, but she continued to lurk nearby, just to watch how events unfolded. She wasn't all that interested in seeing how the pulley was set up or joining the conversation about what supplies the travelers should request from the city first. She just liked to be near the scene with the most interesting action. She drifted a little closer to the hubbub, still keeping to the outskirts.

But her eyes kept cutting over toward the city man who had just made that perilous crossing. He was loitering on the edge of the crowd, just like Jayla, watching them all with a bright, inquisitive interest. His hands were in the back pockets of his loose pants, but Jayla had already learned a little about him by catching a glimpse of his bracelets. She had never seen a bejeweled red bracelet before, so she had no idea how to interpret that, but the metal on his right wrist had been plain enough to see. It was a single gold band with simple silver fluting on the edges, proclaiming him a man who chose women. And the absence of any other personal bracelets indicated he didn't have a wife or children.

Well, if he went around negligently putting himself in danger every day, it was easy to see why no woman would want to tie herself to his fortunes.

A couple of the other stranded travelers had drifted his way. "What are they doing to repair the bridge?" one of them demanded.

The young man put his hands up in a gesture of ignorance, causing his gems to flash in the sunlight. His smile was disarming. "I don't know. But there's a whole committee trying to figure out what to do next."

"What about the other bridges?" a woman asked. "Did they fall, too?"

"They don't seem to be damaged, but they're being checked out. No one is going in or out of the city just now."

The woman groaned. "Then we're stuck here for a while at least. I hope we don't run out of water."

The two of them turned away and were quickly replaced by two teenage boys, eager to talk to the city man. Jayla edged closer to listen.

"How'd you do that?" one of the boys demanded. "Walk across that rope like—like it was just something you'd do every day?"

The man laughed. "I'm courier in the city, so I *do* run along the cables a lot," he said.

The boys looked blank. "What cables?" one of them asked.

"There's a gridway—a cable net that hangs over the whole city. It provides the power for all the light and all the transportation in Corcannon."

"And you're a courier?" the other one said. "What's that?"

"I carry messages and packages. The faster the better. When traffic is slow or there's no direct route from one place to another, sometimes I'll run across the power net instead of along the streets."

"And you never fall?"

"Haven't so far."

"Maybe I'd want to be a courier," one of the boys said.

The city man held out his left wrist, where the bracelet was suitably dazzling. "It's a good life." He dropped his hand. "What are you coming to Corcannon for?"

One of the boys shook his head. "Our dad died. Our mom's got folks here. She'll be looking for work. I guess we all will."

A little nervously the other boy said, "We've never been out of Chibain before."

"Well, I've never been out of the city," the courier answered. "Never saw a reason to leave."

Before the boys could ask more questions, a woman's voice called to them above the ongoing murmur of the crowd. Without a word of farewell, they spun on their heels and darted off.

The city man watched them for a few seconds, then pivoted directly toward Jayla and smiled. She disciplined an instinctive desire to step backward, out of his line of sight. She hadn't realized he'd even known she was there.

"And what about you?" he asked. "Why are you coming to the city?"

She came nearer, since she didn't feel like shouting. This close, she could see the color of his eyes, a clear blue almost as bright as the gems in his bracelet. "Like everyone else," she said. "Looking for work."

Making no attempt to be subtle about it, he dropped his eyes to check out the bands on both her wrists. "Soldier?" he asked, glancing up at her again. He didn't comment on her other bracelet, plain silver edged with a thin line of gold. A woman who preferred men.

"That's right," she said.

Now he gave her a more thorough inspection, as if noting her practical clothing, her soft leather boots, her visible weapons. Maybe assessing her strength and skill, though she wouldn't think a courier would be particularly good at making such judgments. "Doesn't seem like an easy life," was all he said.

A small smile came to her lips. "I haven't noticed too many lives that *are* easy," she replied.

He laughed. "Well, that's the truth of it. Maybe life is easy for rich folk, but I know a couple of those, and they have troubles of their own."

"I've worked for a few," she said. "And I agree."

"Where are you from? By your looks I'd say Oraki, but your accent is more southern Marata."

She nodded. He was quick, this young man, and restlessly observant. Traits she admired, because she possessed them herself, but it was disconcerting to be the one who was observed and analyzed. "Born in Oraki, but spent a lot of time in Marata."

"I'm Cody, by the way," he said.

"Jayla."

"Did you bring family with you, Jayla? Meeting family there?"

She shook her head and gave the briefest possible answer. "On my own."

He looked like he wanted to pursue that line of questioning but read the clear warning in her guarded reply. So he merely nodded and asked, "Assuming they manage to rebuild the bridge, what kind of job will you be looking for in Corcannon?"

"I don't know that I'm going to be too picky," she said. "As long as the work is honest and the pay is reasonable, I'm open to anything. Not sure where to start looking, though."

"There's a training yard I can recommend run by a couple of men who used to be part of the temple guard," Cody said. "You have to pay a fee to work out there, but it's a decent place—everyone knows it—and that's where a lot of the rich folks go to hire their personal guards. There's a kind of cachet to being found there."

She gestured to indicate her slim figure, her plain clothing. "And would you say I have enough cachet?"

He grinned. "I know the owners. They'll let you in."

She met his eyes directly, her own a little hard. "That's a kindness to do for an absolute stranger."

But his own expression was relaxed and easy. "That's a courier for you," he said. "We make friends everywhere. Pays off a lot more than making enemies."

"I don't look to make enemies," Jayla said coolly. "But it takes me a while to make friends."

He glanced around at the small camp, busy with resigned travelers trying to settle in for a long wait, and grinned again. "Looks like we'll have all the time we need."

The first items that came rocking over the chasm were casks of water lashed to mesh cocoons that dangled from the pulley in a precarious fashion. The casks were followed by lumpy bundles of food containing staples like bread, fruit, and dried meat. The travelers who had appointed themselves pulley-masters carefully unclipped the barrels and bags and lined them up on the bank before turning their attention to the next items snaking their way across the gap. Clearly, they didn't figure it was up to them to manage equitable distribution of the goods.

"This might get ugly," Jayla said under her breath as the first casks were commandeered by a group of Maratan traders. The men were burly and efficient, and it wasn't hard to imagine them appropriating everything that made it safely over the canyon, then calmly setting up a booth to sell supplies to the hapless travelers. Well, hapless until thirst or hunger or boiling discontent led to a sudden confrontation.

"I was just thinking that," said a voice over her shoulder, and she glanced back to see who had spoken. She recognized the tall, thin Cordelano man who had worked beside her at the infirmary. Pietro. That was his name. "Somebody needs to organize the allocation of assets."

"If you start, I'll help," Cody offered.

Pietro glanced at Jayla with a smile. There was something about him she couldn't quite place—not an air of command, exactly, not like the captain of a guard or the steward of a great household—but an ease with authority, as if he was used to shouldering burdens and showing people the way. Maybe he was a teacher or a politician, fallen on hard times. His worn clothes were so drastically simple he could have been mistaken for a beggar, but his bracelets gleamed with high-alloy metal. She'd noticed both of them this morning. On his left wrist, a carved and coiled silver band that marked him as a wanderer. On his right, a lustrous gold circlet made of woven strips of hammered gold.

Man who preferred men.

"What about you, Jayla?" Pietro asked. "Will you join in our attempt to keep a decorous crowd?"

"Sure," she said. "Where should we set up?"

In a few minutes, they'd borrowed a table and turned themselves into a tiny distribution center. Cody fetched cartons and bags as they were dumped onto the bank, and Pietro doled out portions. Jayla harried the fretful campers into forming an orderly line, and then patrolled the queue. "Hey now," she said any time someone tried to get ahead in line, and frowned at anyone who looked rebellious.

Only twice did she have to exert a little more pressure. The first time was when a group of teenage boys followed a girl from the distribution site and tried to steal her sack of fruit. But Jayla had already noted them as potential troublemakers, and she was upon them before they could do more than snatch at the girl's hands. They turned on her with snarls of anger, but she faced them down with a professional's cool dispassion.

"Don't start any trouble with me," she warned. One of the boys feinted forward, and she hit him hard enough to get his attention without bringing him to the ground. The other two backed off, eyeing her a little more intently. She made sure they could see the soldier's bracelet welded around her left wrist. "Just get in line if you need supplies."

The girl scampered away while the boys watched Jayla for another tense moment. Then the largest of the three grunted in disgust and motioned to his buddies. They sneered just to show they weren't afraid, then trotted off to the far end of the encampment.

When Jayla returned to patrol the line, everyone else was conspicuously polite. No one even bumped into anyone else for the next thirty minutes.

The second altercation came after they'd been handing out goods for almost two hours. The sun was sinking, the temperature was still a little too warm on this early summer day, and everyone was tired and irritable. Word had made it up from the embankment that the flow of supplies was about to stop for the day, though it would resume in the morning. The last few casks of water had been liberated from their harnesses and set on the ground, and Jayla could only see one more bag of food hanging from the pulley as it eased across the canyon. She was pretty certain that most everyone in camp had been through the line at least once, but the news still caused a murmur of anxiety among the travelers.

Then three men in merchant clothing calmly pushed through the crowd and picked up three of the last casks of water, shouldering them with ease. The onlookers reacted with alarm and disbelief, but no one made a move to stop them as they shoved their way back through the line.

Until Jayla stepped directly into their path and said, "No."

They halted, but in a way that radiated menace, and formed a looming semicircle around her. They were all a good four or five inches taller than she was, muscular, their faces rough with hard travel and harder bargaining. She couldn't tell by their coloring what their heritage might be, but she could read their bracelets, and none of them showed a soldier's glyphs.

"That water's for everybody," she said. "Leave it here."

"Don't see how you can take it from us," one of them said in a matter-of-fact voice.

"I can make you drop it," she said. "And then everybody loses."

"Don't think you can even do that," he said.

He'd barely uttered the last word before she dove at him, ramming her head into his stomach with such force that he fell over backward. He hit the rocky ground so heavily that his bones crunched and the cask splintered, spewing water everywhere. He cried out in pain, clutching his head, but he didn't try to get up. Jayla spun away from him, already in a half-crouch, to face his friends.

"What about you two?" she said. "Want to waste the water?"

They'd hastily set down their burdens and began circling her, their faces creasing with anger. She could see they both had blades in their belts, but they hadn't drawn weapons yet, probably figuring they could crush her easily enough with their bare hands. She didn't think either one was paying much attention to the way the spilled water was seeping into the spare ground, making a slick spot of mud over the hard surface of stone.

"This is none of your mix," one of them said.

"It's everybody's mix," she answered. "We're all trapped here."

That was enough conversation for them. They lunged for her, moving in concert, but they weren't trained soldiers, so they just got in each other's way. One of the blows meant for her landed on the other man instead, and there was a bellow of pain. Jayla spun around and got two good kicks on each of them, one in the kidneys, one in the knees. Each man staggered in first one direction, then the other, and the beefiest of the two stayed half-bent over, trying to regain his balance. Jayla snaked her foot around his ankle, and he went down hard. The third man came boring in, slashing at her with thick, heavy hands; she felt the impact on her right cheek and upper arm. But she danced backward, luring him after her until he was in just the right spot. Then she spun again, came around behind him, and kicked him in the back of his legs. Overbalancing in the mud, he landed face-first on the unforgiving ground.

The second man was up on his hands and knees, but cautiously, as if testing to see whether anything was broken. Big men weren't used to falling, Jayla had always thought; they were accustomed to winning contests just by strength and size, and being on the ground caused them deep disorientation.

If this had been a desperate fight, she would have taken advantage of his loss of focus to leap on his back and crack a few ribs, maybe even twist his neck. But this was just a skirmish. A warning. *Back off. Play fair.*

A movement on the periphery of her vision caused her to swing in that direction, but it was just Cody snagging one of the water barrels. A quick glance around showed her that he must have already rescued the first one, because it was nowhere nearby. He caught her eye and grinned as he heaved the barrel to his shoulder, and for the life of her she couldn't resist grinning back.

He'd made no move to come to her aid. She couldn't remember the last time any man had paid her such a high compliment.

The third assailant had scrambled to his feet, but he didn't immediately advance on Jayla again. She saw him glance around and note the absence of the barrels. His gaze went to the people in line, all of them staring at him and his friends, some in stupefaction, some in anger. His attention came back to Jayla, and his expression was dark, but in it she could also read some of a merchant's cold calculation. *No payoff in continuing this brawl.* His mouth twisted and he took a couple of careful steps forward to prod one of his partners with his foot.

"Enough," he said brusquely.

His friend took a deep breath and nodded, pushing himself upright. The third man had come to a sitting position, his hand still pressed to his head. Jayla saw blood running down his temple. The other two helped him up, and they lumbered off without another word or a backward glance.

Jayla watched them go, then turned around to see if any other kind of trouble might be brewing. But the few people who remained in line were mostly just watching her, and none of them looked inclined to mayhem. She nodded curtly and settled her hands on her belt, adopting the pose of someone waiting and watching. In another ten minutes, the final water cask was empty, the last bundle of dried meat had been handed over, and all the travelers had returned to their individual campsites.

Pietro smiled as Jayla strolled up to the table. "That was impressive," he said. "I can't imagine we'll have any trouble at all tomorrow if you just stand around looking murderous."

Cody pushed his curls off his forehead. He'd been hauling heavy burdens all day; she figured he had to be tired, though his eyes still showed a roving curiosity. "Unless those louts go looking for Jayla in the middle of the night."

She shrugged. "I read them as opportunists, not criminals," she said. "Didn't seem like they really wanted trouble—they just wanted whatever they could get."

"Still," said Pietro. "It might behoove you to bed down near friends tonight. Are you traveling with anyone?"

She shook her head. “I’m fine.”

“You could share a campfire with me,” Pietro offered.

“And me,” Cody chimed in. When the other two glanced at him, he added, “I hadn’t planned to spend the night, but I’m not crossing the canyon in the dark.”

Jayla grinned at him. “And here I thought you were a brave man.”

He laughed. “I’ve run the cables at night,” he admitted. “But there’s not as far to fall.”

“I saved a loaf of bread and a bag of fruit,” Pietro said. “I was assuming the three of us would share after our labors were over.” He rested his gaze on Jayla’s face. “And I would reiterate the thought that you’d be better off tonight with friends at your back.”

She wasn’t worried about the disgruntled merchants—not really—and she didn’t think that either Pietro or Cody would show to advantage in any kind of combat situation. But if she was wrong and the traders came looking for her, they might think twice if they found her with defenders nearby.

“It’s a kind offer, so I’ll accept,” she said.

“And I’m starving,” Cody added. “Let’s eat now.”

Chapter Three:
Jayla

It was another fifteen minutes before they'd gathered Jayla's sparse belongings and arrayed them near Pietro's campsite. Cody built a small fire and they parceled out supplies. The dried meat was surprisingly tasty and the bread was delicious, or else Jayla was hungrier than she'd realized.

"So did any news come across the canyon with the supplies?" Jayla asked. "How long will it be before the bridge is rebuilt?"

Cody spoke around a mouthful of food. "I heard they might not repair it right now," he said. "They might put a temporary bridge across the fissure instead."

"The fissure?" she repeated.

Pietro waved toward something invisible in the gathering dark. "The crevasse on the southern edge of our campsite here."

"A lot narrower than the canyon," Cody said. "If people can cross that, it'll just take them a couple of hours to travel to one of the Maratan bridges." He leaned back on his elbows, too far for the firelight to reach his face. "So I know Jayla's coming to the city to find work as a soldier. What brings you here, Pietro? Unless you don't feel like telling."

"I lived here for a long time. I left for ten years. I missed it, so I'm coming back."

It was an answer that left out more than it included, but since that was obviously deliberate, Jayla was careful about posing the next question. "Do you plan to take up your old life or look for something new?"

"I don't think my old life is open to me," he said, and then shrugged. "I may find that I don't want to stay more than a week or two. I might be crossing back over the chasm before the dust even settles on my shoes."

Cody lifted a lazy hand to gesture in Pietro's direction. "Sojourner."

Pietro touched the twisted silver bracelet on his wrist. "Precisely."

Jayla jerked her head back, her attention caught by a sound beyond the circle of firelight. All around them, other travelers talked and rattled pans around their own campfires, but this noise was different. Closer. Hesitant. Stealthy?

"Who's out there?" she called. Cody rolled to a sitting position, and Pietro casually dropped his hand to his ankle. She wondered if he carried a concealed dagger.

There was another soft footfall and then a small shape moved out of the darkness. It was the little ginger-haired girl who had showed up earlier at the makeshift infirmary. She looked even more ragged and forlorn than she had this morning, her hair unkempt and her face smeared with dirt. She held her bandaged hand carefully against her heart and glanced at each one of them in turn, saying nothing.

"Aussen?" Pietro said in his gentle voice. "That's your name, isn't it?"

She immediately fixed her eyes on him. "Pietro," she replied.

"That's right. Let me introduce you to Jayla and Cody." They all nodded gravely to each other, then Pietro asked, "Are you lost, Aussen?"

"Where are your friends? The women who are watching out for you?" Jayla demanded. The girl just looked at her and didn't answer.

"I don't think she understands Cordish," Pietro murmured. "Or at least not well enough to speak it."

"Who is she?" Cody wanted to know. "She looks Zessin."

"That was my thought as well," Pietro said.

"She was with two women this morning, but they said they barely knew her. They'd started caring for her when the woman she was traveling with died," Jayla explained.

"So she's all alone?" Cody said.

Pietro held up a piece of bread. "Have you eaten? Are you hungry?"

She came deeper into the firelight, her eyes still on Pietro. She didn't answer, but when he leaned closer to offer her the bread, she took it from his hands and quickly stuffed it in her mouth.

"Hungry," Jayla said. "Probably thirsty. *Where* are the women looking out for her?"

Pietro was busy making up a plate of food for Aussen and pouring water into a cracked mug. The girl sat beside him and immediately began eating. "They might not even have noticed that she's wandered off," he said.

"They might be *glad* she did," Jayla said darkly.

"You don't know how heavy their other responsibilities are," Pietro replied. "She might be one more burden than they can bear."

She spared a moment to wonder what kind of life led a man to develop that level of compassion, then pushed herself to a standing position. "I could go look for them."

"You could," he said. "Or you could see what morning brings."

"I don't think that—"

The earth shook beneath her feet, and Jayla tumbled down with a cry. The ground bucked again and she flattened herself against it, arms outstretched and fingers digging into the dirt, trying to anchor herself in place. Pietro grabbed Aussen and cradled her against his chest as if to shield her body from falling boulders. Cody had come to his hands and knees, looking like he was ready to jump up and run, or plaster himself to the ground, whenever he could figure out which option was safest. All around them they could hear the shouts of their fellow travelers trying to ride out the newest tremor.

The shaking lasted less than a minute, but Jayla stayed where she was in case it started up again. Cody had tilted his head as if he was listening to the heartbeat of the world itself.

"Didn't seem as bad as the one this morning," he said.

"Do you think it's over?" Jayla asked.

"Hard to say," Cody replied. "Usually they come in bunches, but each new one is a little weaker than the last one."

Jayla came cautiously to her knees. "Usually?" she repeated.

Cody nodded. "They've been hitting more often. And I've heard that Darrish Mountain has been spitting out ash for the past few months."

Pietro had released Aussen and settled her next to him on the ground. "That's grim news," he observed.

Jayla looked at him. "Why?"

She thought he chose his answer with care. "It's always unnerving when the continent seems to be tearing itself apart."

Cody rearranged himself into a cross-legged sitting position. "There have been a lot of little tremors lately," he said. "But it's been a long time since we had really dangerous quakes in the city."

Pietro nodded. "Ten years," he said.

Cody grinned. "And nothing bad happened."

This time it was even longer before Pietro answered. "Exactly. Nothing bad."

"You think it's worse now?" Jayla asked. "Why?"

"I think—" He paused to refill Aussen's cup of water. "Our whole continent is a precarious construct. Held together by a power none of us understand. I wonder sometimes how long its contours will hold."

The ground felt solid enough now that Jayla felt safe dropping down and copying Cody's cross-legged pose. "But Cordelan put the continent together," she said. "That's what they taught us when I was growing up."

Pietro shrugged. "Oh yes, that's the theology," he said. "The goddesses Dar and Zessaya spent centuries feuding with each other across seas and inlets, but their little fiefdoms were separated by enough open ocean that it didn't really matter. Everyone in Chibain and Marata worshipped Dar, and everyone from the outer islands was devoted to Zessaya. Then Cordelan arrived and raised his hands and declared that he would bind many disparate lands together. And he sewed the mountains to the flatlands, and the islands to the coastlines, and he set Corcannon in the curve of this new continent. And the rivers from Chibain flowed onto the plains of Marata and created lush farmland that burst with new crops. And the minerals from the islands suddenly became available throughout the land. And everyone thrived in this world reshaped by Cordelan's hands." He lifted his eyebrows at her and there was a note of polite disbelief in his voice as he said, "And is that what you believe?"

Jayla shrugged. "In Oraki, we put more stock in small household gods who can make the way smooth or offer a night's protection. It's not that we don't honor Cordelan, it's just that he doesn't seem very present in daily life."

Pietro nodded and glanced over at Cody with his eyebrows still raised. "Do I believe?" Cody asked. He spread his hands. "I don't think about it much, but I always assumed it was all true. Isn't it?"

Pietro made soft scoffing noise. "Our learned scientists have studied the composition of the various provinces of the continent, and they have concluded that, indeed, at some point in the distant past they were separate bodies of land. They say that *something* knitted them together nearly a thousand years ago to create the world as we know it now. Perhaps it was Cordelan. Perhaps it was a natural drift of land masses that caused these bodies to collide. Perhaps Cordelan was an opportunistic schemer who took credit for something he had no hand in at all."

Cody's eyes grew wide. "That's blasphemy! Isn't it?"

Pietro grinned. "It's a topic that is debated with great energy at all our institutions of learning. Since you cannot prove deity, I suppose it will continue to be debated for decades to come. But the point is not really how the continent was created. The point is that it is an assemblage of somewhat incompatible fragments that seem, from time to time, bent on repudiation." When the other two stared at him blankly, Pietro sighed. "We don't know what power holds the separate parts of the continent together, but what if that power is failing? And what if the quakes are warning us that the land is about to split apart?"

Cody dropped his elbows to the ground and leaned back, supremely unconcerned. "There have always been quakes, and everything has held together so far."

"So far," Pietro echoed.

Jayla's mind always focused on practical matters. "Well, if you don't know how the power is supplied, what can you do to fix it even if it is going bad?" she asked.

Pietro gave her a long, serious look and said, "That is exactly the question."

Aussen, who had sat there silently this whole time, set her plate on the ground and stood up. "Are you going back to your friends?" Pietro asked. "You can stay here if you like."

Jayla came to her feet, ready to escort Aussen through the camp. "I'll help her find them. If she—"

Another rumble shook the ground and she dropped hurriedly back to her knees. But Cody had been right: This episode seemed less intense than the last two, almost half-hearted. As if the land was a snarling dog that had snapped at an unwelcome stranger, then continued to growl for the next few minutes just to show it wasn't tame. "Well, that wasn't so bad," she said cautiously.

Halfway across the camp, there was a sizzle and an explosion, followed by a hysterical scream. Jayla leapt up, peering in that direction, hands on her weapons belt. A few feet away, another ominous hiss and the cracking sound of something erupting into flames. Then another, farther away. Another. All over the camp, people were shouting, pointing, and crying out in fear.

Pietro and Cody were on their feet. "What's happening?" Cody demanded.

"I don't know," Jayla answered. "I think—"

Their own small fire gurgled and spit and suddenly bloomed outward in a terrifying flare. Pietro snatched Aussen and stumbled backward as Cody and Jayla scrambled away. Jayla caught a whiff of a marshy, rotting odor.

"The fires! Put out the fires!" someone shouted from ten or twenty yards away. "There's gas rising up from underground! Put out the fires!"

The cry was taken up across the camp, and suddenly there was a frenzy all around them as travelers hurried to douse their flames. Cody cursed and leapt forward, kicking apart the sticks of their own campfire, then stubbing out the flames with the heavy end of an unlit branch. Jayla joined him, rolling the burning logs until they extinguished themselves in the dirt, stomping on the embers that glowed treacherously in the grass.

After a few moments, she heard Cody draw a long breath and she lifted her eyes to gaze around. The whole plateau was completely dark, nothing but shadows filled with shadows. A low rumble of conversation spilled out in all directions, filled half with excitement and half with discontent. *Can you believe that? The air itself just caught on fire! What else is going to go wrong for us?*

"Well, that was something I wasn't expecting," Cody said, and even his cheerful voice seemed strained.

"Yes, we do seem to have collected more than our fair share of adventures," Pietro said. "I could wish for a bigger moon tonight, because I can't even see my hand in front of my face."

"I don't think you're going to be looking for Aussen's friends tonight," Cody said.

"I suppose not," Jayla answered. "I suppose none of us will have a choice but to stay right where we are till dawn."

There was a rustling sound, and she guessed that Pietro had dropped to the ground, Aussen probably still in his arms. Another thump that she assumed was Cody. Jayla resettled herself into a seated pose. Then a flicker at the corner of her eye caught her attention, and she turned her head sharply in that direction.

"Someone's lit a match!" she said. "Who would be so stupid?"

She thought she could sense Cody craning his neck. "It's probably a chemlight."

"A what?"

"It's sort of like a torch—a wooden stick treated with dried paste on one end. You scrape it on a hard surface and some chemicals combine and give off light for a couple of hours. No heat, no fire. Chemlights have become pretty popular."

"I can see why," said Pietro. "I wish we had one."

"As for tonight—nothing left to do but bed down, I suppose," Jayla said. "Aussen can sleep next to me. Aussen, can you find me in the dark?"

A muffled sound of rustling was followed in a few moments by Aussen's small shape crawling up next to her and squirming in place. Jayla spared a moment to hope the little girl wasn't a restless sleeper. It was all she could do to keep from saying *Sit quietly* as the child reached out once, twice, dragging her hand through the thin dirt as if combing it with her fingernails.

"I'm wondering how quickly they might start working on the secondary bridge," Pietro said. "If they build that fast enough—" His voice abruptly cut off.

Aussen had stretched her hands out in front of her, and light streamed from her closed fists. It was a pale, phosphorescent color, blue-white, making Aussen's face look like a spirit from the realm of the dead. In the ghostly glow, her face showed a small smile of satisfaction, as if she had been pleased to be able to summon the light.

"How did she do that?" Cody demanded, his expression both astonished and delighted. "Does she have one of those chemlights?"

"I don't think so," Jayla answered. "I think she just—picked up some rocks or something? She was digging in the dirt a minute ago."

"So maybe there's some kind of stone lying around that you can spark a light from," Cody speculated. "Pietro, did you ever hear of such a thing?"

But Pietro didn't answer. Jayla lifted her eyes to study him across the dead campfire. In the cool, wavering light, his expression was clearly visible and infinitely surprising. He didn't look amazed or impressed or even intrigued. His gaze was fixed on Aussen's face, and he was horrified.

Chapter Four:
Jayla

The second day of being trapped on the plateau was less busy but even more irritating than the first, and Jayla spent hours drifting through camp, looking for occupation. Hardly any patients had sought out the makeshift infirmary, so she wasn't needed there; the crowds lined up to receive fresh supplies from the city were docile and well-behaved, so she wasn't required to keep order. She spent about an hour observing the activity along the southern border of the camp, where workers were building a temporary bridge across the fissure. But the long, slow construction process was maddening to watch, and she couldn't bear to stay for long.

More than once she checked in on Aussen, whose haphazard guardians had come searching for her as soon as the sun made an appearance. Jayla had found herself curiously reluctant to turn the little girl over to their clearly inadequate care, so she detoured past their campsite several times just to reassure herself that Aussen was still alive. The women appeared to be traveling with a group of about fifteen people, more children than adults. *Too many to keep track of,* Jayla thought. *I wonder how many others they've lost along the way.*

Uncharitable. And none of her business.

On another circuit through the camp, she came across Cody sitting by himself on the table that had served as their distribution point the day before. He was in his usual relaxed slouch, idly watching workers gathered at the foot of the broken bridge that led into the city.

"All done for the day?" she asked. "The people of Corcannon have decided we don't need any more supplies?"

He gave her his easy smile. "The cable snapped about half an hour ago, sending a cask all the way down the canyon," he said. "So now everyone is trying to decide if the pulley is worth repairing or if we might get out of here soon enough that we don't need to fix it. How's the temporary bridge coming?"

"Looks like they're making progress." She surveyed him a moment. "If the cable snapped, you really are trapped here with the rest of us."

"I'd rather be trapped here than walking the wire when it broke in two."

She was surprised into a laugh. "I hadn't thought about that."

"Anyway, we'll only be here a few more days. One way or the other, I'll eventually get back home."

"You must not have anybody on the other side who'll be concerned about you."

Now his grin was wider. "Is that your way of asking me if there's a girl waiting for me in the city?"

She shoved him none too gently in the shoulder. "*No.* You could have a mother or a sister who worries about you. An employer, even. Someone you answer to."

"Well, there isn't."

She waited a beat. "Isn't what? A mother? A boss?"

"A girl."

"I don't care."

Still smiling. "Oh. Well. If you did."

She shook her head and changed the subject. "Where's Pietro?"

"He hopped up and left the minute the cable broke."

"What do you make of him?"

"I like him. He's smart. He's thoughtful. And he knows a lot more than he lets on."

She glanced over at him in surprise. "About what?"

"About everything, I imagine." He gave her an appraising look. "Why? Don't you like him?"

"I don't like anybody until I know them really well. I don't trust anybody until I know them really well."

His eyes widened in exaggerated hurt. "What? Not even me?"

"Ha. I don't know anything about you. Why would I trust you?"

He held his arms straight out in front of him so his bracelets caught the watery sunlight. The gems in the red one practically threw off sparks. "You know everything about me!"

"That you have a job—a dangerous one—and that you like women," she said dryly. "I think there's a whole lot more to know."

"Ask me anything."

She tried without complete success to hold back a smile. "Nothing I'm dying to know."

He tilted his head to one side and grinned at her again. "So when we're in the city," he said. "You'll have to let me know where you land. I mean,

I'll give you my address, too, so you can always find me, but I don't want to lose track of you."

Her expression was not encouraging. "And why is that?"

"Well, partly because I like to keep track of everybody. That's what a courier does. Knows where anybody can be found at a moment's notice." The grin deepened. "But partly because I think you're pretty interesting. I'd like to see what you get up to next."

She gave him a long, cool, assessing look. "You know I could do some serious damage to you without even trying very hard."

His smile was gone. He met her eyes unflinchingly. "And why would you want to do that?"

"If you did something careless. If you did something cruel."

"And why would I want to do that?"

"Some people do."

"I've been careless sometimes, I guess," he said slowly. "But I don't think I've ever been cruel. You'll need a better reason than that to avoid me."

"I didn't say I wanted to *avoid* you."

His grin was back. "Well, then."

"But I have no idea where I'll find work."

"Can't wait to see what you figure out."

Jayla was too restless to stick beside Cody much longer, though he seemed prepared to loll on the abandoned table till the world itself came to an end. Pretty soon she pushed herself away and began another circuit of the camp. She was heartily sick of this confined space and this edgy group of people and this sense of absolutely wasted time. She wanted something else to see and something else to *do.* She was never at her best unless she was in motion.

This time, when she made another pass around the Maratan camp, she was surprised to see Pietro was visiting. He was seated on a folded tarp, and Aussen sat right across from him, her knees practically touching his, her eyes fixed on his face. Jayla wasn't close enough to hear, but he seemed to be talking, and Aussen seemed to be listening, even though it wasn't clear that she could truly understand the Cordish language.

As Jayla watched, Pietro reached under the collar of his shirt and pulled out something hanging around his neck. An amulet or a religious pendant, maybe, dangling from a simple leather cord. Pietro tugged it off over his head and held it out so Aussen could examine it, and he continued to talk while she appeared to listen. Then he leaned over and slipped the cord around Aussen's neck, tucking the pendant under her clothing so it lay hidden against her skin.

Jayla took a sharp breath and narrowed her eyes in speculation. No one in the Maratan camp seemed to notice or care that an old man was bestowing gifts on a young girl who had no protectors. Jayla felt her hands clench and her lips tighten. She watched another minute, and then she turned away.

By late afternoon, the temporary bridge was in place, and a few fearless souls had eased themselves across to make sure it was safe. When it was clear the planks and boards were holding, there was a massive bustle across the entire camp as people began packing their belongings and lining up to make the crossing. Jayla glanced at the horizon and estimated that they didn't have more than a couple hours of daylight left. She doubted that even half the travelers could make it across the new bridge before sundown, and no one would risk the attempt in the dark. It would be tomorrow before she was on the other side of the divide.

Restless, she broke free of the crowd and circled the plateau again. At every campsite she passed, she overheard excited groups of travelers speculating about the safety of the temporary bridge and talking about what they'd do when they finally reached the city.

But she didn't see the one person she was actually looking for. She kept moving.

Sunset had just begun uncoiling on the horizon when Jayla found him at the edge of the canyon, staring across the divide into the heart of the city. She glanced briefly at the view, which was admittedly impressive. Every building in Corcannon seemed to be outlined with tiny lights, making a gaudy display against the serrated skyline. The mountain bulked up behind the last row of houses, an impenetrable and looming presence. Against its density, the lights sparkled with an extra giddiness.

Her quarry stood at the foot of the ruined bridge, resting a hand on a twisted curl of metal. Jayla moved up behind him so quietly that he couldn't hear her footfalls or her breathing, not even when she was inches away. Shaking a knife into her hand, she stepped close enough to slip the blade against his ribs through the soft folds of his clothing. She felt him stiffen with shock as the metal touched his skin and held steady. He didn't even try to look over his shoulder.

"I don't have any money," he said, his voice admirably calm. "But you're welcome to my bracelets or anything else you want."

"I think you've given away enough jewelry for the day."

Pietro jerked with surprise as he recognized her voice. "Jayla?"

"That's right."

"What do you—can I turn around?"

She pulled the knife away and said, "Slowly."

He obeyed, turning to face her, his hands held out to show they were empty. In the fading light, she could clearly make out the bewilderment on his face. "What's wrong?" he said quietly. "Why are you angry at me?"

She held the knife so close to his body he would have to realize she could gouge out his heart with a few quick strokes. "I want you to tell me," she said in a low, angry voice, "why a lonely old man like you would be giving presents to a little girl who's all by herself in the world. The only reasons I can think of make me want to run you right through and kick your body into the canyon."

His face instantly showed comprehension and dismay—but not, she thought, guilt or shame. "I swear on my life I mean no harm to Aussen. I am trying to protect her."

She pressed the tip of her knife against his chest just until she could feel the hard resistance of bone beneath his clothing. "That's not an explanation."

He nodded. "No. But what I tell you, you're going to have to take on faith."

"I don't take anything on faith."

He surprised her by suddenly bringing both his hands on either side of hers—not trying to knock the dagger away, but almost as if begging her to *listen* to him as he made a plea. "Jayla. You saw what she did last night. She scooped up a handful of dirt and she turned it into a diamond of light. You saw that."

She jerked her hand away from his, and when he dropped his arms, she aimed the dagger back at his ribcage, but this time she didn't touch him. "I did. So?"

"So that's an ability very few individuals in Corcannon possess. And there are people in the city who would pay any amount of money to get their hands on someone with that talent. They would kidnap. They would kill. Jayla, if these people knew that Aussen existed, they would stop at nothing to get her in their power. Nothing. Do you understand me? Do you believe me?"

She didn't understand him, but she believed him. His passion was entirely convincing. "Who are these people? And why would they want Aussen? What would they do with her?"

"I can't tell you. I can't explain. I'm just telling you it would be dire. You have to keep Aussen away from them at all costs."

"Me? But I'm not her keeper."

Pietro stepped closer and took her hands again, heedless of her knife. "You have to assume that role," he said urgently. "Those Maratan women—they can't protect her. You can."

She wrenched away. "I don't even have a place for *myself* in the city. I can't be responsible for a child."

"Then she'll die," he said flatly.

"Why don't *you* watch out for her if it's so important?" she demanded, conveniently overlooking the fact that her entire impulse had been to keep Aussen *away* from Pietro.

He was shaking his head. "Not me. I am the last man she should be entrusted to. You need to lose yourself in the city, and take Aussen with you, and don't give me a clue where you might be found. If you see me on the streets, you should hide from me. If I come across you somewhere and try to say hello, you should run away. And you should never. Never. *Never.* Tell me where Aussen could be found."

She was beyond baffled. "I don't understand! First you say you want to keep her safe, and now you say you can't be trusted?"

His voice was low, almost hopeless. "I know these people, Jayla, these people who would harm her. They have been—in the past I believed in them with all my heart. I don't like to think it's true, but could they convince me that it would be right for them to take her? I don't trust myself. I trust *you*."

"You don't even know me. You can't trust anyone on a few days' acquaintance."

His laugh was hollow. "And sometimes you can't trust them after a lifetime of intimacy. So I will just say I trust you more than I trust myself. Right now, you're the only person I can think of who can keep Aussen safe."

She ground her free hand into her forehead as if the pressure could help her think. She couldn't possibly take Aussen with her as she tried to build a new life in Corcannon. Her hope was to hire on with the city soldiers or a merchant's private guard. What would she do with a child?

She couldn't possibly abandon the girl to mysterious and nefarious forces. If what Pietro said was true. If he wasn't a complete lunatic.

"What did you give her?" she asked. "I saw you, this afternoon. You handed her a pendant or something. Why?"

He nodded. "Yes. A charm made of a particular type of stone. She's safe as long as she wears it, because it will interfere with her ability to call her power. But she can't take it off, do you understand? Its inhibitory properties will protect her."

Jayla rubbed her forehead and squeezed her eyes shut. Pietro was straying farther and farther into the realm of madness. Or farther and farther into the province of evil. For all she knew, this magical medallion was, in fact, a tracking device that would actually tell Pietro and any of his maniacal friends exactly where Aussen was at all times. Not an amulet at all—a beacon.

"Where did you get this special stone?" she asked faintly, opening her eyes again so she could level an accusing stare in his direction. She could barely see his face in the gathering dark, but she hoped he could see the scowl on hers. "And why did you have it to begin with?"

"I have been wearing it for the past ten years as a sort of penance," he said. "I don't possess this particular ability, so it does nothing for me except remind me how dismally I failed when I could have done so much better."

She dropped her hand and sighed. "You have to stop talking in riddles like that," she said. "Just tell me the things I have to know. Does Aussen understand that she's supposed to wear the pendant at all times? I thought she couldn't speak Cordish."

"I have a few words of Zessin. I think she understood. At any rate, she let me put it on her, and she nodded when I told her she couldn't take it off. When I told her it would keep her safe." His voice roughened with urgency again. "But it can't truly keep her safe. Nothing can, except maybe you."

Maybe me. Clearly he doesn't think even I will be enough if these mad killers come after us. "It's a heavy commission," she said.

"But you'll take it?"

She wanted to refuse. She wanted to explain that she had come this far, managed this long, by caring only for herself, by not taking on burdens that she knew she could not handle. But she couldn't speak the words and had already squared her shoulders to accept the weight. She said, "I don't see that I have a choice."

Chapter Five: Madeleine

Madeleine eyed herself in the full-length mirror and wished gray was not the color of the season. She needed brighter shades for her chestnut hair and olive skin, but this particular shade of iced silver was currently the height of fashion. At least the simple silken sheath draped perfectly over her body and felt as cool as the color itself against her skin.

Her best hope was to accessorize. A filmy scarf of ochre and cinnamon reflected rich tones onto her face, and small bronze clips created curls and coils in her heavy hair. On her bare arms, she added wide gold cuffs above her elbows. Silver cuffs would have been a more perfect match for the dress, but she craved the heat of gold.

Anyway, she had silver enough around her wrists. Around her left was a wide filigreed band studded with dozens of tiny diamonds, proclaiming to anyone who cared to look that she was a member of a privileged elite. She found the bracelet embarrassingly ostentatious, but her father had given it to her on her sixteenth birthday, so she always wore it. Like all his gifts, it had been bestowed on her in an impersonal and unemotional manner. But that didn't mean it was unimportant to him.

On her right arm she wore bracelets of her own choosing. Her favorite was the smooth silver band inset with rows of tiny gold flowers along both edges, identifying her as a woman who preferred men. But she was also fiercely attached to the two very thin, very plain circlets, one gold, one silver, that marked the memories of her brother and her mother. Adults commonly wore wider funeral bracelets to memorialize dead spouses or children, but it was only in recent years that it had become common for people to don slimmer bands to mark losses of siblings or close friends. Madeleine knew her father wished she did not carry her grief so openly, but he hadn't forbidden her to wear the jewelry. He was adorned with two very similar pieces himself.

Her newest bracelet was one she wasn't officially permitted to wear yet, though she kept it in her jewelry case in her bedroom and admired it every day. It had been a gift from Tivol on the occasion of their betrothal; once they were married, it would be welded around her right wrist with her other personal accouterments. It was as wide as the filigreed band, made of a loop of silver and a loop of gold soldered together, with a line of diamonds dancing along the center line. It would mark her as a married woman—*a rich married woman,* she couldn't help thinking—an adult with responsibilities, social standing, a household of her own.

She could scarcely remember a time in her life that she hadn't known she would marry Tivol. She couldn't recall the first time someone had said to her, "Of course, that may change when you are Tivol's wife." He had always been there, as solid and as certain as her father, but so much brighter and kinder and dearer. He was a little too sure of himself sometimes, occasionally wrong about what Madeleine was thinking, and a tiny bit overbearing—but still the person in her life she was most likely to turn to, no matter what the situation. There was no one she knew half so well.

She had been a bit surprised when her father had decreed that the wedding wouldn't go forward for another two years, and even more surprised when Tivol agreed to the delay. "But I've always known I want to marry you!" she exclaimed. "I don't see the value of waiting."

"There is still a great deal of planning to do," he pointed out. "I am still learning about my mother's business and we haven't even *thought* about where to buy a house. And frankly, I'm enjoying all the privileges of a bachelor life. I am loath to give those up before I must."

That had distracted her. "What privileges? You'd better not be consorting with immoral women, or we won't be waiting two years to get married—we'll be waiting *forever.*"

That had caused him to drop a quick, affectionate kiss on her cheek. "Well, if I *was* consorting, I certainly wouldn't tell *you,* but I'm not," he assured her. "But I like being able to dash off with my friends at a moment's notice, and stay up drinking later than I should, and not have to worry about maintaining a household, and all those other boring things that only old men do."

"Very well," she'd said. "I shall enjoy my own two years of freedom just as heartily. But I'm looking forward to living somewhere other than my father's house."

He'd kissed her again. "I'm looking forward to living with *you,*" he said.

There was a knock on her bedroom door before the newest housemaid poked her head in. Her name was Ella, and although she was very sweet, she looked perpetually anxious, even though Madeleine always tried to greet her with an encouraging smile. "Someone's arrived to see you, dona," the girl said. "He's in the gilt room."

Madeleine resisted the urge to correct her. *You should tell me the name of my visitor when you announce him.* She didn't want Ella to become even more uneasy. "Thank you, I'll be right down."

She took a last look in the mirror—the scarf helped a great deal, but the gray was still a terrible choice—then headed out. She paused a moment on the balcony just outside her bedroom door. The central atrium of the house was flooded with light from the glass panels that formed a circle in the center of the roof. The wash of sun picked out all the colors in the mosaic tiles that covered the floors and the walls here on the second story. On sunny days, Madeleine sometimes felt she was inside a jewel box or maybe a fabric-merchant's shop, a mad swirl of hue and texture. Three mosaiced pillars stretched all the way from the tiled floor of the lower level to the supporting beams of the ceiling, adding their own patterns and colors to the general mix.

Madeleine's brother had spent one whole summer figuring out how to rig a rope that would let him leap from the balcony to one of the pillars and slide all the way down. He'd been rewarded with a broken leg and their father's fury, but he had assured her that all the trauma had been worth it. He'd only been ten at the time. He was dead two years later, or who knew what other kinds of trouble he might have gotten into?

Madeleine pushed back the memories and hurried to the stairwell that descended majestically from the second floor to the ground level of the atrium. Here, all the tiles on the floor and the walls were muted, mostly browns and tans with the occasional square of gold or sage. The bottom level of the home was considered the more public space, where strangers might be welcomed or business might be done, so it had to present a more formal air than the upper stories where the families lived.

Passing the tall potted plants that formed rows of greenery along the atrium, she headed for the cozy sitting room where favored guests were always shown. "Tivol, you're early," she said as she burst inside. "I can hardly believe it."

But the man standing just inside the door wasn't Tivol. "Madeleine," he said, coming close enough to grasp both of her hands. "I heard what happened."

For a moment, she was so surprised that she didn't react, not even to yank her hands away. She just stared into his handsome face and felt a blush rising to her own. "Reese," she finally said in a blank voice. "What are you doing here?"

His grip tightened. "I've been in the city a week or two. I had business for my father. I was going to come by one day, but I—" he shrugged and left the rest of the words unspoken.

She could fill them in for herself. *But I thought you would refuse to see me*. She pulled her hands free and stepped away from him, deeper into the room, hoping the color had started to fade from her cheeks. "Yes. Of course. I hope your father is well?"

"He is."

"And your mother? And your sisters?"

"Everyone's fine," he said impatiently. "But Madeleine! I heard what happened to you two days ago! Are you all right?"

She managed a light laugh. "How did that silly bit of news travel all the way across Corcannon to reach your ears? It was nothing."

He frowned. He had the typical Chibani coloring—fair skin, blue eyes, dark hair—but a frown could make him look thunderous. "It didn't sound like nothing. A man comes in off the streets and *attacks* you—"

"He didn't attack *me.* There were five of us sitting at a table and he just ran in our direction. I think he planned to grab as many jewels as he could manage in a few quick swipes, and then run out the door. I just happened to be the first one he reached for."

"He tried to *strangle* you!"

She laughed nervously. "It did feel like that," she admitted. "But the guards were on him almost instantly. I wasn't harmed at all."

"Except for the bruises on your throat that you're trying to conceal with a scarf."

She made a small indignant sound and touched the twisted folds of colorful cloth. "This is a fashionable accent, I will have you know."

He made an imperious motion. "Show me your neck."

"No! Don't be ridiculous! A madman tried to rob a table full of rich women, but he didn't succeed, and none of us are the worse for the adventure. There is nothing in that story to get you all worked up."

He glared at her. "This isn't the first time you've been in danger," he said.

She stiffened. "What do you mean?"

"Two months ago. In the Quatrefoil. Someone pushed you in front of a gridcar."

"Someone tripped, and we *both* fell down, and the car didn't hit us."

"You could have died!"

"He would have died right alongside me! I hardly think anybody would do that on purpose!"

"And there was that physician—"

"Reese! You're being ridiculous! My father called him to the house because I was already ill! He didn't *poison* me, even though the medicine made me sicker."

His fierce gaze was fixed upon her face. "Well, that's three times in the past six months that someone has almost killed you, and in that same period of time, no one has almost killed me once. And I find that very peculiar."

"I find it peculiar, too," she said sharply, "since I want to kill you every time I see you."

Abruptly, his frown lifted and he smiled. "So how are you, Madeleine?" he said simply. "I've missed you."

Her flush reappeared, hotter this time. "I'm well. Busy. I'm—just the same as always."

"I suppose you've been planning the wedding."

"I suppose I have."

"And have you decided yet where you'll live? In the city, or on the Wellenden estates in Marata?"

This was excruciating. "We'll split our time, I imagine. I think Tivol's mother would like him to spend more time in Marata as it is, but he is not as fond of country living as she is, so he's rarely there."

Reese's expression was sardonic. "How surprising."

She felt defensive. "He's quite busy."

"He's a young hedonist who doesn't care about anything except his own pleasure."

"That's not true! Heloise trusts him to conduct all her city business for her, and he works very hard."

Reese made a scoffing sound. "He works very hard four or five hours a week, I suppose. The rest of the time I think he merely enjoys himself."

"Well, since I don't suppose he invites you along on his pursuits, I can't think that you know what you're talking about."

"That's true. Tivol has no use for me."

"If you—" She stopped abruptly, putting her hands up. "This is ridiculous. We don't need to quarrel, and we certainly don't need to quarrel about Tivol. So how long will you be in the city?"

"Only another day or so, but I'll be coming back fairly often, because my father wants me to take his place on the Council." He smiled briefly. "And if you think *I* dislike Corcannon, you should hear my father's rants about the place. He's decided never to set foot off the property again. So I'll be his agent for any business that requires travel."

"Perhaps you'll enjoy that more than you expect."

"Perhaps," he agreed. "I went out to the islands a couple of months ago, and that was quite an experience. Only a handful of people could speak Cordish, but they tended not to be the people who could make decisions, so all negotiations took twice as long as expected. But the place was—" He couldn't seem to find an adequate word, so he settled on, "Amazing."

"I've seen sketches," she said in an encouraging voice. She liked travel much better than Tivol as a topic of conversation. "Those cliffs and the ocean—they seem wild and desolate."

"Even more so when you're actually there," he said. "The colors are—

everything is this slate gray. The cliffs, the beach, the houses and fences quarried from the mountains. The sea is a darker shade of the same gray, and more often than not, the sky is filled with piles of clouds that are almost the same color. And then there will be this burst of greenery or a bush as tall as my head and covered with red flowers, and the bright colors are such a contrast to the dark ones that they can take your breath away. And then the sun comes out and if it hits the water just right, it can blind you. The sky is so vivid you feel like you could dip your hand in it and it would come out stained blue."

"How poetic! Will you be going back?"

"I think so, yes. I think I will be traveling a great deal over the next two to three years."

"Will you go beyond Zessin? Out to the ruined lands?"

He smiled. "The ruined lands are off the eastern coast," he reminded her. "What's beyond the western coast are all these tiny little islands, one right after the other, so small you can hardly believe people live there. My father does run vessels out there to do a little trading, but there's not much commerce out that way. I don't think I'll be doing much sailing. Anyway, I have plenty to do just traveling around the continent."

"Then I hope you travel safely." A memory widened her eyes. "But Reese! Were you on the road when the quakes hit two weeks ago?"

"I was, but we could hardly feel them in Chibain. They were strongest right here at the city border, from what I understand. I should be asking where *you* were."

"Here, still asleep in my bed. I felt the house sway, and a crystal vase on my nightstand fell to the floor. But it was no worse than that."

He was frowning. "Still. Unnerving. I've heard that there have been more rumbles than usual over the past few months."

"Maybe. There are always rumbles, so it's hard to tell."

"I don't like to think of you here in the city if the whole place starts shaking apart. You should come out to Chibain and take shelter on my father's estates. We've barely felt the tremors."

Although he was smiling, she couldn't shake the feeling he was serious. But she adopted a bantering tone. "Well, I heard that Darrish Mountain is spewing ash, and you can practically see it from your front lawns! I would hardly be any safer there if the mountain suddenly erupted."

"Yes, but it lies south of us, and all the land slopes southward," he pointed out. "Any destruction would flow in that direction."

"Toward Marata."

"Indeed." He appeared to be struck by a sudden realization. "Toward Tivol's land! Promise me you won't go visiting his mother any time soon."

She tried to frown at him, but it was all too absurd. As if anyone could truly predict where ash and molten rock would flow. "I'll have to go to Marata sometime. The estates will eventually be ours after I marry Tivol and he inherits the land."

Reese offered her a lopsided unhappy grin. "Maybe you shouldn't marry him," he suggested. "It's too dangerous."

Her breath caught. "Don't be ridiculous."

"Don't marry him," he said. "It will break my heart."

She wanted to reply with another brisk *Don't be ridiculous*. She wanted to respond with a furious scold. *You promised you would stay away. You promised you would stop saying such things. You know you only confuse me and hurt me and make me hurt you in return.* But instead she just stared at him and couldn't summon a word.

"I know your father has always favored Tivol, but I'm from a Council family, too," he went on. "I think your father would get over his disappointment soon enough."

She shook her head. "Reese—"

"You don't have to marry him, Maddie," he said. "Not if you don't love him."

"Of course I love him!"

Reese just looked at her.

"I do!" she insisted. "And we're—we're *friends,* Reese, if you can understand that. We laugh together and talk together and understand each other, and I'm comfortable with him—"

"Oh, and I make you uncomfortable?" he shot at her.

"Yes! Just having this conversation makes me uncomfortable! Knowing you *want* something from me makes me uncomfortable! I can't *give* you that, Reese! I can feel you pleading with me even when you don't say a word, and it *weighs* on me. I'm going to marry Tivol, and that's not going to change just because you—" She tightened her lips over the next impossible words.

But he spoke them anyway. "Because I love you?"

She turned her eyes away. "Because you think you do."

"Because you love me?" he said softly.

She shook her head, still not looking at him. *I don't,* she wanted to tell him. *I don't I don't I don't.* Instead she said, "I'm going to marry Tivol."

There was a moment of silence. "But not yet."

Now she sighed and looked back at him. "Reese."

"Not for another two years, is that right?"

"I don't see what that has to do with anything."

"It means you're not *sure*."

"It means I have a lot of planning to do and Tivol is in no particular hurry."

"It means anything can happen," Reese said. "Two years is practically a lifetime."

"It might feel that way sometimes," she retorted. "Certainly this conversation seems to have lasted for hours."

He surprised her by laughing. "Only because you're savoring every word."

She made a sound of choked fury, and Reese laughed even harder. "I think your arrogance is even worse than your importunities!" she exclaimed. "But at least it helps me to stop feeling sorry for you!"

"Well, I don't want your pity, so I suppose I'll have to flaunt my arrogance more often," he said cheerfully.

"Certainly! That will make you welcome at even more households than mine."

A light voice at the door caused them both to spin in that direction. "What? Reese Curval in town and winning friends everywhere with his mockery and arrogance? I am shocked at such an unlikely occurrence."

"Tivol!" Madeleine exclaimed, hurrying over with outstretched hands. "How good of you to arrive just in time to keep me from quarreling with Reese."

He enveloped her hands in his and smiled at her with his usual lazy charm. "The only way to keep from quarreling with Reese is to deny him entrance to the house," he said. "I thought you knew that by now."

"And yet somehow I forget until he shows up again."

Reese strolled toward the door, his face showing no discomfiture at the interruption—not anger, not remorse, not thwarted passion. For her part, Madeleine was struggling to contain her own emotions. Embarrassment. Dismay at what Tivol might have overheard. Guilt that she had allowed Reese to say such things at all.

And the tiniest bit of disappointment that the conversation with Reese bad been terminated so abruptly. Of course, there was nothing else he could possibly have to say to her, no other answer she could have given him. She should be glad he was leaving without a chance to renew his appeals.

"I enjoyed the chance to catch up this afternoon, Maddie," he said as he reached the door. Ever so slightly he emphasized the pet name that no one else used any more, now that her brother and mother were dead. "I hope we run into each other again soon."

Tivol's voice was casual, but he still kept Madeleine's hands in his, which she couldn't help thinking was a deliberate show of possessiveness. "How long are you planning to stay in town?"

Reese's voice was pleasant as well. "Only another day or two but, as I was telling Madeleine, I'll be back soon on business for my father."

"Well, then, we'll look forward to seeing you next time you're here," Tivol said in his usual blithe way. "Unless—do you have time now? We're off to have lunch. If you're free, you could join us."

For one horrified moment, Madeleine thought Reese was actually considering it, but he finally shook his head. "Not today, thank you," he said. "Too many other demands on my time."

Tivol gently pulled Madeleine toward the door, and the three of them finally left the room. The warm brown tiles of the atrium were turned to gold by the afternoon sun pouring down from the skylights overhead. Outside, it was even brighter and warmer, but Madeleine was so glad to get out of the charged atmosphere of the house that she didn't even care.

Tivol's small, sporty gridcar was pulled up outside in the semicircular drive that accommodated visitors. Tivol owned a larger and more formal vehicle that he used when he was entertaining business contacts or escorting Madeleine to fancy events, but this model was his favorite. It was lightweight enough that Madeleine sometimes felt she could bend the edges of the doors with her bare hands, but Tivol explained that this feature made it twice as fast as any ordinary car. Of course, the main thoroughfares of the city were so clogged with traffic that it scarcely mattered how fast a vehicle could go—but she had heard tales of less crowded, less savory neighborhoods where young men raced their cars down adjacent alleys so fast that sparks flew from the frayed wires overhead. She couldn't imagine why anyone would think such an activity was entertaining.

It took her a moment to realize that there was no second car in the drive. Reese must have walked over, or hopped on one of the big public transports that everyone referred to as chuggers. Tivol seemed to reach the same conclusion, because he said, "Do you need a ride? We're heading toward the Quatrefoil, but I wouldn't mind making a detour."

"Thanks, but I'm going north," he said. "Enjoy your lunch!" And he marched off without another word.

Tivol didn't even bother to watch him walk away. "I'm starving," he said, helping Madeleine into the car and climbing in beside her. "Let's go."

Madeleine dropped to the padded bench, braced her feet, and took a tight hold on the slim metal bar that curved out from the panel in front of her. Tivol was in motion almost before she was settled, pulling out from the drive onto the main road, which was unexpectedly clear of traffic. "Ha," he said and accelerated with alarming speed. On this balmy day, the entire upper half of the carriage was open to the air, and the wind of passage instantly whipped Madeleine's hair into knots. The light car jounced so feverishly over the road that it seemed about to rip itself from the overhead cable and go tumbling down an alley or crashing into one of the manors that lined the boulevard. A particularly hard bounce caused her to slide into the door so forcefully she thought she bruised her hip.

"Tivol! Could you please slow down?" she exclaimed. "You're terrifying me!"

He laughed, but instantly slackened his pace. She straightened on her seat and tried to pat her hair back into place, but she was pretty sure she'd need a mirror and a comb to repair the damage. "Sorry, sorry, sorry," he said. "It's just so rare that you even have three or four blocks where you can travel above a slow crawl."

"I prefer a slow crawl," she said tartly. "I'm less likely to die."

He laughed again and slowed even more. Three cars had pulled into the lane ahead of them and were clicking along at a sedate pace that he had no choice but to adopt. To their left, a large chugger passed, going in the other direction. It was connected to the overhead cables by two thick rods and jammed so full of people that some of them were sticking their heads out of the open windows just to breathe the fresher air.

"I should take you racing with me some night," Tivol said. "Then you'd see how fast some cars can go, the real sprinters. Derrik Bandelo has this little beauty, even smaller than this one, and you'd think it was flying down the road."

"I hate to disappoint you, but that's not a sight that's ever going to interest me."

He glanced over at her with a quick grin. "You can't be certain of that until you see it at least once," he said in a teasing voice. "I'm having a model built that I think will be even faster than Derrik's. Only holds one person, which keeps the weight down, and uses the lightest thickness of metal that will still stand up to the stress of friction. He knows I'm working on it—and he knows I'm going to beat him, too."

"So I finally understand," she said.

"Understand what?"

"Why you don't want to get married for two years. How could you give up such a diverting pastime for the sober life of the married man?"

He grinned at her again. "What makes you think I'm going to give up racing once I'm married? I'm counting on turning you into a convert!"

She thought he was joking, so she laughed—and then she wondered if he wasn't, and she had to hide a frown. She had the sudden, brief, treacherous thought that she didn't want to marry Tivol, she didn't want to marry anyone. She wasn't even sure she wanted to go to lunch. She turned her head to watch the great houses come into view and then drop out of sight as they continued down the wide avenue, and she had to keep working at it to smooth away her scowl.

Madeleine was surprised that night when her father sent word that he wanted her to join him for dinner. She and her father could spend days without encountering each other over a meal or in the hallways. On the rare occasions that he expected her to eat with him, he usually let her know several days in advance and listed the various guests that would be in attendance. She always dressed for the occasion and gladly played her part. Eventually she would be hostess for the dinner parties Tivol held for business acquaintances and Council families; she welcomed the chance to acquire experience beforehand.

Ella had told her that she was expected in the smaller dining room, which pleased her. The casual space with its red and ochre mosaics was much more welcoming than the formal room, which was large, drafty, and oddly austere. She always felt as if she was presiding over some legal proceeding whenever she welcomed guests to the table.

The fact that he had chosen the smaller room made her think her father must be alone, but as soon as she walked in, she realized her error. Harlo turned toward the door as she entered, smiling sweetly and extending his arms. "My dear," he said, and she crossed the room to place her hands in his.

"Harlo! What a treat! It's been ages since I've seen you!" she exclaimed, leaning in so he could kiss her cheek. His lips brushed her skin with the weightlessness of dried rose petals. She pulled back to smile at him, but she was concealing a pulse of alarm. He looked old, she thought—the thin white hair thinner and whiter, the bony face bonier, the dark skin lightening to a faded brown. The hands clasping hers seemed strong as ever, but under the folds of his ivory robe she thought his body seemed more fragile, more bent. It had never occurred to her that Harlo might be mortal. He was known as the high divine because he headed the order of priests that served Cordelan. That made him the most powerful man in the city, and she had just assumed he would live forever.

"Madeleine. How are you?" he asked, releasing her hands. "Although I don't have to ask—you look radiant as always."

She laughed and patted her hair. "I think I look unkempt and disarranged," she said. "Tivol took me out for a drive this afternoon and I feel like I have been buffeted by a windstorm. Had I known you would be here I would have put much more effort into my appearance."

"Nonsense," Harlo said in his gentle way. "I prefer an authentic heart."

Her father had looked over at the mention of Tivol's name. In contrast to the old priest, Alastair Alayne looked to be bursting with health and vigor. He was a big man anyway, with the stocky build of a Maratan blended with the dark hair and deep mahogany skin of a typical Cordelano. He was not above using his size, and the latent ferocity of his natural expression, to intimidate opponents, supplicants, and rivals.

And children and spouses.

"And how did you find Tivol?" he asked.

"As always. Excellent company."

"He's a good boy," Harlo said.

Her father laughed sharply. "Hardly a boy. He's a man grown. One death away from inheriting the richest property in Marata, two years from being a husband—and maybe three years from being a father."

Madeleine laughed lightly. "Well, if I have anything to say about it—as I think I *do*—it might be more than three years before Tivol has children."

Harlo's face crinkled into a grin, and he patted Madeleine on the shoulder. "Oh, your father has wanted grandchildren ever since I've known him," he said.

Madeleine absolutely could not voice her immediate reaction. *I can't think why. He was never interested in his own son and daughter.* Out loud she said, "Yes, he has made it quite clear that he expects me to produce an entire brood! The sooner the better! I think he wants to found a dynasty."

She couldn't quite read the expression on her father's face. Then again, she rarely could. He said, "Exactly right. I've amassed a fortune and I need many heirs to spend it after I'm gone."

"And unfortunately, there is no one but you to present him with those heirs," said Harlo.

Madeleine felt a sudden stab of grief, an emotion that visited her at the most unexpected moments. Logan had been gone nearly eleven years; she would have thought the ache would have worn down to a manageable dullness by now. But it was still a silver knifepoint in her ribs. "Well, I will do my best," she said, speaking around a tightness in her throat. "But I am *not* going to start breeding the instant I get married."

It was clear that Harlo heard her buried pain. His eyes dropped to the slim gold band on her right wrist, and he patted her shoulder again. "You'll carry that forever," he said, so softly her father might not even have heard. "But carry it as a blessing inside your heart."

She was so grateful for the kindness that she felt her eyes burn with tears, but she blinked them away and managed a smile. "I always do."

Her father seemed oblivious. "Let's take our seats," he said. "Dinner is on the way."

Normally, a meal with her father left Madeleine tense and on edge, but Harlo's presence softened everything, even her father's sharp tongue. The old priest had such a soothing presence and gentle humor that people couldn't help but relax around him. When Madeleine was a child, Harlo had been her favorite confidante, and he had been the only person who could comfort her after Logan's death. These days she was much less likely to confide in anyone, and rarely in need of comfort, but Harlo could still make her feel protected and loved.

The conversation revolved mostly around issues that didn't engage her much—business and politics—since Harlo and her father were both prominent members of the Corcannon Council that ran the city. Not until they were finishing up the meal with some sweet lemon delicacy did the conversation turn to topics that more closely involved Madeleine, and then she wished it hadn't.

"But I forgot to ask!" Harlo said. "Are you fully recovered from your terrible adventure? I heard you were attacked in a busy restaurant!"

Apparently, everyone in the entire city had been regaled with the tale. "There was a loud man brandishing a weapon, but he didn't actually attack me," she said. "We were all frightened, but none of us were harmed."

Her father glanced at her before turning his eyes toward Harlo. "That is the way she tells the story, but others tell it differently," he said. "She seems to have been the target of this man's rage."

Harlo held her father's gaze for a moment, his expression severe. "And can you think of any reason someone would have singled out your daughter?" he asked. "Have you engaged in any business dealings that might have left a rival with a grudge?"

Her father didn't seem discomposed by the harsh implications. "No. Nothing. Perhaps this is purely random aggression from someone who doesn't even know who Madeleine is."

"Which is what I've been saying," Madeleine put in.

Harlo looked concerned. "And yet, Alastair, I do not like this! Have you thought about taking steps to have Madeleine more closely guarded?"

"I've thought about it," her father said, which was news to Madeleine. "But it complicates her life to a cumbersome degree."

"Better encumbered and alive than untrammeled and dead," Harlo said. His gentle voice made the words even more chilling.

"So you think I would not be out of line to have her watched around the clock?"

"What? Father! *No!* Harlo, what have you got him started on?"

"One of the temple guards, maybe?" her father asked.

Harlo shook his head. "Think what kind of gossip that would give rise to," he said. "All over the city, they would say I prefer your daughter to all the other lovely young women of the Council families!" He smiled at Madeleine. "It is true, of course, but I don't want everyone to know it."

"But I don't want a full-time guard—from the temple or from anywhere," Madeleine said.

"It would have to be a woman," her father said. "So she could follow Madeleine anywhere. I don't have any female soldiers in my employ at the moment."

"Easily remedied," Harlo said.

Her father nodded. "Well, I'll make that a priority. Tomorrow or the next day."

"You aren't seriously saying that you're going to hire someone to follow me around everywhere I go for the rest of my life," Madeleine exclaimed.

Both the men looked at her. Her father's face was its usual impenetrable mask, but Harlo's expression showed genuine concern. "My dear," he said. "You are so precious. If simple measures could suffice to keep you safe, why would we not take them? Why would you not agree?"

"Because it's ridiculous!" she said. "Because I don't feel like anyone is trying to harm me. Because it would feel odd to be followed around all the time by somebody watching my every move."

"None of those seem like good enough reasons," Harlo said.

Her father nodded. "All right. I'll arrange it."

Madeleine felt alarm. "Wait! Do I at least get some say in choosing the person who is to be my inescapable companion?"

Her father merely looked at her. "What do you know about hiring a soldier?"

"Well—well—nothing, but do I at least get the right of refusal? If it's someone I don't like?"

"No."

"It's a reasonable request, Alastair," Harlo interjected. "Surely she should have the ability to say no."

Her father shrugged. "Fine. But don't think to use multiple refusals to draw out the process so long I abandon it."

It had been exactly what she was thinking, but she assumed an expression of innocence. "Of course not."

"Now that we have settled this most important matter, would it be possible for me to request more wine?" Harlo asked almost plaintively. "Madeleine, could you hand me the decanter?"

"I'll pour for you," she said, jumping up and retrieving the bottle from the sideboard.

He half-turned in his chair to lift his glass in her direction, and she somehow misjudged the height of his arm. The lip of the decanter came down hard on the rim of his goblet, and the glass shattered in his hand. She gasped and made an instinctive grab at the falling fragments, and somehow his fingers were wrapped around her hand and large sharp pieces were digging into her palm.

"Ow—ow—oh, Harlo, I'm so sorry!" she cried, while he was exclaiming, "Madeleine! My dear!" It was a moment before they disentangled and she could set down the decanter. He grasped her hand and appeared distraught over the three deep cuts oozing with blood.

"What have I done? Madeleine, you are hurt!" He snatched up his linen napkin and began winding it tenderly around her hand. "Oh, I'm so clumsy. You poor girl!"

"I'm fine, but look at you! Wine all over your robe—and *blood*—you look like you've gotten into a street altercation! Harlo, I apologize with all my heart!"

Her father was already at the door, calling for Ella to come clean up the mess. "Are you seriously injured?" he asked her, turning to face her.

"Let me see," she said, and Harlo reluctantly removed the napkin. The blood was still welling up, but not very fast, and there didn't appear to be any fragments stuck in the wounds. "I think I'll live."

"You need to get that tended to," Harlo said in a scolding voice. "Can someone on the staff be trusted to dress it, or should we call for a physician?"

"The housekeeper plays nurse for all the servants," she said.

"Then go! Seek her out!"

"But I can't leave you in all this mess—"

"I insist," Harlo said. "And if there is a scar on your hand the next time I see you, I shall never forgive myself."

She hesitated, but truth to tell, the cuts were throbbing a little. And she wanted to finally change out of the gray gown she had worn all day. And she wanted to think over everything that had happened since she left her bedroom this morning, from unexpectedly seeing Reese again to learning she was about to acquire a permanent guard.

"There will be no scar," she promised, leaning over to kiss his cheek. "But if there were, it would just remind me how much I love you. I'm glad we got to visit tonight."

"So am I," said Harlo as she headed out the door. "Let us hope our next encounter is much less dramatic."

Chapter Six: Madeleine

Madeleine discovered it was a bit of a challenge to dress for the day when she had to wear a gauze bandage wrapped around her palm. The housekeeper hadn't been too impressed by the wounds, but she'd applied a smelly antiseptic that hurt far more than the original cuts and advised keeping the whole mess covered for two or three days.

"Gray dress, bandaged hand, and circles under your eyes because you couldn't fall asleep," Madeleine told her reflection. "Good thing you have nothing planned for the day, because you do *not* look like an attractive young lady of fashion."

Almost on the words, Ella knocked on the door. "A visitor to see you," she said.

"Of course," Madeleine groaned under her breath. She took a final look in the mirror, shrugged fatalistically, and headed downstairs.

She was expecting to see one of her friends who happened to be bored this morning, or even one of her father's business contacts, but it had not occurred to her that Reese Curval would be the one waiting. She stopped just over the threshold and stared at him.

He stayed where he was—all the way across the room—and offered her a painful smile. "I came to apologize," he said.

She merely lifted her eyebrows and said nothing.

"I had no right to say any of the things I said. When I stopped by, my intention was to merely visit for a few moments, maybe make you laugh, then leave. I'm sorry that that's not what happened."

"I'm sorry, too."

"I hate that we can't be friends," he went on. "I hate that every time I see you, I just cause you to dislike me more."

She was trying to maintain an aloof expression, but that made her face crease in protest. "I don't dislike you, Reese. I never have."

"You just don't—" He caught himself before he could say more. "Anyway, I couldn't leave the city again knowing that I had upset you."

He was so sincere and so wretched that she felt some of her anger melt away. She stepped a little farther into the room. "Thank you. It was good of you to make the effort to mend the damage."

"I would ask for forgiveness, but maybe I first need to ask for tolerance and work my way up."

She smiled. "Is tolerance the lowest rung? What's the highest?" He just looked at her, and she felt herself blushing. To cover her embarrassment, she said, "Well! I think I can manage that much. At least, as long as you don't say anything else stupid."

"I'm trying not to," he said. He gestured at her. "Is it stupid if I ask what happened to your hand?"

She surveyed the bandage with distaste. "I cut it on a broken wineglass last night. It's most annoying and inconvenient."

"Injuries generally are."

"Oh! But not nearly as annoying and inconvenient as something my father has just decided!"

"What's that?"

"He wants to employ a guard to follow me around. Like you, he's decided that there are too many dangers in the city streets and I must be protected at all costs."

"I'm glad to hear it," Reese said.

"I made him promise that I would be able to approve or disapprove of his choice, but I'm not sure he'll honor the promise. I'm very glum about the whole thing."

"Pick your own candidate," Reese suggested. "Pre-empt him."

She laughed. "As my father pointed out, I don't know the first thing about hiring a soldier."

"I could help you with that. I've hired the last two captains of my father's guard, and half a dozen of the soldiers who protect our shipments. So far they've all proved to be solid choices."

She was intrigued. "*Really.* But—where would I even go to find someone?"

"There are training yards in the southeastern section of town," he said. "Facilities where mercenaries fight and train. You go down there, you watch them work out, you see if anyone catches your fancy."

She stared at him helplessly. "And then what?"

He grinned. "You interview them. See if they seem like sound candidates. See what they're asking for in terms of pay. See if you can agree on terms."

"And you can do all that?"

"Sure. Now, if you like." He glanced around, as if looking for clues that she might be in the middle of some other occupation. "Unless you're busy."

"No, indeed, this is the most interesting activity I can imagine pursuing for the rest of the day! Just let me get a scarf and I'll be right back."

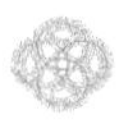

Reese had brought his own gridcar this morning. A sober contrast to Tivol's, it was sturdy and unadorned, though the interior benches were so heavily padded they were actually comfortable to sit on. It was also twice the size of Tivol's, big enough to hold six passengers.

"It's my mother's," Reese said apologetically. "My own is being repaired."

Madeleine squirmed happily on the seat. "I like it! I don't feel like my bones will break as we go bouncing down the streets."

Reese laughed and skillfully guided them out of the drive and onto the gridway. The sun was warm enough that Madeleine caught the faint metallic smell of the overhead wires. Today traffic was heavy in all directions. They clicked along behind a large chugger and four private vehicles of varying sizes, their pace so sedate it might almost be called agonizing. On the other side of the road, a similar parade of vehicles slowly cruised in the opposite direction.

The noise made conversation difficult, so Madeleine relaxed on the bench and idly watched the scenery go by. They started out in the northwestern district of the city, nicknamed Council Row because it was where the prominent politicians and wealthy families had their homes. Most of them were shaped much like Madeleine's own—three- or four-story blocklike structures of white or gray or honey-tinted stones set on expansive lawns. They were generally plain on the outside, with occasional fountains or decorative ironwork fencing to soften their severe edges. It was only once visitors stepped past the imposing front doors that they would get any sense of the colors and styles inside. A great number of the houses were built around central atriums and featured giant supporting pillars that stretched from the floor to the ceiling. In most, the bottom stories would consist of public rooms in prim colors, while the upper stories where family members lived would be decked out in flagrantly joyous hues. But within those restrictions, Madeleine had always found the variety from house to house could be quite amazing. Some manors would be decorated with mosaiced tiles in intricate patterns; others would feature swaths of fabric; still others were painted with landscapes of astonishing detail.

But the view of the grand houses only lasted so long. Once Reese turned onto the main road that headed toward the Quatrefoil, the character of the buildings began to subtly change. For a while they remained in residential districts, but the houses were smaller, a little closer together; it was still impossible to tell from the outside what the personality might be on the inside, but it was clear the level of wealth was not as high. A bit farther east, and the buildings became long rows of connected lodgings. Some were quite fashionable and tended to be rented out to wealthy young socialites who were living on their own; some were a bit more rundown and seemed to be occupied by families that couldn't afford nicer accommodations.

As soon as they crossed a double row of north-south boulevards, the main road bowed out to curve around the Quatrefoil. Here could be found virtually any destination worth seeking out—parks, theaters, restaurants, museums, and of course the vast complex of the Cordelan temple.

It sat at the very heart of the plaza, the heart of the city itself, a sprawling cluster of buildings all constructed of a dense white stone freckled with icy crystals. In the sunlight—even in the moonlight—the walls seemed to glitter with flecks of holy fire. The main feature was the temple itself, a large circular building topped with a stained-glass cupola. Around it were gathered buildings where the priests lived and worked and stored their centuries of records.

Harlo kept an expansive suite in the largest of these structures, and Madeleine had been there dozens of times for lavish dinner parties where most of the wealthiest families were in attendance. She had once heard Harlo laughingly apologize for not being the sort of priest who followed an abstemious path. Her father had replied, "It is not ascetics we need in the priesthood, but men of conviction." It had seemed like an odd thing to say—which was why, she supposed, she remembered it all these years later.

Once they passed the temple, three parks, and a line of exclusive shops, they began to edge out of the central district. The minute they crossed another double boulevard, they were in the professional quarter, where forbidding rows of tall, narrow buildings held the offices of lawyers and businessmen. A few miles later, they were passing through a monotonous landscape of warehouses and factories, trying not to breathe in the fumes of oil, exhaust, and smoke.

A few minutes later, Reese turned the car to the right, and they were soon in another part of town altogether. Here, buildings were all low to the ground, built of brick or wood instead of stone, and clustered together like neighbors gathering to gossip. Interspersed with what might be houses and might be taverns were fruit stands and small vendors selling goods out of carts. Gridcars were scarcer and pedestrians more plentiful. Even the air felt warmer than it had in the northern districts. Madeleine looked around with interest.

"I'm not sure I've ever been to this corner of the city," she said. "It seems friendly, somehow." The noise level had dropped so much she didn't even have to shout.

"Homes and businesses of the workingmen," Reese said. "I won't say it's as safe as your street, but there's a strong sense of community."

"All kinds of people, too," she said. The Council families almost all had at least some Cordelano blood, although their dark coloring was sometimes diluted by the lighter skin tones of Chibani and Maratan ancestors. Anyone in that part of town who looked to be purebred Chibani or Maratan was usually a servant or a merchant making deliveries. But in just a few blocks, she'd seen people of every kind of heritage, including Zessin and even Oraki. It was so unfamiliar.

Reese pulled into a small lot where about a dozen other vehicles were already parked. "Closest place to the leave the car," he explained as they climbed out. "It's just a short walk."

The intensifying heat made it a little unpleasant to stroll down the crowded street, past curious loiterers and an untidy parade of buildings. But they hadn't gone far before they reached their destination. A large well-kept wooden building sat well back from the road, its open doors inviting passers-by to enter, but its real attraction was out front. A rope-and-pole fence enclosed about two acres of land trampled down to hard earth. Within that makeshift arena, about thirty fighters faced off against each other in various types of combat. Some handled swords or knives; others went at their opponents with their bare hands. All of them were on foot, though Madeleine saw a couple of horses tied up near the side of the building.

"Oh!" she exclaimed, because she had never seen anything like this—so much violent, physical, personal action at such close quarters.

"It can be overwhelming at first," Reese said. "But stand here and watch for a few moments, and you'll start to make sense of the contests."

They moved closer to the flimsy fence, where ten or twelve other onlookers were already gathered. One or two of the spectators cast Madeleine an appraising glance, but none of the fighters even appeared to notice they had an audience. Madeleine took a deep breath, curled the fingers of her right hand around the highest strand of rope, and settled in to observe.

It was soon clear that the pairs of fighters all had different styles and motivations. Two men in the farthest corner were wielding swords with frightening energy, shouting and grunting and landing blows that were so hard she could hear them even above the other noise. Other sets of combatants appeared to be working together, showing off various moves, going through the same set of motions over and over. Knives flashed, mud flew, curses rang out, and fairly often someone started laughing. It was a tangled and chaotic and glorious and terrifying scene.

Madeleine had been watching, dumbstruck, for about fifteen minutes before she remembered that she was here for a purpose, and she began to scan the crowd for candidates who might be suitable. At first, she didn't see any women among the fighters, but as she looked more closely, she began to pick them out. In the middle of the arena was a tall, muscular woman of Chibani heritage dueling with a man who was shorter but bulkier than she was. Madeleine knew nothing about sword fighting, but they appeared fairly well-matched to her; at any rate, neither of them took what seemed like a killing blow during the time she watched.

Two other women were engaged in a kind of wrestling match where one would grab the other and try to fling her to the ground. Their expressions were focused and serious, and they paused with some regularity to rehearse their motions again, so Madeleine guessed that one might be teaching the other some maneuver. They were both smaller than the sword fighter but bigger than Madeleine, and all three of them looked powerful enough to crush a skull between their hands. *I'm sure that's a valuable trait in a guard,* she thought. It was still an unnerving notion.

Reese nudged her with his elbow. "See anyone who interests you?" he asked.

"I don't know. It's so hard to judge."

He nodded toward the right-hand side of the yard, the corner that was closest to the building. "She's the one who caught my eye," he said.

Madeleine couldn't see around the heaving, shifting mass of fighters. "Let's get closer," she said, and they circled around the rope fence to get a better look.

The fighter that Reese had picked out was smaller and leaner than the others—about Madeleine's size. What was even more surprising was that she appeared to be a purebred Oraki, her pale skin streaked with mud, her blonde hair braided and coiled on top of her head. She was dressed in worn leather and faded cotton and was slim enough and young enough to pass for a boy.

Her opponent was a Zessin man significantly bigger and heavier than she was, and they were engaged in a knife fight at close quarters. At first glance, it seemed impossible that the woman could have any chance of winning. The man lunged at her with his blade held high—he would only need to fall on her to crush her under the weight of his body, his knife already buried in her heart. Madeleine gasped in terror. But the woman spun effortlessly away, catching his ankle with her foot and tripping him with his own momentum. He fell heavily but rolled quickly to his knees, scrambling to face her as she circled him tightly. She thrust at the back of his neck, but he grabbed her wrist and hauled her over his shoulder, and Madeleine gasped again. But the woman seemed to do a somersault in midair, landing on her feet in front of him, facing him, her knife still in her hand. Another thrust, and this time she connected with his collarbone. He grunted in pain and clambered to his feet. Madeleine saw a line of red collect on the front of his dirty shirt and clenched her fingers over her own much smaller wound.

"Sorry," the woman called. "We weren't supposed to draw blood."

Her partner pressed his hand briefly over the injury and shook his head. "A scratch," he said. "That was a good trick. I'm too heavy for that kind of roll."

"Sometimes it's easier to fight a big man than a small one," the woman said. "Small one is just as fast as I am."

"Try it again?" he said. She nodded and dove at him without another word.

Reese glanced over at Madeleine with his eyebrows raised. "I like her," he said.

Madeleine nodded. "So do I."

They watched for another ten minutes as the woman and her large partner practiced a few more heart-stopping maneuvers, but neither combatant sustained another injury. After one particularly physical exchange, the man paused with his hands on his knees, breathing heavily. He caught sight of Madeleine and Reese and nodded to acknowledge them.

"Looking to hire?" he asked.

Reese nodded back. "Interested in a female guard for a female client."

"Jayla," the man called over his shoulder. "They want to talk to you."

A few minutes later, the three of them were inside, sitting around a small bare table in a small bare room. It was the most impersonal setting Madeleine had ever seen; no niceties at all, not even the offer of a cup of water, just the minimum necessary space to conclude a transaction. Madeline and Reese sat on one side of the table, facing the woman called Jayla. She divided her attention evenly between them, which Madeleine liked. This was not someone who made assumptions about where the power lay.

"You want to hire a fighter?" she asked. Her voice was cool and brisk, with an accent Madeleine supposed was Oraki.

"I do," said Madeleine. "My father has recently become worried about my safety and would like me to have a guard with me at all times."

Jayla focused on Madeleine. "What's caused him to worry?"

A reasonable question. Madeleine found herself wanting to assure the woman that there was no danger, really, it would all be for show, but that seemed like a stupid thing to say. "A few days ago, a madman came at a table of women in a public place. He had a knife. He didn't hurt anyone, but it seemed like he could have. And I was the one he attacked first." She felt Reese glance over at her, so she reluctantly added, "And there have been a couple of other incidents that might have been accidents, but might not have been. For instance, someone pushed me in front of a gridcar."

Jayla nodded. "Would there be any reason for someone to want to harm you?"

Madeleine turned to Reese. "That's exactly what Harlo asked my father last night!" She turned back to Jayla. "I don't *think* so. Unless my father is involved in some dangerous business deal with unsavory people, but that doesn't seem like my father."

"And all of these attacks have taken place outside of your home?"

Madeleine was silent a moment. "Maybe." Jayla just waited for her to go on. Madeleine made a gesture of frustration. "I was sick, and the physician brought me a medicine that actually made me sicker. But that could just have been a mistake on his part."

"And it's not the kind of assault a guard could protect you from," Jayla commented. "Where's that physician now?"

It had never occurred to Madeleine to ask. "I don't know," she said.

Jayla seemed to think it over. "So you might have been targeted three different times, in three different ways. But none of the events was lethal. It's possible there's no connection between them—that things just went wrong on those three days."

"Which is what *I've* been saying," Madeleine interjected.

"But assuming someone really is trying to harm you, two things seem clear."

"Really? Nothing seems clear to me."

Jayla held up one finger. "They're using a variety of different methods because they don't *want* you to think you're in danger. Because they're trying to make the attacks look random and coincidental."

"Which argues a certain degree of planning and malice," Reese said.

Jayla nodded. "It also argues that they will keep trying." She held up a second finger. "Murder is not their primary occupation, or you would be dead already. So either they don't really want you dead—or they just don't have much experience killing people."

"Either the poison or the gridway incident could have been fatal," Reese said. "The knife attack could have been, too."

"So they're inexperienced," Jayla said. A slight frown crossed her face. "But if someone who's not very good at killing keeps attempting to murder a woman, it means that person has a strong motivation to keep trying. That person has a grudge. Or a cause."

Madeleine looked at her blankly. "But—I can't think of any reason either of those things would be true."

Jayla shrugged. "Sometimes people get notions in their head, and those notions don't make sense to anyone else. But those crazy ideas can drive them to do some powerful things."

"Except," Reese said. "All three of these attacks came from different people." He appealed to Madeleine. "Isn't that right? The man who pushed you into the gridway, the man who assaulted you at the restaurant—not the same person, right? And the physician was someone else altogether."

Madeleine felt troubled. "I didn't get a good look at the man who pushed me in the street," she said. "I couldn't tell you what he looked like. But the doctor and the man with the knife were two different people."

"Here's another factor to consider," Jayla said. "In at least two of those situations, someone knew the details of your life. Knew you were sick, knew you would be at a certain restaurant at a certain time. If someone *is* targeting you, it's a person who knows you fairly well."

Madeleine stared at the stranger's calm, pale face and felt her whole body prickle with chill. She didn't believe it, still, not really, this farfetched notion that someone was out to harm her. Mishaps blundered into everyone's life; who *hadn't* fallen down the stairs or accidentally swallowed something toxic? Just yesterday she'd been convinced she and Tivol would die in a fiery gridway crash as they careened down the main boulevard. Would Reese and her father have claimed that was the work of an assassin?

Although she supposed someone could have tampered with the bar that clipped the car to the cable—weakened it in some fashion so that the stress of one hard turn would snap the metal in half and send them spinning into oncoming traffic. Someone who knew Madeleine very well would have known that Tivol was expected at her house that day—would have known that Tivol loved to drive too fast and take ridiculous risks—

"So you're suggesting one of my friends," Madeleine said in a choked voice. "Or one of the servants."

"Could be one of your friends," Jayla agreed. "Probably not one of the servants, because they've got pretty unrestricted access to you. A lot of chances to kill you. Although," she added, "if you're thinking about hiring one in the near future, you might want to be careful."

Madeleine couldn't restrain a shiver. Reese reached over to give her shoulder a comforting squeeze, but he dropped his arm when she gave him a warning look. "I hate the way this is making me think," she complained. "Like I can't trust anyone in the whole world."

"I apologize," Jayla said. "I'm so used to thinking this way that it seems natural to me."

"And yet it's just this kind of thinking that could save your life," Reese said.

"*If* someone is trying to harm me! *If* we're not just overreacting to a few unconnected random events."

"Well, look at it this way," said Reese. "Say we're wrong. Say we hire a guard anyway. What's the worst thing that happens? Your father adds the price of one salary to his household budget—which he can very well afford. But say we're right, but we *think* we're wrong. And we don't hire a guard. And someone kills you next week. Which outcome would you prefer? I know which one *I* would choose."

"Well, it doesn't matter what either one of us prefers, because my father wants to hire the guard, so I will have one no matter what," Madeleine snapped.

Reese smiled at her flash of ill-temper. "Then let's make sure he hires one that you can tolerate."

Madeleine sighed, then looked over at Jayla, who was watching them both. "This is the situation," she said. "My father will make the selection, but I believe he will take my opinion into account. I don't know the salary he has in mind, but he's a rich man, so I'm sure it would be fair. Would you take the job if it was offered? I mean—would you be willing to guard *me?* After meeting me, and learning what the job would entail?"

Jayla nodded, her face grave as if to show them that she understood the seriousness of the position. "I would be glad to take the job. But I have to tell you my own situation."

Madeleine felt her eyebrows rise. "You're not really a soldier?" For the first time, her eyes went to Jayla's wrists. "You certainly looked like a fighter out there in the yard."

Jayla smiled and extended her left hand so Reese and Madeline could see her bracelet. "No, I am. Guild certified."

Reese leaned forward to examine the band more closely, then looked over at Jayla in admiration. "Not just certified, but at the highest level," he said. "I'm impressed."

Jayla's smile went slightly awry. "The rank was hard won."

"Then I'm impressed, too," Madeleine said. "But, wait—if I'm supposed to distrust everyone in the world, shouldn't I question you more closely? Shouldn't I wonder if you earned these glyphs honestly, or if you had them made by a counterfeiter?"

"It's a good question," Jayla said. "And you'll find the occasional charlatan pretending to be a soldier when he's not."

"But we saw her fight," Reese said.

"You saw me fight," she echoed. "And anyone who gets caught in such a deception generally regrets it."

"What do you mean?" Madeleine asked.

"They get their sword hand cut off," Jayla said dryly. "The practice isn't officially sanctioned by the guild, but it happens often enough that most people won't risk it."

"Then what's irregular about your situation? Because the way you spoke, there must be something."

Jayla nodded, and her face because even more serious. "I've become responsible for the welfare of a young girl. She's maybe seven or eight years old. I met her as we tried to cross into Corcannon on the day the northern bridge fell down—"

"Oh, you were one of those poor stranded travelers at the Chibani crossing?" Reese asked. "That sounded miserable."

"It wasn't so bad. But during that time, Aussen came into my care. The woman she was traveling with died on the road, and there was no one else to watch her. My hope is to eventually find her family but—it's tricky. She's Zessin, and she only knows a few words of Cordish. I haven't been able to learn enough about her to know where to place her safely. But I can't abandon her. So any job I take has to allow me to bring her with me."

Of all the things Jayla had done and said since Madeleine laid eyes on her—from vanquishing her oversized opponent to coolly assessing the risks that her potential client might face—this was the thing that made Madeleine like her the best. She matter-of-factly explained her situation, didn't try to glamorize it, didn't complain about it, didn't promise to get it resolved as quickly as possible so her new employer wouldn't be inconvenienced. She just said, *This is who I am and this is what I bring with me,* and waited to see what would happen next.

"I can't think that would be a problem," Madeleine said. "The girl could sleep in your room. If she can understand directions, maybe she could work in the kitchen. That would keep her out of trouble, anyway."

"If your father won't allow her to stay, I could find a place for her," Reese said.

"No," said Jayla. "She's been through too much and I don't want her to be separated from me. If *she* can't come, *I* can't come."

"And my father isn't the one who oversees the servants—I do," Madeleine said. "He won't even notice that she's been added to the household." She took a deep breath and addressed Jayla. "So let me go home and tell my father I have found the person I would like to engage to be my guard. I hope very much that you will have found a place for yourself in my house."

Chapter Seven:
Pietro

Pietro stood with the other volunteers behind the long wooden table and handed out loaves of bread and wrapped rounds of cheese. At nearby tables, other workers were distributing jars of milk, containers of honey, and bags of fruit. There were strict rules about how much food to give to any one petitioner—a solitary man got a single loaf, a small jar; but a woman with three children clinging to her arms would receive as much as she could carry.

Pietro didn't always follow the protocols. If he was approached by a hollow-cheeked teen, he bundled up extra portions and whispered, "Go outside and eat what you want, then come back through the line and I'll give you more." This distribution center was operated by the temple, and Pietro knew Cordelan could afford to give away twice this much food and never notice the cost.

It was the kind of occupation that was virtuous enough to be rewarding, but endless enough to be wearying. There was so much need; there were so many hungry mouths. How could everyone be fed? How could everyone be cared for?

When he had lived in the city ten years ago, he had rarely done a stint at the distribution centers. He had preferred the more intimate ministries—the one-on-one sessions with those who were sick in spirit, gravely ill, or broken-hearted. *It is with people that I feel my calling,* he had explained to Harlo once. *And not with Cordelan himself.*

Of course, people had been his downfall.

Well, Harlo had been his downfall.

He could not resume his priestly duties, but he still felt impelled toward service, so he had settled on handing out food. It didn't satisfy him, but it did quiet that restless, questioning voice in his head that kept asking, *What are you doing here? Why did you come back?*

He honestly had no idea.

"It's not so bad in the mornings," said the woman who had been working on his right-hand side since they both arrived three hours ago. "But it gets so hot in the afternoon. And there are so many people, all needing so much. It gets harder to stand here and feel like you're doing any good."

Pietro glanced up at the high ceiling, where thin lines of sunlight showed through the imperfect join of broad wooden slats. They were in an old storeroom on the border between the Quatrefoil and the warehouse district. The building was completely empty except for the tables, the supplies, and the people, so it should have felt roomy and comfortable. But instead it felt cramped and dreary.

"I imagine there's the opposite problem in the winter," he said. "It's drafty and cold."

"It's worse," she agreed. "But fewer people venture out, so it's not as crowded."

He glanced surreptitiously at the bracelets on her bare arms. On her left wrist she wore a band that proclaimed her a teacher; on her right, circlets that marked her as a woman married to a woman, the mother of two daughters and a son.

"Do you come every week?" he asked.

"I try to. Usually my oldest daughter accompanies me, but she had other plans today." She shrugged, but her face showed disappointment.

"She might be at an age where she finds it tedious to tend to others—she wants to laugh with her friends and not think about all the sadness in the world," Pietro said in his most soothing voice. "But if she has been coming here with you for any length of time, she'll remember the lesson. She'll feel it continue to pull at her—that desire to make life better for those whose need is so much greater than her own."

The woman's face relaxed into a tired smile. "I hope that's true. We try so hard to set good examples for the children, and then one of them does something cruel and shallow, and we wonder, 'How can we have failed so miserably?'"

Pietro handed two loaves of bread to a petitioner who couldn't have been more than twenty, who carried a baby in a sling over her shoulder and held a toddler by the hand. The woman next to him carefully wrapped two rounds of cheese and tucked them into the mother's bag.

"You provide the foundation," he said, still in that gentle voice. "You show them how to build their houses. But they forage for the material themselves, and they build their dwellings out of plaster or wood or wild variegated stone, and you cannot stop them and you cannot change them and you can only help them if they ask for your assistance."

She sighed and then she laughed. "You speak as if you have some experience, but—" She gestured at his hands. The right wrist bare of any family affiliations. The left wrist with its single twisted band. "I'm guessing you don't have children of your own?"

"No. I have spent some time working as a counselor, that is all. Though for the past ten years, I have been a professional wanderer."

"And did you find what you were looking for in your travels?"

Pietro glanced again around the large, depressing room. He had been here almost every day for the past two weeks, and it still didn't feel welcoming or familiar. "I don't think so," he said. "But I'm not sure what I'm looking for."

"Do you think you'll find it in the city?"

"I hope so," he said. "It's the only place I haven't tried."

The woman left about an hour later, but Pietro stayed until the last battered supplies had been handed out—the loaves of bread flattened in the bottoms of the baskets, the clusters of grapes so crushed they were one good squeeze away from being wine. The big building was truly a furnace by now, so the last visitors moved lethargically through the lines and the few remaining workers served them in dazed silence.

It was a relief when the priest who had been overseeing operations all day finally called a halt to the proceedings. "Thank you for your service," he said to the volunteers drooping at their posts. "If ever you feel called upon to join us again, we'll welcome you."

The volunteers responded with a few unintelligible murmurs and drifted toward the exit. Pietro gathered up all the baskets he could find and carried them to the door to be collected and refilled overnight by another army of workers.

"Thank you—most appreciated," said the priest as Pietro added to the growing piles. "It's the kind of work that's never done. There is always one more task."

"Ah, well, that's the nature of life," Pietro said. "We come to resting points, but very few true endings."

The priest laughed. His round, cheerful face made him look youthful, but Pietro guessed him to be in his forties. His ruddy complexion and dark hair defied easy categorization, so Pietro supposed him to be of some complex mixed heritage. The bracelet on his right wrist was hidden by the long sleeves of his tan robe. The band on his left wrist showed him to be a mid-ranked priest with perhaps five or eight years of experience. Exactly what Pietro would expect from someone performing this particular function, since few senior priests were willing to put in the long, grueling hours supervising the distribution center. It was what Pietro had counted on when he began volunteering a week after he arrived in the city. Because of course any priest with ten or more years of experience instantly would have recognized him.

"Well, I suppose there's *one* ending point we all reach, but we shouldn't be in a hurry to get there," the other man replied in a genial voice. "I'm Stollo, by the way."

"Pietro."

"You've been here three days this week, at least that I have noticed," Stollo said, spreading his hands. "The temple thanks you for your service. And if you're hungry, *I* would thank you for service by treating you to dinner."

The casual gesture had lifted his trailing sleeves and revealed the single band on his right hand. Gold, fluted with alternating swatches of gold and silver. A man who was attracted to both men and women. Not that it mattered to Pietro, who was not looking for a romantic partner, especially one so young, and who was not stupid enough to ever get involved with another priest even if he was. Still, he tugged on his own bracelets, just in case Stollo wanted to see them, just in case the other man wanted to assimilate a few bare facts about Pietro's life before they sat down to a meal.

"I'm hungry enough to take you up on the offer," he said. "Do you know someplace good to eat?"

They stayed near the warehouse district, ending up at a snug little alehouse only a few blocks away. The ceiling was low, the lighting was patchy, and the smells of meat and onions were delicious. Most of the other patrons appeared to be working men and women who didn't care who else was there as long as no one bothered them. It seemed like the ideal spot.

While they waited for their food, Stollo and Pietro talked idly and sipped mugs of beer. Pietro hadn't exactly sworn off of alcohol, but he'd indulged in it only rarely in the past few years. He had forgotten how good the rich, bitter brew could taste.

"So, your bracelet," Stollo said as they dug into their main course. "You're a sojourner? On any specific kind of pilgrimage, or simply wandering?"

"Wandering, it seems."

"Where have you been?"

"Almost everywhere, I think. Chibain to the islands, and even as far as Oraki."

"And what did you discover?"

Pietro thought about that while he finished a bite of food and chased it with another swallow of beer. "Both that people are very similar and very different," he said. "Their customs vary. Their rituals. Marriage ceremonies differ from place to place, for instance, yet people always join up in some kind of unit for the joys and rewards of companionship. Attitudes about death change from group to group, and yet everyone mourns a personal loss. I think those were the two things I saw everywhere I went—the capacity to feel love and the capacity to feel pain." He gestured. "And I also witnessed the extremes of kindness and cruelty, which seem to attend love and pain wherever they can be found."

"You are a philosopher," Stollo observed.

"Not so much. A student of humanity."

Stollo grinned. "It's the same thing."

"What about you?" Pietro asked. "What brought you to the priesthood?"

Now Stollo was the one who took time to think over his answer. "I came to it late in life," he said at last. "In my twenties, I was a banker. I was married to a good woman. I was a dutiful son. Eventually none of these roles satisfied me."

"Was it one thing that made you turn your back on all the parts of your life, or many unconnected events?"

"It seemed like many unconnected events, but I suppose they all sprang from the same sense of dissatisfaction," said Stollo. "My father had been a banker, and both of us had always expected that I would join him in the business. It's a good life, if you only care about powerful people. But I was more interested in the powerless, those who rarely had access to money. I advocated a new type of credit with a new type of lender." He shrugged. "The bank wouldn't support my plan and my father was embarrassed that I had even proposed it. We quarreled about it so often that our relationship has been deeply damaged."

"I'm sorry to hear that," Pietro said. "Was your wife also uninterested in your radical notions?"

"No, in fact, she was my strongest supporter," Stollo answered. "But eventually it was the only thing we had in common. Any time the conversation did not revolve around reinventing finance, we had very little to say to each other. When she confessed she had been seeing another man, my first reaction was relief."

"So everything came to an end for you," Pietro said. "And then what?"

"I obviously needed a new career, but what? I didn't have the patience to study medicine and I didn't have the heart to study law. My cousin Danner runs a few small cargo ships out of the Corcannon harbor, and I crewed with him one summer, but I'm not cut out for a life at sea. I decided I wanted to pursue something that had meaning." He sipped his beer. "While I thought it over, I began volunteering. And the more I worked with temple philanthropies, the more I found that my soul was soothed. That I was content."

Pietro toyed with his fork. "That does not sound," he said carefully, "as if you heard a calling from Cordelan himself."

Stollo shook his head. "I had a calling to do good, and I thought I could accomplish that in the temple," he said. "I assure you, I am not the only man who has joined the order because he thought he could achieve some goal other than serving the god." When Pietro looked inquiring, Stollo went on. "Some are like me. They are looking for ways to give their lives meaning. Some are schemers who see that sacred power and secular power go hand in hand, and they want more of that power for themselves."

Pietro leaned back in his chair and regarded Stollo with a smile. Maybe alcohol had loosened the younger man's tongue, or maybe he felt it was safe to share his unguarded thoughts with someone outside the holy orders. Then again, Pietro had spent a lifetime inducing people to confide in him. He had heard more than his fair share of secrets over the years. "I take it you have little liking for that latter group."

"None," said Stollo. "But—I suppose—like any profession, the priesthood needs those with a talent for organization. For managing wealth, training the next generation, and running the city. So while I might feel disdain for those who crave power and prestige, those are the very men who will lead the priesthood in a decade or two."

"Or sooner," Pietro said. "I understand the current high divine is very old."

"Eighty, or thereabouts," Stollo confirmed. "But I hear no rumors of his ill-health."

"Do you like him?"

"Very much. Harlo *is* a consummate politician, no doubt about it, yet there is never any suggestion that he wants power for its own sake. Now, the secretary of the sanctuary—*he's* the kind of man who enjoys controlling other people, all the while pretending like he's just acting in their best interests. But Harlo is genuine. He really does care about the good of the city. He works tirelessly on its behalf."

Pietro waited until the pain around his heart subsided. "He sounds admirable."

"Not that I have many direct dealings with him, of course. I have met him maybe a dozen times, and I would be very surprised if he remembered me."

Pietro would be more surprised if Harlo *didn't* remember him. Harlo remembered everyone and everything; it was his great strength as a leader, that ability to keep track of people and incidents that others might consider inconsequential. Anyway, Harlo had always had an eye for a handsome man, or a charismatic one. The high divine definitely would have noted Stollo's fresh face and general exuberance. "Maybe next time you see him, you should do something memorable," Pietro suggested. "Then he might elevate you to his inner circle."

"Oh, he has plenty of others in that circle already."

Pietro raised his eyebrows as if intrigued by a little light gossip. "A lover or two?"

"One. At least that's what everybody says."

And that remark caused its own pain, though the news was hardly a surprise. "Not one of those power-hungry priests, I hope."

"He doesn't seem to be. Quiet. A little intense. Very handsome." Stollo grinned. "I mean, I can certainly see why Harlo would favor him."

Pietro simply couldn't bear talking any longer about Harlo's possible lovers, so he changed the topic with no attempt at subtlety. "So I understand there are ranks within the priesthood," he said. "Which one have you achieved so far?"

"The third rank," Stollo said proudly. "Which included—just the other day!—a tour of every level of the temple."

"There are levels in the temple?" Pietro repeated, as if he didn't know. "I've only seen the sanctuary on the ground floor, where the public rituals are held."

"There are several levels below it," Stollo confirmed. "One is divided into small cells where priests can go to retreat for days at a time—though I would feel like I was suffocating if I was underground for that long. Another one is mainly used for storage, and you can find the most amazing things down there."

Stollo drew a deep breath. "But below that. There is this *cavern* that seems to have been carved out of the bedrock of the city. And the only thing in it is this strange metal device—Lenno, who gave me the tour, said it was the holiest artefact in the city. He said it was the instrument that Cordelan used to bind the scattered lands together."

"I never heard of such a thing," Pietro said, which was another lie. "I'd like to see it someday."

"I was supposed to receive my own key as part of my investiture, so I can go down to the lower level and meditate whenever I want," said Stollo. "But Lenno told me they'd stopped making new keys so I'll only get my own when someone dies. Well, I can hardly root for that, can I? But if I ever earn my own key, I'll take you to see the god's device."

That invitation was what Pietro had been angling for during this whole conversation—but by the time Stollo was in a position to follow through, Pietro was pretty sure it would be too late. Nonetheless, he smiled and held out his hand. "It's a deal."

Stollo's clasp was firm. "And until that day, you'll still keep volunteering at the food bank?"

"I will."

"Then I'll see you the next time I pull that duty."

Pietro nodded. "I'll look forward to it."

Stollo was not at the distribution center when Pietro returned the next day, so Pietro didn't linger after the food was handed out. But he found equally interesting company awaiting him when he made it back to his rented rooms that evening.

"Cody!" he exclaimed when he spotted the courier lounging outside his door. "I wondered if you would go to the trouble of tracking me down."

Cody grinned and pushed himself away from the wall where he was leaning. "I found you a day after you moved in," he said matter-of-factly. "I've been by a couple of times but you weren't home."

"Come on in. I think I can scrape together a meal if you're hungry."

"I'm always hungry."

The rooms were low-ceilinged and cramped, but since Pietro had no furniture except the few pieces that came with the rent, the space wasn't unbearably crowded. Rather, it was shadowy and hot, though candles took care of the first problem. An open window didn't do much to help the second one.

Pietro rummaged in the small kitchen while Cody looked around with a critical eye. "Do you need me to find you a table? And some chairs? I know shops where you could get them cheap."

"Maybe, if I stay here long enough," Pietro said, cutting up fruit and unwrapping a portion of cooked meat. "I keep thinking I'll find better quarters someday, I just haven't figured out where."

"If you tell me how much you can afford, I can tell you the best places in the city."

Pietro grinned at him over his shoulder. "You are an invaluable source of information."

Cody grinned back. "That's my job."

In a few minutes, Pietro had assembled a couple of plates of food and brought them out to the main room. There was nowhere to sit except the rug, but Cody sank to the floor without even bothering to grimace. Pietro had the feeling that all experiences were roughly equal to Cody—what he cared about was *having* those experiences, no matter how uncomfortable or unconventional.

"So you came looking for me a while back?" Pietro asked. "Did you need something?"

Cody shook his head and talked around a mouthful of food. "Nope. I just like knowing where people are."

"Do you know where Jayla is?"

"Sure. She found a job right away."

"And Aussen is with her?"

"She is."

He did not, Pietro noted with some relief, volunteer any information about where, exactly, Jayla might be employed. He wondered what Cody would say if Pietro asked for the details. *I'd like to look them up and see how they're doing.* But surely Jayla would have warned Cody not to share that information with Pietro. There was a closed, cautious expression on Cody's open face; he knew he was supposed to keep this secret.

"It occurs to me I don't know where *you* live," Pietro said. He munched on a piece of fruit and surveyed his visitor, trying to guess. "Not with your parents. Not by yourself in some tiny place like this one."

Cody grinned again. "Nope. Big old converted warehouse on the edge of the Quatrefoil. About ten couriers live there at any one time, so it's a lively place."

"Ah. I can instantly picture you there in a building teeming with life. You do not seem like a man who is drawn to solitude or peace."

Cody shook his head. "I like it when stuff is going on."

"Do you come from a large family? Is that why you like all the noise and chaos?"

"Yes. Eight brothers and sisters in a very small house. Everyone else liked it better when the older ones started clearing out, but I thought it was lonelier."

"Are you still on good terms with your family?"

He nodded. "All of them. I have a sister and brother who are couriers too. My sister lives in the warehouse with me."

"Sounds like a good life."

Cody shrugged. "It is, but running the cables is a young man's job. My brother and I have been talking about starting a business. A formal service that contracts with a few big firms to carry all their messages. We could build a dorm to house the workers, earn money on rent as well as on the commissions." He shrugged again. "Maybe we'll do it, maybe we won't. But we talk about it."

"It sounds very enterprising," said Pietro. "And very smart."

"So what are *you* planning to do?"

Pietro sighed. "Still working that out."

Cody watched him with unabashed curiosity, but didn't ask any more pointed questions. "You've been keeping busy, though. At least, you've been gone a lot."

Pietro nodded. "Volunteering at a food distribution center." He smiled. "A bit more formal and organized, but essentially the same work you and I did when we were trapped on the other side of the canyon."

"Working at a center that the temple runs, or one of the other ones?"

"I didn't even know there *were* other ones."

Cody nodded. "Sure. There are a couple on the eastern edges of the city. They're a little rougher and they run out of food quicker. But people go there who'd never walk into the temple."

"I'll have to check them out," Pietro said. He gave Cody a closer inspection. "Is there *anywhere* in the city you haven't been—or couldn't get to?"

Cody laughed. "I'd be surprised."

Pietro leaned his back against the rough wall. "There's a place someone mentioned the other day. A room, three levels beneath the main temple where there's some holy relic left by Cordelan."

"There is," Cody said. "I've only seen it once."

"But you've been there? And seen it with your own eyes?" When Cody nodded, Pietro added, "Now I *am* impressed."

Cody grinned. "Well, I wasn't supposed to be there. And I only went because I was told I couldn't. I'd been out drinking with a few other guys, and there were runners from another part of town, and we got into a pissing match about who'd done what and gone where. And someone said no one could get into that room, and I said *I* could, and my brother said *he* could, and then after that we sort of had to do it."

"Of course you did," Pietro murmured. "Overconfident *and* reckless. With an inconvenient kind of male pride."

"It was fun."

"But I was under the impression that you need a key to get into the bottom levels."

"You do."

"And you *have* one?"

Cody's whole face was alight with laughter. Pietro supposed this was his favorite sort of conversation. "I have a copy of a key. But it works."

"So what would induce you—if I said I wanted to see this room for myself—would you—"

"Sure."

"—Take me to see it? You *would?*"

"Sure," Cody said again.

"What would you charge me?"

Cody considered. "I might do it for free. I'd like to see it again."

"But if you get caught—"

"Well, I don't think they'd do anything except throw me out of the temple. What if *you* get caught?"

He said it so lightly, so casually, it was possible to think he didn't realize what a heavy question it was. But Pietro thought Cody had a pretty good idea that the stakes were high, though he didn't know why. "I imagine I would have a lot of questions to answer," Pietro replied.

"Might be worth it, though."

"Might be." Pietro thought it over. "Yes. Definitely worth it. If you'll take me, I want to go."

"Sure. When?"

"I don't suppose you have the key with you tonight? So we can go before I lose my nerve."

For an answer, Cody reached into his pocket and pulled out a ring hung with a truly remarkable collection of keys. He flipped through them rapidly, frowned over one especially ornate example, but then shook his head. "I'm afraid not. But I could bring it tomorrow."

Pietro was momentarily distracted from his main purpose. "*What,*" he said, "are you doing with all of those? I feel certain they were not obtained legally."

Cody was laughing again. "We-elll . . . some of them were. Clients who hire me to make regular deliveries often give me keys to their homes or offices. But in other cases—" He shrugged. "It happens all the time. People flag me down and give me a package and say, 'The gate is unlocked' or 'Someone will be at home to let you in.' And the gate *isn't* unlocked and no one *is* at home, and I can either waste half a day going back to the client for new instructions, or I simply take care of the situation with the tools I have. No harm done."

"Do you make a replica of every key you've ever had in your possession?"

"Well, I do, but I probably don't have to. There are four pretty basic skeleton keys, and if you have them, you can get in most everywhere you need to."

"'Four quarters, four bridges, four keys, four hearts,'" Pietro recited.

Cody just looked at him. "What?"

Pietro sighed and cast his eyes toward the ceiling. "No one reads the classics any more," he said plaintively. Then, more briskly, "It's a line from Alecita Kissidell's masterpiece about the city of Corcannon."

He could see Cody trying to figure it out. "I get the four bridges. I guess the four quarters are the loops of the Quatrefoil?"

"Yes, or the four quadrants of the city—the author wasn't specific."

"What are the keys supposed to be?"

"Love of people, love of knowledge, love of nature, and love of god."

Cody looked unconvinced. "Well, maybe. And the hearts?"

"The four main characters of the book."

"Huh."

"But we stray from our primary topic!" Pietro said. "Which is what kind of key a person might need to get inside the temple."

"A skeleton won't do it," Cody answered. "For that you need the real thing. Or a really good copy."

"Which you have."

"Which I have."

Pietro took a deep breath. "Well, I'm free tomorrow if you are, but I'm new at criminal activity," he said. "Is it better to go in boldly during the day, when anyone might see us, or try to sneak in at night?"

"Daytime, I think," Cody said. "There are a lot more people around, but no one's paying attention. At night, you just *look* guilty, even if you're not."

"All right then. Should we meet at the temple tomorrow—say, around three?"

"Sounds good."

Pietro put his hand to his heart. "I'm actually terrified."

"It'll be fun."

Chapter Eight: Pietro

Fun wasn't the word at the top of Pietro's mind the following day as he waited for Cody at the temple. It was an unexpectedly gloomy afternoon, the sun taking cover behind a towering bank of clouds, so the white walls did not glitter with their usual blinding shine. Still, the tall, graceful building was soaked with such accumulated light that it seemed to gleam beneath the pewter skies.

Pietro had arrived an hour early because he could not stay away. Since he had arrived in the city, he had felt the pull of this building, this entire complex; it had exerted a pressure on his body so strong that any time he walked within a half-mile of its boundaries he could feel his bones bending in that direction. He had, until today, managed to fight that urgent longing. He had traveled miles out of his way to avoid any route that would take him past this spot; he had eschewed the Quatrefoil altogether, forfeiting any chance to frequent its shops and restaurants.

But now here he was, just outside those familiar walls, and the insistent drag of desire had almost lifted him off his feet to carry him inside without his physical volition.

To distract himself, he made a game of studying the dozens of people who came and went through the temple doors. Those two men looked to be lovers who might be reserving a date for their marriage. That solitary woman, stooped and shuffling, could be coming to pray for her husband's recovery from illness. The couple with the three children were clearly tourists, taking in the grandest sight the city had to offer.

It was easy to spot the priests, garbed in their robes of ivory and tan, with quatrefoil patterns embroidered along their collars and sleeves. Their heads were bare, their faces serene. Pietro had stayed some distance from the entrance, deep in the shadow of a nearby building, so that no one entering or leaving the temple was likely to notice him. But this meant he was too far away to see faces clearly. From this distance, he thought there were one or two priests he could identify by their silhouettes, by the features he could almost make out.

Anyone he recognized would surely recognize him.

He had taken some pains to appear anonymous. He had donned the trousers and rough cotton shirt that a working man would wear, and he'd put on a soft cap to cover his hair and shadow his face. Still, anyone who took a close look at him—anyone who *knew* him—would not find this much of a disguise.

But no one would be expecting to see him today. In the temple. In the city. And wasn't expectation half the requirement for recognition? One day in the islands, Pietro had come across a merchant he'd known well back when he lived in the city. They'd stared at each other a good three minutes before either of them could recall the other's name.

And Pietro didn't plan to stare at anyone for even half that long. If he could manage it, he wouldn't make eye contact with anyone.

"Here you are," said Cody, stepping up beside him. "I thought maybe you'd changed your mind."

"No," Pietro said. "This is something I need to see."

"Then let's go in."

They crossed the wide flat apron of stone that fanned out from the open doors, passed under the tall lintel, and stepped inside. It was like color suddenly developed a voice and burst into song inside Pietro's head. Every surface of the interior was alive with vibrant hues—worked into stone mosaics, crafted from heavy fabrics, painted on walls and screens and furniture and doors. It should have seemed like a wild cacophony, but instead it felt like a joyous symphony, with many disparate parts melded into a glorious harmonic whole.

Pietro had always thought the colors were shouting *See how amazing the world can be*. He had felt an instant uplift every time he walked into this whirling, chaotic, gorgeous place.

Cody was looking around with a more critical eye. "I always think I'd get a headache if I was here too long," he remarked.

"You don't like all the color?"

"I do—but there's a lot of it."

"You get used to it."

Pietro paused long enough to glance around, simply enjoying the pleasing proportions of this grand space. Topping that distant ceiling was a cupola constructed almost entirely of stained glass, which admitted enough jeweled sunlight to paint gaudy patterns on the tiled floor. The roof was supported by a ring of grooved columns that formed a huge circle in the center of the round temple; each column was so thick it would take two or three people to put their arms around it, and each one was adorned with streamers of gold or crimson. Most of the activity of the temple occurred within that ring of columns, directly under that flamboyant glass. In one quadrant were rows of heavy wooden pews facing a central dais; no officiant was leading a service right now, but plenty of visitors were sitting on the benches, or talking to priests, or visiting with each other, or merely looking around. In another quadrant was a small fountain enclosed by a circular bench. As usual, half a dozen people bent over the low lip of the basin, scooping up water to sip from their hands or splash on their faces.

The rest of the central space was mostly open, except for the occasional slim statue or ornate candelabra—and the constant parade of people crossing it to peer at treasures scattered throughout the temple. Many of those could be found in the shadowed perimeter of the building that lay between the curved outer walls and the inset circle of pillars. They included more fountains, paintings on easels, carved and gold-leafed wooden cabinets, statuary of all sizes and materials, chairs so elaborate that no one had the nerve to sit on them, and ten-foot-high ornamental shrubs planted in pots the size of wine barrels. A visitor could spend a whole day here and not have time to examine each item in detail.

"That's always been my favorite thing in the temple," Cody said.

He was pointing toward the far wall, marked as off-limits by a discreet rope fence and a stern temple guard. The entire surface, floor to ceiling, consisted of some reflective metal incised with a complex landscape of ocean, mountain, forest, and sunset. None of the city's learned scientists had ever been able to identify the metal used for the base; none of the contemporary artists understood the method that had been used to transfer the materials to the substrate. The temple records showed that the artwork had been in place since the building had been constructed a thousand years ago.

"Yes, that's an impressive piece," Pietro said. "The story goes that it was created by Cordelan himself. He mined the ore and smelted it by hand and spread the molten material over the wall and traced the designs with his fingertips. No one has been able to replicate any part of the installation, from the metal to the dyes."

Cody eyed the huge mural with more respect and a bit of speculation. "How can that be?"

Pietro smiled. "He's a god. He can do whatever he likes."

Cody resettled his weight and did a slow, casual pivot. "The door we want," he said in an undervoice, "is over there. Behind the pillar that's closest to the statue of the kneeling woman. I'd say we should stroll around the whole place, pausing to look at paintings and sculptures, then spend a little time looking at the kneeling woman. When it seems like no one is watching, we'll just step behind the pillar and open the door."

Pietro nodded as if his heart wasn't beating too fast for him to take a breath. "Let's do it," he said.

Accordingly, they began a slow pilgrimage around the interior of the building. Pietro had to admit he didn't look too closely at the objects he was supposed to be admiring. He was always half-turned toward that central dais, keeping an eye on the crowd, trying to keep track of how many priests were mingling with the parishioners, and how many might be taking note of *them.* But he only spotted five priests, all of them deep in conversation with very somber-looking visitors, and none of them seemed to have any attention left for sightseers bent on mischief. Even the temple guard appeared to ignore anyone who didn't draw too close to Cordelan's masterpiece.

Cody and Pietro spent what seemed like an hour memorizing the features of the kneeling woman. "No one's looking this way," Cody breathed. "I'm just going to slide into the shadow of the pillar and unlock the door. You stay where you are until I wave you over."

Pietro nodded because he couldn't speak. As naturally as fog lifting, Cody eased away and drifted out of sight. Pietro shifted his body so he could simultaneously watch the door and observe the broad open spaces of the temple. The guard was frowning at a small boy who clutched the rope barrier and stared with longing at the god's landscape. Two of the priests were conferring with a concerned-looking man. Another comforted a sobbing woman. Two others sat with their backs to Pietro, holding intense conversations with petitioners.

A flutter caught his eye, and he looked over to see Cody waving from the half-open door. Keeping all his attention on the interior of the temple, Pietro sidled backward blindly until he felt Cody grab his arm. They hurriedly ducked through the door and shut it behind them.

"I can't believe that worked," Pietro whispered. His heart was hammering so hard that he could feel his heavy pulse at his throat, at his elbows, in his palms. "I can't even believe your *key* worked."

The door had led them to a dark hallway that appeared as if it might circle the entire perimeter of the temple. The only light came from widely spaced opalescent disks set in the walls at irregular intervals. More of the god's handiwork, or at least Pietro had never learned what material was used to keep the sconces perpetually lit. They could be found in every tunnel and chamber of the entire complex.

"We still have a lot of turns to take," Cody said, his voice just as quiet. "And anybody we run into will know we don't belong."

"Do you know the rest of the way?"

Cody nodded. "Pretty sure. After I've been somewhere once, I can always find my way back."

"Then let's go."

The route was straightforward enough, if nerve-wracking to navigate. The hallway curved invitingly ahead of them, but Cody only followed it for a few feet before he used the same key to unlock another door. It led to a steep stairwell lit by only a single glowing disk. They followed it down and exited into another hallway.

The minute they emerged, they could hear the low buzz of voices, and they both froze. This corridor ran perpendicular to the upper one, seeming to lead right back under the temple itself. It was much wider and more welcoming than the hallway above, with more lights and a few decorative touches to soften the bleak stone walls. It was lined with closed doors along either side, and the voices were coming from behind some of the nearest ones.

"I was told that this level was where priests would go for retreat and meditation," Pietro murmured in Cody's ear. "While they're at their prayers, it should be safe for us to slip by."

They glided down the hall, scarcely daring to breathe. Pietro cursed his heavy, sensible boots but he managed to set each foot down with a minimum of noise. Cody made no sound at all.

It seemed like they had traversed the entire width of the temple three times over by the time they finally made it to the end of the hallway. Cody's invaluable key unlocked that door, too, and they both sagged with relief when they ducked into another shadowy stairwell.

"It was night last time I did this," Cody said. "And no one was awake singing."

"And you were drunk, so you weren't too nervous," Pietro retorted.

Cody grinned. "I was drunk the night I said I'd do it. Dead sober when I was walking these halls."

Pietro took a deep breath. "Shall we go on?"

Cody nodded, and down they went again. This time, the door opened onto one huge round space as big as the entire temple, but much less appealing. The ceiling was barely a foot above Pietro's head, and the supporting pillars were squat and unadorned. The area was crammed with piles of cloth, stacks of furniture, wooden crates, and unidentifiable shapes that loomed menacingly in the cool light of the phosphorescent disks.

"Storage," Pietro said. "Wouldn't think anyone would be down here unless he was looking for something specific."

Cody snorted. "Wouldn't think he could find it even if he was. Look at this mess!"

"I don't care about the mess. Where's the door?"

Again, they had to cross the entire space to find the exit at the other end of the room. Pietro had completely lost track of where they might be in relation to the first door they'd entered a couple of levels up. Cody's key made a metallic scraping sound, but the door didn't open.

"Stuck," Cody grunted, and began gently rocking the key in the lock. Pietro felt his heart seize up again. To have made it this far undetected, only to meet some impassable barrier!

"Can you pick it?"

"No, can you?" Cody retorted, still teasing the key back and forth. "Shouldn't have to. It worked last time."

"Maybe someone changed the locks. Maybe that's how they keep the place secure."

"Or maybe no one comes down here very often and it's rusty—ah."

Pietro felt a rush of excitement as he heard the tumblers falling, and the door made a low groaning protest as Cody swung it open. They cautiously stepped through, entering a stairway that was barely more than a jagged fault in the stone of the mountain. The narrow, unnerving downward spiral was more of a ramp than a series of steps. The disks of light emitted such weak illumination that Pietro couldn't tell the color of the rock that made up this sloping tunnel. He was immeasurably grateful when, after rummaging in his pocket, Cody produced a flash of light that modulated into a steady glow.

"You brought a chemlight!" Pietro said.

"I remembered this part from my last trip," Cody said. "This time, I wanted to be able to see."

They carefully felt their way down the curving path. The air felt thin and dusty, as if very little of it filtered down through the layers of heavy stone. Maybe that was why Pietro was having trouble breathing. Maybe there was another reason.

The tunnel abruptly ended in a cramped well of space guarded by a heavy wooden door. "If I remember right, it's not even locked," Cody murmured, and pushed on the handle. The door creaked open, swinging inward. Cody hesitated for a second before stepping through, Pietro at his heels.

Just across the threshold, they stopped and looked around. They were in a dim chamber faintly lit by three more of those iridescent disks. It was approximately rectangular in shape, maybe eight feet high, twelve feet lengthwise, eight feet across—but the walls were so rough that outcroppings and protrusions destroyed any sense of symmetry. Pietro could almost imagine that the chisel and hammer marks were still visible in the stone, that the work of hacking out this small cell was still in progress. It would be a relief if it was wider, taller, more open; it felt too narrow, too confined.

In the middle of the room, skulking under the unnatural light, squatted a stone structure a little more than knee-high—a solid base topped with a wide, shallow bowl. The basin was largely obscured by a spoked metal wheel that lay flat across it as if it had fallen from a passing carriage. An ancient pitcher sat on the floor in front of the base, completely black from tarnish.

"So here we are," said Cody. "What's so important about this place?"

Pietro stepped close enough to touch the wheel, though he didn't. A plain metal handle had been welded to one spot on the rim, clearly inviting someone to wrap his hand around it and tug the circle into motion. "That's the question, of course," Pietro said. The thin air or the close walls robbed his voice of any resonance; he sounded strange to himself. "What exactly is this shrine used for?"

"Don't you know?" Cody asked. "You seem to know a lot of other things."

"This is still mysterious to me."

Which was true. To some extent. Mostly because what he thought to be true was unbelievable.

Cody crowded up next to him. "I wonder what would happen if I spun the wheel."

"My guess is you would find it impossible to budge."

Cody curled his fingers around the welded metal handle. When Pietro didn't protest, Cody pulled gently—and when that had no effect, pulled harder. In a few moments, Cody had wrapped both hands around the handle, braced his feet against the uneven floor, and was straining with all his weight to force the wheel to turn. But it didn't shift by a fraction of an inch.

"Might be soldered in place," Cody panted. "It doesn't give at all."

"That's what I expected."

Cody gave up and began wandering around the small space, inspecting each of the disks of light and running his fingers down a few of the raw scrapes visible in the stone. "Hey, look at this," he said, fitting his palm to a spot on one of the shorter walls. "This looks like a hand print. See this? Like someone put his hand to the stone and *pushed,* and it left a mark."

Pietro came over to see for himself. His own hand was too large to fit inside the mold, his fingers too long and his palm too broad. "The story I heard was that Cordelan and Dar were arguing. She was so angry that she slammed her hand against the mountainside, and she left behind a perfect imprint."

"Well, I suppose a goddess can do anything."

"Except stop a god," Pietro said. "Dar ruled Chibain and Marata until Cordelan showed up."

"But then she married him," Cody said. "So it worked out all right for her in the end."

"I suppose."

Cody was looking around again. "There's nothing else to see. How long do you want to stay down here? I'm starting to feel like the place is haunted or something."

"I agree," Pietro said. "I've observed enough. Let's see if we can get out of here with as much stealth as we employed to get in."

The journey upward seemed both faster and less perilous, though they faced the same hazards and checkpoints. No one challenged them at any turn; Cody meticulously locked every door behind them; and they stepped with relief back into the gaudy confines of the temple.

"It seems easier to breathe up here," Cody said. "Probably just my imagination."

"Maybe," Pietro said, "but I'm imagining the same thing."

"Not even the guard seems to have noticed where we went," Cody said with satisfaction. "I told you we could pull this off."

"I will feel more like a success once we've left the temple and no one has come after us to arrest us," Pietro said.

Cody laughed, but they wasted no time crossing to the main door and exiting. After the time spent in the dark underground and the vivid sanctuary, the overcast skies outside seemed both dull and soothing. Once they were a block away from the temple and no one had challenged them, Cody and Pietro paused to suck in several deep breaths. Pietro still felt like his heart was racing, and he wasn't sure it would ever again resume its accustomed pace. But he smiled as if everything was fine.

"Thank you so much for taking me on this adventure!" he exclaimed. "I know you said you would do it just for fun, but I still feel like I owe you something. A meal, if nothing else?"

"I'd take a meal," Cody said, "but not tonight. I've got a job to get to in about an hour."

"Some other time, then."

"And I was glad to go," Cody added. "Glad to see it again. Though it's funny."

"What is?"

"I thought it would be bigger. I thought it *was* bigger, last time I was there."

Pietro felt his heart stop, simply pause in its accelerated rhythm and crouch there, quivering in horror. "Really? How much bigger?"

Cody spread his arms in an inadequate attempt to convey a sense of space. "I thought it was more like a square last time. It's like some of the walls are closing in." He dropped his hands. "But that's ridiculous. Isn't it?"

So it hadn't been Pietro's imagination. It hadn't been his faulty memory. The chamber really had shrunk in size. The walls really had moved closer. Over what period of time? Was it years or was it months? Were they still moving?

What would happen when they finally ground together, crushing the tool of the god between them?

How much time was left?

Chapter Nine: Brandon

Brandon stood for a long time outside the mansion, just staring. It looked much like every other house on Council Row, with its clean lines, its gracious proportions, its self-contained secretiveness; there was no way to know from the outside what it might hide on the inside.

Not that ~~that~~ he had entered any of the other houses along this street, in this part of town. He'd just heard stories the other guards told about the times they had accompanied one of the priests on their visits to wealthy parishioners. *Nothing much to look at on the outside, but inside it was like a flower market had exploded. Cordelan strike me dead if there weren't plants growing on the ceiling. . . .Gold leaf on every wall and every pillar and every bannister, so bright in there I thought I might go blind. . . . Stark. Nothing but black and white tile anywhere you looked.*

He had not, until he pulled this assignment, strayed too often into this part of town during his two years in Corcannon. He had been hired on by the temple guard within a week of arriving, a stroke of great fortune that had colored all his days. Good pay, good accommodations, and a ready-made cadre of companions. They teased him for being a country boy, but at least half of the other soldiers came from the more rural parts of Chibain and Marata. City men didn't often sign up to be fighters. They wanted to better themselves in other ways.

Brandon had had plenty of interesting tasks since he'd been hired. Providing an honor guard for the high divine when he made public appearances, patrolling the temple complex at night to keep looters at bay, accompanying the purser when he visited the bank to withdraw funds to cover another week's worth of operating expenses.

But this job would be like none of those. For one thing, it was a semi-permanent posting. He would be living here, in this house, for the next six months, along with two other temple guards who would be sharing the duty with him.

For another, he would be guarding a woman. A woman who rarely had visitors and never left the premises and could not be left unattended for a single minute.

The sergeant who made the assignment hadn't been forthcoming with details, merely telling Brandon when and where to report. Brandon had ventured to ask a single question: *Am I keeping this woman safe or am I keeping her a prisoner?* And the sergeant had simply answered, *Both.*

Brandon had packed his gear and taken one of the chuggers to the northwestern edge of town, trying not to gawk at all the big houses as they went by. How much money would a man need to have in order to own a place like this? One year of upkeep would probably cost more than Brandon would make in a lifetime.

Six months of living in such a house would make a memory that could also be measured by a lifetime, Brandon thought.

Now that he had arrived at his destination, he took a long time just to get his bearings. The house sat on spacious grounds, maybe twice as big as the properties of most of the nearby houses. The lawn was not particularly well tended, being largely given over to shrubs and vines that were a few half-hearted pruning attempts from taking over. Like many of the other rich estates, it was enclosed by an ornamental iron fence; unlike the other borders, this one looked like it would actually keep an intruder out. The thick bars were too slick to easily grasp, too high to easily climb, too close together to permit even a child to squeeze through. They were also topped with sharp finials that could probably slice a man's hand right open. Even so, Brandon thought, the fence wouldn't be impossible to breach with the right tools; he was pretty sure he could make it over if he wanted to badly enough.

But a pampered rich woman without the proper training would probably find it an insurmountable barrier.

The tall gate was locked, as he had been warned, so he pulled on the rope that should set off a bell in the interior. A moment later, the heavily carved front door swung open to admit a stocky young woman dressed, like Brandon, in the dark blue livery of a temple guard. She was of average height and athletic build, and she moved with the lithe assurance of a dancer or a fighter. Her hair was a muddy brown and her skin the indeterminate color he had come to associate with someone of mixed heritage.

"You're the new guard?" she said as she approached the gate.

He showed her the gold bracelet on his left wrist. It was stamped with the temple's quatrefoil pattern, interrupted in four spots by the crossed swords that denoted his status as a soldier. Next to it he still wore his guild bracelet incised with another series of crossed blades.

The woman flashed her own jewelry, a matching temple cuff and a guild bracelet showing a higher rank. "I'm Finley," she said.

"Brandon."

She nodded. "That's the name they told us."

She unlocked the gate to let him in, then locked it behind him. "You'll have your own key so you can come and go," she said as they strolled up the walk. "Only when you're due for a day off, of course."

"What's the schedule, then? Sergeant didn't say."

"There's three of us here. Two have to be on the premises at all times. We generally pull twelve-hour shifts. One on guard, one as backup, though he can be sleeping. The third one can be gone when he's not guard or backup, but he still has to be ready to take his turn on the next shift." They had arrived at the front door, which had swung shut upon her exit; she did not immediately reach to open it again. "Mostly, we stick around three or four days in a row, but then one of us will get restless and take the night off, leaving the other two behind."

Brandon nodded; he was sure there was a constant tradeoff between staying sharp, which meant not wandering away during those off-duty stretches, and not going mad from boredom. "How often do the guards change over? I was told it was a six-month posting."

"That's about average. There've been a couple who only stayed a month." She made a face. "Or a week."

Brandon raised his eyebrows. "She's that bad, then? The woman we're watching?"

Finley rested her hip against the door and settled in for a little gossip. "Her name's Villette Rowan, though we only ever address her as dona." It was the common honorific for wealthy women, though Brandon had never had cause to address anyone by the respectful term. "Oh, she's all right. Keeps to herself, mostly, but she's always courteous when she speaks to any of us. And I've never lived in a place so grand!" Her hand made a sweeping gesture toward the walls.

"But—?"

Finley grinned. "*I* don't see the attraction myself, but apparently the lady is so appealing that half the soldiers fall in love with her and want to set her free. That's why the postings are always temporary—so she won't have time to win over some fresh new farmboy who's so dazzled by her smile he'll do anything she asks."

"Maybe they should stop hiring men to watch her."

Finley laughed. "Oh, they tried that! Brought in a set of female guards with gold all over their bracelets, who swore they'd never in their lives lusted after a woman. But Villette won them over in a matter of weeks. The story goes that they were going to help her escape until the high divine got wind of their plot." She grinned at him. "So you just be careful any time you're alone with her."

Brandon couldn't tell how much of this story was true and how much was Finley just spinning wild tales to see if he'd fall for them. All he said was, "Thanks for the warning. I'll be careful. How long have *you* been here?"

Finley finally tugged the door open. "About two months. I think Nadder's been here almost four months. They like to rotate the guards a lot, to make sure none of us get too friendly. To make sure two of us don't start an alliance against the third."

Brandon felt his eyebrows rise again, but all he said was, "Lot of precautions."

"Yeah," said Finley. "It makes you wonder why she's so special."

"You don't know?"

Finley shook her head. "All I know is that she's not supposed to leave. And no one's supposed to see her without the temple's consent."

"Hard way for her to live," Brandon commented as he followed her inside.

"Then she shouldn't have done whatever she's done."

Brandon had no answer for that because he was too busy looking around. The atrium that opened off the doorway was the most elegant place he'd ever seen. There was none of the garish brightness he'd heard about—just stone walls in a shade of aged ivory, banners and floral arrangements of a soothing dusty blue, floor tiles picked out in patterns of cerulean and bronze. A thin floral scent drifted through the air; the skylights overhead admitted shafts of filtered gold. Tall archways heightened the impression of airiness; a spiraling staircase added to the elegance. It might have been the most restful architectural spot Brandon had ever seen.

"It's pretty, isn't it?" Finley said. "The garden's just as nice." She gestured toward one of the archways. "It's out through there. Villette spends all her time in the garden when the weather's nice. Even when it's cold, she's out there, that's what the winter guards told me."

"I guess she feels less like she's in a prison if she's outside."

Finley shrugged. "I guess. Come on, I'll show you your room." She headed toward an archway directly across the atrium from the garden, speaking over her shoulder. "Most houses like this, the guards and the servants sleep on the upper floors, and the lower level is full of parlors and dining halls and public rooms. But Villette doesn't do any entertaining, and the guards always have to be at the ready. So the downstairs rooms have been converted to bedrooms."

She stopped in front of a polished wooden door and pushed it open to reveal a large chamber flooded with light from a window that stretched from the ceiling to the floor. The narrow bed and wide chest of drawers were so incidental to the space that they looked like furniture someone had accidentally left behind.

"You could house a battalion in here," Brandon remarked.

"You could! But you have it all to yourself. Better enjoy it, 'cause you'll never bunk so solitary again as long as you're with the temple."

"And your room is just as big?"

"And just as empty. Here, drop your gear and I'll show you around."

The rest of the ground level held more bedrooms, a kitchen, a laundry, and a parlor where the lady could meet with the few approved temple visitors who might arrive. The second story consisted of a series of bedrooms—all of them furnished, though only one was occupied. "And you aren't permitted to enter Villette's," Finley said, though she showed him the other rooms. All of them were busily furnished with generous beds and upholstered chairs and tables and bookcases and armoires. Each room had a silent, haunted air that Brandon found increasingly unnerving as they continued their tour.

"How long has she lived here all alone?" he asked. "Did other people used to live here with her?"

"I don't know. I never asked."

"It just seems—I've never seen such a lonely place."

Finley shrugged. "I guess. Do you want walk around the third floor? That's where the cook and the maid and the gardener have their rooms."

"Might as well. I need to know the layout of the whole house in case there's ever trouble."

Finley nodded approvingly. "I usually make at least one pass a day upstairs. Just because."

The upper story was utilitarian and spare, though the harmonious blue and cream colors continued even on this level. Brandon noted the placement of the windows, gauged whether it would be possible to leap from the skylights to the third-floor balcony if someone happened to breach the roof, and leaned over the banister to assess how hard the drop would be from this level to the ground.

"Might not kill yourself, but you'd break something," he decided.

Finley nodded. "To do it safely, you'd need to slide down a rope." She pointed to one of the closed doors. "There's one in that room. No one sleeps there, so we've stashed a few supplies."

"That was smart."

"Wish I could say it was my idea."

The tour completed, they headed back to the kitchen, where the household staff members were sitting around a scarred wooden table, finishing up a noon meal. Finley made brisk introductions in a tone that made it clear the guards and the servants had only the most cursory dealings with each other. The housekeeper and gardener both appeared to be in their sixties, sturdily built but hardly physical threats, which Brandon supposed was why they'd been hired. The maid might have been in her twenties and looked thin as a newel post, so she presented no menace either.

"Eat something—get settled in your room—then maybe you should nap if you feel like it," Finley instructed him. "New man always takes the nine-to-nine shift for the first week, so you need to be wide awake by sundown."

"All right," said Brandon. He was hungry, so a meal sounded good, but he'd never been less sleepy in his life. He settled at the table and Finley sat across from him. The cook silently brought him a plate of food, and he tucked in. "Any protocol for how to spend the night watch?" he asked. "Any particular patrol pattern? Inside and outside?"

Finley shook her head. "Nadder usually prowls around. I mostly sit in the atrium. You can see—and hear—most points in the house from there. I get up every hour or so to walk the perimeter. Sometimes I go upstairs, sometimes I go outside, sometimes I don't bother." She filched a crust of bread from his plate. "I'm backup tonight, so if there's any trouble, you wake me up first."

"Is there ever? Any trouble?"

Finley shook her head again. "Not since I've been here. Not that I've ever heard of. No one's ever tried to break in."

Which meant there was only a guard on Villette Rowan because she wanted to leave. Which meant this lovely mansion wasn't a vault to be protected but a prison to be secured. Brandon ate the last of his meal and felt more curious than ever about the woman he would be guarding for the next six months.

To his surprise, Brandon did manage to catch about an hour's worth of sleep before emerging from his room around eight that night. Through the glass panes overhead, the sky looked dark already, but through the doorway that led to the garden, sunset was just beginning to paint the horizon in melodramatic hues. Nightfall soon.

He had another quick meal in the kitchen, then loitered in the atrium waiting for his shift to begin. It wasn't long before the third guard made his way in from the garden. He was a good-looking, dark-skinned man who might be in his mid-thirties. His sleeveless vest showed off his muscular arms, so bulky that his bracelets appeared to be almost uncomfortably tight. On the left wrist, the expected temple circlet. On the right, a solid gold band. Brandon wondered if the temple officials might someday decide to have Villette Rowan watched solely by men who preferred men. Surely such a cohort was less likely to succumb to her charms.

"You're the new guard?" the other man greeted him.

"Brandon."

"Nadder. Finley show you around?"

"She did. Anything I need to know about our charge tonight?"

"Quiet as always. Hasn't said a word to me."

"How long will she stay out there?"

"Could be five more minutes, could be another three hours. Long as she doesn't try to leave the house, it doesn't matter to you."

"All right. Guess I'll see you in the morning."

Nadder nodded and headed toward the kitchen. Brandon stepped through the archway and down a short hallway. An open door admitted the heavy, dreamy scent of summer blossoms and the pattering melody of a small fountain. The transition from the brightness of the interior to the dark of the exterior was stark and sudden, and Brandon paused just outside the spill of light to let his senses adjust.

He appeared to be standing in a square, walled enclosure that might have been fifty feet in each dimension. The tiled patio just beyond the door was connected to a couple of brick paths that curved through a half-hearted array of bushes, flower beds, and stunted trees. To his right was a small pavilion that seemed to hold tables and chairs and a few potted plants. It was covered with a heavy linen canopy, but was otherwise open to the night air. The tinkling of the fountain seemed to come from under its protection.

The walls were high enough to be difficult to scale, and Brandon guessed they were slick as marble, though he couldn't tell in this light. They were innocent of any vine that might offer a handhold to a desperate climber. There was no gate to admit visitors directly to or from the yard; anyone who wished to take refuge in the garden would have to access it through the house.

It was hard to tell if anyone actually *was* out here enjoying the night. Brandon stood there for five minutes, then ten, trying to probe the shadows, but he saw no one moving, heard no one breathing, could not locate any shape that he could definitely identify as a woman.

It would be funny—and horrible and disastrous—if, on Brandon's very first night on this assignment, Nadder had arranged for the prisoner's escape, and Brandon spent his entire watch guarding over empty air.

Then there was a sound from under the canopy, the slightest scrape of metal against stone, and Brandon peered more intently through the darkness. Yes—that looked to be a seated figure, barely distinguishable from the feathery mass of the potted plant behind her. The sound came again as the woman rearranged her chair. Those sinuous shapes must be her arms, uncrossing and recrossing as she rested her wrists on the table before her. That slight bobbing motion was her head as she glanced around.

Brandon waited, wondering if she would speak to him, but she was silent. So he was silent as well. It was not up to him to introduce himself as her latest jailor. She might not even notice, or care, that someone new had joined her household.

He was obscurely disappointed. He realized he had been bracing himself to resist her advances, to remain impenetrable to her guile. But she was not bent on winning him over. She didn't even realize he was there.

Brandon's next two shifts at his new job were equally uneventful. Both nights, when he stepped out into the garden, Villette Rowan was so still that he had to strain his senses to make sure she was actually present. She never bothered to speak to him, not even when, after an hour or two of silent contemplation, she came to her feet and swept into the house. He bowed as she passed, but he got very little more than an impression of her size and a glimpse of her features.

He could tell she was delicate and slim, with light bones and small hands. Her hair was dark and her skin was a deep brown. When she passed him, the floral scent of summer intensified, sweeter than honeysuckle, and faded once she entered the house. He always waited a moment or two, then followed her inside to watch as she made a slow, graceful climb to her room.

He spent the remainder of those nights patrolling the interior of the house, making at least one pass around the exterior grounds, and trying not to yawn. It was always a relief when the servants began stirring shortly after first light. Even though he was still on duty until nine o'clock, at least he was no longer the only one awake. And breakfast helped him keep his eyes open until his shift ended and he could seek his bed.

"How do you like the job so far?" Finley asked at the end of the third day. She was on duty, though she was pretty relaxed about it, lounging on one of the wrought-iron chairs set before a matching table in a corner of the atrium. He had dropped into the chair across from her, making sure not to obstruct her view of the garden. He was backup for these twelve hours until his own shift began.

"So far there's not much to it," he said.

"Has she talked to you yet?"

"Not a word."

"Maybe she's given up. Nadder says she ignores him like he's not even there, and she's always treated me like I'm invisible. Maybe she's decided it doesn't do any good to try to seduce the guards."

"Just as well."

Finley yawned. "I agree."

At nine, Finley headed down the hall to her room and Brandon walked the short route out to the garden. As always, he stood still a moment just to get his bearings, to make sure nothing and no one had breached the small space, to locate the shadowy figure sitting under the linen canopy. Then he took his customary stance—legs spread wide to keep him steady, hands crossed behind his back, ready to sweep down and grab weapons from his belt—and settled in for a long, uneventful wait.

The next hour passed in silence except for the rasping of insects, the scurrying of night creatures, and the rustling of shrubs and flower stalks. Then from under the awning came the faint screech of metal against stone. Another slight sound heralded a small burst of light, and Brandon realized Villette had struck a match. And lit a candle. Two. Three, before blowing out the match.

"So you're the new guard," she said.

As soon as she'd moved, he'd swung around to face her, and now he bowed in her direction, in case she could see him. Her own face was tantalizingly illuminated by the flickering candlelight—a swatch of cheek, a crown of hair, a single oval eye—each feature briefly appearing, then quickly fading into darkness.

"I am," he said.

"What's your name?"

"They call me Brandon."

She considered him. "You have an unusual accent. Where are you from?"

"The islands."

"Ah. Then your name isn't Brandon after all, is it?"

He was so surprised he almost didn't respond. "I'm sorry?" he said at last.

"The Zessin people have their own language, don't they? Full of lots of s's and l's and hissing sounds. What's your real name?"

"No one in the city has ever been able to say it," he told her before pronouncing it.

"You're right. I can't say that. So I suppose Brandon will have to do. How long have you been in Corcannon, Brandon?"

"About two years."

"Do you like it?"

"I do."

"What do you like about it?"

All the other questions had been simply worded, simply answered, but this one required more thought and a longer reply. "I like the possibilities," he said. "I like the thought that any day I might learn something that I didn't know before. Something that matters."

"So it's not the crowds and the fancy restaurants and the cultural delights that appeal to you. It's not the *place.* It's how the place might help you define *yourself.*"

"I—yes. I suppose so," he said, unnerved again. Never would it have occurred to him to describe his reaction that way, but she was absolutely right.

"Have you *seen* many of the attractions?" she asked. Her voice was warm and interested, with the barest edge of laughter. It didn't feel like mockery, but Brandon could hardly tell. "Or have you spent all your time in soldierly pursuits?"

He could feel a grin shape his mouth. "Mostly the soldierly pursuits."

"And now you're stuck here for the next six months. Not much chance of visiting the sights while you're guarding me."

"I have a night off now and then. I can head down to the Quatrefoil." As soon as he said it, he wished he hadn't, since she wasn't allowed any such privileges.

"I recommend the museums of art and history. You learn so much in a short period of time."

"Maybe," he said doubtfully.

Now she laughed softly, but the tone still didn't sound unkind. "You're not much of one for artistic or intellectual amusements? You prefer physical action and tangible gains?"

"Rather build something than look at something someone else built," he explained.

"Now that's very interesting," she said. "What *have* you built?"

"I helped two of my brothers build their houses. Worked on boats my whole life with my father and my uncles. Gathered the stones and built a water garden for my mother. Things like that."

"A water garden!" she exclaimed. "I wonder if you could create such a thing here. What are the requirements?"

"Well, water, of course."

She laughed again. "Yes, of course! Would it use the same kind of pumping system as my fountains?"

"Probably."

"Then that's easily taken care of. What else?"

"And then you'd need to decide how big you want it to be, and what kinds of flowers you want, and whether you want to keep fish in it—"

"Fish! Of course. I must have fish."

"I built a little bridge for my mother's. It doesn't go anywhere, it just crosses over the water. But she can stand on it and look down and see the fish swimming by."

"I am entranced! I must have such a treat! When can you start construction?"

Brandon pulled himself up short. *How did she do that?* he wondered, ever so slightly dizzy. *How did she that quickly get me to talk about something I love? How did she get me to forget who I was even talking to?*

"I don't think I would be permitted to build such a thing for you," he said stiffly. "That's not how my time is supposed to be spent."

"Well, I don't see why not," she said. "If all you're supposed to be doing is keeping me from running away, and I'm not trying to run away, you may as well work on some projects. Otherwise you might die of boredom."

"So far I haven't been bored," he said.

He heard the scraping sound again and her face moved out of the candlelight; he thought she had probably leaned back in her chair and was surveying him. "So what terrible things have they told you about me?" she asked abruptly.

He was taken by surprise. "Nothing. Nothing terrible, at any rate."

"Surely they've warned you that I am always trying to befriend the guards, and that you should never show me a single kindness."

"Well," he said cautiously, "something like that."

She didn't reply and a long silence stretched between them. Brandon didn't know why it made him so uncomfortable, but he was convinced she was waiting for him to speak again, and after a while he couldn't bear the waiting.

"Is it true?" he asked.

"That you should never show me a kindness?"

"That you always befriend the guards."

"The ones who seem willing to be befriended," she said. "But since I have no other friends and very little other company, don't you think my life would be woefully sad if I couldn't have an agreeable conversation with one or two other human beings? Ever?"

Over the past three days, he had just about come to that conclusion on his own. "It would," he said. "Very lonely, too. But—"

"But what?"

"They told me that you try to make friends so they'll help you escape."

Her laugh was so low it might not even be a laugh. Certainly it wasn't mirthful. "Oh, I'll never escape this house."

Another long silence fell between them. He was burning to ask more questions—starting with the biggest, the most obvious one. *What have you done to cause you to be locked up here for the rest of your life?* Finley would tell him it didn't matter; it was his job to carry out the assignment he had been given and not ask for the reasons behind it. The prisoner, he thought, could not be counted on to tell him the truth.

But he really wanted to know.

The chair moved more decisively across the tile, and he could see Villette's silhouette stand up. "Well, it's late and I'm sleepy," she said. She bent over to blow out the candles before stepping out from under the canopy and toward the door.

But this time, unlike the other three nights, she moved at a measured pace, her head lifted, her attention fixed on Brandon where he stood near the door. He watched her slow journey from the complete darkness of the pavilion to the moon-streaked shadows of the open patio to the almost-light thrown by the interior sconces. With each step, her shape became more distinct, her features more discernible. He couldn't help staring intently at her face, which so far he had seen only in glimpses and which even now was not wholly visible in the dimness.

The high cheekbones, the rich skin, the dark hair coiled at the nape of her neck—yes, those were exactly the way he had envisioned them after those few brief impressions. Her eyes were a velvet brown under elegantly arched brows; her mouth and nose were daintily shaped. He wouldn't have called her beautiful, exactly, but there was something winsome about the arrangement of her features. It was hard to read her expression, yet he couldn't shake the thought that her face was shuttered with sadness. As if no other emotion would ever be able to break through.

And then she smiled and the expression was so inviting it almost chased away the sadness. Almost. "I wonder about you," she said softly. "Do you wonder about me?"

Without waiting for an answer, she brushed past him and went into the house.

This night he didn't follow. He was too busy catching his breath.

Chapter Ten: Brandon

Brandon could hardly sleep the following day for wishing the sun would race through its customary perambulations and plummet toward the hard line of the horizon. Finally, knowing he would have to be alert for all the long hours of his shift, he willed himself to doze in the early afternoon, only to wake up a few hours later. It would have to do. He rose and shaved and put on his navy uniform with extra care.

Then there was just an hour of desultory conversation with Finley to get through, and a solitary dinner to consume as slowly as possible so the activity filled the last empty hour. Finally, finally, the clocks showed five minutes to nine, and Brandon could march under the archway that led to the garden.

"I'm here," he announced unnecessarily to Nadder. The other man nodded and left.

Brandon stood at stiff attention as he waited for the echoes of Nadder's footfalls to fade. He was positioned so that, with one twist of his head, he could glance into the house or directly into the shadows under the pavilion. He could make out Villette's slim seated shape, though she hadn't bothered lighting candles this night. He thought she, too, was waiting for Nadder to be out of hearing before she resumed last night's conversation.

But five minutes passed, and then ten, and then an hour, and Villette didn't speak at all.

Brandon was dismayed at the strength of his disappointment—shocked, actually, to discover how much he had looked forward to hearing her voice again. His whole body had been strung with excitement when he first took up his waiting pose, but as the night wore on, he felt his hands unclench and his shoulders droop and the corners of his mouth turn down.

Stupid. What had he expected? What had he *wanted,* even? He couldn't even put it into words.

He tensed up again when he caught the sound of her chair moving against the tile, but all it signaled was that she was rising to her feet. She stepped out from under the awning, but she didn't look his way as she passed by him so closely he was for a moment enveloped in her honeysuckle perfume. Then she was gone and the scent was gone and he was left with the whole night to get through before he could seek his bed and try to forget that he was an idiot.

The next day passed in exactly the same manner, except that Brandon was so tired he managed to sleep heavily for nearly nine hours before emerging from his room. Again, he killed the time before his shift by chatting with Finley and slowly eating dinner. But when he stepped outside to relieve Nadder, the other guard greeted him with a yawn.

"She's not out here," Nadder said. "She went in after lunch and hasn't left her room since. I stayed outside because it was too hot in the house."

"Oh. All right," Brandon said blankly. "I guess I'll do a patrol or two outside but mostly keep to the house."

"Sounds good," said Nadder, yawning again. "See you tomorrow."

It was the second-longest night Brandon could ever remember.

But he slept more reasonably the following day and felt more like himself when he woke up. Not hopeful, not disappointed, just ready to do his job. Which did *not* require conversation with his charges.

He and Nadder did some training exercises together in one of the unused ground-floor rooms, lifting weights and going through some basic fencing moves. When they emerged, they found Finley eating dinner in the atrium. A large tureen of food and extra plates had been laid out on the table beside her, so they pulled up chairs to join her.

Brandon didn't recognize the spices or even the meat in the stew that he ladled out, but he had to say he liked it. "This is *good,*" he observed. "I don't think I've ever had it before."

"Comes from southern Marata," Nadder said. "Cook makes it specially for me."

"Gotta be as boring here for her as it is for the rest of us," Finley said. "So she doesn't mind if you ask her to make you something different once in a while."

"I'll remember that. There are a few dishes from the islands that I've been missing."

"Well, if they're too exotic, she won't have the ingredients," Finley warned.

Brandon nodded enthusiastically. "She could get them! In the southeast district there's a whole Zessin neighborhood. You can get food—clothes—anything."

"Never been there," Nadder said.

"I'll take you sometime, if you want to go."

"You can't both be gone at the same time," Finley pointed out.

Nadder shrugged his muscular shoulders. "We can go once I'm off the assignment. Couple more months."

"Not like you're counting every single day."

"I don't think it's so bad here," Brandon volunteered.

"I didn't either, my first week," Nadder agreed. "But day after day after day of *nothing*. It wears on you."

"Well, there'll be *something* tomorrow," Finley said.

"What's that?" Brandon asked.

"Visit from the temple. Someone comes every couple weeks to check on Villette—usually the high divine. He's supposed to get here sometime in late afternoon."

"How long does he stay?" Brandon asked.

Finley shrugged. "Around an hour, unless Villette is being uncooperative. Then maybe ten minutes."

"But it's not like she has a lot of other visitors, so even though she hates him, she usually lets him stay and talk a while," Nadder added.

"Why does she hate him?"

Finley looked expressively around the atrium, all mellow gold and restful blue in the softening twilight. "Because he's the one who keeps her here?"

Brandon took another bite of stew before casually asking, "Does anyone know why?"

Finley shook her head. "And I don't care. I'm not even curious."

"I'm curious," Nadder said, "but I don't really care."

I'm curious, Brandon thought, *and I already might care too much.*

About thirty minutes later, when Brandon stepped outside, he looked automatically for Villette's shadow under the pavilion. It took his eyes a few moments to adjust, but then he peered harder. He couldn't make out her solid shape against the ruffled darkness; was she even there? Had she somehow slipped over the wall while the three guards were laughing over dinner? He took a step toward the awning, narrowing his eyes as if that would improve his vision.

Her voice came from somewhere to his left. "I'm over here."

He spun in that direction. The moon was about half full and not particularly helpful, but it gave off enough light to show her silhouetted against the high stone of the enclosing wall. He felt like he should answer her but he didn't know what to say, so all he managed was "Oh."

"Sitting made me feel anxious," she explained. "So I've been pacing instead."

"Has it helped?" he asked.

That made her laugh. "A little."

It seemed like she might be willing to engage in conversation again tonight, so he risked another question. "Why are you anxious?"

She began a slow promenade along the edge of the garden. He heard a slight crunching sound with every footfall and remembered that the perimeter near the wall was lined with gravel. "I shall be meeting with my enemy tomorrow. It always makes me fretful."

"The high divine."

"So someone told you."

"Just that he was coming. Not why he's your enemy."

Her deliberate pace had led her far enough away that she now had her back to him. He saw her slice a hand through the air as if to indicate the story was too complex to relate. "He wants things from me I cannot supply," she said, the words floating back to him. "Or refuse to supply, if you believe his version of events."

"And would he release you if you could—or would—supply them?"

Now she responded with a muffled laugh. "Oh, he would put me in a different sort of prison altogether. A worse one, if you can believe it. There is no advantage to me in acceding to his demands."

It didn't make any sense, and Brandon figured it wouldn't unless she wanted to sit down and explain exactly what her situation was. Which he was pretty sure she wasn't planning to do. He stopped asking questions.

She reached the far wall of the garden, sighed, and turned back in his direction. "But let's not talk about the high divine," she said. "Let's talk of more interesting topics. Tell me about yourself."

"I don't think I have a single story that you would call interesting," he replied.

"Oh, that can't be true. Tell me about a time when you were growing up. Some game you played with your brothers."

He grinned. "Mostly we didn't play games. We were fighting or wrestling—it was always 'see who can punch the hardest.'"

"And who could?"

"My oldest brother, because he was the biggest. Until I was about twelve, and then I was the biggest. *And* the one who hit the hardest."

She was drawing nearer with every step. "And that's why you decided to be a soldier?"

He shrugged. "It seemed to be a road out."

She stopped when she was only about five feet away. This close, even in the thin moonlight, he could almost make out her features. Those slanted cheekbones. Those sad eyes. "Did you leave the islands and come straight to Corcannon? That must have been a shock."

He shook his head. "Spent a couple years in southern Marata working for different landowners. There's a lot of unrest in that part of the country—people poaching off each other's property, and brigands on the road. So there was plenty of work."

"But you got restless again, so you came here."

"Not that, exactly. I took a job with a merchant hauling cargo to Corcannon. After my third trip across the canyon, I decided to stay."

"Do you miss the island life?"

He hesitated. "I want to say I don't," he answered honestly. "I couldn't wait to get away. The place where I grew up is so small. There's nothing to do but fish or work in the mines or spend all day trying to scratch a living from the land. But the city—" He gestured uncertainly. He didn't have the words to explain. "It has things I never knew I'd want to know about," he ended lamely.

"And yet sometimes you lie awake and miss that old life so much your ribs hurt," she said softly. "Is that it?"

"It's the small things I wouldn't even have said I'd noticed," he said. "The way the waves sound at night when everything else is quiet and you can hear them. The way the air feels so heavy against your skin. There's a coshichi bush outside my mother's house—it's the first thing to bloom every spring when everything else still looks lost and dead. Big purple flowers that smell, I am not lying, like vinegar. How could you miss something like that? But they don't have any coshichi bushes in Corcannon. Spring arrives here before I even remember it's coming."

"Ah, those details are very specific to the place," Villette said, nodding. "Smells and sounds—you couldn't import them the way you could import a piece of clothing or a type of food."

"So that's what I miss."

She tilted her head. "What about the religious rituals? Don't they worship Zessaya on the islands? Don't you miss her?"

He grinned. "Well, I was never as observant about Zessaya as my mother wanted," he said. "But I promised her that I'd at least wear my chazissa every day."

Villette looked intrigued. "What's that?"

He slipped a finger under his collar and pulled out the short leather cord hung with a charm about half the size of his thumb. "It's a representation of the goddess in one of her poses," he explained. "If you want protection, you pick a pose where she's holding a shield. If you want peace, you pick the one that shows her holding a sleeping baby. There are twelve of them."

"And which pose do you favor?"

"The one for courage. She's holding a spear and looking fierce."

"May I see it? Can I hold it?"

"Sure." He slipped the cord over his head, untied the knot, and let the charm slide free onto her outstretched hand.

She held it up to the pale moonlight, turning it this way and that. "It seems like it's made of carved stone—is that right?"

"Cherloshe," he said. "You can find it all over the islands. And only in the islands, or so I've heard. People say cherloshe rocks are the bones of the goddess."

"It looks like there's a little loop at the top, carved from the stone itself, and that's what the cord goes through?"

"That's right. You never use even the smallest scrap of metal on a chazissa."

"Really? Why?"

He laughed. "Because Zessaya hates Dar, of course, and Dar is the goddess of the mountains and the ore mines."

"So I suppose the people who worship Dar never use cherloshe in any of their rituals."

"I wouldn't know," he said. "I've never been in a Darrish temple."

"Neither have I," she said. She was still holding his chazissa, turning it over in her fingers as if trying to feel how the stone carver had rendered the serious features and flowing robes. He didn't know how to ask for it back. "So you're a Zessin man working in Cordelan's temple and you wear a chazissa. Does that bother your fellow guardsmen?"

"I thought it might," he answered honestly. "But a lot of the guards are from Chibain and Marata, and they carry Darrish amulets, and nobody seems to care. It's like as long as you're willing to say that Cordelan is the supreme being, you can worship any other god you like."

"Oh, that is so very much in line with Cordelan's philosophy!" she exclaimed. "Bow down before him! Show reverence to the high divine and his favorite priests! Acknowledge them as your masters, and then all will be well. But just once say you don't believe in them and you don't consider their word to be law—well, then, you will be crushed into dust beneath their feet."

Brandon stared at her. "Is that what you did—defied them?" he asked. "Is that why you're here?"

"It's one of the reasons," she said. "I refuse to give such a selfish, arrogant god complete power over my life."

"What are you going to do?"

For an answer, she popped the chazissa in her mouth.

And swallowed it.

Brandon was so astonished he could only stare. Villette turned away from him, struggling for breath, possibly choking on the small figurine. He leapt to her side, prepared to pound on her back to make her spit up the charm, but she pulled away violently. "Water," she gasped. "On the table."

He lunged over to the pavilion, felt around on the table for a pitcher and glass, and sprinted back to her so rapidly half the water spilled out over his hands. Villette gulped what was left in the glass and coughed a few times, then crossed her hands over her stomach and leaned over. After panting heavily for a few moments, she straightened up and took in one long breath of air.

"Well," she said. "That wasn't as smooth as I'd hoped."

He was still stunned. "Why did—why did you do that?"

Her dark face seemed to have paled with exertion, but the expression in her eyes was as fierce as ever Zessaya's could be. "Defiance," she said.

Brandon shook his head. "That doesn't make any sense."

"Well, you know the stories," she said, lightly enough. "When Cordelan decided to remake the continent, he also chose to make Dar his wife, and together they ruled the united lands. And together they were so powerful that Zessaya had no choice but to cooperate with them. But Zessaya is an insolent, subversive goddess, and she refused to be completely controlled by her old enemy and this new god. So she made cherloshe impervious to Cordelan's power. And anyone who wears cherloshe is protected from Cordelan's vengeance."

"But you aren't *wearing* it," Brandon pointed out. "You *ate* it."

Now he saw a new look on her face—half anger, half fervor. "You want the truth? All right, I'll tell you. I have a condition. There's something in my blood, and the high divine wants to exploit it. And I have spent all my adult life trying to make sure he doesn't. And the one thing in this world that can counter the condition in my blood is cherloshe. Cherloshe nullifies it, or changes its composition or—something. I don't know. But it keeps me safe from the high divine's machinations."

Brandon didn't know what to think. It seemed like the most elaborate, the most ridiculous, of lies. What possible condition could she have? How could the priests exploit it? And how could an ounce of rock dissolve into her blood in a way that would protect her?

"It sounds mad," he said.

She actually laughed. "It does! I will grant you that. But it's the truth."

"How long does it last? The—the effects of the cherloshe you swallowed."

"Usually a month or two."

"What happens once it wears off?"

This laugh was a little wilder. "Oh, I've been wondering that for the past few weeks, ever since I lost my last source of supply. When the high divine comes tomorrow, you see, he will test my blood. He will check to see if it is—at the optimum condition for what he wants. It won't be, because of your chazissa, that miraculous bit of stone with powers you didn't even know it possessed. But if it was—if it *was*—" She shook her head. "My life would be over."

He was shocked. "He would *kill* you?"

"Oh, no. No no no no. I am so much more valuable to him alive than dead. He would rather see half the city murdered than to see me harmed in the slightest way. But I would be unhappier than anyone in the course of human existence."

Privately, Brandon thought that was another exaggeration. There were plenty of miserable people in the world and, despite the fact that Villette was imprisoned, she didn't seem as bad off as some people he could think of.

But he found that he did not want the high divine to do anything that made her unhappy.

"How did you get cherloshe before?" he asked.

"A friend of mine would bring some when she visited. But she was discovered and she has been banned from the house. So not only do I not have the cherloshe, I don't have the pleasure of her company."

"Would you like—I mean, I could get you some more. If you wanted."

Her face softened; her lips parted. "Brandon," she said in a wondering voice. "If you would do that for me—"

"It wouldn't be hard. I'll just buy another chazissa or two in the island district. Then you'll have them on hand when you need them."

"That would be—I can't even tell you how amazing that would be!" She clasped her hands under her chin, and he couldn't tell if she was thanking him or praying to the goddess. Maybe both. "You're so kind."

He was embarrassed. And pleased. "I'm happy to do it."

She took a deep breath. "Then—if you're willing—I would be so *grateful.* I would be so *relieved.* This will give me a kind of hope I haven't had in months."

"I'm happy to do it," he repeated.

They stood there for a moment, smiling at each other in the dark. The honeysuckle smell of her perfume seemed stronger than any other scent in the garden, in the city.

"Well," she said. "I have to go in and prepare myself for my dreadful day tomorrow. Thank you again. You have given me so much courage." And she bowed her head to him, as if he was a rich landowner and she was a servant girl, and hurried into the house.

Brandon was left standing there, the leather cord curled in his hand, the night heavy around his shoulders. The ground shifting beneath his feet. The world completely remade. He could not explain it, but he knew that during one simple conversation, he had irreversibly shifted his allegiance. Perhaps Villette couldn't be trusted. Perhaps her every word was a lie. Perhaps the high divine—whose role as head of the temple mandated that Brandon be loyal to him above all others—perhaps the high divine had a very good reason for keeping Villette locked away, separated from friends and family and any kind of reasonable life. But Brandon was on her side now. If she needed him and he could help her, he would contravene his professional oaths, he would risk his nascent career, and do so gladly.

It seemed impossible that he would not come to regret it.

It seemed impossible to make any other choice.

Chapter Eleven: Jayla

Within her first week as Madeleine's personal guard, Jayla had drawn a host of conclusions.

The woman lived an entirely frivolous life, filled with nothing but luncheons, dinners, shopping excursions, and outings with friends. Jayla had accompanied her to private houses, open-air markets, fine dining establishments, and one concert hall, and never did anyone do anything except eat, talk, buy, or dance. It was hard to have much respect for such a meaningless existence, though Jayla certainly respected the amount of money it represented. Someone, somewhere, must be dealing with merchants or meeting with bankers or overseeing profitable farmland, because otherwise this lifestyle could not be sustained.

She had quickly learned that that someone was Madeleine's father, Alastair Alayne—who, it turned out, enjoyed not only wealth but political power. He was a cold and taciturn man whose presence always set the tone, even the temperature, for the rest of the household. When he was home, even if he was locked in his office where no one saw him, every servant moved soundlessly through the halls and Madeleine mostly confined herself to the colorful rooms on the second story. When he was gone, the sun shone more brightly through the skylights in the high ceiling. The servants called to each other across the atrium. Madeleine laughed.

Jayla had had almost no dealings with the man. He had interviewed her for fifteen minutes, inspected her bracelets for authenticity, and outlined the terms of the job before hiring her on the spot. Since then, she had passed him in the halls maybe ten times, and never exchanged a word with him, which suited Jayla just fine.

Madeleine never said she was afraid of him—never acted nervous or cowed when he entered the house or called her in to dinner—but it was clear she wasn't close to her father. It was also clear that, despite the superficiality of her life, Madeleine was a kind soul with a sunny temperament. She greeted everyone with a cheerful word, maintained excellent relations with the entire staff, and had more friends than Jayla would have believed any one person could manage.

Madeleine had been the one to welcome them when Jayla presented herself at the Alayne house, Aussen in tow. Jayla had been trying hard not to gawk at the graceful archways, the colorful columns, the sheer grand elegance of the place, when Madeleine stepped into the atrium.

"Here you are! I'm so glad, because I've got an appointment in an hour and I was hoping you could accompany me," Madeleine said. She bent down to look into the little girl's eyes. "And you must be Aussen."

Aussen pressed up against Jayla and stared at Madeleine without making a sound. The child had been overwhelmed by the color, noise, size, and motion of the city. Ever since they had arrived, she had to seemed to shrink in on herself, growing timid and silent. As they took the noisy chugger from their rented rooms to the Alayne property, Aussen had gripped Jayla's hand and stared around her apprehesively. Jayla had started to wonder if it had been a mistake after all to sign up for this job.

"I think I mentioned that she doesn't speak many words of Cordish, though she seems to understand them," Jayla explained.

"You did," Madeleine replied, still leaning over to watch Aussen. Then she produced a few slow, uncertain syllables that Jayla didn't recognize.

Aussen's face lit with a smile and she answered in a torrent of words. Madeleine laughed, threw her hands out, and straightened up, shaking her head. She said something else, and Aussen stopped talking, but the little girl was still smiling.

"What did you say?" Jayla demanded.

"Our cook speaks a little Zessin, so I asked her how to say 'welcome to your new home,'" Madeleine said. "I wasn't sure I got it exactly right, but Aussen seemed to understand me."

"She definitely did. Your cook speaks Zessin? Maybe she can help me communicate with Aussen a little better."

"I'm sure she'd be happy to. Now let me show you your quarters."

They had been given a room on the third floor, small but well-kept, with two narrow beds, a single chest of drawers, and even a window. Jayla had held posts where eight people might be crammed into a space this size, so she was pleased and grateful at the accommodations.

"Aussen can be trusted to stay here by herself and not get in trouble when I'm busy with you," Jayla said.

"Good, although she might go mad if she's cooped up here alone all day," Madeleine answered. "The cook said she'd be willing to train her if

Aussen was willing to work. The housekeeper, too."

"Then maybe I can take her down to meet with them when we get back from your outing," Jayla said, making it clear that she knew her foremost duty was to her employer.

Madeleine answered, "This ought to work out splendidly."

And it had, really. The cook was a brisk, friendly woman named Norrah who seemed ready to handle any crisis with ease. Her Zessin vocabulary was limited, but far better than Jayla's, and she immediately was able to find out a few critical details about Aussen's life.

"The woman she'd been traveling with—the one who died—was a neighbor. She doesn't know where they were supposed to go once they arrived in Corcannon, but she knows her mother is supposed to arrive in two or three months. She's eight years old. Also, she thinks you're really nice."

Jayla was surprised into a laugh. "I wouldn't have expected that. All she's seen me do is brawl and worry."

"Well," said Norrah, "I wouldn't be surprised if she's seen a lot of brawling and worrying in her time."

The other servants were a little less friendly than Norrah, but that didn't bother Jayla. Her goal was always to maintain cool, professional relations with the people around her. That made it easier to get along, while she was there; made it easier to go, when she wanted to leave.

She'd had no occasion to interact with anyone else in Madeleine's life—a personal guard was as invisible as a servant, or should be—but she had drawn some conclusions about the ones she'd observed during small, intimate luncheons. The young women were mostly flighty and empty-headed, though one or two seemed as kind as Madeleine, which boosted them in Jayla's estimation. The young men were similarly unimpressive, appearing to waste their lives drinking, gambling, and engaging in sports; if any of them spent time working in their family businesses, they never mentioned it in conversation.

Jayla had been surprised, two days after taking the job, to discover that Madeleine planned to marry Tivol. He had driven them to and from a large, merry luncheon at an establishment deep in the Quatrefoil, so Jayla had had a chance to observe him at close quarters. She liked his friendly, easy style and the affectionate way he treated Madeleine, but there was a carelessness about him that she found irksome. Probably because she herself was never careless.

Shortly after they'd returned to the house, as they'd climbed upstairs, Madeleine had said, "If I need to travel outside the city, you'll accompany me, won't you?"

"Of course. Where are you going? And when?"

Madeleine paused outside her door. "To Marata, but I'm not sure when. Tivol's mother keeps inviting me to visit."

Up till this point, the two of them hadn't had much conversation that could pass for personal. Jayla preferred it that way—but she also didn't mind a chance to get to know a little more about a client's life. Sometimes the information came in handy. So she repeated, "Tivol's mother?" in an inquiring voice.

"She wants me to understand all the intricacies of running the property so that I know what I'm doing once I marry Tivol."

"Tivol? Not Reese?" Jayla said without thinking.

Madeleine made a sound that could have been a laugh or a sigh. "No, although Reese would like to change my mind."

Jayla's face burned; she had been unforgivably rude. "I'm sorry, dona, I didn't mean—"

"Actually, it's a relief to talk about it," Madeleine confessed. "All of my friends adore Tivol, because he's so charming and cultured. And because he flirts with them, but that's harmless. Reese is—not quite as refined as most of them like."

"I only met him once," Jayla said. "The day you came to the training yard. He seemed very interested in your well-being. And—" How could she phrase this without risking offense? "He seemed sensible and solid. Maybe not the kind of person who is at ease in a ballroom."

"Exactly! He'd rather be mucking around on his father's farm than accompanying me to a dance."

"I don't know how the wealthy families of the city plan their marriages," Jayla said. "Do the parents arrange for their heirs to marry? Or do you get to choose who you fall in love with?"

Madeleine leaned against the wall, looking like she was prepared to talk all night. "A little of both," she said. "Since I was quite young, it was clear my father wanted me to marry Tivol. I've known him my whole life and he's always been my best friend. It seemed like the most natural thing in the world that he would propose to me and I would accept."

Jayla just raised her eyebrows and waited.

Madeleine sighed. "And then, Reese . . . I've known Reese my whole life, too, of course. But he was hardly ever in Corcannon, and when he was, he didn't play around with the rest of us much. He was always so serious. But then last year, he was here all the time, and I would see him at a ball—or he would come to the house to visit—and we would go for walks—"

"You fell in love with him," Jayla said, because otherwise it seemed like Madeleine would never get to the point.

"No! Not exactly. I mean—well, he did kiss me."

Jayla tried to hide her smile. "I suppose you can kiss a man you're not in love with."

"Oh, I've kissed dozens. But this was—different."

There was a silence. "But you still want to marry Tivol," Jayla finally said.

"I do! But Reese doesn't want me to."

"What would your father say if you told him you were going to marry Reese?"

Madeleine shivered. "He would be so angry. He and Heloise—Tivol's mother—have launched any number of business deals partly because of the wedding. We're both the sole heirs of our families, so all the property we have will be combined."

"I can understand your father's reasoning, then."

"But Reese comes from a wealthy family, too, so he's certainly an *eligible* match."

"I suppose it comes down to which one you would rather marry."

"Tivol, of course," Madeleine said a bit too quickly.

"Well, then, everything seems to be taken care of."

"It's just that Reese can be unsettling."

"You could refuse to see him the next time he comes to the house."

"That would be so rude! And he's been so kind lately—" Madeleine fell into a brief and somewhat melancholy reverie. "I've just never been one of those *romantic* girls," she said at last. "I've always thought liking someone was more important than having a grand passion that would burn out in a couple of years. Running an estate and managing a business takes work, and that takes compatibility. I can picture living happily with Tivol for the next sixty years. Whereas Reese and I argue all the time."

Jayla felt like she needed to say something, so she commented, "That's certainly a consideration."

"My parents married for love, but I don't know how happy they were together."

This was so astonishing that Jayla couldn't let it pass. "Your father married for love? It's not what I would have expected."

"No! He is so closed and cool-headed you would hardly think he had any emotions at all."

"Do you know how the marriage came about?"

"My mother was an orphan who was—oh, the third cousin of one of the Kissidells. Something like that. So the Kissidells took her in and raised her, though I never had the impression they were particularly generous to her. My father met her at some ball he hadn't even wanted to attend, and a few months later they were married."

"How long were they married?"

"Almost twelve years. She died in childbirth."

"With your brother?"

"No, actually, with her third child. She and the baby both. Apparently my father wanted a houseful of children—though I don't know why, since he was never that interested in spending time with the children he *did* have. She'd had a difficult time with the other two births and the doctor had told her not to get pregnant again, but she did."

"How old were you?"

"Nine. I remember her, but not as clearly as I wish I did. I don't have any memories of her laughing or singing. Mostly when I see her face in my mind, she looks sad."

"Maybe life as a rich man's wife wasn't much better than life as a poor relation."

Madeleine sighed. "Maybe life as my father's wife was too hard for anyone to bear. I never got a chance to ask her. Anyway, the point I was making was that my father's marriage was romantic—but maybe not successful. So I hope mine will be more successful even if it's less romantic."

"I think you know Tivol well enough by now that there will be no surprises," Jayla said. "That sounds like a good way to start a marriage."

"It does. You're right. Yes," Madeleine said. "And I'm very much looking forward to my wedding day."

She smiled, nodded a goodnight, and slipped inside her room. Jayla continued up the next flight of stairs to her own room, wondering if Madeleine really had convinced herself that she was marrying the right man.

Jayla and Madeleine didn't have any more extended private conversations over the next few days, which were filled with excursions and parties. Tivol was present at most events, Reese at none of them. At one of the balls, where Jayla stood in the shadows watching the dancers, she amused herself trying to guess which of the other young men Madeleine had kissed. Frankly, she found it hard to tell them apart. Maybe Madeleine had kissed them all and not known the difference.

Once Jayla had been working at the mansion for two weeks, she earned a day off. Norrah agreed to watch Aussen, so Jayla made plans to explore the city. With Cody.

She had thought about it a long time before she sent Cody the details of her new position. She had been on her own long enough, had been traveling long enough, to know that an acquaintance of the road should never be considered a true friend. Situations arose on a journey that made it advisable to work with others, and those encounters were often enjoyable, but the man who helped you free your wagon from a ditch might be a thief or a liar or tedious political fellow that you wouldn't want to welcome into your life. Friendships formed from expediency tended to fall apart under the stress and wear of ordinary life. Jayla was always ready to move on.

But Cody had asked her to stay in touch. And she didn't know anyone else in Corcannon. And she might be a tiny bit lonely.

So she'd sent him a note to tell him where she was, and he'd replied the very next morning, and they'd agreed to meet on the first day she had free.

She stepped through the front door of the mansion to find Cody waiting for her in the circular drive. He wasn't wearing the red vest that marked couriers as they dashed through the city, but he might as well have been, since his bracelet full of gems flared with sunlight every time he moved his wrist. By contrast, Jayla was out of her Alayne livery, wearing her old worn leather clothes. Any casual passer-by would have a harder time assigning her an identity.

"You found the place," she greeted him.

He nodded. "Knew where it was. I've brought messages to Alastair Alayne plenty of times."

She waited a beat. "Did you know *I* was here? Before I told you?"

He narrowed his eyes, as if trying to determine whether his answer would anger her, then nodded.

"Would you have come looking for me? If I hadn't gotten in touch with you?"

"Thought about it. But I didn't."

"But if I hadn't?"

"Maybe. Once."

She was trying not to smile. "Just once?"

"Well," he drawled. "You seem to know your own mind pretty well. I don't see you changing a no to a yes just because someone keeps asking you the same question."

That made her laugh out loud. "That's the second-best compliment you've paid me."

"What was the first?"

"Not trying to protect me when I was in a fight."

He opened his eyes comically wide. "*I'm* no good in a fight."

"So you've *never* thrown a punch?"

Now he grinned. "Hardly ever. Anyway, you're a professional. I didn't figure you needed my assistance."

"Well," she said. "If there were five people coming at me at once. Then I might need some help."

"Five. Good to know," he said. "I'll keep an eye out."

And she laughed again.

"So where do you want to go?" he asked, turning toward the street. "What do you want to see?"

"East side," she said. "The Zessin district."

He gestured for her to follow him to the side of the road, where one of the big public transports was racketing into view down the gridway. "You're trying to find out about Aussen," he guessed.

"Seems like the place to start."

The chugger stuttered to a stop barely long enough for them to swing on board before it lurched forward again. All the seats were filled, so Jayla grabbed a metal pole and braced herself against the uneven motion. Cody had also wrapped one hand around the support, and he swayed easily with every bump and jounce.

"I know you can take care of yourself," he said over the noise of transit. "But there's a few things you ought to know when you start exploring the city. The northeastern district can be pretty rough, so be careful any time you go there. And maybe don't go alone."

"Do *you* go there alone?"

"I have," he admitted. "But I don't like to." He grinned. "And I bet I'm faster than you. I can outrun most anybody."

She tightened her grip on the rail and deliberately gave him a thorough inspection. Muscular and lithe, with a runner's trim build and loose physicality. "I bet I'm almost as fast," she said.

He laughed out loud. "Maybe if there's time at the end of the day, we can have a race. Or maybe we can—" He paused, and now he was the one to look her over with a critical eye. "Or maybe not."

She knew he was goading her, but she couldn't let it pass. "Maybe what?"

"Back at the house. We have a training area set up where couriers can practice running the wires. If they're brave enough."

Jayla pointed at the roof of the car. "Those wires? The power lines?"

"That's right. Have you been here long enough to see a courier running along the cables?"

She nodded. "I want to do it."

He laughed again. "I knew you would."

"Can you teach me? Really?"

"I can *try*. Some people never get the knack." He appraised her again. "You've got the right build for it. And a good sense of balance, would be my guess."

"Usually."

"And you're not afraid of anything."

She felt her lips move in a wry twist. "Well, I'm not afraid of heights, if that's what you mean."

"Oh, so there *are* things that scare you?"

She had one free hand, so she poked him sharply in the ribs. "Nothing I'd tell *you* about."

He grinned. "Not yet," he said. "But maybe someday."

Chapter Twelve: Jayla

The ride to the island district took close to an hour, although Jayla and Cody were able to snag seats after the first twenty minutes. Unlike Tivol's little sprinter, the chugger pulled over every few minutes to allow more riders to board, and this slowed their progress considerably. Jayla didn't really mind. She was enjoying looking out the open windows at the changing architecture of the city. Since she'd arrived at the Alayne house, she hadn't strayed farther east than the Quatrefoil, generally taking routes that led straight down the middle of the city. Cody had put them on a transport that appeared to be circling to the north and east before it carried them to their destination. She could feel the chugger strain as the road made a gradual ascent where the edge of the city met the mountain. This was as close as she'd gotten to the flinty black wall of stone, and she briefly stuck her face out the window so she could get a better look.

As soon as they passed the center point of town, the road began descending, and now the squeal of brakes was added to the clacking of wheels, the rush of air, and the rumble of conversation. Around them, the city changed again, the buildings growing first larger and more impersonal, then smaller and dingier. The wealthier-looking riders had all disembarked before they crossed the center line, and most people who boarded now wore shabby clothes and expressions of exhaustion. Jayla noticed that while the more affluent passengers had mingled relatively freely, these riders tended to cluster by race. When a Zessin woman boarded, she would pass up three empty seats by Chibani women to sit by a Zessin man. No one seemed overtly hostile, but no one appeared particularly friendly, either.

They passed through a district that looked to be nothing but cramped, crumbling buildings and empty alleys for as far as Jayla could see. The transport had slowed to a crawl because it passed over pavement so cracked and buckled that to take it at any speed would probably cause the vehicle to overturn. People hopped off or jumped on without waiting for the chugger to come to a complete halt. As it creaked around a wide curve in the road, two young men swung on board. They were both Maratan, lean and feral, wearing long cloth coats even in the summer heat. Moving casually, Jayla shifted her arms to check the placement of her hidden weapons. Everyone else watched the newcomers covertly while pretending their attention was somewhere else.

"This is the northeast district, I take it?" Jayla breathed in Cody's ear.

He nodded. "It gets better in a couple miles."

Sure enough, about ten minutes later, the pace of the transport picked up. The buildings visible on either side of the road seemed to shake off a creeping malaise and straighten to their full height. The dangerous young men exited without a backward glance, and the sense of relief among the other passengers was palpable.

"Come on," Cody said, nudging Jayla to her feet. "Next stop is ours."

The chugger came to a stop long enough for eight or ten passengers to hop off and a handful to climb on. As the transport sparked away, Jayla stood on the side of the road and looked around.

They were in a small, lively urban plaza that had a distinct and unfamiliar look to it. While the buildings were constructed with the same stone, plaster, and wood that made up the rest of the city, there was something markedly different about this section of town. Maybe it was the colors of the curtains in the windows or the flags over the doors. Maybe it was the exotic flowers growing in the pots and small plots of land. Maybe it was the heavy, spicy aromas that seeped out through open windows.

Most everyone Jayla could see looked like Aussen—small-boned, freckle-faced, and auburn-haired—though there was much variation in height and weight and individual features.

Jayla took a deep breath. "These are Aussen's people, all right."

"Now if only we can find the ones she belongs to."

Jayla did a slow pivot, trying to determine the purpose of each different structure. Some were houses, she thought; a couple appeared to be storefronts. "I'm supposed to be looking for a temple."

"How do you know that?"

"Madeleine's cook speaks a little Zessin, and Aussen told her that's where her mother is going to look for her."

"That's useful," Cody said. "Let's see what we can find."

They tried the largest of the three shops, because Jayla reasoned anyone who planned to sell to the public could probably speak a couple of languages. The interior was overloaded with goods—swaths of fabric, shelves of books, stands of spices, counters full of jewelry. The scents of leather, paper, and food combined into a dizzying incense.

Several people, all islanders, moved through the narrow aisles, casting suspicious looks at Jayla and Cody, but no one approached them. Jayla headed toward the center of the shop where a heavyset woman of late middle age appeared to be arranging necklaces in a display case.

"Do you speak Cordish?" she asked.

The woman gave Jayla a quick inspection before nodding. "Well enough. What can I help you with?"

"I'm looking for a temple that I believe is in the area. I'm hoping to find someone there who could give me information I need."

The woman pointed. "Go that way for a block, then turn right. Three buildings down from that, on the left. Out front there will be a statue of the goddess, about so tall." She held her hand at waist height. "The guardian should be able to answer your questions."

"Thank you," Jayla said. She was about to turn for the door when her attention was caught by the necklaces on display under the glass of the case. She bent closer to get a better look. They all appeared to be pendants strung on simple leather cords. Each one was made from the same pitted white stone and featured a woman in various poses.

Each one looked very similar to the necklace Pietro had given to Aussen.

"Can you tell me—what are these?" she asked.

The woman seemed surprised that anyone could be so ill-informed. "Chazissas, of course."

"I'm sorry, I still don't understand."

The clerk pulled a chazissa out of the case and let Jayla handle it. Yes, very similar to the necklace that Aussen always wore tucked under her clothes. "A representation of Zessaya in one of her poses. Most islanders own one or two and wear them every day."

"And these are—good things? Helpful things?" Jayla didn't know how to phrase the question. *Nothing in these chazissas could harm a lost little girl?*

The woman looked at her as if Jayla might be crazy. "They are amulets of protection," she said. "The goddess watches over anyone who wears one."

"That's all right, then," Jayla said.

Cody had sidled up next to her. "What's wrong?"

There was no reason to believe this woman could ever have desire to harm Aussen—but there was no reason to trust her, either. "I'll tell you later," she said.

The clerk put the chazissa away, since it was clear Jayla wasn't planning to buy it. "Is there anything else you wanted?"

Jayla glanced around the shop, suddenly realizing she had been presented with an opportunity. "A young islander girl has come under my care. Is there something I could give her that would make her happy?"

"I know just the thing," the clerk said, stepping out from behind the counter. She returned a moment later carrying a toy fish made of shiny gold fabric. It was about the length of Jayla's hand, stuffed with so much padding that it was half as fat as it was long. Its eyes were represented by wooden buttons painted emerald green; its mouth was an embroidered red. Triangular patterns woven into the gold fabric looked as if they were meant to represent scales.

"Keshalosha," the shopkeeper explained. "Zessaya's lucky fish. It swims in the waters just off the shoreline, and if you see it, you will have a blessed life."

"And how often does anyone see it?"

The woman laughed. "Never! It does not exist! Though people often *claim* to have seen Keshalosha on the day before they marry or the morning before they start some new venture."

"How much?"

As soon as Jayla had handed over her coins, Cody took the toy from her and slipped it inside a flat leather bag buckled over his chest. "You don't have any way to carry it," he pointed out. "I always have my messenger pouch."

"Thanks," Jayla said, the brief word directed at both Cody and the clerk, and then she led the way out of the shop.

Cody fell in step beside her as she headed in the specified direction. "Why were you concerned about the chazissa?"

"Because Pietro gave one to Aussen and told her to never take it off. He told *me* it would keep her safe."

Cody looked thoughtful. "Do you think he just meant that Zessaya would watch over Aussen as long as she wore the amulet?"

"No. He meant it literally." She added, "I don't trust him."

They walked on three steps in silence. "I saw him the other day," Cody said.

She came to an abrupt halt, causing two men walking behind them to almost run them over. "You did? Where?"

"I went to his place to see how he was doing."

She felt like her legs had become as heavy and unmovable as the stone beneath her boots; she would never be able to lift her feet again. She stared at him, wondering what he might be hiding behind his amiable face. "Why?"

"Because I always like to keep track of people."

"Did he ask about me? Or Aussen?"

"Asked if I knew where you had landed, and I said yes. He didn't ask where you were—and I wouldn't have told him anyway. I told you I wouldn't."

Indeed, he had agreed to keep that secret weeks ago as the whole group of stranded travelers finally entered the city via the alternate bridge. She hadn't told Cody why he needed to conceal Aussen's whereabouts, and he hadn't inquired. But he *had* promised.

Still, people broke promises all the time. She kept her troubled gaze on his face. "Maybe *you're* the one I shouldn't trust," she said.

His own gaze was steady in return, his face unusually sober. "What have I done to make you say that?"

"*Why* do you like to keep track of everyone?"

He spread his fingers wide and touched them to either side of his head. "It's how I think," he said. "It's like my mind is one big map, and I have to know where to put people and things. Every time I go to a new building, every time I meet a new person, I fill in the map some more. I might have only met a man once when I delivered a message to him ten years ago, but if you say his name, the map comes up in my head and I remember where I saw him. And I can take you right there. That's just how I see the world."

"Maybe," she said doubtfully. "But Pietro?"

"You don't trust him," Cody said. "Isn't that a good enough reason to know where he is? So we can find him if we need to?"

"That's not why you went looking for him," she challenged.

He grinned. "No. I like him. He's interesting. But I'm not going to tell him anything about you."

"Then why—" She shook her head. "I don't understand you."

He spread his hands in a helpless gesture. "If you don't want me to come to the temple with you, I won't. I think I should make sure you get safely back to the Alayne house, but after that—you don't have to see me again if you don't want to. Just tell me to go away."

She had been about to say just that. *You may as well leave right now, and don't bother getting in touch with me again.* But the minute he made the offer, she changed her mind. "No, I want you with me," she said. "It's just that you don't make sense to me."

His grin was back. "Then I guess you need to spend more time with me until you figure me out."

She snorted, but she almost smiled. Her feet had transmogrified back into flesh, so she was able to resume striding along the street. "The shopkeeper said we should take the next turning—here. And look, I can see a building that must be the temple. There's a little statue out front, anyway."

A few moments later, they were inside. They had entered a small, round space, dimly lit by a few pillar candles placed on low tables. Jayla looked around swiftly, taking in impressions. The walls were covered with a series of fabric wall hangings featuring a handful of people in deliberate tableaux. Each scene included a depiction of the same woman—small and graceful, with emerald eyes and ginger hair. In one image she carried a spear; in another, a basket of bread; in another, an armful of long-stemmed purple flowers. The borders of each hanging were worked with repeating motifs of fish, stylized ocean waves, and twelve-pointed stars.

There was a plain fountain in the middle of the room, nothing more than a stone basin and a simple spray of water. Three curved wooden benches were placed around the fountain, forming a circle with three wide gaps. Two women sat together on one, quietly talking. They ignored the newcomers completely.

A third woman stood at the fountain, her eyes closed, her hands stirring the water as she soundlessly moved her lips. She wore an unadorned black dress, sleeveless in the heat; its collar and hem were embroidered with gold and green fish. Jayla's bet was that this was the woman the clerk had referred to as the guardian. She guessed it was rude to interrupt the cleric at her prayers, so she took a seat on a bench right in the woman's line of sight. Cody settled beside her.

Fifteen minutes after they arrived, the other two visitors had left and the guardian was still at her ritual. Jayla was silently debating the merits of knocking over a candle or dropping something loud and metallic on the floor, but Cody—usually so restless—seemed perfectly content to just sit there, so she tried to hold onto her patience.

After another five minutes, the guardian pulled her hands from the fountain, flicked off the water, and opened her eyes. She was looking straight at Jayla, and her expression was unsurprised, so she had clearly heard them enter. She surveyed them for a moment, then she smiled and asked a question in a language as soft and sibilant as ocean spray.

"I'm sorry," Jayla said. "Do you speak Cordish?"

"Yes, but not very well," the guardian answered. "You look like someone who has come here with a question." She misplaced the accents on a number of words, but her voice was low and lovely.

"I have. If you can spare me a few moments."

The woman nodded serenely and seated herself next to Jayla. "What is it you need to know?"

"My name is Jayla. On my travels here, I took charge of a young islander girl whose companion had died on the way. I believe her mother is supposed to meet her at this temple, but I don't know when and I don't know how to get in touch with her. I am hoping to leave a message that will find her when she arrives."

"What are they called?"

"The girl is Aussen and the mother is Tezzel."

"Both common names among the islanders." The guardian shook her head. "But there have not been any recent inquiries about anyone with those names. And I would be certain to know of it if such a search was under way."

"Then, with your permission, I will return every week or so until you have news."

"Of course." The guardian took a moment to scan Jayla's face, and then went on. "But perhaps there is a better arrangement? You do not speak Zessin, and I would guess a young girl from the islands does not speak Cordish."

"You would be right."

"You have done this girl a kindness by escorting her to Corcannon, but perhaps it is time to turn her over to people who might understand her better?"

Beside her, Jayla felt Cody stiffen, though he still seemed to sprawl at ease on the bench. Her own face creased into a frown. She hoped it looked more like concern than suspicion. "Thank you. That is generous," she said. "And I admit that I am not used to caring for children."

"I know several young mothers who would be happy to take her in."

"But—" Jayla let worry seep into her voice. "There was a man who traveled in the same group. I thought he took an odd interest in Aussen. I thought he frightened her. He learned that she was supposed to meet her mother at the temple, and I'm afraid he might come looking for her. If I keep her with me, he won't be able to find her."

"That is indeed disturbing," the guardian agreed. "If you told us his name or described his appearance, we could be watching out for him."

"I'm sorry," Jayla said. "I don't want to take the risk."

The guardian nodded, seeming to accept that far more easily than Jayla might have in her position. "Zessaya put the girl in your hands, and you want to honor the goddess's will. Then you should do so."

"So if I come back every week—"

"You could let me know where to send word if her mother arrives," the guardian said.

Jayla smiled apologetically. "But then I have the same worry," she said. "What if this man found out where Aussen was staying and came for her there?"

The guardian widened her eyes at that. "You seem to think this man is capable of an astonishing level of stealth and evil."

"I don't know what he's capable of," Jayla said. "But he himself told me he has powerful friends."

"Then we will rely on your visits to reunite mother and child."

"Thank you," Jayla said. "I will hope that day comes soon."

They took a different route from the Zessin neighborhood to Cody's part of town, boarding a transport that followed a more central road. Jayla was getting a better sense of the city's layout, and she thought Cody lived in the warehouse district just east of the Quatrefoil. At any rate, once they hopped off the chugger, they walked through row after row of big, boxy buildings and throngs of people dressed in the loose, rough clothes of physical laborers.

"Here we are," Cody said, guiding her to a building almost indistinguishable from all the others. It was four stories high, made of rough gray stone with absolutely no ornamentation. Two or three windows on every level appeared to be original to the house, but intermixed with them at irregular intervals were another ten or so that looked like they had been hacked out of the thick walls at a later date. Each window was open to the heavy summer air.

When they stepped through the door, they were instantly in a big open chamber that contained the entire ground level. The high ceiling was supported by a series of columns made of stacked stones the same color as the exterior. There were no mosaics or paintings on the walls or pillars—nothing to brighten the unrelenting gray—but the floor was a mad jumble of dilapidated chairs, fat pillows, colorful rugs, tables, shelves, baskets, and the odd bit of broken statuary that looked like it had been appropriated from the garbage heap of a second-rate temple. Six or seven people lounged on the furniture in various spots, talking, arguing, or playing games; none of them seemed to notice when Cody walked in. Even in the low light, Jayla could see that they all wore bracelets set with the highly reflective gems of the professional courier.

"This is the common room," Cody explained, guiding her toward a corner where a sturdy metal stairwell made a switchbacked ascent. "There's a kitchen against the back wall and we take turns cooking, though none of us are very good at it."

"How many people live here?"

"Ten right now. Sometimes there have been as many as fifteen, but that feels like a lot."

At the base of the stairwell, Jayla glanced up, tracing the crisscrossing black struts up three more stories. "Where does everyone sleep?"

"We've put in walls on the third floor to make six bedrooms. Some people have their own rooms, some share. On the fourth floor, it's mostly just a big empty space, like it is down here, but some people prefer to camp out up there. Rig up blankets for privacy if they feel like it. Those tend to be the people who don't stay too long."

"And what's on the second floor?"

He lightly touched the small of her back, urging her upward. "That's what we're here to see."

The second floor was a giant playroom, or training yard, or some combination of the two. Like the bottom level, it was one large open space filled with a collection of oddments, but here Jayla was sure there was a purpose behind each accumulated piece. In one section were hand weights and pulley contraptions the couriers probably used to build up their strength. In another corner, a system of ladders and hanging nets seemed designed for runners to practice their climbing skills. Down the center of the room was a narrow lane, wide enough for two people to travel side by side; it was completely free of debris. Jayla suspected it was a short track designed for running abbreviated races. Around the perimeter was a longer track, similarly free of clutter, for practicing endurance runs.

Fully half of the space was given over to a low web of cables and wires suspended about a foot off the floor between the supporting pillars. Jayla headed over to inspect it, and Cody came behind her to explain.

"We tried to replicate the wires the way they hang over the city," he said. "Those heavy black cables—those are the power lines the cars run on. Most of them have a weave of smaller wire cables that run along them on either side, so there's a mesh a couple feet wide with the cable running down the middle. The weave is pretty open, though—if you're not careful, your foot will slip through, and then your whole leg will go through, and it's hard to pull yourself up and regain your balance. At that point, it's usually better to free your leg and drop to the street."

"How often does that happen?"

"When you first start doing it, all the time. After your first year or two, hardly ever."

"So you run along the mesh, not the cable."

"Mostly. But sometimes, especially on the narrower routes, there's no mesh. Just the cable. That's a lot trickier because you have to go slower and you have to be a lot more careful about your balance."

She glanced over at him. "That's what you did when you crossed the canyon. When the bridge came down."

He nodded. "I like walking the wire. I practice almost every day. But it's not really that useful. If you're carrying a message all the way across the city, it's usually just as fast to follow the streets or hop a transport. But if you're taking something from one edge of the Quatrefoil to another, or out to Council Row, and traffic is heavy, overhead is the way to go."

"How do you get up to the mesh?"

He gestured toward the corner of the room with the ladders and netting. That was when Jayla spotted a sturdy pole with a T-shaped crossing at the top. "All along the roads, there are poles that support the cables. You pull yourself up one of those, then swing onto the web. It's not easy, so it's better to practice here first."

"I bet," she said. "I'm pretty coordinated and I'm not sure I could do it."

"Harder to walk the wires," he said. "If you can't master that, no point in climbing the pole."

She nodded. "All right. What do I need to do?"

"I'm going to start you on the cable, just because it will give you a sense of how good your balance is. If you can master the slow walk on the cable, you should find it easy to run the mesh."

"All right. So I just—climb up there?"

"First you need different shoes. Thin soles, so you can feel the wire. So you can grip it with your feet. We've got a box over here."

In a few minutes, she had donned borrowed shoes with soft leather soles and tied her hair back to keep it out of the way. Cody held her wrist as she cautiously stepped up to the cable, placing one foot in front of the other and trying not to ignominiously tumble over into the webbing.

"Two things to remember," he said. "You want your weight to be as low to the wire as it can be. So flex your knees a little to bring you down. But keep your back straight—keep your weight dead center over the cable, or you'll overbalance and fall. Feel the wire through the soles of your shoes. It'll sway as you move. It might roll a little beneath your feet. You have to be aware of all those things, all the time."

She stood there a moment, holding her pose, feeling the way her body adjusted to the slight movement in the wire. Cody still held her arm and she didn't pull away because she could tell she was leaning into and away from him to keep her balance. She slowly shifted her weight to her front foot, slowly lifted her back foot and brought it around.

Too far, too fast. Her arms flailed and she crashed into the webbing. She felt the rough strands dig grooves into her ribs and thighs and cheek.

"Damn it," she said, rolling to the edge and standing up.

Cody was laughing. "Everybody falls. A lot."

"I want to be better than everybody."

"Yeah, that's what I like about you."

This time she took hold of him so she could let go when she wanted. Again, she placed both feet and stood for a moment, getting her bearings. Again, she shifted her weight to her front leg, but brought her back foot around with more care. This time she didn't fall, though her grip on Cody's forearm tightened to a clutch.

"Better," he said.

"Does it get easier when you have some forward momentum going?"

"Yeah. But it still doesn't go fast."

She took another step, feeling her feet curl around the edge of the cable. Feeling the wire sharp beneath her soles, even through the leather. If she spent too long on this exercise, her feet would be bloody. She couldn't afford to lame herself just to prove she could acquire this spectacularly useless skill. But she could practice for a little while.

"Another step. Good," Cody said. "And another one."

She fell three more times before she managed to walk the length of the cable from one pillar to the other—and even at that, she never let go of

Cody's hand. But she was developing the beginnings of a sense of balance, an understanding of how the cable swayed beneath her weight. A remote idea of how she might train her body to perform this trick.

"Excellent! You're a natural," Cody enthused as he helped her down. For a moment, her feet couldn't lie flat against the smooth surface of the floor. She flexed her toes and stretched her spine.

"That's hard," she said. "But fun."

"I thought you'd like it. When's your next day off? You can come back and practice."

"Maybe two weeks from now? I'll let you know."

He was smiling. She realized that she had just committed to another outing with him before she'd even had time to decide how she felt about this one. It wasn't just the heavy cable that was making her reassess her sense of balance.

"Unless something comes up," she added. "For either one of us."

"Right," he said. "I won't count on it."

But he was still smiling. And even though it annoyed her, she could feel herself smiling back.

Aussen loved the stuffed golden fish. Her face broke into a smile of delight when Jayla offered it to her, and she instantly cradled it against her cheek.

"Keshalosha?" Jayla said hesitantly, and Aussen replied with a spate of happy words, none of which Jayla understood. She crouched down so she was at eye level with the little girl, and said in a slow voice, "Do you still have your necklace that Pietro gave you?"

Aussen instantly pulled out the amulet from under her shirt. Jayla examined it briefly, but it was exactly as she remembered—a white stone figure that she now knew to be a representation of Zessaya. For the first time, she wondered if Aussen had been so willing to wear it because it was familiar to her—because most people she knew already owned something very like it. She might even have a pendant of her own back home.

That still didn't explain why Pietro had given it to her or why he wanted her to have it or how, in fact, it could protect her. But at least it made Jayla feel a little better. It had to be a good thing to be watched over by a goddess, didn't it? Maybe she should buy a chazissa of her own the next time she was in the islander district. She wouldn't mind a little protection herself.

Chapter Thirteen: Jayla

Two days later, Jayla was accompanying Madeleine to a grand affair at the residence of the high divine.

"Everyone will be there," Madeleine said as they swept down the grand staircase. She was wearing a flame-colored dress and a shawl woven of so many vivid colors it was impossible to pick out a pattern, but the bright hues suited her better than the grays she had favored ever since Jayla arrived. "It will be quite the gala."

"It seems odd to me that a priest would put on lavish entertainments," Jayla remarked. "I think of religious folk as being more austere."

"Not in Corcannon!" Madeleine replied. "The high divine of the temple always presides over the Council, so he's very active in city politics. Which means he's deeply involved with all the Council families."

"I haven't spent much time learning about city government," Jayla admitted.

Madeleine laughed and led the way outside. The sunset was so gaudy it looked like a mosaic in the Alayne house, but night crouched overhead, ready to swallow every bright streak. The air was still warm with the day's accumulated heat, but Jayla thought it would cool down appreciably once the sun disappeared.

"Naturally, Tivol is late," Madeleine murmured, then turned back to Jayla. "It's pretty simple, really. There are a couple of dozen wealthy families who have historically held positions on Corcannon City Council. Every five years, twelve people are elected to serve for the next term. The high divine has a permanent seat on the board."

"Who decides who's eligible to be a Council family?"

Madeleine laughed again. "Well, I don't know, but it's been the same set of families ever since I can remember! Some of them only own property in the city, but most of them have estates out in Chibain or Marata. But they come to Corcannon all the time for business."

Jayla was still trying to work it out. "So—you must have aunts and uncles and cousins somewhere?"

"Dozens! Most of them are in northern Marata, but a few of them live in Corcannon year-round."

Tivol's sprinter rattled up as she finished speaking. Traffic was unusually light, and he took the turn from the main road so fast that the overhead rod threw off sparks. Both Madeleine and Jayla instinctively jumped back, but the vehicle didn't overturn as Jayla half expected.

"Tivol!" Madeleine exclaimed. "If you don't promise me right now that you will drive in a more reasonable fashion, I am not getting in this car with you—not tonight, and not *ever!* You're going to kill yourself one day, and I don't want to be with you when you do."

He was laughing but contrite. "Sorry, sorry. There was no one in front of me and I couldn't resist kicking it up to full speed. I shall be utterly sedate while I have a passenger beside me."

Jayla noticed, although Madeleine probably didn't, that Tivol didn't seem to recognize that there would be *two* people riding with him tonight. She said nothing as she climbed into the back seat—which was really a cramped space designed to hold small personal possessions, and not a live person.

"You better be," Madeleine said, settling in front. "I am not joking. I'll get out on the street and wait for a chugger if you don't behave."

He leaned over and kissed her cheek. "I am properly chastened," he said. "And may I say how very beautiful you look."

Madeleine smiled back. "You may. You look very nice as well."

"Of course! The social event of the season!"

The two of them teased each other for the rest of the drive, during which time Tivol obediently drove at a reasonable rate of speed. He didn't have any choice about slowing down once they turned onto the main road that bisected the Quatrefoil, because it was already jammed with so many private vehicles that traffic was almost at a standstill.

"At some point it would be quicker to get out and walk," Madeleine observed.

"We're going to leave the car a few blocks away, so we *will* be walking," Tivol said. "But not quite yet."

After they had inched forward another half mile, Tivol pulled off into a parking area and they all disembarked. Jayla glanced up at the tightly packed grid of cables that allowed gridcars to maneuver fluidly across the plaza, then she fell in step a couple of paces behind the other two.

It was almost full dark now, but artificial lamps lined the streets and provided decent visibility. Still, Jayla was on high alert. There were so many shadowed doorways to pass, so many lightless alleys. Too many places for an assailant to lurk. This would be a perfect place to stage an attack.

But they made it without incident to their destination. It was a long, white stone building several stories high. Unlike the plain exteriors of the mansions that lined Council Row, this building was highly ornamented with fluted columns, carved friezes, and lacy grillwork. More of those artificial lights had been strategically placed on the grounds to illuminate both the façade and the walkways leading up to the grand entrance.

From all directions, people on foot were converging on the doorway. Jayla was pleased to spot eight or ten temple guards in their distinctive dark blue livery. Some stood at the doors, watching people as they entered; some patrolled the edge of the street, making sure none of the drivers had any trouble.

Madeleine took Tivol's arm, then turned back to look for Jayla. She smiled to see the guard right on her heels. "It's quite a sight, isn't it?" she said.

"It's impressive," Jayla said. "And this whole house belongs to the high divine?"

"No, it's part of the temple complex. His lodgings are on the third level, but most of the building is used for other things." She waved a hand toward the open doors. "We'll all be sitting down to dinner in the big conference hall on the bottom floor."

Within a few steps, they had fallen in with the rest of the throng all vying for the best spot in the line that was slowly being funneled through the doors. Madeleine greeted some of her friends with cries of delight, as if she hadn't just seen them a day or two before. Tivol dropped her arm and turned aside to joke with one of the men waiting in line next to them.

A hooded figure slipped between Tivol and Madeleine, raising its arm in one smooth, swift stroke. Jayla's body was in motion before her brain even registered the threat. She flung herself forward as the arm sliced downward, the chilly artificial light running like silver along the curved blade. She felt the impact as her shoulder crashed into the assailant's chest, heard the faint *oof* of a high-pitched voice. She had collided with a small, wiry body, and she could feel it bunch and coil as the other person tried to spin away.

Clamping her hand around the assailant's wrist, she wrenched her arm downward and sent the knife flying. It skittered across the pavement with a musical clatter. She followed up with a punch to the jaw, then hooked a foot around the attacker's ankle. They both went down hard.

Jayla was dimly aware of screaming all around her, of bodies shifting away in alarm, but all she cared about was containing the thrashing form beneath her. She was pretty sure her opponent was a woman, but she couldn't pause long enough to rip off the concealing hood. Whoever it was bucked frantically beneath her, clawing at Jayla's face, trying to get free. Jayla countered with a fierce blow to the chest that caused the woman to gasp for air.

Then suddenly temple guards were on either side of her, shoving Jayla to one side and hauling the woman up by both arms. Jayla rolled to her feet and glanced around quickly to locate Madeleine. Yes—just a few steps away, staring fearfully from the shelter of Tivol's arms. All around her were privileged rich couples dripping with silk and jewels, gaping at this sudden eruption of violence. People who weren't near enough to see were calling out, "What happened?" More temple guards were abandoning their posts to race over and assist.

Jayla ignored them all. "Are you hurt?" she asked Madeleine. "Did the knife touch you?"

Madeleine shook her head in a slow, disjointed motion. "No—I—I didn't even realize he was there until you hit him—" She brushed at her neck, as if she felt where the phantom blade would have come down.

"She, I think," Jayla said.

"*She?* A woman assaulted Madeleine?" Tivol demanded. "Why?"

Jayla shook her head, but there was no time to answer. Two of the temple guards, satisfied that the attacker was under control, hustled over to Madeleine. "Best for you to get inside," one of them said. "In case there's more."

That had been more or less what Jayla was thinking, but she wouldn't have said it in a way that made Madeleine shrink back into Tivol's embrace, looking more fearful than ever. But Madeleine didn't argue. Still huddled under Tivol's protective arm, she followed the guards as they cleared a forceful path through the crowd of revelers. Friends called out to them as they passed through—"Madeleine, are you all right?" "Tivol! What happened?"—but neither of them answered.

Jayla came behind them, close enough to touch the fringe on Madeleine's gaily patterned scarf. But her eyes darted from side to side, assessing each young woman as she reached out toward Madeleine, each young man as he stepped close enough to catch Tivol's attention.

No doubt about it now, she thought. This wasn't some random act of aggression or some unfortunate accidental encounter. Someone was definitely targeting Madeleine. Jayla remembered the conversation she'd had with Madeleine on the day they met. Jayla had speculated that the attackers were amateurs who weren't used to killing, but who were so caught up in a cause that they would keep trying until they got it right. She'd also suggested that whoever was behind the assaults was acquainted with Madeleine, well enough to know when she might be where.

Tonight's events had confirmed rather than disproved these suspicions. Someone had known Madeleine would be attending the gala tonight. Had slipped silently through the excited crowd, waiting for the right victim, the right moment, to strike. Could have gotten lucky with one good slice, but more likely would have botched the job and needed several desperate blows before managing the fatal thrust. Probably wouldn't have had enough time before the screams of the crowd alerted the temple guards.

Was already planning to try again.

It didn't matter that this attacker was already in custody and could do no more harm. This made at least the third and maybe the fourth different individual who had attempted to murder Madeleine.

If there were four, there were probably more. A circle of potential assassins. A mysterious group with an unfathomable hatred for a young woman who, as far as Jayla could tell, had never done a single thing in her life to make her remarkable, let alone despicable.

Jayla found herself less concerned with *who*. What puzzled her most was *why*.

What worried her most was *when*.

Chapter Fourteen:
Madeleine

Everyone thought she should go straight home, but Madeleine refused. "I'm staying," she said to Tivol, to her friends, even to Harlo when he pushed through the party-goers to find her in a corner of the crowded hall.

"But my dear," Harlo said, taking her hands and surveying her with concern. She hadn't realized how cold her hands were until she felt the warmth of his. "You must be so shaken up! You *think* you're fine, but in an hour, suddenly you may find yourself trembling and incoherent."

"Well, if that happens, then in an hour I'll go home," she said.

"I just think your father will consider me most remiss if I do not insist that you depart at once."

She actually managed to laugh. "My father would think me very poor-spirited if I ran home merely because someone *tried* to hurt me but didn't even manage to tear my dress. If someone had attacked *him,* he would have just grunted—" She made the appropriate sound. "And kept walking."

"Nevertheless—"

"I think she is determined to prove how brave she is, and it does us no good to argue," Tivol interrupted.

Harlo squeezed her hands and let them fall. "I'll make sure the guards know you should never be out of their sight."

"Thank you," Madeleine said. She didn't even try to be surreptitious about it—she deliberately turned her head so she could make eye contact with Jayla, discreetly standing a few feet behind her. If no one else here realized why she had survived the night, Madeleine did. "Thank you," she said again.

"I must attend to my guests," Harlo said. "If you *do* decide to leave early, let me know. Otherwise, I will worry when you are missing."

He swept away with his usual grace. Madeleine turned to Tivol. "And it's not that I'm trying to be brave," she said. "It's that I'm so *angry.* Someone wants me to be afraid—someone wants me *dead.* I am filled with such rage that I want to hit that person in the face. But instead, I'll attend a party."

Tivol sighed and kissed the top of her head. "Then let's go make merry."

They stepped out of the corner and into the mass of revelers, where they were instantly enveloped in a circle of well-wishers. For the next hour, the same scenario played out over and over. A few of Madeleine's particular friends would spot her and come running over, emitting little shrieks and drawing her into quick embraces. They would demand to know what had happened, how she felt, what she was going to do next. She held her head high and answered steadily. *It was terrifying. Yes, I am a little frightened, but I know I am well-protected. I imagine Harlo and my father will have the assailant interrogated, and we will learn the reasons behind the attack.*

And then she would change the subject. *I love your necklace! Is that a new perfume you're wearing? Oh, I hope your mother is coming to town soon.* It always worked. People invariably were more interested in talking about themselves than about anything else.

Despite her defiant words to Tivol, she didn't feel brave at all. In fact, she wanted to cower under his arm for the entire night. If he was standing on one side of her, then danger couldn't come from that direction, and she could watch the other side. She continually glanced behind her to make sure Jayla was nearby and was always immensely comforted to find the guard only a few feet away, ceaselessly scanning the crowd.

She wanted to protest when Tivol eventually dropped his arm and joined an animated conversation with some of his friends; she wanted to wail out loud when he moved off with them to explore something on the far end of the room. But she didn't. She drew herself taller and smiled brightly at her father's cousin and asked her neighbor's daughter when the baby was due.

It was a staggering effort. Someone wanted her dead, and it made no sense, and it filled her with an uncontrollable, uncontainable sense of panic. This was worse than grief, in a way, because grief was so real and implacable and incontestable. This—this—formless, inchoate fear didn't quite settle in her lungs, in the base of her throat. It shrouded her like a wispy fog, made it harder to see the world around her, uncertain of where to set her foot—uncertain, even, if there was a stable surface for her to set her foot upon.

But she was too proud and too stubborn to turn back. She was too angry to give in. She smiled, and she chattered, and she tilted her head to listen to her friends. And—always mindful that she might be at the edge of a precipice—she continued to move forward across the room, step by measured step.

Harlo came back to check on her twice, accompanied the second time by Benito, a junior priest who was widely rumored to be his lover. Benito's dark complexion, silk-black hair, and vivid green eyes bespoke a mixed heritage that had yielded exquisite results. He was, in fact, one of the most beautiful men Madeleine had ever seen. A number of her friends often sighed over the fact that the bracelet on his right hand was solid gold without a thread of silver.

"Madeleine," Benito said in his sweet voice, laying his cheek briefly against hers. "What must we do to keep you safe? Shall Harlo assign a handful of temple soldiers to follow you any time you set foot out of your house?"

She laughed shakily. "My father has already hired a personal guard for me, and she does indeed follow me everywhere!" she replied. "In fact, she is the one who stopped the attacker tonight. I had been somewhat annoyed to have the constant shadow, but tonight I was most grateful."

"But maybe Benito is right," Harlo said with a frown. "Maybe one guard is not enough. Perhaps you need a pair."

"A troop. A contingent!" Benito suggested with a smile.

"Certainly not! I can barely tolerate one. But maybe this will be the last time I am in any danger."

"I certainly hope so, but why do you think that?" Benito asked.

She gestured vaguely toward the door. "This time they captured the attacker, didn't they? I saw the temple guards haul him off—haul *her* off. Once she's been questioned, maybe we'll find out—" It was surprisingly hard to say the words. "Why anyone would want to murder me."

Benito looked quickly at Harlo, trying to hide an expression of dismay. "Of course," Harlo said smoothly. "We may learn a great deal."

But Madeleine wasn't fooled. "What? What's wrong?"

Harlo hesitated, then nodded at Benito. "The young woman apparently did not want to be questioned," Benito said. "Before they could even get her inside the guardhouse, she had ingested a fatal poison."

It was a moment before Madeleine could make sense of the words. "She—what? She *killed* herself?"

"So it appears."

"Because she didn't want to explain why—explain why—"

"There could be many reasons she did not want to face an interrogation," Harlo said. "She may have been a criminal wanted for other infractions. Or perhaps she is simply unstable, and she planned suicide no matter what the outcome of tonight's events. Sadly, we will never know."

"No—I suppose not. Well, I admit I am disappointed," Madeleine said. She hoped she sounded composed, but in truth this news was almost as upsetting as the attack itself. She found herself wondering how Jayla would interpret this information, but she thought she could guess. *Someone would rather die than reveal who sent her to kill you. That means she is a fanatic. That means everyone else who tried to kill you is a fanatic. That means they will try again.* Aloud she said, "I really did hope for some answers."

Benito gave her arm a comforting squeeze. "There may yet be some clues," he said. "In her clothing, in whatever items she had on her body. We might be able to track down where she lived and who her friends are. Don't lose heart."

She smiled at him gratefully. "No, I won't. Thank you."

Harlo was looking over his shoulder, clearly receiving a signal from someone on his staff. "Ah, my dear, I am needed. I will talk to you again before the evening is over."

"Of course," she said, and kept the smile on her face as they turned to go. The minute they disappeared into the crowd, she felt the panic claw its way back up her throat. Dead! The attacker was dead! Who would be sent after her next? Someone stealthier, more determined, with a steadier hand . . . She looked around frantically for Tivol, desperate to seek comfort from his presence, take refuge against his shoulder. Three of his friends stood nearby, laughing immoderately at some private joke, but Tivol wasn't with them. He wasn't talking with the older men clustered near the wine buffet—he wasn't paying exaggerated compliments to any of the pretty young women scattered around the wide room. Madeleine felt her breath shorten as her lungs refused to fill; she felt her hands curl with anxiety. Where was Tivol?

"Madeleine," said a low voice behind her, and she turned practically into Reese's arms. His face was a study of horror and worry. "Madeleine. I just got here five minutes ago and I heard—"

"Oh, Reese," she said, and it was an effort to keep her voice level. Her need for solace was so great she had to fight the urge to fling herself into his arms. As it was, she instinctively extended her hands, and he took them in a reassuring grasp. "I can't even tell you—"

"Should you be standing here? You look so pale," he interrupted. "There are a couple of chairs over there. Let's sit down."

She would have protested, but he was already shepherding her to a row of plush seats set invitingly against the wall. He kept his hold on her hands as they dropped onto the padded cushions. Madeleine couldn't keep herself from checking to make sure that Jayla had followed. She had.

"Tell me about it," Reese demanded.

"It happened so quickly. We were outside, with the crowd, everyone pressing to get inside. And then this small creature—it was a woman, Reese! A woman!—she just slipped up beside me and struck at me with a knife—"

"*Madeleine!*" He brought her hands to his mouth, kissing her knuckles, but never letting his eyes waver from her face. "Are you hurt? Everyone said you weren't, but—"

"No. The knife never touched me. Jayla—my guard, you remember the guard we hired—"

"Of course I remember."

"She was right there. She stopped the attacker. It was so fast I almost didn't realize what was happening."

He kissed her knuckles again. She felt the strain in his arms, the tension in his hands, and she had the fanciful thought that he was forcibly restraining himself from sweeping her into a hard embrace. "If something had happened to you—"

She managed a woebegone smile. "I am so very glad it didn't."

"I hope your father gives a *bag* of money to Jayla as a reward. If he doesn't, I'll do it. *Two* bags."

Madeleine tried to assume a bantering tone. "Well, of course it's her *job* to protect me, and she does get paid for that."

Reese glanced around with disfavor, as if he found the opulent room and the gaily dressed party-goers far from his taste. "I suppose you can't go straight home. I suppose you have to stay and show everyone how calm and collected you are. An example of strength to all the women of the Council families."

That actually made her laugh. "I don't feel strong. But I do want to stay. I told Tivol that I wasn't being brave, I was just feeling rage."

Reese glanced around again. "And where is Tivol?"

"Here somewhere," she said lightly. He turned back to her, his face creasing with anger, but she forestalled him before he could speak. "But I wasn't even expecting to see *you* here tonight! When did you get back to the city?"

"Yesterday afternoon. I was going to call on you in a day or two."

"You still could," she said, the words just slipping out.

He gave her a long look before answering. "If you'd be willing to see me."

She tried to make her voice casual. "Of course."

"Madeleine—"

She had never in her life been so happy to hear the chime of dinner bells. The people standing around the room began turning toward the double archway that led to the adjoining dining hall. Faint, delicious aromas wafted through from the other side.

"Finally!" Madeleine exclaimed, jumping to her feet, which caused Reese to release her hands at last. "I'm starving."

Reese stood a little more slowly. "Sometimes stress will do that to you," he said. "Give you a ravenous appetite."

She patted her stomach. "Stress, or perhaps the fact that I didn't eat much all day because I wanted to make *sure* I fit into my dress."

"And a lovely dress it is."

"I had it made especially for tonight. I thought—"

A tremendous crashing sound came from beyond the archway. Madeleine cried out and threw herself blindly at Reese, clutching his sleeve and hiding her face against his jacket. She felt his arms tighten around her, felt him swing her in a half circle, so his back was to the archway and his body would shield her from danger. Maybe that was his mouth against her hair.

Around her, she first heard muffled shouts of alarm and then a wave of nervous laughter. "Some poor servant dropped a whole tray of wine glasses," a man said, and there was another round of mirth.

It still took her longer than it should have to stop trembling and raise her head. Reese stood unmoving, limitlessly patient, still holding her close, still absorbing half her weight. She had the impression he would stand, just so, for the rest of the night if that was how long it took her to regain her composure.

She was tempted, for a moment, to take him up on his silent offer.

But she drew in a deep breath, she lifted her chin, she stepped back, and he let his hands fall. "That was a little unexpected," she said. The noise. Her reaction. The feel of his arms around her.

"*Now* do you want to go home?" he asked.

She stood even straighter. "*Now* I'm hungrier. Let's have dinner."

Madeleine had expected Tivol to be remorseful that he had abandoned her for most of the evening, but she had not reckoned with the allure of midnight racing.

At the dinner table, she had been seated between one of her father's cousins and Tivol's oldest uncle. Across from her, but three seats up, Tivol lounged between Madeleine's elderly neighbor and a nervous young Kissidell girl who had to be at her very first social outing. Tivol glanced over frequently to give Madeleine an encouraging grin or toast her with a glass of wine, but they weren't close enough to have a conversation.

She had always thought this room was beautiful, but tonight she was ready to change her mind. Three of the walls were covered from floor to ceiling with bits of mirrored glass, and the endlessly reflective mosaic flickered with so much light and movement that Madeleine had a headache within twenty minutes. Once she'd consumed the first two courses and had a glass of wine, her stomach started to turn on her as well.

Now I want to leave, she thought. *But people have stopped suggesting it.*

Well, she could make it through the meal, and then she would beg Tivol to take her home. The party would go on past midnight, but Madeleine was suddenly quite thoroughly done.

During one of the brief pauses between courses, Tivol came to his feet and circled the table to bend solicitously over her shoulder.

"You're starting to look tired," he said in her ear.

She was grateful that he had noticed. "I am. I'm ready to leave at any time."

"Excellent. So is Coretta," he said, naming Madeleine's ancient neighbor. "She just sent for her driver. You can ride with her."

She twisted around in her chair to get a look at his face. "You don't want to take me home?"

His smile was half sheepish and half excited. "Denton has his new sprinter here. Fastest one yet, he says. He wants a few of us to go out and test it. Night's the best time to race, you know, because there's almost no traffic—"

She couldn't believe it. "You're leaving Harlo's party—to go *racing?*"

He misunderstood her anger. "I know. I know. My mother would say it was unforgivably rude, but look around!" He made a sweeping gesture. "There are so many people here! Harlo will never know I've left."

"*I'll* know."

He gave her a conspirator's grin. "But you'll never tell. Shall I let Coretta know you'll ride home with her?"

She hated manipulative, petty people, but she found herself saying, "No need. Reese is here, and I'm sure he'll take me."

Even that didn't seem to catch Tivol's attention. "All right. I'll come by tomorrow and check on you." And he patted her shoulder and strolled away.

It was all she could do not to stare after him with such blazing fury that he erupted into a pillar of fire that burned out within seconds to a pile of abandoned ash.

Tivol was probably right not to worry. Madeleine felt so tired and so wretched during the ride home that she couldn't even flirt with Reese, and Reese seemed to be so worried about her that he didn't even bother hinting that he loved her. Then, too, Jayla was sitting right behind them, close enough to overhear every word. It didn't feel like the right time to indulge in dangerous dalliance.

Madeleine did, however, allow Reese to help her from the car and into the house and all the way up the stairs to the door of her bedroom. She didn't actually need to lean on him for that whole journey, but she did it anyway. Jayla loitered in the shadows on the bottom story, either courteously giving them time to talk privately, or implacably waiting for him to leave so she could be sure he no longer posed a threat.

"I want to come check on you tomorrow," Reese said as Madeleine transferred her hand from his arm to the doorknob. "But my schedule is already crammed full. The day after?"

"The day after would be good. Maybe we can go out for lunch."

He offered a short bow. "I'll look forward to it."

She let herself into her room and managed to maintain a neutral, almost cheerful, aspect while the maid Ella undressed her. It wasn't until she was finally alone, with the lights out and the curtains drawn and the soft covers pulled up to her chin, that she finally allowed herself to start crying. She couldn't tell how many of the tears came from terror, how many from rage, how many from stark disillusionment, but they rose from an apparently bottomless source. Her body was exhausted before her passions were, and when she finally fell asleep, she was still curled around all three of those cheerless companions. Fear. Fury. And a sense of inconsolable loss.

Chapter Fifteen: Madeleine

In the morning, Madeleine discovered it was just as well that Reese wasn't planning to visit her, because her own day had gotten unexpectedly complicated.

Her father, who usually left the house quite early, was still on the premises when she went looking for breakfast at an hour so late it was almost lunchtime. She checked involuntarily upon seeing him in the small dining room, perusing some official-looking papers but clearly waiting for her.

"Madeleine," he said, laying the papers aside. "How did you sleep?"

She sank to a chair across from him and spread a napkin across her lap as he studied her. "After tossing and turning for hours, I think I dropped off right before the sun came up," she said. "Had I known you would still be here, I wouldn't have come down in my robe and slippers!"

He waved this aside. "From all reports, you weren't harmed. Is that true?"

The footman brought her a glass of juice and a plate of toast. She took a sip and nodded. "Untouched."

"But I suppose there is no longer any ambiguity," he answered. "This person was sent specifically to do you harm."

"That was my conclusion as well," she said as steadily as possible. "I had hoped that they would be able to question my attacker, but Harlo said—"

"She poisoned herself rather than submit to interrogation," her father interrupted. "That is also what I was told."

Madeleine spread preserves on her toast and took a small bite. Last night she had been ravenous. Today, still wrung out from the hours of weeping, she felt lethargic and ill. She'd been awake less than an hour and she already wanted to go back to bed. "So it seems we were right to hire a guard," she said.

He drummed his fingers on the table. "I wonder if you would be safer at the Wellenden estate."

She stared at him. "What?"

"Even a determined assassin might find it difficult to travel five hundred miles to track down his target. And Wellen House is staffed with an extensive personal guard. I think you would be safer there."

"But I don't want to go to Wellen House. And I doubt Heloise would want the responsibility of protecting me. She has plenty of other concerns."

"You can discuss it with her this afternoon."

"This afternoon?"

"She's in town. She wants to see you."

"But I—"

Her father tossed back a last swallow of water and came to his feet. "We can talk about it more tonight. I'm late."

And without voicing the slightest concern about Madeleine's state of mind after last night's trauma, without expressing relief that she was unharmed or gratitude that she was still alive—without another word—he left the room.

She stared after him with so much stupefaction she didn't even have the energy left to burst into tears.

Tivol arrived while she was still getting dressed, so she took some satisfaction in making him wait half an hour while she put on the finishing touches. As the summer reached its zenith, the chilly gray that had been considered the ultimate in fashion was modulating to a light yellow that was kinder to Madeleine's complexion. But she still felt the need to pile on brighter colors. Cinnamon. Tangerine. A splash of cherry. It was like she had a sliver of ice at her core and she was trying to warm herself from the outside.

Tivol was pacing the gilt room, and he looked up swiftly when she walked in. "Madeleine!" he exclaimed, flinging himself across the room to hug her.

She didn't push him away, but she turned her cool cheek to his impetuous mouth and stood unresponsive in his arms. He dropped three kisses on her face, held her close a moment, then gripped her shoulders as he pulled back to survey her.

"I was right. You're angry with me," he said.

"What could I possibly have to be angry about?"

He groaned and folded her back into his arms. "Oh, I'm such a boor. A cad. An insensitive boorish cad! I never should have left you at Harlo's last night. I realized that the minute I woke up this morning. I opened my eyes, and I thought, 'I hope Madeleine has recovered from yesterday's terrible adventure,' and then I thought, 'I don't even know if she made it safely home!'

And then I realized—I mean, it was selfish and stupid and *unforgivable* of me to abandon you yesterday, and I am here to make it up to you in any way you require."

She found herself losing some of her stiff reserve and leaning slightly into his embrace. *This* was what she had needed last night, Tivol's arms around her; *this* was where she had always felt safe. "It was not unforgivable, but Tivol, how could you have left me like that? Didn't you know how much I wanted you with me?"

"I should have, but I didn't!" he exclaimed. "You always seem so calm and so sure of yourself, and last night was no different. You were so strong and serene that I just stopped worrying."

"I didn't feel as calm and strong as I wanted everyone to believe," she said. Maybe he was right. She had insisted she was fine and he had believed her; should she have expected him to read her mind? If she'd asked him to stay by her side, if she'd asked him to take her home, he would have done it. She knew that for absolute fact. She melted a little more in his arms, lifted her head to nuzzle the base of his throat. "But I *was* angry when you left me."

"I won't do it again," he promised. "You'll see—I'll follow so close behind you everywhere you go, you'll be embarrassed. You'll have to explain to all your friends that I'm a lovesick idiot who's afraid to let you out of his sight. It'll be inconvenient, I know, but you'll have to get used to it."

She laughed. "I think I'll like it," she said. *I won't like it tomorrow when Reese shows up,* she found herself thinking, but she shook the thought away.

"So what shall we do this evening?" he asked. "How shall I prove to you how much I love you?"

"Why wait till this evening? Let's go right now to the temple gardens. The weather is perfect for strolling along and admiring flowers."

His face showed a comical, exaggerated level of dismay. "Yes, a perfect day for it, but—I suppose I forgot to mention that my mother's in town. And she's expecting us this afternoon. We could go to the garden *after* we visit her."

Madeleine freed herself from his arms and sighed. "That's right, my father mentioned it this morning. When are we supposed to see her?"

Tivol caught her hands. "At two, but—we can go tomorrow! I know she has a meeting scheduled with—but we can work around it."

For a moment she was tempted. Tivol so rarely defied his mother that she was moved that he would even suggest it. It proved he was serious about atoning for his transgression; it showed he valued Madeleine over everyone else in the world. "She will be displeased with you," she said tentatively.

"Not at all. I'll let her know you're too worn out from yesterday's events."

Madeleine frowned. "Oh, no. That makes me sound like some poor helpless creature who can't handle the slightest adversity."

Tivol kissed her hands. "Then I will come up with some other excuse. Today is *your* day, and I will do whatever makes you happiest."

She smiled and kissed him. "But then I would spend all day today dreading tomorrow's visit," she said. "Let's get the obligation over with this afternoon and *then* go somewhere special."

"That's my Madeleine," Tivol said in an admiring voice. "Always doing the right thing. I wish I was half as good as you are."

She laughed. "I wish you were a *quarter* as good as I am."

But what she was really thinking was, *I can't go see Heloise tomorrow because I am going to spend the day with Reese.*

The Wellendens' town house was close enough to the Alaynes' that Madeleine and Tivol could have walked the distance in fifteen minutes. But they took Tivol's little sprinter, Jayla riding silently behind them. Tivol had frowned slightly when the guard followed Madeleine out the front door.

"We're just going to my mother's," he said. "Surely you don't expect to be under attack there."

"After last night, I am feeling a little vulnerable," Madeleine answered. "I don't even like to step outside my bedroom unless I know Jayla is there. Anyway, if we go somewhere else directly afterward—"

"You're right. The guard shall accompany us everywhere!"

In just a few minutes, they were parked in the circular drive before the Wellenden mansion. If anything, its lines were even boxier and more severe than those of the Alayne house, and behind the high grillwork fence the lawns were green but unadorned.

Inside, it was not much better. Heloise Wellenden had always had a reputation for austerity, and amongst a set of people who had made opulence a lifestyle, she had chosen to be extravagant in her plainness. So the wide, airy atrium featured white marble floors and white tiled walls and white stone pillars that supported two levels of white balconies. Swaths of diaphanous curtains softened a few of the archways; dozens of ceramic vases held lilies and gardenias in the palest shades. In certain moods, Madeleine found the very spareness of the place to be restful to her senses—but more often she missed the gaiety of the more familiar colors of home.

Theoretically, this was where Tivol lived, and he certainly had a suite of rooms here. But he had confided to Madeleine long ago that this wasn't the kind of place where a dashing young man felt comfortable inviting his friends over for a night of socializing. So, like many of his peers, he also had rented rooms in a fashionable building on the west side of town, and that was where he spent most of his time.

"She'll be waiting for us in the sun parlor," Tivol said as they stepped inside. He gestured at a pair of stiff white ladderback chairs set under one of the overhanging balconies, and said, "Your guard can wait for us here. Unless you think she needs to accompany us into my mother's presence?"

Madeleine exchanged a nod with Jayla, who made her way silently toward the seats. "No, I think your mother is quite capable of fighting off an assassin with a butter knife and a look of frigid disdain."

Tivol gave a crack of laughter. "Oh, absolutely. My money's always on her."

They headed down a white-tiled hallway and entered a room almost as sunny and airy as the atrium. More of those flimsy curtains fluttered at the high windows, more vases of flowers added warmth and fragrance to a setting that was just as monochromatic as the foyer. White tile on the floor, white paint on the walls, furniture upholstered in white cloth of a heavy weave.

And sitting in the center of the room, Heloise Wellenden.

In the pristine setting, it was almost a shock to see a figure of such color. She had the deep mahogany skin and silky black hair of the pureblood Cordelano; her lips and nails were painted a vivid red. She wore a flowing pantsuit of cobalt blue silk belted around her waist and a loose scarf in aqueous hues. Her arms were laden with bracelets—the ornately filigreed one on her left hand proclaiming her a member of a Council family, the seven on her left hand detailing her personal story. A widow, a mother of one, a daughter who had lost both parents, a sister who had lost three brothers. Madeleine had often wondered if it was grief that made Heloise so difficult, or if she had always been unlikable.

Still, this was her future mother-in-law, and Madeleine could get along with anyone. She crossed the room and kissed the older woman's cheek. "Heloise. How good it is to see you."

Heloise didn't bother to stand up, but she took Madeleine's hands in hers and gave her a searching look from her deep brown eyes. "Madeleine. You look tired."

Madeleine knew it was true, but she still found the comment irritating. Nonetheless, she tried to respond lightly. "It's been a tumultuous couple of days."

Tivol pushed a couple of chairs over, and they took their seats. "Yes, yesterday was quite a shock," he said. "But Madeleine was magnificent. No crazed woman with a knife could shake her poise or cause her to run and hide."

"Tivol makes me sound bolder than I am," she said with a smile. "I *was* unnerved by the attack, but since I hadn't actually been harmed, it seemed silly to miss out on an evening I had been looking forward to."

"But this isn't the first time someone has tried to hurt you," Heloise said, still watching Madeleine intently. "You must be very careful. You are quite precious, you know."

It was the kindest thing Heloise had ever said to her. "Why, thank you," Madeleine replied. "And I am being very careful indeed."

"There's a guard," Tivol said helpfully. "She follows Madeleine everywhere."

"I wonder if you would be safer out of the city," Heloise said. "At Wellen House, perhaps. The estate is remote and well-guarded, and I think intruders would find it difficult to reach you."

So my father and Heloise have already discussed this, Madeleine thought. Had they been dashing off notes to each other as soon as the sun came up? Perhaps her father had stalked the short distance between their properties so they could confer in person over the best way to handle this inconvenient turn of events. She could almost hear them saying, *Each of us has only one heir, and we cannot merge our business interests if one of them is dead.*

She hated herself for the thought. But it made her reevaluate what Heloise had meant by calling her precious.

"You can't send her off to be locked away in Marata!" Tivol objected, reaching for Madeleine's hand. "I need her! If I don't see her every day, my life loses meaning."

"You could join her at Wellen House," Heloise suggested.

Tivol showed a face of exaggerated shock. "Move out of the *city?*"

"Well, eventually you'll have to."

"Nonsense. You're going to live forever."

"I admit that would be my preference, but I fear it is unlikely."

"Well, I'm not ready to move to Wellen House yet, and I doubt Madeleine is."

"You could let her answer for herself."

Madeleine tried to summon a convincing smile. "Indeed, it is very kind of you to make the offer," she said. "But I'm not ready for country living, either. And now that I have my own personal guard, I feel safe enough in Corcannon. I do appreciate the thought."

"If you change your mind—"

"I'm sure she won't," Tivol interrupted. "Let's talk of other things! How was your trip? How long are you staying?"

They struggled through a few minutes of polite conversation before a servant entered with refreshments. At the center of the tray was a large, lumpy loaf of brown bread, its thick crust sprinkled with silvery seeds. It was a traditional menu item in Marata, and Tivol's favorite dish.

"You brought some cardu!" Tivol exclaimed. "You really do love me!"

"The cook is the one who thought of it," Heloise said.

"Well, she *does* love me. Does everyone want some? I'll slice it up."

The tray came equipped with an alarmingly large serrated knife and three delicate china plates. Heloise poured glasses of water for each of them while Tivol attacked the cardu.

"That's a tough crust," he said, as the blade failed to pierce the top. "Here, Madeleine, can you hold the bread steady?"

"I should have had them prepare it in the kitchen," said Heloise, watching with faint amusement as Madeleine ceremoniously set her hands on the two ends of the loaf. The crust felt hard as a clamshell beneath her fingers.

"Nonsense! Cardu's at its best when it's freshly sliced." Tivol carefully placed the knife in the center of the loaf and used both hands to saw through it. "Success! Hold on to the left side while I whittle off a piece for you."

Maybe Madeleine didn't move her hands fast enough; maybe Tivol was just careless. But the blade slipped and the knife skittered over a heavy ridge of baked dough, and the serrated edge ripped a long gash through Madeleine's thumb. She yelped with pain and jerked her hand back, putting her hand to her mouth to suck away the blood.

"Madeleine!" Tivol exclaimed, dropping the knife with horror. "Are you all right? Show me, show me! I didn't cut your finger off, did I?"

"No, but Tivol, that hurts!" she replied. "How did that even happen?"

"I don't know, but I shall never eat cardu again in my life. Here—let me see."

He took her hand and cupped it in his own, right over the refreshment tray. More blood immediately welled up from the cut and dripped onto the cardu, which made Madeleine obscurely happy. Tivol made a *tsking* sound and grabbed an embroidered linen napkin to wrap it around her injury.

Heloise had already rung for the servants to request salve and bandages. "How very ironic that we were just discussing how much safer you would be on my property in the country," Heloise said. "Since I can't even seem to guarantee your safety in my own parlor."

"I'm beside myself with humiliation and remorse," said Tivol. "Madeleine, my dear, my darling, can you forgive me?"

She was trying to be cheerful and nonchalant, but in truth, she wanted to start crying. "And to think that someone who hates me attacked me last night without doing me the slightest harm," she said, trying to make a joke of it. "But someone who loves me says he wants to feed me, and suddenly I'm bleeding everywhere."

Tivol tossed aside the soiled napkin and picked up a fresh one. "It doesn't look that deep," he said. "But you might get this tended to so it doesn't get infected."

"I'll do that," she said. "As soon as I get home."

A maid arrived bearing gauze and antiseptic cream. In a few moments

Madeleine was sitting in one of the white upholstered chairs, her thumb bandaged to comically large proportions, a plateful of cardu on her lap.

"I don't think I can choke down a scrap," Tivol said, staring at his own portion.

Madeleine had already had her first bite, so she could speak with conviction. "Nonsense. It's how you get revenged upon it," she said. "Besides, it's very good."

"Next time I am certainly having it sliced in the kitchen," said Heloise. "But it *is* very good."

Tivol sighed and sampled his own slice. "Oh—an exceptional example of the art form," he said with his mouth full. "It would be a shame to waste it."

"My son," said Heloise, a faint smile on her face. "Always practical."

They labored through another fifteen minutes of conversation, but everyone seemed relieved when Madeleine rose to her feet and said she wanted to go home. "I don't think I'm up for a visit to the gardens after all," she said to Tivol as he stood beside her. "And I've got obligations all day tomorrow. Perhaps we can do something the day after?"

"Of course. I am at your disposal."

She turned to her hostess, who had not bothered to stand. "It was good to see you again, Heloise. Thank you for thinking of me."

"Of course," Heloise said, echoing her son. "I am glad you were free."

Madeleine's eyes fell on a drop of red perfectly centered on the empty seat nearest the serving table. "Oh no! Heloise! It looks like I have bled all over one of your beautiful chairs!"

Heloise flicked a dismissive glance in that direction and shook her head. "It doesn't matter. It is easily repaired or replaced."

"I'm so sorry."

Heloise fixed her with those dark, unreadable eyes. "My dear," she said, "it's a piece of furniture. Nothing is more important than your blood."

Chapter Sixteen: Madeleine

In the morning, Reese arrived bearing a bouquet of roses in an astonishing array of hues. "I had the florist pick out all the wildest colors in the shop," he informed Madeleine as she buried her nose in the velvety petals. "Because that's always what I think of when I think of you."

"Reese. That's so sweet," she said. She snapped off a dark red bloom veined with streaks of orange, because it perfectly matched the scarf she had draped over her shoulders. "Let me just pin this in place."

She struggled with the clasp of her brooch; it was a clumsy task to attempt with one thumb in a bulky bandage.

"Do you need help?"

"No, no, I've got it. Thank you!"

He came closer. "What did you do to your hand?"

She didn't want to relate that story. "Cut it accidentally on a knife."

"Every time I see you, you've been wounded!" he said. "Last time I was here, you had a gash on your hand from a broken decanter. Maybe it's not just street assassins who are trying to harm you."

"This really was an accident," she assured him. "And I am determined that nothing terrible will befall me today."

"No," he said. "I've made certain of that."

She gave him an inquiring look. "And where are you taking me?"

He smiled and held out his hand. "You'll see."

She was amused to find that he was still driving his mother's gridcar. She wondered if it was because his own was still being repaired or because he remembered that Madeleine liked it. She suspected the latter, but didn't remark on it one way or the other, just settled onto the thickly padded bench. Reese waited until Jayla had climbed in before he took his own seat and put the car in motion, turning carefully onto the street.

She was intrigued when he passed the road that would take them to the Quatrefoil with its multitude of attractions, and not long after, she guessed their destination.

"We're going to the lake!" she exclaimed. "What a splendid idea! The weather is perfect."

"I thought you might be uncomfortable in the plaza with all those people around," he explained. "So I rented a small excursion boat for the afternoon, and brought in all my own staff. No one can approach us on the water without being seen—and no one on board will mean you any harm."

It was so thoughtful that she wanted to start crying—something it seemed she was ready to do at a moment's notice these days. "Reese. That's so kind. I don't know what to say."

He glanced over at her. "You don't have to say anything. Just enjoy yourself."

She already knew she would.

Chrission Lake was at the northwestern edge of the city in a small cup of a plateau where the mountain first began its jagged ascent. The power lines for the gridway didn't run that far, but a few enterprising souls operated a stable yard at the foot of the mountain, renting out horses, carts, and drivers to take visitors to their destination. The day was so fine that the stable master was doing a bustling business—but Reese had made advance reservations, so their party had only a five-minute wait before they were enjoying a rather bumpy ride up the mountainside.

The discomfort of the journey paled to insignificance as they topped the rise and caught their first glimpse of the lake. It was small enough that visitors could see its entire perimeter, but big enough to not seem crowded by the twenty or so boats that floated lazily across its dappled surface. Two more boats were tied up at a long dock, awaiting new arrivals. On the rocky, slanted surface of the nearest bank, groups of visitors had spread out festive blankets where they could recline to watch the play of sunlight over water.

"Reese," Madeleine said. "*What* a marvelous idea this was."

He took her arm to guide her down the narrow and somewhat treacherous path that led to the dock, then glanced behind him once. "Do you need any help?" he asked Jayla.

"I'm fine," Jayla said. Madeleine thought she sounded amused.

In a few moments, they had boarded their rented boat. It was about forty feet long and half as wide, with an open doorway that led to a lower level. Above the main deck was an elevated station where a captain already hovered at the controls. Set against the railing at the bow was a small linen-covered table flanked by two chairs. In the middle of the table was a vase filled with more vivid roses.

"Let's cast off," Reese said, "and then have lunch."

It was the best day Madeleine had had for longer than she cared to remember. The weather was ideal, sunny without being oppressively hot; the boat rocked so serenely across the water that the wine in their glasses barely trembled. A silent footman brought them food at discreet intervals, but otherwise no one came near them. Even Jayla, who had taken a seat near the captain, appeared to be staying as far away as possible.

The combination of sunshine, wine, and isolation made Madeleine feel like her whole body was unclenching from a pose she had held so long she hadn't even been aware of the effort she was making. It seemed easier to breathe, somehow, even though it hadn't seemed hard before. Easier to smile. Possible to relax.

They talked idly, trading stories about growing up, Reese on his father's extensive property in Chibain, Madeleine in the city house with its bright mosaics. Reese admitted that, as a child, he had been terrified during his rare visits to Corcannon when he had to take noisy rides on the confounding gridway. Madeleine had enjoyed her trips to family properties in northern Marata, tumbling through the sprawling mansions in the company of her brother and an undifferentiated host of cousins.

"Once Logan died, I didn't want to go any more," she said with a sigh. "The first year, my father insisted, but after that he gave up. So I haven't been back to Marata for years. I see my cousins when they come to town, of course, but it's easier somehow."

"How long has it been now?" Reese asked.

"Ten years. He was twelve, I was fourteen."

"How did he die? I remember getting the news, but not the details."

She made a small sound that might have been a laugh. "Given his general fearlessness and *stupidity,* you'd have thought it was from some kind of crazy stunt—"

"Like swinging down from the pillars."

"Like swinging down from the pillars, which he *did!* And he also learned how to run the cables, just like a courier."

"I didn't know that! I'm impressed."

"It was so typical of Logan. He wanted to *be* a courier. He couldn't believe it when our father told him Council families don't do menial work."

"So what happened?"

"He was out with my Uncle Archer—my father's brother. They were in the Quatrefoil—I think he was taking Logan to some special exhibit at the museum. They were crossing the street in front of a fleet of parked gridcars. There was some kind of electrical malfunction and the lead car came loose and went careening down the street. Archer jumped out of the way but Logan—" She shook her head. "His body was so mangled they wouldn't even let me see it. My father said it was better that I never had those pictures in my mind. But I wish—I really wished they'd let me say goodbye."

She fingered the slim gold bracelet on her right wrist. "For *years,* I let myself believe he wasn't really dead. That some other poor boy had gotten run over by the gridcar. That someone had scooped Logan up just in time to save him, and in all the confusion he got separated from my uncle, and he was so disoriented he couldn't remember his name or where he lived, so this kind man took him home and raised him like his own son. . . ." She shook her head again. "I still can't help myself. When I'm out in public, and I see a young man who's about Logan's age, I study the shape of his face, wondering, 'Is that him? Would I recognize him after all this time? Would *he* recognize *me?*' But I've never seen anyone who looks enough like him for me to go over and strike up a conversation."

Reese reached across the table to cover the hand that still toyed with her bracelet. "I'm so sorry," he said.

She tried to shrug. "It's a stupid little fantasy."

"It's a form of hope, and hope is never stupid."

She wanted to reply that hope was the stupidest emotion in the whole human repertoire, making people pine for impossible things, but she didn't want to give Reese an excuse to talk about impossible things he still hadn't quite given up on. Or maybe she did, but she shouldn't. She gently pulled her hand away.

"Well, you've had your own losses," she said. "I know your grandfather's death was hard on you."

He nodded. "As if the world broke into a thousand pieces and reassembled itself in the wrong configuration," he said. "It's still never gone back to its proper shape, and that was five years ago."

She echoed his own words. "I'm so sorry."

"I worry about my father," he added. "He's been turning over more and more responsibility to me, and I know he's constantly tired. The last few times I've been home, he's said he needs to talk to me about something—and then changed his mind and said he'll tell me next time. So I know something is weighing on him, but I don't know what."

Madeleine rested her elbows on the table and laced her fingers together. "Oooh, a mystery! Maybe he's going to confess that you have an illegitimate half-sibling somewhere."

Reese laughed. "Hard to imagine which of my parents is *less* likely to have produced that child."

"Maybe the whole estate is in debt and you're about to be a pauper!"

"Don't sound so excited about it."

"No, of course not, but it would be very dramatic."

"Well, since I have access to all the books and bank statements, I can assure you that the estate is in sound financial shape."

"Maybe he murdered someone and buried the body on the property."

He regarded her with misgiving. "You have some very lurid ideas."

She bubbled over with laughter. "Well, but your father is so proper and kind. I just can't imagine what sort of secret he could be keeping from you."

He was grave. "It's more likely that he's nursing a serious illness and is trying to summon the courage to tell me."

Madeleine instantly sobered. "Oh no! I hope that's not true."

"So do I. But even if it is, I think I have to wait until he is ready to talk to me."

"If it is—if it is, please come tell me. I would want to know."

"Thank you. I will."

A moment of silence passed between them. Madeleine shook her head and tried to brighten her voice. "Well! We've stumbled onto some dark topics. Let's think of something more light-hearted to talk about and then, I'm afraid, we'll have to start making our way home."

"I was regretfully thinking the same thing," Reese said, raising his hand to signal the captain. The floor of the deck thrummed below them, and the boat began making a slow circle in the water. "I actually have business to attend to this evening, though I set the appointment for as late as possible."

"And my father is entertaining clients at the house tonight and wants me to be present," she said. "So I must go home and comb the tangles out of my hair and scrub the sunshine from my face."

"Nonsense. A look of windblown carelessness inspires confidence in the most severe and judgmental man."

She laughed, but Reese frowned. "Although—are you up to playing hostess for your father? We haven't talked about how you're doing after your scare the other night."

"I'm fine. Well—I admit I've been a little edgy. A little more emotional than usual. But certainly I'm well enough to make polite conversation with a few people over dinner."

"And I suppose they've learned nothing more about the person who attacked you."

"She *died.*"

"I heard that."

"She took poison rather than let them interrogate her. That's probably what frightens me most about this whole situation. What was she afraid to reveal?"

Reese was frowning. "That's not right."

"What? She's not dead?"

"No, she is, but—she didn't take poison."

Madeleine was bewildered. "What? How do you know that?"

Reese made an impatient gesture. "One of my men used to be a temple guard and still has friends in the ranks. He said her throat was cut."

"But—"

"He seemed pretty certain. He said there was an investigation under way to determine who had been with her and how it could possibly have happened."

"But then why would Harlo have told me that?" She thought about it some more. "Although, it wasn't actually Harlo who told me. It was Benito. But Harlo was standing right there."

"My guess? They thought you would be even more upset to learn she'd died violently. So they came up with a different story."

Madeleine found herself shivering, even in the warm sun. She wrapped her arms around her body and found herself clenching up in an instinctive protective pose. "Well, I'm more upset to learn they lied to me," she said. "And—what does it mean that her throat was cut? Did she do it to herself? Or—did someone do it *to* her?"

Reese looked grave. "It wouldn't be my own choice for suicide. But she did have at least one knife on her when she attacked you, so maybe she had two. And maybe she had decided that, one way or the other, someone was going to die by a blade that night." Madeleine's face must have looked wretched, because his own creased with remorse. "I'm sorry. I shouldn't have told you. I should have let the fiction stand."

"No," she said sharply. "Whatever else passes between us, don't you lie to me. I couldn't bear it."

He nodded and touched his hand to his heart. "Thank you," he said. "It means a lot to me that you trust me with the truth."

"It means a lot to me to know you will tell it to me."

They disembarked without incident, though Madeleine found her legs were somewhat unsteady once she was on solid ground. Jayla strode confidently up the hill, but Madeleine swayed uncertainly as she took her first few steps up the rocky slope. That meant Reese had to take her hand, which meant she hung on to him for the whole short ascent. Naturally, they sat a few inches apart in the cart on the way back to the stable, and even farther apart once they were in the gridcar. But in some strange way, Madeleine felt as if she was still clinging to Reese, still leaning on him for support.

They were about a mile from her house, inching along in a slow line of heavy traffic, when the ground shook beneath them and tumbled them around the interior of the car. Madeleine cried out in alarm and heard an answering cacophony all around her—metal wheels shrieking across the pavement, overhead wires hissing and sparking, passengers in the nearby vehicles shouting and cursing. She felt Reese clutch her arm and yank her out of the car just as a second tremor rumbled beneath them. She tripped to the ground, breaking her fall with her outstretched hands, rolling aside in time to see Reese haul Jayla to safety. As Madeleine scrambled to her feet, he charged forward and grabbed her hand. The three of them raced to the side of the road to crouch against the spiked-metal fence surrounding the nearest property. All around them, riders from other cars did the same.

They huddled there for ten minutes, hands over their heads, feeling the ground shake and steady, shake and steady, each time less violently, until the last little shimmy was so slight Madeleine thought she might have imagined it. She saw their fellow travelers rise cautiously to their feet and look around, calling out to each other to check on their condition.

Madeleine allowed Reese to tug her upright and then turned instantly to Jayla. "Are you all right?"

The guard nodded and brushed dirt off her knees. "Yes. You?"

"Yes." Madeleine glanced around. The square house behind them looked relatively unharmed, though a decorative statue had toppled onto its side. The state of the road was a different story altogether. The knot of gridcars had been knocked into each other, creating a big untidy mess. Two of them were facing the wrong way and one was lying on its side, its connector pole bent in half.

"*That* will take some time to clear up," Madeleine observed.

The strangers nearby had reached the same conclusion, because they were starting to mill around the crashed vehicles, pointing and lamenting and strategizing.

"Yes, but at least the power lines appear to be intact," Reese said. "A bad enough quake could rip them down, and then the city would come to a standstill."

"Then we've been lucky!" Madeleine exclaimed.

Reese took her arm. "Come on. I'll walk you home and then I'll come back here and see what I can do."

Madeleine shook her head and pulled away. "Nonsense. It's less than a mile home, and I have Jayla with me. I'll be fine."

"All right. But be careful."

"I will. Thank you, Reese, for a most wonderful day."

"Wonderful until this happened, anyway," he said.

She squeezed his arm and quickly dropped her hand. "Wonderful without qualifications," she corrected. "I appreciate it so much."

Before he could say anything else, she turned and began walking down the street in the direction of her own house. Jayla fell in step beside her, glancing around continuously to make sure trouble didn't come pouncing from one of the gated lawns. The guard didn't seem interested in talking, for which Madeleine was grateful. She had too much on her mind to be able to make rational conversation.

They passed dozens of gridcars out of commission, either spun out of alignment or ripped from the overhead wire or flipped onto their sides. Around each knot of upended vehicles were clusters of drivers and passengers, working together to try to restore order. A few people were yelling, and several were crying, but for the most part, strangers appeared to be working together to solve the crisis. Madeleine assumed that city maintenance workers would also be dispatched to help clear the roads and get traffic moving again.

By the time they arrived home twenty minutes later, Madeleine was sticky from the heat and shaky from the accumulated shocks of the day. She had never been so grateful to step inside the cool, quiet calm of the atrium. The stairwell looked almost insurmountable, but she took the steps slowly and ultimately made it to the top. Another few moments and she was in her own room, safe, alone, with time and space to think.

She had hardly been surprised when the quake came ripping down the boulevard; at first it hadn't even registered with her. Her mind was in such tumult already that she thought maybe the heaving ground was just a matter of her own perception, an outward manifestation of her inner turmoil.

It was the best day she had had in ten years. And the worst.

She might be in love with Reese Curval. And she had no idea what to do about it.

Two days later over breakfast, everything got worse.

"I've changed my mind," Madeleine's father said. "You should get married now."

Madeleine was so surprised she choked on her morning juice and coughed for a full minute. The two of them had been sitting at the table for half an hour, and these were the first words either one had spoken.

"What?" she was finally able to say.

Her father looked at her with his usual inscrutable expression. "You should marry Tivol. As quickly as possible. Next month, perhaps."

"*What?* I can't possibly plan—and *why* would you want—I don't understand."

He touched a napkin to his mouth and dropped it to his lap. "The planning is the least important part. You should marry and begin your new life."

One last cough to clear her throat, then she gazed at him across the table, her face tense and serious. "Tell me what this is all about," she said. "What's happened to change your mind?"

"Nothing's happened. But there seems no reason to delay."

"Is the business in trouble? Are you worried about debts? Is there—"

"This is not about me," he interrupted. "Don't you want to marry Tivol?"

Oh, she wished she knew the answer to that question! But naturally she pretended she did. "Of course I do, but—"

"I have already checked with Harlo. The main sanctuary is booked for months, but you could arrange a small ceremony in this house. Harlo said he would officiate no matter what day you chose."

"Father! I am not going to have a headlong, scrambling wedding! I'm happy enough to move up the date, but I'm not going to just throw together a ceremony at the last minute—"

"Two months. No longer."

She stared at him. "Or what? You'll throw me out of the house?"

He stared back and didn't answer. Madeleine felt her warm indignation turn to something chilly and uncertain. She couldn't even name the emotion.

"Even if I wanted to marry so quickly, Tivol does not," she said, trying to keep her voice level.

"Heloise will be able to persuade him, I'm certain."

"So there *is* a business reason behind this decision," she said. "If this is something you and Heloise are plotting together."

She saw his face roil with denial and possibly anger, but then he smoothed out his features. "Yes," he said. "I have discussed it with Heloise, and we have very strong economic reasons for advancing the timetable."

It was the only thing that made sense, yet she couldn't shake the notion that he was lying. Her thoughts were racing so fast she couldn't catch hold of one long enough to examine it. Married to Tivol within two months! How could she manage the preparations—the details of the event itself, the massive effort of moving her life from her father's household to Tivol's? Where would they even live? She refused to share a mansion with Heloise Wellenden for a day, even if meant she had to live in Tivol's cramped bachelor lodgings.

How long would it take her to get over this inconvenient, this ridiculous, this impossible feeling of affection for Reese? She had loved Tivol her whole life and she had always found Reese to be so difficult and contrary, and yet in the past few weeks—

But that didn't matter. She couldn't think about that. She wanted to marry Tivol, she *had* to marry Tivol, and her secretive and controlling father was not going to tell her why she had to do it in blinding haste. She would do as he commanded, because she always had, but she couldn't suppress a small rebellious flare of satisfaction at the thought that she would finally be out on her own, no longer answerable to his demands or tiptoeing around his moods.

"Then there is nothing left to discuss except the arrangements for the wedding itself," she said coolly. "I suppose you are willing to leave all those decisions up to me?"

"Of course. I just want the event concluded as soon as possible."

She wondered if she could shock him. "You realize what everyone will assume when they hear the news," she said. "All my friends—all my cousins. They'll think we're getting married so abruptly because I'm pregnant."

He wasn't shocked. He wasn't even angry. He just gave her a dead-level look and said, "I wish you were."

Chapter Seventeen: Brandon

Brandon was taking his afternoon nap when the tremor shook him roughly awake. For an instant, he didn't know what was happening. He rolled out of bed and into a crouch, grabbing for the knife that was never more than a few inches from his fingertips. But as the walls danced around him, as an earthenware bowl slipped off a table and shattered on the floor, he realized the house wasn't under attack—or at least, not from a foe that could be defended against.

Someone pounded on his door, and Finley called, "Brandon! Outside! Now!" He caught up his boots and skidded out the door in his sock feet. As he raced toward the atrium, he heard footsteps converging on this central point from all over the house, and he realized everyone was headed for the same exit into the garden.

"Where's Villette?" he called when he saw the maid rushing down the steps.

"In the garden already," she panted back.

In a few moments, they were all there, huddled in the center of the enclosure as far as possible from the high stone walls, the heavy linen canopy, and the bulk of the house itself. Far from anything that could fall on them, crushing them beneath its weight. Brandon glanced fearfully at the grass beneath his feet. Couldn't the ground open up just as easily and swallow them whole? Was any place truly safe once the world was determined to shake itself to pieces?

"When can we go back inside?" the cook asked after a few moments had passed and nothing else had happened.

"Not yet," came Villette's voice, sharp and clear. Brandon let himself look at her as she stepped out from behind the maid's shadow. He had never given up the night shift, much to the delight of Finley and Nadder, and so he had never had a chance to see Villette in full daylight. That creamy brown skin. Those deep-set eyes, dense with sadness. That rich dark hair braided away from her face. Too beautiful to look at straight on. He shifted his position so he could watch her from the corner of his eye.

"Not yet," Villette repeated. "Give it a few minutes. The tremors tend to come in—"

A hard shiver ran under their feet, throwing them all off-balance. The little maid screamed and pitched to the ground; the sound of breaking glass came from inside the house. Brandon found the gardener clutching him for support. Nadder had one hand around Villette's arm to hold her steady.

This tremor didn't last as long as the first one and didn't feel as bad. "How long till it's over?" Brandon asked.

The gardener shook his head. He was a stooped older man of indeterminate heritage, always civil if not particularly talkative. He had told Brandon his name was Abenza, but everyone called him Abe. "No telling. But usually if there's nothing for a half hour, you can say you're safe for the day."

"It's been a while since we've had quakes this often," Finley said. "At least ten years, yeah? I was a kid."

"We *never* had anything this bad down in the islands," Brandon said.

Nadder had released Villette, though he still stood near enough to catch her if another tremor set them all careening. "Really? I thought they shook the whole country."

"It's the seams," Abe explained. "Sometimes they can't hold together."

Brandon just looked between the two of them. "I don't even know what you're talking about."

He thought he heard faint amusement in Villette's voice. "When Cordelan knit the lands together, he couldn't bind them all perfectly. So there are seams between Marata and Chibain, for instance, and Marata and Oraki. There's also the long crevice that divides Corcannon from the mainland. Sometimes the world shifts, and the lands shove up against each other, and then we get quakes." She arched her dark brows and smiled at him. "Aren't there seams between the islands and Marata? I would think you'd have just as many quakes as we do."

He knew what she was talking about now. The borders between the five islands, and between the islands and Marata, were stony, inhospitable stretches of land sometimes more than a mile wide, sometimes narrow enough to toss a rock across. His father had always maintained that Zessaya had made those passages so difficult to traverse because she wanted to keep Maratan marauders from slipping over to the islands. It happened anyway, of course, but never at night, when a man or a horse could easily go lame trying to make one of those crossings.

"We have—seams, as you call them," Brandon said. "But I don't recall the land ever rolling like that. Maybe the islands are just floating on the ocean, so they don't shake so much when there are tremors."

On the words, the ground rumbled again, just enough to let them feel it, not enough to make any of them lose their balance. Brandon thought he heard Finley curse under her breath before she looked apologetically in Villette's direction.

"Once it stops, when will it start up again?" Brandon asked.

Abe shook his head again. "Nobody knows. Could happen again tomorrow. Might not happen again for a decade."

"Unnerving, isn't it?" Villette said. "Especially for people who like to know exactly what the future holds."

"Nobody ever knows what the future holds," the cook said briskly.

"Then why does anyone ever seek to control it?" Villette asked whimsically.

No one tried to find an answer for that. The group was starting to pull apart, the servants edging toward the house, Villette drifting toward the patio.

"I wouldn't sit under the canopy. Not just yet," Brandon cautioned her. "If there's another quake and that comes down, it could suffocate you."

"I'm just going to fetch a chair and bring it back out," she promised. "I'm tired of standing."

Finley and Nadder were advancing on the tall stone wall, their heads canted back as if they could see over the top. "Can't tell if that's a crack or not," Finley said, raising herself to her toes and lifting her hand as high as it would go to trace some pattern in the material. "Feels pretty solid."

"I'll go outside and check from the other side," Nadder said, heading for the door.

Villette emerged from the patio, carrying one of the lacy ironwork chairs that usually sat in front of her table. "Certainly! You must make sure the wall can't possibly be breached by any random resident of the household."

Brandon hurried over to take the chair from her hands. "Where do you want to sit?"

She smiled at him. "By the fish pond, of course."

He tried not to, but he smiled back. "Well, then."

He had not, after all, built a water garden for Villette. Over the past few weeks, they had had only a few conversations, random, unexpected, intriguing. She might go days without acknowledging Brandon's presence at all, then spend two hours one moonless night quizzing him about his life back on the islands. He never knew whether her mood would be expansive or contained, so every night he made his way to the garden determined not to give in to his mounting excitement. Every night he failed.

Some nights he was rewarded.

Perhaps a week after he had first discussed the idea of a water garden with her, he came out for his evening shift to find that someone had started digging a large, shallow hole in the open ground between the patio and the fence. When he went over to inspect it, Villette's voice sounded directly behind him.

"I so much loved the idea you proposed," she said without any preamble, and he whirled around to try to make out her face in the dark. "But I was certain Finley and Nadder would find it odd that I had asked you to undertake such a project. And they might mention it to the high divine. And the high divine would be afraid you had become fond of me, and you would be sent away, and I would never get my water garden, and I would be very sad."

He had to admit that this was exactly how events might unfold. "I suppose you're right."

"But once I had the notion in my head, I could not give up on the idea of fish! So I asked Abe if he could construct a pond for me, and he was most willing."

"Well, I don't mind that *I'm* not the one to complete the project for you," he said. Though that was a lie—he had loved the idea that he would be the one to create a small, beautiful spot that would bring her joy. She would think of him every time she studied the rippling water or caught a flash of color under the floating lilies. Long after his stint was over, she would remember him. "But I'm happy you're getting a pond."

"I am quite looking forward to it! You will have to tell me what kinds of fish I should stock and what I should feed them. I am innocent of any knowledge whatsoever on this topic."

They had passed a few agreeable evenings discussing the fish breeds she might invest in. He had even told her the legend of Keshalosha, the lucky fish that supposedly swam in the waters off the Zessin islands. She had wondered what kinds of plants might add an aesthetic appeal to the pond, but Brandon suggested that Abe would be a better one to ask. "I'm not sure what grows well here," he admitted. "The soil is different where I'm from."

And that had led to another long discussion about life on the islands—the common flowers, the typical foods, the favorite holidays, the variable weather conditions. At the end, Villette had sighed and said, "I would love to visit that spot someday."

He had kept his voice steady as he replied, "And I would love to be your guide on that visit."

She laughed and said something almost under her breath. He thought it might be "sweet Brandon," but maybe it was "sweet dreaming," or maybe it was nothing at all. But he felt his face flush and his heart race at the mere thought that she might someday be free, walking along those dear familiar roads, clinging to his arm and exclaiming in delight as he introduced her to beauty after beauty.

The next ~~night~~ two nights, she didn't speak to him at all. The third night, she wasn't even in the garden. He might as well be guarding a fantasy, or a ghost. He might as well be obsessed with a creature he had simply imagined.

But now the pond was finished, and stocked with a variety of fish—some languid and silver, some quick and blue, some shaped like golden triangles, others like red snakes. The pond had become the favorite spot of everyone in the household, and any time anyone from the guards to the servants had a free moment, they could be found standing on the brick lip, tossing scraps of food into the ripples. Abe had suggested they place a pair of stone benches on either side of the water, but they had not yet arrived.

So Brandon carried the heavy chair from the patio and placed it where Villette indicated. "I want to watch them," she said, settling in so she could follow Nadder and Finley as they checked the integrity of the stone wall. Brandon took up a stance beside her chair.

"Can you hear that?" Nadder shouted from the other side. "I'm tapping at a spot about two feet above ground level. Might be a crack."

Finley bent over and ran her hands around the specified location. "It looks fine on this end, but right above—near the top. I can see a line in the mortar."

"Hang on. Let me check."

Villette leaned back in the chair and stretched out her feet so they were almost at the water's edge. "This is very entertaining," she said. "I wonder if they expect me to shove at the wall with such force that I bring the whole thing tumbling down."

"I think they just want to be able to assure the high divine that they are taking all precautions where you are concerned," Brandon said.

"Ah, yes, the high divine," Villette said. "He is convinced that I am a wily woman, always scheming."

Brandon didn't know how to answer that, so he said nothing. He thought maybe the head priest was right. He thought that, given her circumstances, Villette had every right to scheme.

Villette stirred in the chair. "He'll be back next week, you know."

"Who? The high divine?"

"Yes."

For no reason that made sense, Brandon felt a spurt of fear. "Testing your blood again?"

"Yes. That's exactly what he'll be doing."

"And will he find what he's looking for?"

Nadder's voice came from over the wall. "Here! About halfway up. Does that look like a crack to you?"

"It does. But I can't feel any give when I push on it as hard as I can."

"No. I can't either. All right, move down a little ways."

Villette shifted in her chair again, straightening up and tucking her feet beneath her. She had never turned her head and lifted her eyes to meet Brandon's. "He might. I don't know. Or maybe the cherloshe I swallowed is still having an effect. I suppose I'll find out."

Finley was on her tiptoes, stretching as high as she could go, which apparently wasn't high enough. She turned and motioned to Brandon. "Hey, give me a boost, will you? Nadder thinks he sees a crack near the top."

He had no choice but to join the other guards in making sure Villette's prison was secure. They spent another thirty minutes poking and prodding at the stones and mortar, but nothing appeared to be seriously out of place. By the time they finished their inspection, Villette had gone inside.

And she didn't come back down for the rest of the day.

Later that week, Brandon had his rare day off. He normally slept from about ten in the morning until five or six at night, but he wanted to make productive use of daylight hours, so he forced himself awake shortly after noon. Yawning, he gulped down a hasty meal, then headed out into a gloomy, overcast day. Finley had said this was a signal that summer was more than half over and autumn would quickly descend. The seasons weren't as pronounced on the islands, where the ocean kept temperatures relatively even most of the year, but Brandon had already spent two winters in the city. He shivered at the memory.

He caught a chugger headed east and settled in for a long, tedious ride. The only excitement came when they were almost at the Quatrefoil. The other passengers began murmuring and pointing, some of them sticking their heads out of the window to get a better view. Brandon craned his neck to see what was causing all the commotion, and then he caught his breath in an admiring gasp. One of the city couriers was skimming along the overhead wire, graceful as a dancer, racing toward some unknown destination. Brandon watched until the slim swift figure was out of sight.

After that, there was no way to pass the time except by watching the architecture subtly change as the transport moved between neighborhoods. Once they left behind the soaring roofs and steeples of the Quatrefoil, the buildings became shabbier, dirtier, more workaday. Brandon started paying more attention to the interior surroundings as a rougher clientele began climbing aboard. He wasn't wearing his temple livery, but anyone looking for clues would spot the soldier's bracelet on his left wrist and mark him down as a poor candidate for robbing. Even so, best to be careful. He was carrying a fair bit of money and he'd just as soon keep it.

Eventually, the slow transport reached Brandon's destination—the Zessin district on the southeastern edge of town—and he disembarked. The heavy gray clouds cast early shadows across the streets and storefronts, but even so, Brandon felt his heart lift as he glanced around. All the people he saw were strangers, of course, but they looked familiar, their faces brown or freckled, their wavy hair every shade of red. Even the way they walked, with an easy loose-limbed gait, seemed different from the purposeful stride of the impatient city dweller.

He had come here with a specific intent, but he first detoured through a small open-air food market that dominated the south edge of the main street. It was a transient affair of rickety booths and upended carts—they probably came together every morning and were dismantled every night, but, oh, what delights they offered! Brandon browsed through the makeshift stalls, paying for and gulping down small portions of salted fish, herbed bread, and fermented milk. There was even a vendor selling seagrass wine, and Brandon purchased a canvas rucksack just so he could carry two bottles home with him.

"You want to be careful with that," admonished the vendor, a stooped old man whose unruly white hair still showed streaks of ginger. He wrapped both bottles in dirty squares of canvas to keep them from breaking against each other in the bag. "If you're not used to it, it'll knock you flat in three swallows."

Brandon laughed. "You don't have to tell *me*. My dad used to make it in a shed out back."

"Oh, well, then, you know."

Next, he stopped at a booth where a middle-aged woman was selling packets of dried spices. He wasn't sure Villette's cook would know what to make of any of them, but he purchased the four that had always been in his mother's kitchen, then stood there a moment merely inhaling their scent.

Maybe this is what homesickness feels like, he thought. At any rate, he didn't have another word for the emotion.

He finally forced himself away from the market and continued down the short street that constituted the heart of the Zessin district. Another block took him to a small shop that sold fabric, clothing, and accessories. He headed straight to the table in the back where the jewelry was sold.

A rather formidable-looking woman about his mother's age materialized beside him before he'd had time to do more than bend over and glance at the necklaces on display. She was dressed like an island woman, in soft, loose fabrics that appeared weathered from an incessant assault of sea air. She had a solid body, big hands, and a suspicious expression on her face.

"Is there something I can help you with?" she asked in a tone that indicated she highly doubted it.

It took him that long to realize he was the only man in the shop and that most of the items for sale were intended for women. But he refused to be intimidated by a seawife. He straightened up and said, "I'm looking for a gift for my mother. A chazissa."

The seller's countenance warmed slightly. "Well, that's all right, then. Which of the goddess's incarnations were you interested in?"

"I'm not sure," he admitted. "She's been going through a rough time lately, so maybe the pose of protection, but—I haven't decided."

Reaching under the table, the seller drew out a large, flat wooden box and cleared space for it on the counter. Inside were at least twenty chazissas lined up on a black cloth surface. The white stone amulets were crisp and pristine against the dark fabric, the leather cords almost invisible.

The woman lifted a chazissa in each hand. "The pose of protection. The pose of nurturing." When his face showed uncertainty, she returned them to the case and held up two more. "The pose of courage. The pose of generosity."

"I'm thinking—I don't know—I might need to get her a couple different ones. She might need a lot of help right now."

The seller studied him for a moment, the amulets dangling from her hands, and then she nodded. "Well, it's very expensive, but some of my customers indulge themselves with a cycle chazissa," she said.

"I don't know what that is."

She rummaged under the table again and came up with another box, smaller than the first and set with a lock. Fishing a key from her pocket, she opened the lid, and drew out one of the treasures inside. "A cycle chazissa," she repeated. "Featuring all the goddess's poses."

This leather cord was longer than the others and hung with twelve distinct amulets, each one carefully spaced from the others and knotted in place. These charms were smaller than the typical ones, a little more delicate, but so beautifully rendered that Brandon could make out the goddess's features, varying from fierce to tender. He reached out as if to stroke a carved cheek, a tiny hand, but didn't bring his finger close enough to touch.

Such a chazissa could bring Villette months and *months* of protection. And she would find the small, slim figurines so much easier to swallow. He didn't care how much it cost. He would pawn his soul for such a prize.

"That's it," he said. "That's the one I want."

Chapter Eighteen: Brandon

Brandon was back in the mansion in time to take a nap before his shift began, but he was too keyed up to sleep. He could have joined the others for dinner, but he didn't want the inquisitive Finley to ask him about his afternoon off. He thought he might look too elated, or answer too evasively, or in some other way signal that this had not been an ordinary day. So he lurked in his room until he heard the others leave the kitchen and scatter to separate realms of the house. He emerged thirty minutes before his shift, giving him just enough time to gulp down a quick meal before Nadder came in from the garden.

"All yours," said the other guard through a yawn.

"She's out there tonight?"

Nadder nodded. "Just sitting under the canopy, hardly moving a muscle, but she's there."

"All right. See you tomorrow."

Even so, Brandon lingered in the atrium, waiting as the rest of the house settled down for the night. The servants slept upstairs and were always quick to seek their beds, but Finley often wandered around until nearly midnight. Not today, though—she had the morning shift tomorrow and clearly wanted to get a full night's rest. So it was only another hour or two before everyone else in the house seemed to be asleep.

Brandon returned to his room to fetch his new rucksack before heading out to the garden. The air was cool, but the day's cloud cover had dissipated, leaving the night sky brilliant with constellations. He tipped his face up, as if he could feel starlight on his skin, then glanced into the shadows under the canopy. He couldn't immediately make out Villette's form, so he stepped closer, peering into the dark.

"Over here," came her voice from the direction of the fish pond, and he hastily turned in that direction. She was sitting right on the brick border that circled the pond, and she was trailing her fingers in the water.

Brandon hefted his rucksack and went over to join her, coming to an easy crouch a few feet away. "Careful. Those fish might bite."

"They never have before."

He touched a finger to the brick to steady himself, and asked with some diffidence, "Can I sit with you a while?"

"Of course."

He settled into a cross-legged pose, still keeping his distance. Despite their canvas wrapping, the bottles clinked together in his bag.

"What do you have there?" she asked.

"I was in the Zessin neighborhood this afternoon and I bought some seagrass wine. I wondered if you'd like to taste it. It's the unofficial drink of the islands."

"Seagrass wine!" she exclaimed. "Oh, something with such an exotic name must be either exquisite or hideous. Of *course* I want to taste it."

He smiled. "You'll get people who take one position or the other. My mother can't stand the stuff, but my father used to make some every year, and he had a long list of faithful buyers."

"Do you like it?"

"Love it. But you have to be careful, especially the first time you try it. It can go to your head faster than you think. And go to your stomach not long after," he added conscientiously.

She laughed. "So I should limit myself to a glass or two?"

"Half a glass. Maybe a few swallows."

"Come now. I'm not that susceptible."

"Trust me." He drew himself back up in a crouch. "I'll go to the kitchen and get a glass."

She seemed to be in a playful mood. "Nonsense. If I can only have a couple of mouthfuls, I'll drink from the bottle."

He laughed. "Just like an island girl."

"I have no higher aspirations."

He sat back down, pulled out a bottle, and pried loose the stopper. Instantly the aroma drifted out, tangy and sharp. Brandon briefly closed his eyes, smelling salt air and wood fires and the sour fragrance of the coshichi bush. Then he opened his eyes and handed the bottle to Villette with a flourish.

"One swallow," he admonished.

Her fingers fleetingly touched his as she took it from his hand. "Will you have some, too?"

"I'm on duty."

"If I promise not to try to climb the fence while you're sprawled, drunken, on the edge of the pond?"

"Someone could still break in and try to hurt you," he pointed out. "I have to be ready to fight them off."

She made a scoffing sound. "No one has ever tried to break *in,* " she said. "Although the high divine assures me it could happen. He says the guards are here to keep me safe because there are people who want to kill me."

"*Kill* you?" Brandon repeated, horror igniting along his bones. "Who? Why?"

She shrugged pettishly. "Some group of malcontents who believe that the blood in my body renders me an abomination. They want the world to go back to a time before people like me existed. He even has a special name for them. The Reversionists. Which sounds so much nobler than deranged murderers, don't you think?"

"Are you afraid? That he might be telling the truth?"

"No. The only person who's ever offered me any threat is the high divine himself." She lifted the bottle to her mouth and took a slow, deliberate taste. Brandon could just make out the expressions that crossed her face—surprise, uncertainty, intrigue. She took another guarded swallow.

"That's strong stuff," she said, clearly trying not to cough. "And it tastes like—I can't even describe it. Like a fruit that almost rotted, but then got burned in a fire instead."

"Not a bad description," he said, laughing.

She raised the bottle again, but he pulled it down before she could drink. "You shouldn't have any more. You'll be sorry in the morning."

"I've barely had any!"

"Trust me."

She held it out to him. "Then you have some. Or I swear I'll gulp the whole thing down."

It was an empty threat, because he could have wrested the bottle away from her before she managed more than a few sips, but he took it from her hand anyway. "Oh, all right. One drink."

"And then I'll have one more. And then we'll be done because—you're right. I can already feel it."

He put the bottle to his mouth, unable to ignore the fact that her lips had touched the rim just moments before. If he was going to get drunk on anything tonight, he knew, it would not be the wine. He held the liquid on his tongue for a moment, savoring its rich and mournful taste, then let it scald down his throat. Not as good as his father's, he thought, but potent anyway.

"That'll warm you up on a cold night," he said, setting the bottle down between them.

"So is this how you spent your day off?" she asked. She had leaned forward again to trail her hand in the water. He saw the faint ripples from the movement of her fingers under the surface. "Stocking up on Zessin alcohol?"

"And a few other things."

"Are you homesick?"

"I wasn't—until I got there."

"What else did you buy?"

"Some spices for the cook, if she wants to try them. Some food in the market. And a present for you."

"For me? How delightful. I love presents."

He reached into the rucksack again, finding the zippered interior pocket where he had carefully stowed the chazissa. He had insisted that the shopkeeper wrap it in two layers of fabric to protect the charms against the jostling of travel, so what he handed over to Villette was a lumpy parcel of worn cloth.

She took it a bit gingerly, shaking the water off her fingers. "And will I know what I'm looking at when I open this?"

"I think so, yes."

She slowly peeled back the layers to reveal the coiled chazissa inside, the white charms nesting against each other as if the miniature goddesses were whispering secrets in each other's tiny ears. She caught her breath and stilled her hands and sat there absolutely motionless, transfixed.

The silence stretched on too long for Brandon. "It's a cycle chazissa," he said anxiously. "Twelve pendants, each one made of cherloshe. I thought—I don't know how often you need to eat one—but this would last you a year, maybe."

"*Brandon,*" she breathed, staring down at her lap. She still hadn't looked at him or even moved. "I can't tell you—this is *amazing.*"

"But then I started to worry," he said. He could tell he was talking too much, too fast. "Does the maid search your room? Do the priests? Is there somewhere you can hide it? Because it won't do you much good if there isn't."

Villette nodded slowly. "There is. In the bedroom down the hall from mine, behind an old armoire. They search *my* room on a regular basis, but never that one."

"That's good, then," was all he could think to say.

She lifted the cord by two fingers and held the necklace up to examine it by starlight. The twelve white charms seemed to generate their own luminescence, as if they really might harbor divinity. "But *this* is so precious I might have to divide it into parts and hide it in several spots. In the spare bedroom. In the garden. In a little glass jar that I drop into the fish pond."

"Don't get any of the charms wet," he said instantly. "They'll dissolve."

She laughed, still admiring the chazissa as it dangled from her fingertips. "Maybe that's what I'll try next time," she said. "Melting one in a glass of water first."

"Tastes terrible."

"I promise I won't mind."

He wasn't sure how to reply to that, so he just said, "Well, good."

A moment more she studied the charms, then she slipped the chazissa over her head and tucked it under her clothing. "Help me up," she said.

Brandon scrambled to his feet. Despite her obvious pleasure, he felt obscurely disappointed, as if he had expected her to show more emotion, more relief, more gratitude. As if he had expected her to look at him as her defender. Her savior. The most important person in her world.

To cover his uncharitable thoughts, he extended a hand and said, "I thought you were going to have another drink of wine."

"Oh, I am." With one hand, she grasped the neck of the bottle, and with the other, she took hold of Brandon and let him pull her to her feet. Her fingers were cool against his warm palm. Without releasing him, she raised her eyes to his and took a long slow pull from the bottle.

"Careful," he said, using his free hand to take the wine away from her. "You'll be sick."

Her fingers clung to his; she came one dizzying step closer. He was enveloped in a heady mix of seagrass and honeysuckle scents. "I can't be sick," she whispered. "I am *saved.* I am ecstatic. I am glorious."

And she leaned in and kissed him on the mouth.

It was the end of one life as he had known it and the beginning of another. She tasted like desperation and euphoria, starlight and fire, mystery and cruelty and defiance and hope. Still holding the bottle in one hand, he crushed her close, feeling the heat of her skin and the soft curves of her body. He kissed her again and again, but every time he pulled back, she lifted her face for more.

"I don't know how I'm going to do it," he whispered gathering her even tighter, staring down at her with a madman's conviction. "But I'm going to get you free of this place."

She kissed him one more time. "I know you are."

A week later, a delegation from the temple arrived. Brandon had been sleeping during the high divine's previous visits, but this time he was determined to be standing guard when the cleric was on the premises. He knew he couldn't protect Villette from the high divine's machinations, but he thought she might feel better if she could see that Brandon was present—unable to help her, maybe, but watching over her nonetheless.

So he'd told Finley to wake him as soon as the head priest arrived. "I've never seen him close up," he told her. "I'm curious."

"He's just an old Cordelano man."

"A *powerful* old Cordelano man," Brandon corrected. "That makes him special."

She'd shrugged, but promised. Nonetheless, Brandon slept lightly in case she was too careless to keep her word. He had just stirred on his bed, wondering if he had heard the sound of new arrivals, when someone pounded on his door.

"Wake up—he's here," Finley called. Less than two minutes later, he was in the hallway with Finley and Nadder when Abe opened the doors to the arriving delegation.

Three figures swept in with ceremonial pomp. Two—a man and a woman—were dressed in the dark livery of temple guards. The third wore an ivory robe heavily embroidered with stylized quatrefoils, and glanced around with an air of supercilious command. But he was neither old nor Cordelano. Brandon would have put him down as a mixed-blood Chibani who was about forty years of age. He had very blue eyes in a very pale face and a smile that suggested he enjoyed seeing people in pain.

"That's not the high divine," whispered Finley, who waited between Brandon and Nadder as they stood at strict attention.

"I know," Brandon whispered back. "I've seen him at the temple before. He's the secretary of the sanctuary."

"Michalo," Nadder named him. "If the high divine died suddenly, he'd be in charge."

"Let's hope the high divine doesn't die," Brandon muttered, and was rewarded by Finley's snort of amusement.

The secretary paused halfway across the atrium to glance at the guards. "I'm here to see dona Villette," he said. "Could someone tell me where she might be found?"

Brandon only stepped forward because he wanted an excuse to be present during Michalo's conversation with Villette. Otherwise, he never would have done anything to draw the secretary's attention. "She's in the garden. I'll show you the way."

Brandon led the visitor down the arched hallway and into the enclosure. It was a beautiful afternoon, with a hazy cloud cover preventing the sun from generating an uncomfortable level of heat. Villette must have persuaded Nadder or Abe to set two of the metal chairs on either side of the pond, and she sat in the one facing the door. She was dressed in some pale, floaty fabric that made her look fragile and sweet, and she didn't bother to stand as Michalo marched her way. Brandon took a position just under the canopy, a shadowed spot that he hoped rendered him almost invisible while allowing him to overhear every word.

"Oh, it's you," Villette said, making no attempt to hide her disdain. "Was the high divine so unnerved by our last conversation that he didn't have the courage to face me again?"

Michalo sank gracefully into the opposite chair and lounged back, completely at ease. "I don't think it takes courage to face one selfish, recalcitrant girl," he replied. "He has so many duties more important than cajoling you."

Villette laughed. "Ah, that will deflate my vanity! And here I've been thinking that the world itself will end if I don't do everything the priesthood requires."

Michalo touched the tips of his fingers together and studied her over his hands. "You are certainly valuable—or you could be," he answered. "But you are not our only opportunity."

"Your only commodity, you mean. Your only—*thing* to be used and discarded."

"Nobody wants to discard you," Michalo said mildly. "On the contrary, all of us wish you to live a long, healthy, productive life."

She offered him a smile of such rage and hatred that Brandon wondered that even the arrogant Michalo didn't cower before it. "I know you do," she said. "Which is why, every night, I contemplate ending my life and destroying all your dreams."

Brandon's head jerked up and his heart nearly stopped. Villette thought about killing herself? Every night? Did she have a weapon that could do the job? Did she have the cold nerve and iron resolve to carry out her threat? He couldn't bear to entertain the thought.

"You won't do that," Michalo said with gentle certainty. "You would much rather live to see how frantic we become when you spite us."

Her laugh was surprised and genuine. "I would much rather live," she agreed, "but in a world where I do not have to care about what you think or say or want from me."

"Unfortunately," said Michalo, "that is not the world we find ourselves in."

Villette shrugged and glanced away from him, letting her eyes wander around the shrubs and bushes. Brandon thought her glance rested on him as he stood, glowering, under the linen canopy, but if so, it was just for a moment. She made no other attempt at conversation; her attitude made it clear that she had already dismissed Michalo from her thoughts.

Michalo sat there a few minutes, as if passing the time in companionable silence, then he roused himself and sat up. "Well, you know why I am here," he said. "Let's get it over with."

Now Brandon was sure of it; Villette flicked a glance in his direction before turning her attention to Michalo. "And if I refuse?"

Michalo's voice was weary. "Oh, must we go through this every time? I have two temple guards with me, and I cannot think your household staff would rally to your defense. Do not make me take by violence what I would much rather take by consent."

She regarded him steadily. "I wonder if it is possible that you understand how very much I hate you," she said.

"I know that you do," he said. "I wonder if you understand how impossible it is that this can progress in any other way. Now give me your hand."

Another second or two she glared at him, then she abruptly extended her arm. Michalo rose and crossed to her side, pulling a little bundle from a pocket of his robe. The items he shook out were too small for Brandon to see from this distance, but he saw the effects.

Michalo touched something to Villette's fingertip and a bright dot of red welled up. The secretary blotted the blood with a square of fabric that he carefully folded and slipped back in the packet. He handed another bit of cloth to Villette, and she pressed it against her finger as she dropped her hand to her lap.

"All done," Michalo said. "As always, thank you for your patience and generosity."

Villette did not answer. She had turned her head and now she was gazing down at the fish pond, watching the shapes flit by. Michalo seemed to give up on the notion of any further conversation, because he returned the small bundle to his pocket and headed back to the house without another word.

Brandon fell in step behind him, but in truth he was so shocked he almost could not move his feet. Blood? They were cutting open Villette's body and taking her *blood?* Why would the temple of Cordelan need such a thing—demand such a thing—hold Villette prisoner for such a reason? She had told him that the temple officials tested her blood, but somehow he had not realized how exactly they obtained it. He still had no idea what they were looking for in its ruby depths.

And he hoped with a ferocity that left him dizzy that the cherloshe in Zessaya's amulet concealed whatever treasure they hoped to find.

As soon as Michalo entered the atrium, he nodded at the temple guards and said, "Search her room." Wordlessly, they climbed the stairs and pushed open the door to Villette's bedchamber.

Michalo dropped into a chair by the table where the guards often sat to have dinner. Everyone else had dispersed, so Brandon was the only other person in the atrium when Michalo glanced around as if he was bored. The secretary motioned Brandon over.

"You're the new guard, aren't you?" Michalo asked.

"Yes, patri."

"You've got the look of a Zessin man. Are you from the islands?"

"I am."

"How long have you been employed by the temple?"

"Almost two years."

"Like the work?"

"The best job I've ever had."

Michalo nodded. "And how long have you been on this assignment?"

"About five weeks now."

"What do you think of your charge?"

Brandon let his voice hold the faintest note of surprise. "I—don't think of her, patri. I just watch the house."

Michalo gave a little grunt that Brandon couldn't read as either satisfaction or displeasure. "She is widely considered a beautiful woman."

Brandon kept his eyes respectfully on the secretary's face, but the phrasing made him wildly curious about the composition of Michalo's right-hand bracelet. Probably gold through and through. A man with no interest in women. "That's not for me to notice. I just watch the house," he repeated.

Michalo regarded him steadily. "She has a reputation as someone who tries to make friends with all her guards. Develop personal relationships. Has she made any overtures to you?"

Brandon met Michalo's intent blue eyes with an unwavering gaze of his own. Strange, that midnight kiss with Villette did not render him stupid and stuttering, as he would have expected; it made him steadier, more confident, more resolved. "I think we've exchanged twenty words. One night she asked if I was cold. One day I helped her move a piece of furniture, and she said thank you. Another time she asked if I had any bread she could throw to the fish. I don't think we've had any other conversation."

The degree of specificity seemed to reassure Michalo, because he relaxed into his chair. "She can be a rude one, that's certain," the secretary said. "But she can also be charming. Even the high divine will admit that, when she exerts herself, she can be delightful."

"I'm sure the high divine talks to her more often than I do," Brandon said.

"Well, if she ever does start to favor you," said Michalo. "If she starts telling you stories about her life, you should know that everything she says is a lie. Everything. She has spun a fantastical tale for some of the other guards and they were foolish enough to believe it. Don't you make the same mistake."

Brandon hesitated a moment. "If I knew why she had been placed here. What her offense was. It would make it easier to know when she was lying."

Michalo nodded. "I understand that. Unfortunately, these are matters that are too dangerous to be discussed except with a few priests and Council members. Just know that she has contemplated actions that would bring the whole city of Corcannon to its knees. And if she leaves this place, she will attempt those actions again."

"I understand," Brandon said. "Thank you for warning me."

Just then, the two temple guards came clattering down the stairs, and Michalo stood up. "It was important that you know."

The female guard approached the secretary. "Nothing suspicious in her room, patri."

"Good," said Michalo. "Then let's go." He strode toward the door, the temple guards following in his wake. Brandon followed them outside so he could lock the gate behind them, then he trudged back to the house.

He wondered what fantastical tale Villette had told the other guards when she was trying to convince them to help her escape. He knew exactly why Michalo had mentioned that story to him—to sow a seed of doubt in Brandon's mind in case Villette ever tried to win him over. *The things she is saying are so ridiculous they can't possibly be true. Don't be stupid enough to believe her!*

One of them was clearly lying—and in the biggest, boldest terms, not just with subtle gradations of the truth. Michalo claimed Villette had evil intentions toward the entire city. Villette maintained that the temple wanted to use her in some unspecified but degrading fashion. It seemed impossible that they were talking about the same thing, even from opposite perspectives.

A holy man would seem to have less incentive to prevaricate. The high divine was supposed to be Cordelan's representative in the city, a man of wisdom and honor and good intent. Cordelan had united the scattered lands to create a wealthy and fertile continent that would nourish and sustain all his people, and the cleric who served Cordelan similarly had the welfare of every living creature as his primary goal.

And yet . . .

Why would Michalo call her valuable? Why would he describe her as an opportunity? Why would he complain that she would not do as she was asked? If she had tried to destroy the city, as Michalo asserted, that would be a reason to keep her incarcerated and powerless—but it would not be a reason to keep returning to her, trying to force her to cooperate in a scheme she clearly resisted.

If she had tried to destroy the city, the temple would have destroyed her. She had tried to *withhold* something, something that the high divine wanted.

Something in her blood.

No, Brandon was sure, whatever her unlikely tale might be, it was true. And he was more committed to her than ever.

Chapter Nineteen:
Pietro

It wasn't long before Stollo convinced Pietro to begin doing volunteer work on the eastern edge of the city. The worst part of town.

Pietro had continued to show up regularly at the temple's distribution center, in part because he didn't know how else to spend his days. Now that he wasn't wandering the length and breadth of the continent, he no longer had travel as his occupation; he needed some kind of purpose. The city library had a gloriously diverse collection of books, and he had made reading a staple of his evenings. Additionally, he had started to cook elaborate meals, an activity that had never before interested him in the slightest, and shopping for ingredients could take even longer than preparing any dish. And every once in a while, Cody dropped by to spend an hour talking or to take Pietro on an improbable tour of some unfamiliar part of the city. It was through Cody's efforts that Pietro had finally managed to acquire a few more furnishings for his apartment, including a comfortable sofa and a kitchen table and chairs.

But many hours still stretched out before him, empty and echoing. And lonely.

Stollo was the easiest of companions, always cheerful, always filled with so much enthusiasm that he never required an infusion of energy from anyone else. They had fallen into the habit of going out for dinner once or twice a week, and over their meals they would debate philosophy, dissect history, and discuss books. Now and then they touched on religion, but in an abstract fashion, never talking about the activities of the current temple administration. Nonetheless, Pietro came away with the impression that Stollo didn't agree with many of the high divine's policies or practices. Stollo was a reformer who believed the temple should serve the poorest and most vulnerable populations, regardless of cost. Harlo tended to take a conservative approach to problems—until he embraced shocking, extreme solutions. Even Stollo, Pietro thought, would not approve of some of the high divine's actions.

During one of their outings, Stollo casually mentioned that he spent his free hours volunteering at a school in the eastern slum. Pietro tried unsuccessfully to keep the astonishment from his face. He had lived in the city most of his life and spent only a handful of uncomfortable hours in that part of town.

"Assuming you survive your trips there," he said, "what do you do?"

"Whatever they need. Sometimes teachers ask me to meet with a student who is struggling to read or to understand simple math. Sometimes they ask me to talk to a whole classroom about how to run a business or how to present themselves to strangers when they're looking for employment. Sometimes I just sit in the hallway and talk to anyone who seems to need a conversation."

Pietro nodded. He was familiar with that last part of the job. He had provided plenty of impromptu counseling to teen girls or middle-aged men who approached him with some kind of casual, innocuous remark, acting as if they didn't need insight from anybody. He had often thought this was the most valuable work he had ever done. "And this is part of your temple duties?"

"Oh, no. I go on my own."

Pietro shook his head, holding back a smile. "You are clearly trying to enter the lists as the holiest and kindest of men."

Stollo laughed. "No! I assure you, I am as selfish and mean-spirited as the best of them! Just this morning I was very put out when the laundress didn't arrive in time with my clean robes and I had to put on the same one I wore yesterday."

"But then you reminded yourself that you had clothes and shoes and decent food and a warm bed, when so many don't, and your mood instantly improved."

"Well," Stollo said. "Yes."

"And you didn't actually rebuke the laundress."

"Of course not! She tries so hard. And she's practically a child still."

"I hold to my original opinion."

"You could join me some afternoon, if you like," Stollo said. "They always need more volunteers. And you're good with people."

"I'm good with people when I'm not fearing for my life."

"Nonsense. You'll be with me. No one ever harms a priest."

That was pretty close to the truth—Pietro couldn't remember the last time anyone wearing the temple quatrefoil had been attacked in the city. And it was false to imply that he was worried about his safety—these days he was so conscious of the ephemerality of life that the specter of death seemed like a familiar and unalarming companion. "I just never considered going down there before," he admitted. "It just seemed like a place to stay away from."

"It's not," said Stollo. "It's a place where you can do real good."

So Pietro had accompanied Stollo on his next outing to the eastern neighborhood, a place so ramshackle and tumbledown it looked like it had been hit by a localized quake. He had entered the sagging brick building that served as a school and watched several dozen ragged children swarm around Stollo, clamoring excitedly for his attention. He had observed Stollo laugh and extend his arms, trying with a single gesture to embrace them all. He had thought, *I was never this good. Even when I was a good man.*

Pietro had done his part, too, reading stories aloud to the class and conducting private tutoring sessions in the hallway with young boys who seemed less interested in learning how to read than in holding the undivided attention of an adult. Was he having any effect on their well-being, doing any good at all? It was impossible to tell. Yet the work soothed him. At least he could say he was doing no harm. That was more than he could claim about some of his activities in the past.

At any rate, he liked the way this new commitment shaped his life and became part of his routine. Now he was spending three days a week at the temple distribution center, two days at the school. That meant that he saw Stollo five times every week, though they didn't end every one of their outings with a meal. In fact, there were many days at the distribution center that they only exchanged a few words before one of them took off for another appointment.

Well. Before Stollo took off. Pietro didn't really have other appointments.

"I'm afraid you look on me as a charity case," he said lightly over dinner one night.

Stollo swallowed a big bite of fish and showed disbelief. "How so?"

Pietro made a vague gesture toward his own body. "You worry that I am pitiful and lonely, with no other friends, and so you kindly spend half your days with me, ensuring that I am occupied." He forked up a slice of meat. "And fed."

Stollo laughed heartily. "I think of you as a man who could make friends anywhere he wanted," he answered. "For some reason, right now, you have decided not to. And for some reason, right now, you have decided my company is safe. I'm honored to be the one you've chosen as a friend."

The meat still speared on his fork, Pietro stared at Stollo for a long moment. "How odd," he said at last.

"That I enjoy your company? You're educated and articulate, interested in everything, knowledgeable about many things, insightful and humorous. Who wouldn't enjoy conversations with such a man?"

Pietro chewed his food while he thought that over. "No," he said at last. "How odd that you have so exactly described a state I was not even aware of being in. Deliberately closed off from most of my fellow men. When that is not my natural state."

Stollo took a sip from his beer and eyed Pietro over the rim, clearly trying to decide whether or not to say something. "I have always thought," he said at last, "you had a reason for coming back to Corcannon. But it wasn't a reason you liked."

Pietro considered that, too. "I left so abruptly," he said. "I wanted to see what had changed while I was away." Stollo waited silently, so Pietro sighed and went on. "There's more to it, of course. But unfortunately, I don't think I can talk about it."

"I mean, I know you were in love with someone. And you feel like he betrayed you."

Pietro flinched back, but Stollo kept his gaze steady. "True on both counts," Pietro said. "But it wasn't just that he betrayed me. It's that he did something—unforgivable. And not to me."

"Are you going to see him while you're here? Is that why you came back? To tell him what you think of him?"

"Oh, he knows what I think of him."

"That didn't answer the question."

Pietro took a taste of his wine. "I don't want to see him," he said. "I admit—now and then—I've placed myself in venues where he might—it's possible he could have seen me, or someone who knew me once might see me and report back to him—"

"The temple."

Pietro caught his breath. "What?"

"You were a priest. Obviously."

Pietro managed a long, slow exhalation. "How long have you suspected that?"

"From the minute I met you."

"Why didn't you say anything?"

Stollo shrugged. "It was pretty clear you didn't want to talk about it. I don't care what you did with your life before. We all have a past, and lots of us are trying to leave that past behind."

"Though the past is like a shadow," Pietro said. "It's always attached to you."

"So what brought you back to the city?" Stollo asked again.

"I was in Oraki. And there was a quake. A small one, but I could feel the ground shudder beneath my feet. And it frightened me."

Stollo nodded. "There have been more quakes in the past few months than I can ever remember before."

"Ten years ago," Pietro said. "That's the last time they were so frequent. And so strong."

"So?"

Pietro drained the last of his wine in two long swallows. "So that's why I came back."

One evening when they left the school, Stollo needed to return directly to the temple, so Pietro headed back to his lodgings alone. The first chugger to come clicking along was the one that would make the entire loop around the city at a maddeningly slow pace, but Pietro wasn't in a hurry and it had been a while since he made this particular journey. So he climbed on and secured a seat by the window and prepared himself for a very long ride.

But a few stops later he was pushing through the knot of standing riders who were holding onto the overhead rail near the exit. "Excuse me—please, I need to get off—excuse me!" After some grumbling, they let him through, and Pietro stepped off into the Zessin district.

He'd rarely spent much time here, so he took a moment just to look around. It was strange to see so many people with similar features and coloring, but familiar, too, from the time he had spent wandering the islands. He caught the scent of specialty spices and the aroma of cooking meat, and he took in a deep, appreciative breath. It didn't smell exactly right without the seasoning of the ever-present salt breeze, but it still made him hungry. Maybe he'd stop at the outdoor food market and pick up a meal to take back to his rooms tonight.

He strolled slowly down the short road that seemed to form the heart of the district, glancing in store windows and pausing to admire a few lingering purple blossoms from a flowering bush. Lovely color, terrible scent. A few feet away was a clothing and accessory shop, so he pushed the door open and went in.

He had had some vague idea of buying one of the loose sets of cotton shirts and belted trousers that served as standard attire for islander men. But as soon as he noticed the jewelry counter in back, he realized what he had really come here to find.

He made his way to the back of the shop to examine the chazissas on display. Did he need Zessaya in her martial pose, a spear clutched in her hand and a look of ferocity on her face? He was somewhat more inclined to the goddess in her comforting mood, cradling a baby to her breast. Cordelan knew he'd had very little in the way of comforting in recent years—and none at all from the god himself.

A middle-aged man came over to see if he needed help. Automatically, Pietro checked out the man's bracelets. Shopkeeper, according to the circlet on the left hand; married man with four children, according to the right.

"I'm interested in a chazissa," Pietro told him.

The shopkeeper tried not to look skeptical. "For a friend?"

Pietro smiled slightly. "For myself. I had one and then—I gave it to someone who needed the goddess's intervention more than I did."

"You do not look like an island man."

"No, but I spent some time there and grew to respect Zessaya very much."

"Oh? Where were you living?"

Pietro listed the small towns he had visited, and the shopkeeper grew friendlier as it became clear Pietro wasn't lying. They even found a few people they knew in common, at least by reputation.

"Which pose speaks to you?" the shopkeeper finally asked.

"I have been trying to decide," Pietro said.

"Is there a particular challenge you're facing? I find that when people can figure out the focus of their lives, it helps them choose a chazissa."

"Very wise," Pietro approved. "Let's see, my challenge." He laughed softly. "Coming to an understanding of the way the world works. Sorting out the true from the false. Recovering my faith that there is a sense of order to the days. Is there a pose for that?"

But the other man was reaching into his case and pulling out one of the leather cords hung with a cherloshe charm. He held it up so the small stone figurine was at Pietro's eye level. The goddess had her head bent down so that her eyes appeared to be reading a tiny book that she held open in her two white hands.

"The pose of knowledge," the shopkeeper said. "It's very popular among students and teachers, but I have also found that it appeals to sojourners such as yourself." Clearly he had been checking out Pietro's bracelets just as Pietro had been studying his.

Pietro closed his hand around the little charm and instantly felt better. "Most excellent! A perfect choice!"

Pietro wouldn't even let the shopkeeper wrap the necklace for him; he just slipped the cord over his head and tucked the amulet under his shirt. It felt briefly cool against his skin, but quickly warmed to his own body temperature.

"You will have to write the friend you gave your chazissa to, and tell him that you have found one even better," the shopkeeper said.

"I'll have to do that," Pietro said. Against his inclination, against his will, against all his better instincts, he found himself digging for information in the most casual voice. "I keep thinking he might come to Corcannon someday. He's an islander, so he'd probably end up in this district. Is there anybody who keeps track of who comes and goes? Who might be able to tell me if he's in town?"

"Most islanders stop by Zessaya's temple pretty soon after they arrive. The guardian, she'd probably know if your friend was here."

"The temple guardian! Of course. I'll check with her. Thank you most sincerely."

"You're welcome. Come back if you decide you need another pose!"

Pietro laughed and headed for the door. "And I just might!"

He stepped outside, striding off confidently even though he had forgotten to ask where the temple might be. But after a few steps, he slowed and then stopped, pausing to lean against a shop wall as he reconsidered what he was doing.

If Aussen's family had sent her to the city in the company of a trusted friend, it made sense that this friend would take her to the island district—and that Aussen's family would eventually show up and start looking for her here. If Pietro had figured that out, Jayla undoubtedly had as well. The odds seemed very slim, but it wasn't out of the realm of possibility that Jayla would drop by the temple at the very moment Pietro was talking to the guardian, trying to look all innocent as he asked about the child in Jayla's keeping.

He did not want to know where Aussen was. That was a piece of knowledge so dangerous that just having it in his possession would put Aussen at incalculable risk. He would turn around right now and catch the next transport home. He would maintain ignorance, and Aussen would be safe.

But would Corcannon be safe?

It was a long time before he could force himself to stand away from the wall and turn his feet back toward the gridway, back toward more familiar streets, back toward the false sanctuary of home.

Chapter Twenty: Pietro

I've found a new restaurant," Pietro told Stollo two nights later as they were packing up at the distribution center. "I have a young courier friend and he knows the most *amazing* places. This one isn't much to look at, but the food is outstanding."

"I'd love to go! Not tonight, though, sorry. Next time?"

"Of course."

Stollo headed toward the door, then turned back with a smile. "A young courier friend?" he repeated. "Should I be jealous of how you're spending your time?"

Pietro's breath caught. Stollo was teasing, of course—he was laughing, wasn't he?—but there might be a shade of anxiety in his warm eyes. "I'm probably forty-five years older than Cody, and so decrepit he's always ready to catch me if I stumble," Pietro said roundly. "I hardly think he views me as a likely prospect."

"Sometimes you're surprised to find out who's attracted to you."

Now it took some effort to still the pounding of his heart. "I suppose that's true. I'll have to start paying attention to all my casual interactions."

"Not a bad idea," Stollo said. He smiled again and strode off to get the center ready to shut down for the evening.

Pietro shambled out into the night, feeling tipsy as a teenager who'd misjudged his tolerance for alcohol. Oh, pointless to pretend he hadn't felt a growing affection for Stollo, but he had managed to keep the feeling in a small woven basket inside his heart, an object too compact to take up much room but decorative enough to catch his attention every time he peered in that direction. He was too old and too sad and too damaged to be pursuing romances right now. Stollo would be much better off with someone whose heart was as generous and whole as his own.

But it was hard not to feel a certain triumphant glee at the notion that someone might love him—impossible not to feel marked by a peculiar radiance that was both universal and entirely unique to him. Of course, he would not—should not—act upon any offer that Stollo might extend. But how delicious to think that such an offer might be made. That someone wanted to make it. And Stollo, of all people! Anyone would be lucky to have caught the attention of such a man.

He was so happy he almost walked right in front of a private sprinter that came speeding down the gridway just as Pietro was trying to cross. "Hey!" someone called, and a stranger jerked him out of the way as the vehicle came to a screeching, bumpy halt. The driver leaned through the window to shout invective, but Pietro just shook his head and mouthed an apology.

"Thank you so much," he said to the man who had saved him. "I don't know what I was thinking."

The stranger was about Stollo's age and looked like a banker or some other respectable soul. He shook his head. "You need to be careful," he said. "Those gridcars can't stop as quickly as you think."

Pietro thanked him again and continued on his way home, both shaken and sobered. He wondered if this was some kind of broader message from the gods themselves, warning him that his carelessness could usher in the end of the world. Or merely emphasizing that he didn't have the right to happiness any more. At any rate, he paid strict attention to every noise and movement for the rest of his journey home, and nothing else untoward happened.

Until he unlocked the door of his small apartment, walked in, and found Harlo sitting at his kitchen table.

For a long time, they merely stared at each other. Pietro was too dumbfounded to be slammed by any of the emotions he would have expected, such as pain or longing or despair. Harlo had aged visibly in the intervening decade. Pietro could see marks of time in the sparseness of the white hair, the gauntness of the severe cheeks, the slight tremor in the thin, beautiful hands. He wondered what changes Harlo noted in his own face; he could hardly remember what he had looked like ten years ago. Inside, he felt so old he would not have been surprised to learn a century had passed.

It seemed Harlo would not be the one to speak first, so Pietro finally shut the door, crossed the room, and sat down across from his visitor. Not too close; he had an urgent feeling that he must keep his distance.

"Somebody must have recognized me at the temple."

"The library, actually," Harlo replied. His voice was exactly as Pietro remembered, resonant and soothing. A voice you would trust to tell you the truth as handed down by the god himself. "Renato. You remember him?"

"Of course."

"He followed you home one night."

"How enterprising of him."

"That was three weeks ago. Until then, I had no idea you were back in the city."

"I've only been here a couple of months."

"I waited," Harlo said. "I was sure you would get in touch with me. But you didn't."

Pietro spread his hands. Not much to say to that. It was obviously true.

Finally, Harlo went on. "If not to see me again, why did you return to Corcannon?"

Pietro certainly wasn't going to give the answer he'd given Stollo. He certainly wasn't going to talk about tremors in the ground and what might happen if the continent tried to shake itself apart. "I'm still trying to work that out for myself."

"I looked for you, you know. It was months before I was convinced that you had deserted the city altogether."

"I left the next day."

Harlo went on as if he hadn't spoken. "Of course, I feared the worst. I thought—I had the men check—any corpse that showed up in an alley or a morgue, I made sure it wasn't you. For a whole year, Pietro."

Pietro wondered if he was supposed to feel sorry for Harlo and his deep grief or if he was supposed to be moved by the level of devotion that implied. "Doesn't Cordelan teach us that we should be at peace in our souls before we embark on the journey toward death?" he asked. "I am so far from being at peace that I will doubtless live forever."

Harlo's sorrowful expression looked entirely genuine. "I could not believe you would hurt me that way," he said softly. "I thought you loved me."

"And I thought you wouldn't murder children," Pietro snapped. "I suppose we were both wrong."

Harlo gripped the table. "I did not murder that boy."

"I saw you do it."

"I employed him as a tool to save us all. How can you not understand that?"

"I cannot understand that even a god could require such a sacrifice."

Harlo gazed at him a moment in silence, his face slowly losing the softness of grief and taking on the hardness of conviction. "You say you have been in Corcannon for a couple of months," he said. "You must have felt them. The quakes. Have they woken you up at night? Shaken you off your feet as you were walking down the road? Have you thought, 'How strong was that one? Has it knocked over a few buildings? Compromised the gridway?' Have you wondered, 'When will the next one come? Will it be even more powerful?' Have you asked yourself, 'How can I make the tremors stop before the whole city tumbles to the ground—before the continent itself is ripped into pieces?' Have you once asked those questions of yourself?"

Pietro didn't respond. But he had, of course, and Harlo could see the answer in his eyes. The high divine leaned closer.

"I ask myself those questions every day. I am the voice of the god, the human incarnation of his will. And I do not believe he wants to destroy the very land that he so painstakingly put together. Which means he wants me to save it in any way possible."

Pietro's breath was coming shallowly, but he was trying to maintain a relaxed pose, a slightly bored attitude. "And have any ways presented themselves to you?"

Harlo shook his head, and now his face showed real distress. "There is only the one girl, and we cannot forfeit her. We would mortgage the future to pay for the present."

"What a reversal of policy! You allow someone to live!"

"I would sacrifice the one life to save millions of others, except we eventually would be worse off than before."

"Then abandon your policy of secrecy," Pietro suggested. "Announce to the whole city the danger that lies ahead, and urge everyone to flee now and rebuild their lives elsewhere."

Harlo leaned forward again and spoke with bitter intensity. "Move where? Rebuild what? Don't you understand, Pietro, it is not just the city that will be destroyed? The entire continent was knit together by the god's hands. If one part of it unravels, the whole place falls to pieces. Chibain separates from Marata, the islands detach and float away. The world is remade."

"The world was remade once when the god stitched it together," Pietro said stubbornly. "Why not let it return to its former state?" He flung a hand out as if pointing. "There are lands far beyond our western border where people appear to live happily and well. The Zessin people trade with them all the time."

Harlo nodded, but he wore a sardonic expression. "Oh yes. Thousands of people living on hundreds of islands, none of them bigger than thirty square miles. Not one of them with a society as rich and sophisticated as ours. Not one of them with our industry or our culture. Their small size constrains their progress, Pietro. But the god *enabled* us. He left us with technological gifts that we still don't entirely understand. If this land falls apart, you will see our civilization fade in a generation."

"You don't know that."

Harlo cut him off. "But before that," he said, "you will see destruction on a scale you have not imagined. Have you ever sailed the eastern seas? Visited the ruined lands?"

"No."

"Well, I have. Years ago, when I was a young priest with grand ambitions. I had some of these very same conversations with the high divine of the time. He thought that I might someday rise in the ranks and take up his own office, and he believed it was essential that I understand how very serious his responsibilities were. He hired a ship and sent me out to tour those broken islands. Dozens of them. Some of them no bigger than the Quatrefoil itself. All of them—" He waved a hand. "Lifeless. Black. Beaches like melted stone."

"What does that have to do with—"

Harlo's frame was practically vibrating with intensity. "That was the *first* continent that Cordelan attempted to sew together from many small pieces. Did you know that? No? Very few people do. But something went wrong—we can only guess what—and the land tore itself apart. Leaving absolute destruction in its wake."

Pietro's body hurt from his attempt to hold it still, to keep his hands open and relaxed on the table. His stomach had clamped down to a small hot mass of boiling pain. It could not be true. And yet a part of him knew it was. If the quakes were not stopped, the entire continent could be destroyed. *One life to save millions of lives,* Harlo had said.

If Aussen's death could protect the world—

No.

Pietro finally managed to speak, keeping his voice as even as possible. "You have a very hard choice. I do not envy you."

Harlo studied him. "And yet you judge me."

"It is not my place to judge."

"You forsake me."

That suddenly they shifted from the apocalyptic to the personal. It was almost a relief. "I could not endure what I had learned about you."

"And I was not sure I would endure your leaving."

Pietro's voice was sharper than he wished. "Yet I hear you have found ways to console yourself."

That surprised a crack of laughter from the older man. "What, you won't sully your pure soul by coming to see me of your own free will, but you'll gossip about me with strangers?"

"I didn't ask for information," Pietro said stiffly. "Someone supplied it in the course of conversation."

"I hope the description was sufficiently titillating. Of a handsome young man eager to please a powerful old cleric. I hope you had a hard time dismissing the images from your mind."

Pietro was stunned. "You're angry."

Harlo spread his hands with his usual graceful elegance. "Angry! Hurt!

Bewildered! You were *everything* to me! And you told me you despised me and you vanished without a trace. That is a wound I will carry with me to the grave. Forgive me if I cannot help wanting to wound you in return."

Pietro rested his elbow on the table and dropped his face in his hand. He was so weary. He was so sad. He was so confused. "You don't have to bother with that," he said in a low voice. "I have never recovered from the blow I suffered that night."

"Damage done to all contestants," Harlo said. "And no victors in sight."

They were silent for a moment. Pietro wanted to demand *Why are you still here?* Yet part of him wanted to plead *Don't leave.* He couldn't think clearly with Harlo in the room. Maybe he didn't want to think. Maybe thinking had always been his problem.

He straightened up and said, "So what are you going to do now?"

Harlo shook his head slowly. For a moment, he looked even older than Pietro felt. "I have no idea. I cannot see my way clear. And—it's even worse than you know."

"I don't see how that could be possible."

Harlo said simply, "They're back."

No explanation, no details, but Pietro instantly knew what Harlo meant, and he felt the bony hands of dread coil around his throat. "The Reversionists?" he managed.

Harlo nodded. "And they're trying to kill her."

"I thought they had all been identified and disbanded! *Years* ago!"

"So did I. I thought the histories had been erased from our archives. Yet someone must have told someone who told someone who passed the knowledge down."

"Do you suspect a member among the priesthood?"

Harlo shrugged, his face showing infinite weariness. "Possibly, although there are only a handful of us who know the full truth. Maybe a dozen members of the Council families also know, and they may have told others. Whether inside or outside the temple, there appear to be fanatics on the loose."

"But do they know—do these Reversionists understand the consequences?"

Harlo's smile was bitter. "That they would be bringing about the end of the world? *You* do not truly understand, and you are more educated than most. I have no idea what they think they know or what they believe or even which god they honor. I know only that they could destroy us all, and I have no idea who they are."

Pietro took a long, slow breath, though he wasn't sure why he bothered. The entire conversation was undermining his will to live. "You have to tell her," he said. "She might—if she understands the situation—she might be a willing martyr."

"In my experience," Harlo said, "people aren't nearly as civic-minded as you'd hope. They'd much rather live for themselves than die for the good of the world."

"Would *you* do it?" Pietro challenged. "Sacrifice yourself?"

"Now that I am an old man who has already seen too much? I would lay down my life tomorrow. But when I was young and hale and had my whole existence before me? I would like to think I would give myself willingly to the requirements of the god. But I suspect I would try desperately to think of another solution."

Harlo did not turn the question back on Pietro, but he mulled it over anyway. He had been a passionate and overly dramatic youth, and the abstract idea of protecting a loved one with his life would have held a sweeping romantic appeal. "I think I would have *believed* I would do it right up until the very moment the blade came down," he said. "I would have gloried in the idea—and quailed at the execution."

"Which is why we proceed in secret." Harlo sat there for a moment, seemingly lost in thought, then shook his head and glanced around as if seeing the apartment for the first time and not finding himself particularly impressed. "Is there anything you need?"

Pietro was at a loss. "Need for what?"

"Need from here. From this place. Before we go."

"Go where?"

Harlo gazed back at him, looking as bemused as Pietro felt. "Back to the temple, of course."

"But—I'm not going back to the temple."

It was like they were speaking to each other in different languages, both incomprehensible. "But I've found you. There's no reason to keep hiding."

"I'm not hiding. I'm just living."

"But you can go on living once you're back at the temple."

"I'm not—" Pietro flattened both of his hands on the table and leaned forward, trying to speak clearly and precisely. He wasn't sure if he was laying out the argument for Harlo or himself. "I can't be a priest anymore. I don't know what I am now, but I can no longer serve Cordelan. I'm not coming back to the temple." He made himself keep his steady gaze on Harlo. "I'm not coming back to you."

Harlo held his eyes for one interminable, heartbreaking minute. The older man's face, already grooved with age, seemed to wither; his thin body shivered once, as if all his bones splintered simultaneously beneath his skin. It was not as if his expression had been optimistic before, but now it seemed to lose its last faint trace of hope, as if he had witnessed every accumulated bleakness of the human condition. He looked extinguished.

"I see," he said at last.

Pietro wanted to take it back—he wanted to promise to reconsider—he wanted to say anything, do anything, to ease that pain from Harlo's face. But he had no words. He had no solutions. He couldn't live with what he knew and he couldn't support Harlo's actions, and he honestly didn't know how to go forward from this time and place. He just knew he couldn't do it at Harlo's side.

Harlo pushed himself to his feet and Pietro leapt up, afraid the old man would topple over, dizzy from the emotional blow. But Harlo stood with his usual straight spine and squared shoulders.

"Sometimes I wonder why I try so hard to avert the end of the world," Harlo said. "Sometimes I think it's already occurred."

Chapter Twenty-one: Jayla

Although Jayla would have preferred to keep Aussen safely locked up in the Alayne mansion where no one could ever see her, that seemed unfair both to Aussen and the cook who looked after the little girl whenever Jayla was gone from the house. So on her next couple of days off, she took Aussen with her and they explored the city. They visited parks and museums, sampled food from street vendors, and even strolled through the great temple so Aussen could gawk at the high pillars and gorgeous walls.

But they never took a chugger all the way to the island district. When Jayla visited that part of town, she went alone.

Cody accompanied them on almost all of their outings. He had picked up a few words of the Zessin dialect, and Aussen had been practicing her Cordish, so they managed to have halting but enthusiastic conversations as they tried exotic new foods or wound through the flower banks in the public spaces. He even raced with her down some of the graveled paths in one of the larger parks.

"You're fast," he told her after he'd let her win. "You can be a courier one day."

"She's not going to be a courier," Jayla said.

"Why not? What *is* she going to be?"

Of course Jayla couldn't answer that. Her visits to the Zessin district had yielded her no new information, even though she always asked the temple guardian the same set of questions. *Has anyone come looking for Aussen? Have you learned anything about her family?* The guardian always gave the same replies.

Once Jayla had thought she spotted Pietro strolling down the main boulevard of the district, looking around with deep curiosity. She couldn't be sure; she had quickly ducked into an alley so he wouldn't see her, and when she peeked out again, his face was turned away. But the man she spotted had the same slim build and confident stride.

Why would Pietro have gone to that part of town if not to look for Aussen?

She had posed the question to Cody but he didn't have an answer for her, either. "You still see him, don't you?" she'd said almost accusingly.

"Sure. I like him."

"Does he ever ask about me?"

"No. And he never asks about Aussen."

"What does he want from you?"

"Friendship, I think. Do you want me to drop him? I will if you say so."

"I don't want anyone to do anything just because I asked it," she said quickly, which made him laugh. Which made her angry. "Anyway, it's *Aussen* I'm worried about," she said huffily. "I don't want him to know where she is."

"Jayla. I'm not going to tell him."

It was so hard to think it through. "Maybe it's better if you stay in touch with him. Maybe it's best if we know what's going on with him."

"That's what I always say. I like to keep track of people."

So Cody kept track of Pietro and Jayla kept track of Aussen. And Cody and Jayla kept track of each other.

It annoyed her, how much she liked Cody. And he knew it annoyed her, which amused him. He told her once she was like a feral cat sitting on top of a shattered brick wall, hissing at anyone who came too close. "Well, you're one of those big friendly dogs who runs up to total strangers and slobbers all over them," she shot back.

"That's exactly what I am," he replied enthusiastically. "I'm glad it's so obvious."

She wasn't sure exactly what he wanted of her. Maybe just friendship, as he claimed he wanted from Pietro. He never sat too close, never surprised her with a hug, never embarrassed her with compliments or declarations. But she'd met a couple of the women who shared his house with him, and she'd seen how he joked and roughhoused with them, and it was clear he treated her differently. She couldn't describe that difference exactly. But she had to admit it pleased her.

When it didn't annoy her.

But she still found herself including him any time she had a day off.

One unexpectedly cool and rainy afternoon, they decided it would be too miserable for them to enjoy their planned excursion to Chrission Lake. Cody suggested they return to his house, where Jayla could practice walking the cable, so they caught a chugger back to the warehouse district. The skies opened up and soaked them just as they disembarked, so they sprinted the last few blocks to his place. The lower level of the big building was almost deserted, since couriers were in high demand during bad weather when no one wanted to run their own errands. Cody waved at someone sitting on the far side of the large open space, but didn't pause to talk.

"I think we all need dry clothes," he said. "Will you wear one of my shirts or sweaters just to get warm?"

Jayla's instinctive reaction was to say no, because that seemed oddly intimate, but she was freezing, and Aussen was shivering. "Sure," she said casually. "That would be nice."

She tried not to be too interested in the small room that he had to himself on the third floor, but she couldn't stop herself from looking around. There was a mattress on the floor, covered with a rumpled quilt in shades of blue and green. Shelves that displayed a variety of objects, from books to small figurines to a sizable collection of antique clocks. An enormous wooden chest held shut by a padlock. And an assortment of crates that seemed to hold his clothing.

He pointed. "Clean. Dirty. Not so dirty I wouldn't wear them again. Let's see what's in the clean box."

He found a sweater for Jayla and a heavy long-sleeved shirt that would do for Aussen if they rolled up the sleeves five times and allowed the hem to hang past her knees. But she seemed more interested in another item hanging from a hook on the wall—his red courier's vest.

"You want to wear it while you're here?" he asked. When she nodded, he carefully fitted it over her shoulders and snugged it tight. It was almost as long as the shirt and practically obliterated her in a weave of scarlet.

"She is *not* going to be a courier," Jayla said again.

He paused to admire Aussen and spoke an approving word in Zessin before turning back to Jayla. "Why not? It's a respectable profession."

"Because her mother's going to find her and take her home, that's why."

"But if she doesn't?"

Jayla shook her head. "Don't say that. She has to."

Cody shrugged and let it go. "Come on. Let's go downstairs."

They had the big exercise room all to themselves, which pleased Jayla. She much preferred not having an audience when she was learning new skills and likely to look ungainly or incompetent. It was ridiculous, she knew, but felt like she already ought to be good at everything.

She was confident enough on the cable by now that she didn't need Cody to hold on to her as she made the crossing. So she took off her boots and walked the wire, back and forth, back and forth, feeling the twisted strands through her knit socks. Then she put her boots back on and practiced running on the stretched webbing. She still couldn't move as quickly as Cody, but she was faster than she'd been, and much steadier than she was on the wire. She almost thought she would be able to run the along the gridway if she ever wanted to.

While she worked on balance, Cody and Aussen indulged in faster pursuits. They first raced a few times down the short, straight center track, then they began a methodical jog around the perimeter of the building. Once Jayla was done with the wires, she fell in step behind them and began a slow, steady run of her own. It was good to feel her muscles stretch and loosen, her lungs and her heart respond to the extra demands. Her body felt strong, healthy, finely tuned. A tiny sense of euphoria began to build under her ribcage.

Cody and Aussen had pulled off the track so they could climb ropes, but Jayla was still running, when three figures burst in from the stairwell. Two were women, but Jayla wasn't sure about the third. All three wore damp street clothing and red courier vests, so Jayla assumed they were some of Cody's housemates that she hadn't met yet. They'd probably come here to work out, which meant this might be a good time for the visitors to leave. Jayla slowed down gradually, then came to a stop right next to Cody and Aussen.

The newcomers had already joined them, clustering around Aussen with friendly laughter. "Look at that! Our youngest recruit ever!" one of them exclaimed.

"We might need to get you a smaller vest, though."

"Have you learned to run the wires yet? You're so tiny you might slip through the webbing."

Aussen smiled up at them, liking the tone even if she didn't understand all the words. One of the women patted Aussen's head, glanced at Jayla, then turned her attention to Cody. She had a lanky build, ragged dark hair, an open expression, and a courier's bracelet on her left wrist. Her right-hand bracelet was pure silver, worked with an intricate floral design.

"Why don't you introduce your friends? Don't you have any manners at all?" she asked.

Cody grinned. "The courier-in-training is Aussen. The fierce young woman is Jayla. This is my sister Tokah. She lives here, because she wants my life to be miserable."

Tokah laughed. "Is it working?" She turned to give Jayla a relaxed smile. Her expression was casual, but Jayla had the sudden conviction that Tokah was hiding intense curiosity. What had Cody told his sister about his new friend? "Why would he call you fierce? You look perfectly nice to me."

"I think he's afraid of me because I threatened to beat him up once."

All three of his housemates laughed heartily at that. "Oh, see, Cody's not used to that," said one of the others. This one had a Cordelano's dark hair and skin but the stocky build usually found in Marata. "Woman are usually fawning all over Cody and telling him how adorable he is."

"That's Kammi," Cody announced. "Kammi hates me." This earned him a more-or-less affectionate punch in the arm. The motion showed off Kammi's right-hand bracelet, an exuberant swirl of silver and gold in shimmering loops and patterns. Someone who was sometimes male, sometimes female, and open to loving anybody.

"You think people hate you if they're not besotted with you," Kammi said.

"He has to be everybody's favorite," Tokah chimed in. "And if he's *not* your favorite, he'll work night and day to win you over."

Kammi gave Jayla a wide-eyed innocent glance. "Is that how he's treating *you,* Jayla?"

"Jayla's not good at silly banter," Cody interjected.

"But she can speak, can't she?" Kammi asked. "Is Cody being extra nice to you?"

"I was under the impression Cody was extra nice to everyone."

That earned a chorus of *oohs* from Kammi and Tokah. "You keep being difficult," Tokah recommended. "It's good for him to have to try a little harder."

Cody shook his head and gestured at the third new arrival. "This is Rovyn. She's much kinder than Kammi and my sister."

Rovyn was almost as dark as Kammi, but smaller boned, more delicate. Jayla's guess was that she could travel over the gridway as lightly as a child. She was smiling as pleasantly as the other two, but Jayla thought the huge brown eyes were wary and the thin frame was strung with tension. "You think I'm kind because I occasionally feed you. And help you mend your ripped clothing. And remind you when you're about to be late for an appointment. That's not kindness, that's pity."

Again, the others all laughed. Jayla managed a discreet glance at Rovyn's bracelet. A wide band of silver decorated with large buttons of gold. Woman who definitely preferred men. Jayla shifted away from Cody to make it clear she didn't have any claim on him.

"I knew I never should have let any of you move into the house," Cody muttered.

Rovyn turned to Jayla with a smile that seemed wholly insincere. "How did the two of you meet? Cody collects people from all over, and the stories are always so interesting."

"I was trapped on the western side of the northern bridge when there was a quake a couple months ago," Jayla said. "Cody came over to bring us supplies."

"Oh, I remember that!" Tokah exclaimed. "I watched him walk the wire across the canyon! I didn't breathe until he was safely across."

"Tokah's too dizzy in the head to walk the wire," Cody explained.

Now she was the one to slug him. "Too smart to risk my life that way."

Jayla decided not to mention that she was trying to learn the same skill.

Rovyn's hand rested briefly on Aussen's head. "And is this your little girl? She's so pretty."

"That's Aussen, and she's not mine. I'm taking care of her until her mother arrives."

Kammi had dropped to a crouch and smiled at Aussen. "And how do you like it in the city so far?"

Aussen listened carefully and answered slowly. "I like it. I like the food."

Kammi's head tilted to one side. "Islander, right?" Kammi said, following up the question with a spate of liquid words. Aussen's face lit up and the two of them launched into an animated conversation.

"I didn't know you spoke Zessin," Cody said in an accusing voice. "You'll have to give me lessons." Kammi waved a casual hand in his direction without looking away from Aussen.

"This is good," Jayla said. "Maybe now we can learn if there's anything important that Aussen hasn't been able to tell us. The cook speaks a little islander, but not enough to really hold a conversation."

"So, Jayla, how do *you* like the city?" Tokah asked.

"I'm still getting used to it. Still finding new places to explore."

"Where are you from?" Rovyn asked. She let her gaze wander deliberately from Jayla's blonde hair to her borrowed sweater to her worn leather leggings. Her expression implied that she had never seen anyone so exotic.

"Oraki," Jayla said. "By way of Marata and Chibain. I've traveled a bit."

"That must have been exciting," Rovyn said.

"More exciting than I would have wanted, sometimes."

"Oh, now I want to hear the stories," Tokah said.

Cody turned a look on Jayla. "Oh, don't you dare," he said. "Don't you sit down and tell my *sister* all the stories of your life when you'll hardly tell me a thing."

She made her voice as sweet as she could. "But your sister seems so much more interested than you do."

His expression was so incredulous that even Rovyn had to laugh. "You're as irritating as the rest of them," he said.

Kammi jumped up, smiling broadly. "Enough arguing. What Aussen wants more than anything is lemon cakes. I've got time to go now if everybody else does."

"It's raining," Rovyn said. "I'm not setting foot outside again."

"It's almost stopped," said Tokah. "I'll go."

Cody looked at Jayla and she nodded. She was more than ready to leave, and happy to have Kammi and Tokah join them. Even happier that Rovyn would stay behind. "Sure," she said. "Sounds good."

The bad weather had kept most people indoors, so the five of them were able to find a table big enough to hold them all at the pastry shop that Aussen liked. Cody offered to treat, and Kammi and Tokah took the opportunity to order the most expensive items on the menu. This answered a question Jayla had had at the back of her mind about whether or not Cody was in a financially sound situation. He'd never seemed to worry about money—but then, Cody didn't seem to worry about anything. She had no idea how much a good courier could earn, but it was clearly enough to afford the occasional pricey outing.

The conversation was so light-hearted and the company was so affable that Jayla found herself relaxing more than she had in weeks. Months. Kammi had taken a spot next to Aussen and made a point of quickly translating any bits of conversation that were especially funny—or appropriate for a child's ears. The three couriers traded stories about some of the worst clients they'd had or most peculiar deliveries they'd made, and Kammi in particular could be hilariously graphic.

"And then he said, 'I don't have any money for a tip, but if you want part of the shipment, I'll give you one—'"

Tokah whooped. "Did you *take* it?"

"Sure I took it! I was curious, you know? Though I have to say I didn't think it was quite as—" Kammi glanced at Aussen and carefully chose a word. "Effective as a human hand. Or—other body part."

Now Cody and Tokah were doubled over and even Jayla was laughing helplessly. Kammi continued, "Then maybe six months later, I had another shipment. Same guy. And he *remembered* me! And he said, 'Oh, did you get a chance to use it? What did you think?' Like he wanted a product review that maybe he could share with his other customers—"

"I'm dying," Tokah gasped.

"And I said, well, it wasn't bad, but I'd had other experiences that were better, and he offered to *show me how it worked.* 'If you've got time, you could come back to the other room—'"

Now they were all in convulsions. Aussen looked brightly between them, but Kammi just patted her head and said, "Some other time, baby. Like, ten years from now. I'll tell you then." She repeated the promise in Zessin.

Once they had managed to control their mirth, Tokah turned to Jayla and said, "Enough of our stories! Tell us about you."

"Oh yes, *do* tell us about you," Cody said.

She ignored him and answered Tokah. "What do you want to know?"

"You're wearing a soldier's wristband. And I know you work as a guard somewhere in the city, but that's *all* I know. How did you come to be a fighter?"

Jayla half didn't want to answer and half did. Cody had been careful about trying to pry information from her, always respecting her silences and changes of subject, and she felt a little bad about that. It wasn't that she had secrets, she just wasn't used to sharing out bits of herself. But she did understand that real friendship was largely dependent on knowing some of those bits.

"I grew up in Oraki, near the Maratan border. Sometimes the Maratan folk we saw were friendly, and sometimes they weren't. My father used to call it 'trade or raid.' You'd see a party of mainlanders coming toward you, and you wouldn't know which way it was going to go."

"What was your family like?"

"Just my parents and brother and me, though I had aunts and uncles and cousins nearby. Most everybody worked on nearby karka farms—planting in the spring, harvesting in the fall, and making charcoal from the shells over the winter. Whole caravans would travel to Marata to sell the harvest and buy goods to get us through the next season." She took a sip from her water. "I was traveling with the caravan once, with my father and my uncle, when we were raided. Nobody was killed, but we lost everything we'd brought with us. My father said it was because none of the desert folk knew how to fight. So I decided right then I was going to learn."

"I don't even know how somebody sets out to do that," Kammi commented.

"There was a guild house in one of the bigger towns a couple hundred miles away. My mother didn't want me to go, but my cousin went with me. He dropped out after the first month, but I stayed. I liked it. There's a different rhythm to the work than there is to farming. A whole different set of skills you need. And there's freedom, because you're not trapped on the same piece of land. Some people like the soldier's life for the fellowship, but it's a good life for a loner, too. I liked being strong. I liked knowing that I could take care of myself. I liked knowing I could take care of other people."

"Did you go back to the village to protect your family?"

Jayla grinned. "No. The guildmaster recommended me for advanced training in southern Marata and I wanted to go. And once I earned my bracelet, I got job offers that took me to northern Marata and then Chibain. I went back for visits every year until my parents died."

"Oh, I'm sorry to hear that," Tokah said. "Where's your brother?"

"Married and still living in the village. We stay in touch but we're not close."

"So you don't really have ties anywhere," Kammi said.

"I like the freedom," Jayla said. "If a job goes sour, I can move on. If I'm curious about seeing a new town, I can just go. So far I haven't come across a place I've liked so much that I wanted to stay forever."

"Not even Corcannon?" Tokah said, appearing shocked.

"I do like it," Jayla admitted. "But I don't know how long I'll stay."

"I don't think I'd ever leave the city," Kammi said.

"I'd like to see the mountains in Chibain," Tokah said. "But I think Marata sounds boring."

"It is," said Jayla. "But you eat well there. Sometimes food is scarcer in Chibain."

They asked more questions about where she'd traveled and what she'd seen. It didn't escape her notice that Cody didn't pose a single query, though he appeared to be listening intently to everything she said, storing up every word. She was pretty sure he was afraid she'd stop talking if he seemed too curious, and she was a little sorry she'd made him feel that way. On the other hand, she never would have volunteered any of this information to Tokah and Kammi unless she trusted Cody. She wasn't sure how she'd be able to explain that to him.

So instead she turned to him and asked directly, "Did that answer all your questions?"

He rewarded her with a brilliant smile. "Enough of them, anyway," he said. "I'm sure I'll think of more later."

"Just ask."

His smile was even brighter. "Count on it."

She thought he might wait a few weeks, but in fact he barely held off until the end of the day. As he sometimes did, he accompanied them back to Madeleine's house, then encouraged Aussen to run inside while he talked to Jayla for a bit. So she had a moment to brace herself.

When he turned to face her, his expression was unwontedly serious. "What's the rest of the story?" he asked.

"Why do think there's more to it?"

"Because no one gets to be as wary as you unless something happened. You don't trust anybody. That means someone, sometime, betrayed your trust."

She nodded, then shrugged. "Second job I took. Big guard unit for a well-connected shipping company, good place, had a real sense of camaraderie. I liked it and thought I'd made friends. And there were two other guards, they'd been friends a long time, but they treated me like I was one of them, and I liked that too." It wasn't an easy story to tell. She still felt stupid, and she still felt angry. "Then they told me they'd been cheating the company, stealing small items from every cargo shipment and selling them to their own buyers. They invited me to join them. It had never occurred to me that anyone would do that. I was so shocked I didn't even try to cover my reaction. They knew I was going to turn them in—so they turned me in instead. I was the new person, the company believed them instead of me." She shrugged again.

Cody was indignant. "An accusation like that could follow you for the rest of your career!"

"Oh, it could. So I went to the guild house in the nearest city and put the case before them. It was a serious accusation, you understand, and if they'd decided I was lying, they could have cut off my bracelet and cast me out. But they interviewed some of the other guards at the shipping company—and some of the buyers—and they got enough evidence to exonerate me. The company offered me my job back, but by then I didn't want it."

"Well, I'm glad the terrible story didn't have a terrible ending."

"So that's the reason I don't trust anybody."

He eyed her for a moment. "Well, that's one of the reasons," he said.

She was immediately defensive. "What do you mean?"

"Something else happened. Something that sent you away to begin with." When she didn't answer, he said, "I'm guessing it was your brother."

Her lips twisted in a wry smile. "He was a bully. And whenever we argued, my parents took his side. I had gotten used to not being believed—but I never learned to like it."

"The pieces are starting to come together now," Cody said.

"Any surprises?"

He smiled at her. "There are always surprises," he said. "That's the fun part."

Chapter Twenty-two: Jayla

Jayla wasn't sure if her recent confessions to Cody would make her more eager to spend time with him or more reluctant—relieved to have found someone who could know her so well, or unwilling to be stripped so bare. But she didn't have a chance to find out over the next week, because Madeleine's life had become a scene of chaos.

Every day, Madeleine had to meet with a dressmaker or a wine supplier or a baker to discuss details of the upcoming wedding; she was entertaining an endless stream of curious friends, gossiping neighbors, and eager vendors hoping to secure her business. Jayla accompanied her on all her buying jaunts and generally lurked nearby whenever there were guests in the house, even ones who didn't seem particularly dangerous. But Jayla was enough of a cynic to believe anyone could pose a threat.

She tried to stay far enough away from open doors to avoid eavesdropping, but it had been hard to miss Madeleine's first conversations with Tivol and Reese once Alastair Alayne had announced that the wedding would be imminent. The one with Tivol had been emotional but fairly civilized.

"Darling, why are you so upset?" Tivol had asked. "I'm delighted!"

"No, you're not! Just a couple of weeks ago you told me you weren't ready to give up the bachelor life, and now suddenly you'll be saddled with a very difficult and demanding wife—"

"Don't make me laugh. There will be adjustments, I'm sure, but we're such good friends, Madeleine! We'll figure it out! We'll just have to be patient with each other—"

"And where will we live? I am *not* staying in your mother's house, but I would rather live in the street than move into your lodgings."

"We'll find a place to rent. Small, just temporary. We'll live there until we can buy our own house. Really, some of the apartments in the south-western corridor are elegant. And neither your father nor my mother will be anywhere in sight."

"It just doesn't make any *sense.* Why now? The fact that both of them are in favor of a hasty wedding makes me think there's some economic reason behind it, which infuriates me—"

"Madeleine. Darling. Just be calm. We're getting married. Don't worry about why. Just concentrate on being happy."

It was the first time Jayla had actually almost liked Tivol.

The conversation with Reese had been far more dramatic. Jayla had been in the atrium, on her way to the kitchen with Aussen, when Reese came bursting through the main door and demanded of the nearest servant, "Where is she?" When Ella just gaped at him, Reese said, "Never mind," and went bounding up the stairs.

"Go see Norrah," Jayla said, giving Aussen a push, and then she ran up the stairs after him.

She heard Madeleine's squeak of surprise when Reese stormed into her room, but it wasn't followed by a cry for help or even a furious demand for him to leave. Instead, there was only a moment of charged silence. And then Madeleine's voice, low and wretched. "Oh, Reese."

"You can't marry him," Reese said.

Another silence and then, "Of course I can. I have always planned to."

"But you *can't!* You don't love him!"

"I've always loved him."

"You're *used* to him. He seems safe to you. I don't seem safe. But Maddie—"

"No! You don't seem safe! You *throw* yourself into my room and you *demand* I listen to you and you think—just because you want something—that I want it, too—"

"You can't stand there and tell me you don't love me."

"I'm not even having this conversation."

"You can't say it, can you? Say it, if it's true."

"It doesn't matter if I love you or not! My life does not accommodate you! And I will thank you not to make my life any harder than it is right now!"

"Maddie." More calmly. "You don't have to be afraid of your father. I know he is a powerful and terrifying man."

"I'm not afraid. It's just that he—"

"It's just that he has always told you what to do and you have always done it. But I can take you away from this house—this day, this minute—and he won't be able to stop you. He won't be able to hurt you. You can marry me instead, and we can live in Corcannon or Chibain or anywhere you want, and you can *do* whatever you want, and he won't ever be able to control you again."

"And if I marry Tivol I will also be out of this house and away from my father, and I will be able to do whatever I want."

"Yes, but you will be married to Tivol."

"*I want to be married to Tivol!*"

There was a longer silence this time.

Finally Reese spoke, his voice hoarse, as if the effort of forming words was actually painful. "Well, I hope you've managed to convince yourself. You haven't convinced me."

There was the sound of footsteps as he moved toward the door. Jayla spun around to race down the staircase, hoping to be unobserved, but Madeleine's cry of "Wait!" stopped her as well as Reese.

"Wait," Madeleine said again. "I can't—I won't be able to bear it if you're angry with me."

A sound that might have been an attempted laugh. "I'm not angry. I'm heartbroken. Can you really not tell the difference?"

"I never set out to hurt you. I never tried to—I never pretended—"

"No. I can only blame myself for wanting something that was never promised to me. Never even offered."

"Reese—"

Yet again, silence from beyond the door, this one the longest yet. But this time Jayla was fairly certain the two speakers weren't simply staring at each other across the room. She decided that any danger Reese might still pose would be to Madeleine's heart, not her person, so she made her way silently down to the atrium. Just in case she was wrong and Madeleine cried out for help, she lurked at the bottom of the stairwell until Reese emerged about an hour later. His face was closed and set, and he left the house without a look back.

For the rest of the day, Madeleine refused to come downstairs, even when the dressmaker showed up for a fitting, even when one of her cousins dropped by to visit. Even when her father wanted her to join him for dinner with Harlo. Norrah sent up a tray of food, which was returned largely uneaten. It seemed clear Madeleine didn't need Jayla's protective services, but Jayla still stayed within easy call in case Madeleine suddenly changed her mind and wanted to dash out of the house. But it never happened.

A couple of hours after dinner, Jayla rescued Aussen from the kitchen and took her upstairs. They spent a few minutes practicing Zessin and Cordish so they could both improve their language skills. Then Jayla kissed the girl on the forehead and put her to bed.

A few moments later, she was standing outside Madeleine's door. It had become their custom for Jayla to drop by every night to inquire about Madeleine's plans for the next day so she knew how to prepare. Madeleine usually greeted her cordially, and they often talked for a few minutes on topics not strictly related to Jayla's job, but they had never developed what Jayla would consider a true friendship. Well, Jayla knew better than to presume that even a close relationship with an employer could ever amount to friendship. She was probably even more interested than Madeleine in maintaining a professional distance. She could be fired at any time; she could quit at any time. A contract made everything perfectly clear.

Still, she would have had to be an absolute stone not to realize Madeleine had had a trying day and to wonder if the other woman actually wanted a visitor at this hour. So her knock was soft and she did not plan to repeat it.

But Madeleine answered instantly. "If that's Jayla, come in."

She stepped inside to find the room lit by a single low lamp. Madeline sat by the open window, the outline of her profile barely discernible against the night sky. She didn't turn to face Jayla, just sat there in silence a moment. Jayla waited.

Eventually Madeleine said, "I suppose you heard all of that."

It seemed pointless to pretend not to know what she meant. "The first part of it, anyway."

"It doesn't seem like I have to ask you not to repeat it to my father, but—"

"Of course I won't."

There was another long wordless stretch. Jayla would have offered to leave, but she suspected that Madeleine had invited her in because she wanted to talk. Finally, Madeleine stirred on her chair and turned in Jayla's direction. "I don't know what to do," she said simply.

I can't possibly advise you, Jayla wanted to reply. *I'm not your cousin or one of your friends. I'm not your confidante.* But, again, only a stone could be so heartless. "Is it that you don't really know what you want?" she asked. "Or is it that you're afraid you can't *have* what you want?"

Madeleine caught her breath, as if she had not considered her dilemma that way. "It's that—I'm not sure what I want is the right thing to do," she said at last. "It is not just my own life that matters here. So many things are connected."

Jayla nodded. "I see that. But I suppose I wonder—"

"Wonder what?"

"How terrible would it be if you did *not* do as your father wished? Would it destroy Tivol's life?"

"He loves me."

"He might find someone else he loves just as much."

"And there are business interests to consider. If the Alayne and Wellenden fortunes are not merged, I believe a lot of money could be lost."

"Couldn't your father find another business partner? Couldn't Tivol's mother?"

"I don't know. I suppose so."

"If you weren't alive to marry Tivol, all of them would survive in some fashion," Jayla said. "You can't be the only thing that keeps the world going."

That made Madeleine laugh—a faint but genuine sound. "No, indeed! You're right. How very vain I must be to think I am that important."

"That's not what I meant."

"No, but it's a very freeing thought! I could vanish today and the world would keep spinning."

"Vanishing is harder than you might expect," Jayla said with a trace of amusement. "But I do think you could make some of your own choices and find that the outcome is not as terrible as you fear."

Madeleine sighed. "It would seem terrible to my father," she said. "And it is very hard for me to go against his wishes."

Jayla weighed her words carefully. "Are you afraid of him? Do you think he would harm you?"

"No. Of course not. He wouldn't hurt me, I'm sure of it," Madeleine said. She did not sound sure. "He might lock me in my room. Or something. I don't know. He's a very hard man to withstand."

Jayla waited a moment and then said, "If you need assistance leaving the house, you realize I will help you."

Madeleine stared at her a long moment, her eyes pools of darkness in the shadowed room. "My father pays your salary," she said at last. It was a question, although it wasn't phrased as one.

"He pays me to keep you safe," Jayla said. "If he's the threat, I'll keep you safe from him."

Madeleine exhaled on a long tense gust of air. "He's not a threat. Really. But it's good to know that you—I will keep that in mind if I decide that—I have to think about things very carefully."

"You don't have a lot of time."

"I know. But I still need to think."

"Of course." Jayla waited a beat, then said, "I came by to see if you knew what your plans were for tomorrow."

"Oh yes," said Madeleine with the ghost of a laugh. "I'm meeting with Harlo to discuss my wedding vows."

It might have been a week later, sometime around midnight, that Jayla was jerked awake by a percussive boom followed by a sinister sizzle. She leapt from her bed and flung herself across Aussen's small form before another, slightly softer detonation sounded in the distance. Aussen curled up beneath her, clutching her Keshalosha fish in one hand and clinging to Jayla with the other. She asked an urgent question in words Jayla didn't understand, but it wasn't hard to interpret.

"I don't know," Jayla said. "Something exploded."

She stayed where she was, making her body a shelter for Aussen's, but listening intently for any clues as to what had happened. In a few moments, she started hearing sounds from the house—voices raised, calling from room to room—and even softer and farther away, the noises of neighbors opening their doors and shouting to each other across their lawns. Jayla lifted her head so she could hear better, and that was when she realized the world was in total darkness. The windows of her room usually received faint illumination from lights in the street; a small artificial lamp was always set near Aussen's bed in case she woke up and was afraid. Sconces stayed lit around the clock in the atrium and along the stairwell, providing a faint ghostlight that spilled in under the door. All of these were powered by the same great engine that fed the gridway—and all of these had been extinguished.

Jayla didn't know what catastrophe could have knocked out the engine or how difficult it might be to restart, but that wasn't her concern at the moment. The sounds hadn't come from someone breaking into the house to harm Madeleine or steal Aussen, so she could relax.

"Everything will be fine," she said, repeating the phrase in halting Zessin. "Go back to sleep. I'm going downstairs to look around."

In the perfect darkness, Jayla glided through the room, pulling on yesterday's discarded clothes and tucking a knife into her waistband. Just in case.

She stepped through the door and paused to get her bearings. A three-quarter moon dripped a gauzy, mostly useless phosphorescence through the overhead skylight, but it was enough to suggest where the bannister and the stairwell lay. Jayla could see shapes outside some of the servants' doors as the maids and footmen clustered in the hallway, wondering what to do next. She felt her way carefully down to the second level and arrived at Madeleine's door just as it opened.

"What do—" Jayla started, and Madeleine responded with a little shriek. "Sorry, I thought you could see me."

"Jayla? Oh, I'm glad you're awake. I was just going to come get you."

"What do you think happened? It looks like the power was knocked out."

"Yes, that's my guess. It's happened a couple of times before, but it usually only lasts an hour or so."

"Is it safe?"

"Do you mean will the city catch fire or something? I don't *think* so, but since I don't really understand how it works—"

"Or looters might take advantage of the darkness and try to break into houses and businesses."

"Of course that's the first thing you'd think of!"

"I just might sit downstairs and wait until sunrise."

Their voices attracted attention, and a few more shapes drifted down the stairwell.

"What would you like us to do, dona?" asked the junior footman.

"Do we have candles? Jayla's right, it wouldn't hurt for a few of us to keep watch in the atrium."

"There are candles in the kitchen," Norrah said. "If I can find my way there."

"I can walk the house blindfolded," said the footman. He was young and a bit of a braggart, but Jayla had always thought he was sharp and capable. "Hold on to me."

They led the way, and Jayla and Madeleine followed them down the stairs. "You don't have to sit up with us," Jayla said to Madeleine once they reached the ground level.

"I can't sleep, so I might as well."

Jayla glanced around as if she could see through the shadows piled under the archways and behind the broad pillars. The distant moonlight gleamed like frost along the polished floor and created feathered halos around the decorative plants in their heavy stone vases. "Where's your father? Didn't the noise wake him?"

"He's not home."

Jayla nodded, knowing the movement was invisible. Every few weeks, Alastair Alayne would be absent from the house overnight. No one specified where he spent his time, but Jayla had always assumed he had a lover or at least a temporary paid companion. At the back of her mind she tucked away the thought that his next absence would provide a perfect time for her to spirit Madeline out of the house. If Madeleine decided she wanted to go.

"Is Aussen all right? Is she afraid?"

"She woke up but I told her everything was fine. I'll check on her in a bit."

They stood in silence for a moment before Madeleine exclaimed, "You just never realize how *dark* it can be. I'm so used to the sconces always being on."

Jayla was amused. "Well, that's the advantage to growing up in the desert," she said. "No artificial light, so if you didn't have a candle and the moon wasn't out, you learned to move through the darkness. You get so you can sense where things and people are, even if you can't see them."

"I'm not sure I'd ever get good at that."

They waited a bit longer, hoping someone would emerge from the kitchen with a few lit tapers. Jayla's hearing was always sharper in the dark, and she could catch a few snatches of conversation down the hallway.

"I think they're having trouble finding the candles," she said. "It might be a while."

Madeleine made a small sound of irritation. "All right, just a minute—

where's the nearest planter?"

That made no sense, but Jayla just gave a mental shrug. "Take my arm. I'll lead you over." They crossed the floor in a cautious step-and-glide, then Jayla guided Madeleine's hand to the stone lip of one of the big pots. "Feel that?"

"Yes, thank you." There was a faint sound of digging, a barely discernible movement in Madeleine's dense shadow—and then a small globe of cool light bloomed between Madeleine's fingers.

Jayla stared at her in absolute shock.

Madeleine responded with a merry laugh. "If you could see your face!"

"What are you—what did you—"

Madeleine twisted her hands back and forth, pivoting in a slow circle, and the icy light created swooping shadows across the surfaces it was strong enough to reach. "Isn't that a fun trick? My brother and I were always able to do it, but I've never met anyone else who could. Give us a patch of dirt, and we can squeeze it into a ball of light. It was very handy when we were children sneaking around the house at night."

It was hard to know how to phrase the question, hard to even form the words. "Why do you think this is something *you* can do? And no one else."

"I don't know! Just something we inherited. From our mother, I suppose, since my father can't do it." A pause. "Well, he says he can't. But I'm not sure he always tells me everything."

He absolutely doesn't tell you everything, Jayla thought. "And you're sure your friends can't do it? Your cousins? Tivol? Reese?"

"Oh, I'm sure. When we were children, our cousins would try and try, and get so mad when they couldn't make anything happen. Tivol always says it's one of the things he loves most about me, because it's such a pretty and useless skill." Madeleine was silent a moment, perhaps remembering something Reese had said on the same topic, but deciding not to repeat it. "Anyway, since I've been an adult I haven't had too many occasions to go around creating my own personal ball of light! But it's good to know I still can."

"Yes. I imagine it is."

A flicker caught the corner of Jayla's eye, and she turned to find Norrah and the footman making their way from the kitchen, lit candelabra held triumphantly aloft. "Excellent," Madeleine said. "Now we can all see."

Jayla felt she was more in the dark than ever.

It was noon the next day before power was restored, but none of the city's systems appeared to have sustained any permanent damage. Rumors filtered through the streets about what had caused the breakdown, some speculating that it had been sparked by a small quake, and others insisting it had been purposeful destruction by petty criminals. Madeleine's father dismissed all the theories, saying the problem had been caused by normal wear on the power core and that city workers were figuring out ways to prevent the problem from happening again.

It was a week before Jayla had an unexpected free day when Madeleine came down with a headache and moaned that she would not set foot outside the house for any inducement. Jayla left Aussen with Norrah and took a chugger to Cody's house.

"You're lucky," said Kammi, who answered the door to Jayla's knock. "He'd have left in another ten minutes."

Rovyn was peering over Kammi's shoulder, and she looked as though she wished Jayla had not been so fortunate. But she managed a civil, unsmiling nod, and Jayla responded in kind.

Cody appeared surprised but happy to find Jayla had sought him out. "Did I forget I would be seeing you today?" he asked.

"Madeleine's sick, so I got the day off," Jayla replied. "Do you have to work?"

"I was planning on it, but I don't have to. Is there something you'd like to do?"

"I want you to take me to see Pietro."

Chapter Twenty-three: Jayla

If Cody had been surprised to see Jayla, Pietro was astonished. He'd answered her urgent knock by throwing the door wide open—this clearly was not someone who was afraid thieves or murderers might be awaiting him on the other side. When he saw her, his eyes widened and he stepped back as if her presence had hit him with the force of a blow.

"Jayla." And then, suddenly alarmed, "Has something happened to Aussen?"

She brushed by him to enter his rooms without an invitation. One quick glance showed her a small, spare living space, clean and uncluttered. The place of a man who was rarely home or who craved order in at least one corner of his life.

"Not yet," she said. "But you owe me some explanations."

Pietro must have given Cody a searching glance as he followed her across the threshold, because she heard Cody say, "I don't know why we're here, either."

She spun around to face Pietro. She had had a few days to consider, and she thought she had come up with a safe way to ask this question. "I met a woman the other day. And it turned out she had this amazing skill. She could take a lump of dirt in her hand and make it glow with light."

Cody seemed impressed. "Really? I didn't know anyone but Aussen could do that."

Pietro closed his eyes. "Ahhhh." He thought for a moment, nodded, and opened his eyes. "Let's sit down and talk. Would you like something to drink?"

They gathered around his small table and sipped at a lukewarm beverage that Jayla didn't like very much. Neither she nor Cody said a word while Pietro appeared to gather his thoughts. She thought he looked noticeably older than he had when they camped out by the bridge. Although that was ridiculous; that had been less than three months ago.

"Of course you know the story of Cordelan," Pietro began.

"Of course," she said impatiently.

"But just for context, let me recite it again. The world was a wide expanse of many small islands and land masses, separated by a tempestuous sea. Some of the lands were ruled by Dar and some by Zessaya, and nothing changed for centuries. Until one day Cordelan made himself known to the world. And he said, 'I will knit together the scattered lands. I will bring water to the desert and stability to the islands and prosperity to the united people.' And so he stitched the mountains to the midlands, and the desert to the islands, and the city to the larger mass."

"We know all this," Jayla said.

Pietro sipped his drink before continuing. "Now, the religious doctrine tells us that Cordelan was, indeed, a deity, though the sacred texts are unclear on why he chose that moment—after eons of silence—to step forward and reshape the world. There are some historical scholars who posit that Cordelan was not a god at all, but a visitor from another world, who had crossed the unimaginable miles of space to land on our planet."

"Really?" Cody said. He sounded delighted. "I like that!"

Jayla was confused. "Would something like that even be possible?"

"Who knows? But many of the things that seem to be explained by divinity make even more sense if you view them as technology created by people who were advanced enough to travel across the stars."

"Such as?"

"The power core that drives the city, for one thing. No one truly understands how it works. The story is that Cordelan created that power core after he sewed the continent together. But maybe a visitor from another world took whatever energy source he used to travel here, and buried it beneath the land, and set it up to sustain us for untold generations."

"That sounds—impossible," Jayla said.

Pietro shrugged. "More impossible than a god creating the power core by simply waving his hands and willing it to be so? Maybe. I would think advanced technology also would explain how our own world could be so forcefully reconstructed." He took another sip. "And the theory about a visitor from another planet is attractive for other reasons. Historical artefacts dating back for millennia show that the Chibani and the Maratans and the Oraki people and the islanders—everyone except the Cordelanos—have lived on this world almost since it was formed. But there is no evidence of Cordelanos living here until a thousand years ago."

"How can you know that?" Jayla objected. "It's not like you can dig them up and see the color of their skin."

"The shapes of their skulls are slightly different and they have a particular bend to their index fingers. More than that, we have drawings that have survived since ancient times that we can date with passable accuracy. It's only about a thousand years ago that Cordelanos appear in any of these pictures. It's not unreasonable to assume that Cordelan came here with some contingent of others—dozens, maybe hundreds. They settled onto this planet and began intermarrying with the natives. Cordelan himself is supposed to have taken Dar as his wife and fathered ten children with her."

"I don't understand what any of this has to do with Aussen. And the trick with the light."

"I'm getting to that. It's complicated. Whether you believe Cordelan was an alien visitor or an actual god doesn't entirely matter, because the rest of the story plays out the same either way. He rearranged the world and he locked the new continent in place with a very peculiar device."

Cody looked up at that. "You mean, the one we visited under the temple?"

"Exactly."

"Just *tell* me," Jayla said.

"The device is a lever that is tied to the mechanism that holds the pieces of our world together. Every few years that lever must be oiled to keep it functioning. If it is not oiled, the stone walls that surround it move closer to each other—and closer. Eventually they will crush it. And the lever will shatter, and the lock will fail, and the land masses will break apart—probably with a great deal of violence."

"The quakes," Jayla said.

"The quakes, indeed. They are a precursor of what could come."

"So then—the quakes are letting us know that the mechanism needs to be attended to."

"And very soon. Or our world will rip apart at its literal seams."

"So then why hasn't it been done?"

"Because the substance that is used to keep the instrument turning is blood."

Jayla stared at him. She couldn't figure out where this was tending, but she had a feeling it would be terrible. "What kind of blood?"

"From a direct descendant of Cordelan himself. No, even more specific than that. From someone born to a *woman* who is a direct descendant. The religious scholars believe this was a condition that Dar imposed, to acknowledge the importance of the female line. But the blood itself could come from either a man or a woman."

Cody leaned forward. "You said he fathered ten children. I suppose someone kept track of them?"

"Yes—very close track! The priesthood was formed in part to watch over these very precious descendants. And for years—decades—many centuries—all was well. As soon as the priests detected a tremor, they would draw a few ounces of blood and pour them into the basin, and the mechanism was placated and everything went on as normal. But over time, it took more blood to pull the lever and settle the walls back in place. And then a little more blood. Maybe the mechanism began to degrade—to rust, perhaps. Or maybe whatever compound made Cordelan's blood so special was diluted with every new generation. But eventually the lever would only move if what amounted to the blood of an entire person could be poured into the basin."

Jayla knew her own face was horrified. When she glanced at Cody, she saw his expression mirrored hers. "People were *killed?* To do this?" she said.

"Well, not at first. Generally, the older members of the family—the ones who were sick, or exhausted, ready to go—when their time came, they volunteered. Except, something else had happened."

"This keeps getting worse," Cody muttered.

"It does," Pietro agreed. "Cordelan's descendants were fewer and fewer with every generation. Some women had only a single child. Some had none at all."

He paused, lifted his cup as if to take another swallow, and set it down untouched. "Up until this point, the children of Cordelan had always known their role. Their fate. And they felt—privileged—to partake in this sacred ritual. But as their numbers dwindled, and the quakes kept coming, and there were not enough older people on the verge of death, the priests became desperate. They convinced a man in his fifties to sacrifice himself years before the natural end of his life. But a few years later, they needed another volunteer, and no one would agree. And so—one was taken. And a few years later, another one. Each one younger than the last. And each one unwilling."

Cody murmured some phrase that sounded like a ritual prayer, but Jayla didn't recognize it. Pietro nodded in his direction. "Exactly. Now Cordelan's few remaining descendants were keenly aware of their dire fates. They knew that when they married and had children, their daughters would be forced to give birth to the *next* generation of sacrifices. And their sons, once they were old enough and big enough to produce the required quantity of blood, would be taken away and killed."

"How old?" Cody asked, seemingly unable to help himself. "How big?"

"It would vary with the individual, of course, but roughly one hundred pounds."

Jayla had to fight to keep her voice even. "So the boys were murdered and the girls were bred like farm animals," she managed to say. "And they knew this was what would happen to them."

"And they did not like it. As you can imagine. So they rebelled, and several of them tried to run away, but none of them were successful. Ultimately, all of them became prisoners of the priesthood. Very valuable, very well-kept prisoners."

Pietro paused, but when neither Jayla or Cody spoke, he sighed and went on. "At this point, it seemed to the man who served as high divine that it would be a good idea to *not* tell the next generation what fate lay in store for them. At the time, Cordelan's only surviving heirs were two sisters—one a grown woman, who already knew what her life held in store. And one a girl too young to have heard the story. The younger one was separated from her sister and raised by another family. Never told who or what she really was. And her daughter was raised by another family. And *her* daughter. The various high divines wanted to be very certain that none of them could piece the tale together and figure out what might lie in store for them."

That first woman must have been Madeleine's grandmother, Jayla thought. Or great-grandmother, perhaps. Pietro had not been specific about the timeline. But Jayla was absolutely certain this story was going to end with Madeleine being a descendent of Cordelan—and destined to die on his barbaric altar. She asked, "Did the foster families know who the women were and what was intended for them?"

"Oh yes. The heads of all the Council families know the truth. They have always worked with the high divine to keep the city functioning."

Alastair Alayne. He had married one of these doomed women, knowing perfectly well that his heirs would be given over to the god. Then he had plotted his daughter's wedding so that the children she produced with her husband—

Jayla's mind skidded to a stop. Tivol. Did *he* know? Did *Reese* know? Jayla felt her body fill with rage and fear and something very like panic. She could not take it all in. She could not bring herself to entirely believe it. She had to work very hard to keep her breathing deep and even.

"And now?" Cody asked. "Are any of Cordelan's descendants still living in the city—with no idea of who they are?"

Pietro nodded in Jayla's direction. "The young woman Jayla just met. Madeleine Alayne. As far as the Council families know, she is the last surviving child of Cordelan and the goddess Dar."

"That sounds like there might be more," said Cody.

"The high divines have always been very crafty. Let's face it, they've been peddling a lie for centuries. Some generations back, they claimed that their last prisoner had died without giving birth, leaving only the girls who had no idea about their fate." He spread his hands. "But I wonder if that's the truth. Somewhere in the city, might there be a young woman living under heavy guard, awaiting her fate with horror? It would be a deception entirely in keeping with the highest circles of the priesthood."

Cody said, "And you know this because—" He waited.

Pietro managed a faint smile. "I was a priest, yes. Not in the very highest circles, but high enough to learn this story."

Jayla thought she had her voice under control now. "So this woman. This Madeleine. She will marry someday and have children, and then—what happens to them? What happens to *her?*"

"If she has sons, they will be taken from her when they are old enough—or when the high divine is desperate enough. If she has daughters, they will be married to Council family men who understand where their duty lies. When she is past her child-bearing years, and if there is an emergency, it is very likely she will find herself sacrificed on the altar of common good."

Jayla pretended to be thinking something over. "If it is so urgent for her to be producing children, I would think she would have been married off when she was quite young. But the woman I met looked like she was at least twenty or twenty-two."

"She is twenty-four," Pietro said. When they both glanced at him, startled, he responded with a painful smile. "I knew her. Back in my former life."

"That must make this hard for you," Cody said.

"It makes it unendurable," Pietro replied quietly.

"So why isn't she married?" Jayla asked. Silently she added, *Yet.*

"Oh, the requirements of the mechanism are so very precisely calibrated!" Pietro exclaimed. "For the blood to turn the lever, it must be present in a specific quantity, and it must include a compound that apparently does not develop in a woman's body until she has reached a certain maturity. Any children she bears before that time will never have the chemicals in their blood, so they are useless to the temple—which is why Madeleine has not been encouraged to marry sooner. Generally, a woman's blood will reach the desired composition when she is about twenty-five, unless her development is inhibited by certain external factors."

So much information. Jayla was starting to feel like she was drowning in awful details, but she forced herself to focus and asked, "What factors?"

"How healthy she was as a child, whether she ever had certain illnesses. But the biggest factor is whether or not she has been exposed to cherloshe."

Jayla fixed her eyes on him. "Cherloshe," she repeated. "I don't know what that is."

"Oh, but you do," he said with another painful smile. "It's what Zessaya's followers use to make the chazissas they wear to honor her. You saw a cherloshe charm on the necklace I gave to Aussen."

"Wait," said Cody, wrinkling his forehead.

Jayla was just as confused. "I don't understand."

"Cordelan and Dar banded together to rule the continent that he had made—but Zessaya still had plenty of power of her own. She threatened to rip the islands from their seam along the mainland if Cordelan didn't promise that he would never harm her people. So he agreed that anyone would be safe from his justice if they wore an amulet crafted from her body—that is, made from the cherloshe stone that forms the bedrock of the islands. And it turns out that if any of Cordelan's descendants are exposed to too much cherloshe, their blood does not develop the necessary compound until the influence is removed."

Cherloshe, Jayla thought. *That's what I'll do. I'll get a chazissa for Madeleine.* Out loud she said, "So when you gave the necklace to Aussen—"

"I was hoping to make her invisible to Cordelan," he said, nodding.

"But that means—do you think that *Aussen* is—"

He spread his hands. "No one except one of his descendants has ever been able to do that particular trick of picking up a fistful of soil and turning it into a beacon of light. No one."

"It doesn't seem possible," Cody asked. "She's an islander. I don't see how Aussen's mother could have taken a lover who was descended from Cordelan. Not if all the boys are sacrificed the minute they're old enough to give enough blood."

"I know. I was shocked myself when Aussen managed that feat. But I am convinced she comes from Cordelan's stock." He shrugged. "Maybe, decades ago, when there were still plenty of heirs, the priests lost track of someone. A young woman escaped their close attention and ran away to the islands. And generations later, Aussen is the result."

Jayla fixed him with a hard stare. "You said you had powerful friends and they would want to hurt Aussen. You said you didn't want to help them, but that they might persuade you to change your mind. That's why you told me to take her. That's why you told me to keep her away from you."

Cody looked between the two of them but kept his mouth shut. Pietro sighed and rubbed his eyes with his finger and his thumb. "And all of that is still true," he said quietly. "Just the other day I had a visit from one of them, and he is so desperate that if he knew of Aussen's existence—"

She was on her feet with a knife in her hand before he could finish the sentence. "Maybe I should kill you first," she said. "Before you can tell anyone anything."

She heard Cody's shocked voice pronounce her name, but Pietro just looked up at her, weary and somber. "Maybe you should," he said. "It's not like I'm loving any part of my life right now."

"*Jayla,*" Cody said again.

She turned to him, the blade still in her hand. "I don't trust him."

"He doesn't know anything."

"All he has to know is that Aussen exists. All he has to do is tell someone." She gave Pietro another cold look. "Maybe he already has."

Pietro shook his head. "If my word means anything to you, I can swear I haven't. And my intention is to never speak of it to anyone." He closed his eyes. "But I still recommend that you never tell me where she is."

"But what happens now?" Cody demanded. "What if the quakes keep getting worse? What if the device gets crushed? How do we stop that?"

Pietro shook his head again, the slow, hopeless movement of a man who saw absolutely no options. "I have no idea. The priests could take Madeleine and throw her body to the god, but then what? Unless they truly have another descendant stashed somewhere in the city, they have only bought themselves a few years. They could sacrifice Aussen—"

"No they couldn't," Jayla growled.

"But she's too small. Her little body doesn't hold enough blood to move the lever. And they can't wait until she's old enough and big enough, because they don't have that kind of time."

"So then what?" Cody asked, his voice even more strained. "If we can't figure it out?"

"The continent tears itself apart. In a matter so violent it perhaps is not survivable. We become just like the lands to the east. Ruined by the god's hand."

Jayla was in a daze as they left Pietro's small apartment. She honestly didn't think she would have been able to find her way back to the Alayne house without Cody's hand on her arm. Even so, she was clumsy and unsteady, blundering into small hazards on the road and bumping into people striding in the other direction. They had elected to walk, at least for part of the way, and in absolute silence they made their way out of Pietro's neighborhood and into the wide bustling avenues of the Quatrefoil.

She felt Cody tug her to a fancifully carved wooden bench that overlooked a small patch of green and was currently unoccupied. "Let's sit for a minute," he said, and so they did.

Jayla stared blindly ahead of her, barely registering the play of sun and shadow on the street or the clicking of the cars as they passed along the gridway nearby. She had leaned forward and rested her elbows on her knees, and now she was not sure she would ever have the strength to push herself to an upright position again.

"What are you going to do?" Cody asked.

She just shook her head, and they sat there in silence a while longer.

"Do you want me to get you something to drink? There's a vendor selling bottles of something."

Her stomach was in such turmoil that she might throw up anything she swallowed, but her mouth was so dry that her lips felt cracked. She nodded. She didn't look up when he left or returned, but she did straighten her back and take the bottle when he handed it to her.

"Just water," he said. "He had juice if you'd rather. Or wine."

She just shook her head and took three cautious sips. The water tasted almost sweet on her parched tongue, washed some of the horror down her throat. Her stomach tensed, then quieted again.

"Each part of that story was more dreadful than the last," Cody said. "And I have this terrible feeling it's all true."

Jayla addressed the patch of grass at her feet. "I can't let either one of them die."

"Of course you can't!"

"I mean. He says the world will end if one of them isn't sacrificed, but I—I can't let them be sacrificed." She turned her head just enough to see his face from the corner of her eye. "Maybe you think that's wrong of me."

"What? No! How can you even say that?"

With the hand that didn't hold the bottle, she gestured at the busy square, filled with such energy and motion and life. "This beautiful city. All these people. How do you weigh that? The life of one person against the value of all this?"

The glib and light-hearted Cody shook his head and showed her the most somber look she had ever seen on his lively face. "I don't know how to make those calculations. All I know is that if the person to be killed was my sister or my roommate—if that person was you—I would do everything I could to save them. I don't know how to think about—" His hands made circles in the air, trying to shape the city or maybe the entire planet. "Everybody, all at once, in the abstract. All I know is how to take care of one person at one time. All I know is to watch out for the people who matter to me."

"I have to tell her." At his gasp of horror, she quickly added, "Not Aussen. I would never put this nightmare in her head. But Madeleine has to know."

"You think she doesn't have any idea? No suspicions at all?"

Jayla shook her head. "I don't think so. Tivol, though—the man she's supposed to marry—I would bet everything I own that he knows."

"Tivol Wellenden?"

She nodded, a little surprised. "You know him?"

Cody shrugged. "Not to speak to. I've made deliveries to him. And of course, everyone in the city knows who all the Council families are."

"I don't like him. I could never figure out why."

Cody managed the ghost of a smile. "You don't like anyone."

"But if he knows what's supposed to happen to Madeleine—and he has kept it a secret from her all these years—"

"What do you think she'll do? When you tell her?"

"I have no idea."

He took a deep breath. "And after you tell her. What will *you* do?"

She turned to look him more directly in the eyes. "I have no idea," she repeated. "But it sounds like it won't be safe to stay in Corcannon."

"It sounds like it won't be safe anywhere."

She was silent a moment. "If the quakes start getting worse—I think I might take Aussen and head to the islands. See if I can find her family. I have to think—"

"What?"

"The islands might be the safest place of all. If Zessaya had enough power to make bargains with Cordelan, maybe she has enough power to protect her own lands when the tremors come. Maybe. At the moment, it's the best plan I can think of."

Cody nodded, his face determinedly neutral. "When would you leave?"

"I don't know. I don't know how long we have until the quakes start tearing the land apart."

"Don't go without letting me know."

She shook her head, looked away, and finally said, "You'd be welcome to come with me."

He didn't respond for so long that she had to turn back to face him. He had managed another smile, this one warmer and sweeter. He took her hand and carried it to his heart, and she let him hold it there. "That's an amazing offer, coming from you."

She tried her own smile, though it wasn't as successful. "Easier to travel when there's two of you on the road. Two adults, I mean."

"I'm not sure I can do it," he said. "Leave everyone behind. All my family."

"They could come," she said. "*Everyone* should be leaving the city."

"Can I say that I'll think about it?"

She couldn't tell if her swift reaction was surprise or hope. "You mean, you might?"

"If I tell the others. If they know why I'm leaving. If they can choose to leave too. Then I think—it seems to me—I'm not sure I can bear if it if you just walk away—"

Before she could stop to think about it, she leaned forward and pressed her lips against his. She thought she could taste first his amazement and then his delight. He put his free hand around her shoulders and drew her tightly against his body, but she didn't try to pull away; she wriggled against him, trying to get closer. The kiss seemed to last forever.

"Who would have thought I could be grateful for the end of the world?" he whispered against her mouth.

"It does change a person's perspectives on certain things," she whispered back.

"Though all in all, I still wish it wasn't going to happen."

She sighed and freed herself from his embrace, though she let him bend in for one more quick kiss. "I have to say I agree. But I need to go. I still have one very hard task to do today, and I don't think I can put it off."

He stood up and pulled her to her feet, since it turned out he still hadn't released her hand, and they started strolling slowly toward the nearest gridway stop. Jayla wondered how long it would take to walk the whole way back. A couple of hours, maybe. Half of her wanted to take the slowest possible route home, put off the terrible conversation as long as she could. And half of her wanted to scale the nearest pole, climb onto the support webbing, and run as fast as she could to Madeleine's house. She compromised by waving down a chugger clacking in her direction.

"I can come with you if you want," Cody said.

She shook her head. "I need to think about this. I'll do that on the ride. But thank you."

He nodded, kissed her again, and let her go.

The transport was crowded. Jayla had to shove her way on, then stand for the duration of the trip, clinging to a handrail and sightlessly staring out the window. When the car rounded the bend onto Council Row, she felt another swell of cowardice and the craven desire to just keep riding. But she took a deep breath, excused herself as she pushed past the other riders, and swung off in front of the Alayne mansion. Another series of deep breaths and she had made herself cross the street. Open the gate. Enter the house. The faint smells of a savory dinner drifted from the kitchen to the atrium; the youngest housemaid was sweeping the highly polished floor.

"Is Madeleine in her room?"

The girl nodded, and Jayla ran lightly up the stairs. Her heart was pounding and her hands were clenching. She could not remember the last time she had had to do something she so much did not want to do.

She knocked, and when there was no response, she knocked again. "It's Jayla," she said. "Can I come in?"

She took the muffled response as an affirmative, so she steadied her nerves and entered the room. "I have something I need to tell you," she began.

But when Madeleine turned to look at her, Jayla knew her mission was unnecessary. Madeleine already knew.

Chapter Twenty-four: Madeleine

Madeleine was almost grateful for the headache, because it gave her a reason to not leave the house. It forced her to stay inside, to think hard about the sudden dramatic acceleration of her life and how she really felt about that. It gave her time to breathe.

But her head hurt too much for her to think clearly, so all she actually did was sit in the window seat, watch the cars wind by on the gridway, and mope. She did wash her face and comb her hair and put on her plainest gown, because who knew when she might have to run outside in the middle of a quake, but the mirror showed her such a wan, bruised countenance that she hoped she wouldn't have to see another living soul. The maid brought her a lunch tray, but she barely bothered to eat. A couple of times she got up and paced, but that made her headache worse, so she sat down again and leaned against the window casement. And tried again to think.

She would be marrying Tivol in a month. She should be happy and excited, full of longing and excitement. Instead, she was anxious and uneasy, full of worry and despair.

Of course she knew the reason. But that only made things worse.

If she wanted to marry Reese instead, she couldn't. Or even if she could, she didn't want to. She wasn't sure; she wasn't able to think it through. He infuriated her and he unsettled her and he had no right to tell her he loved her, but when he was gone for more than a few days at a time she missed him so much it was like his absence carved a physical hole in her body. At times she thought she might put a hand to her heart and find that her fingers sank all the way through her hollow ribcage and out past her spine. She couldn't even put into words what it was that she missed about him, what she might say to him if he was standing right beside her. There was simply this ceaseless echo inside her head that went knocking through her empty bones. *Reese. Reese.*

Reese. She didn't remember ever having Tivol's name reverberate through her body like that.

There had been this—connection—between them last year. An unexpected flare of warmth she experienced whenever he stepped into the room. A sense of dizziness when they danced together. An unspoken but powerful emotion one afternoon when they strolled through a temple garden for more than an hour, saying almost nothing, occasionally glancing at each other, then looking quickly away. She had not examined her feelings too closely at the time, hadn't questioned those little spikes of happiness. They'd always been friends, in the loose, easy way people of their class were friends. She didn't want any more, expect any more. Didn't think about it.

Reese had ruined everything by declaring he loved her and asking her to marry him. She had been utterly shocked—because it hadn't occurred to her to put a name to the emotion, to consider a course of action that would permit it. Because he had made her examine her heart and then forced her to make a choice based on actual knowledge, not self-deluded innocence. Because he had made her hurt him.

She had told herself that she wasn't just as hurt.

It hadn't been that difficult, a year ago, to resume her old life and remember that she had always loved Tivol. She hadn't thought Tivol was even aware of the sad little romance, though every once in a while he said something pointed and sarcastic about Reese that made her wonder if he had noticed more than she realized. But everything soon seemed back to normal. She was even able to have light, impersonal conversations with Reese when they were both at some social event together. It helped that he was so rarely in town.

But everything had changed that day a few weeks ago, and she didn't know why. Maybe because Reese had stopped pretending that he didn't care. Maybe because her life had been threatened and Reese was the first one who seemed to think that the risk was real—and that her life was precious. Maybe because she had let her guard down.

Maybe because she had stopped loving Tivol.

Oh, but that wasn't true. She had always loved him. She still loved him.

Well, it didn't matter if she loved him. She was going to marry him. Plenty of people made good marriages based on nothing more than a shared sense of duty and a baseline amiability. She and Tivol had always been *friends,* that was the important part. She was comfortable with Tivol. Reese made her nervous.

Reese made her feel like her veins ran with molten silver and her ribs formed a cage for fluttering songbirds.

Those didn't seem like good reasons for marrying *anybody.*

She shut her eyes. If she married Tivol, she wouldn't have to keep worrying about Reese. She would be launched on her new life. She would be a happy bride. Her mind wouldn't keep circling and whimpering in this unpleasant way. Everything would be settled. Everything would be clear. That's what she wanted. She would marry Tivol.

It didn't help that her eyes were closed. The tears leaked out anyway.

She hadn't managed to sort anything out by early afternoon, when there was a tentative knock. "There's a visitor," Ella called through the closed door.

Madeleine jerked upright and came to her feet, smoothing down her skirt, then running her fingers under her eyes to make sure they were dry. She must look disastrous. "I don't think I'm well enough to see company," she called back. "Who is it?"

There was a small commotion outside—footsteps, a surprised gasp from the maid, and then a man's voice. "It's Reese. Let me in. I have to talk to you."

Madeleine had to bite back her own exclamation of surprise. She could feel her cool face flush with heat. "Reese! No! You can't come in."

"It's important. It's about—it's not about—let me in."

She was seized with sudden terror. What dreadful news had Reese been authorized to deliver? "What is it?"

"I have to talk to you," he said. He tried the door, which of course she hadn't locked, so he came right inside. "It's important," he repeated.

Ella was peering in, looking frightened and just the tiniest bit intrigued. "Should I fetch the footmen?" she asked anxiously.

Of course, *this* would be the day Madeleine had let Jayla leave the house, thinking she had no need for a guard. But she was not going to subject any of them to the indignity of having the servants throw Reese out of the house when he clearly was unwilling to go. "No, everything's fine," she said. "Don't raise an alarm."

The maid curtsied and withdrew. Reese shut the door firmly, then turned to stare at Madeleine. The window was still open, admitting enough light for them to see each other plainly. She stopped worrying about how awful she must look, because he looked even worse.

"Reese. What's wrong?" She had been about to warn him to keep his distance, but now she took two steps toward him, extending her hand. His face was ravaged.

"I've just come from my father's—"

"Oh no! Reese, has something happened to him? Is he—"

He shook his head impatiently. "No, he's fine. Well—he's fading, but—

that's not what I came here to talk about. I saw him and he told me—what apparently he's been trying to work up the nerve to tell me for the past six months. And I—Maddie, I—it's too terrible."

Now she took his hand in hers and held it in a comforting clasp. His other hand came up and clutched hers. "Tell me," she said. "I'll help you through it."

"You can't," he whispered.

"Just tell me."

He stared at her a moment, his blue eyes burning into hers. His expression was so complex it was hard to decipher, but she thought she saw anguish. And fear. And rage.

"There is a secret that the heads of all the Council families know," he began. "And because my father's death will make me the head of my family, he wanted me to learn it. I swear to you, Maddie, I never—not once, not *ever*—did I have the faintest idea about any of this."

"All right. I believe you. What is it?"

"The city—the whole country—it was all stitched together by Cordelan centuries ago."

She was completely bewildered. *This* was what had upset him? Some ancient religious mythology that everybody already knew? "Reese, what in the world—"

His hands tightened painfully on hers. "But there's a cost to it," he said, speaking over her. "The world is held together by some strange device that Cordelan left behind. And every few years it has to be primed with the blood of one of his descendants. And right now, the only one of his descendants who is still living is you."

The words were so nonsensical she could hardly take them in. Maybe Reese was experiencing a temporary bout of madness. "That's just ridiculous," she said.

"Outrageous," he agreed. "Almost incredible. But you know my father doesn't lie."

"But Reese—what—tell me again, only this time make sense."

"It doesn't *make* sense!" he exclaimed. "It seems the god created some mechanism that would hold the whole continent together. But it has to be fed every few years with blood, and that blood can only come from someone related to him. And if the blood isn't poured into this device, the world comes apart at the seams. Tremors. Geysers of fire. Destruction."

"The quakes," she whispered.

"Exactly. The quakes. And they're only going to get worse."

"But then—what—*whose* blood? How much of it?"

He looked as wretched as she had ever seen a person look. "The blood of someone who is directly descended from the god. Whose heritage has been traced for generations and generations. And apparently the only person left alive in this whole world who meets that requirement is you."

She just stared at him. After a long silence, he said, "Did you understand me? Say something."

"I'm not descended from Cordelan," was all she could come up with.

"Everybody seems to think you are."

"*No one* thinks it! My mother was an orphan, raised by the Kissidells out of kindness. No one even knew who her parents were."

Reese raised his eyebrows. "Someone knew. My father says that, decades ago, the Council decided to conceal the truth from these descendants because—understandably—they would not be eager to embrace their fate—"

She wrenched her hands away and threw herself across the room. "This is too fanciful to be believed! First you say the world will be destroyed without some blood sacrifice, then you say that I'm the one who will be that sacrifice—oh, and right, the reason I'm qualified is that I'm related to the *god?* Do you have any idea how insane you sound?

"I know. It sounds crazy. I know. But look at the facts—"

"There have not been any *facts* in this wild tale you have brought me!"

He held up a finger. "The world is being shaken by tremors."

"Yes, as it has been in the past!"

He nodded. "The last bad burst of quakes was ten years ago. Remember that." He held up a second finger. "Alastair Alayne, who is not the most romantic of men, married a young woman with a mysterious background who knew almost nothing of her own heritage." A third finger. "They had two children. One was a boy who died under tragic and unusual circumstances ten years ago."

"Yes, he was hit by a gridcar—" Her voice trailed off.

"But you never got to see his body. Because he wasn't killed accidentally. He was taken to the temple where he was drained of blood to appease the god."

And even though this entire story was farfetched, ridiculous, overwrought, impossible—at that moment, certainty clicked in place for Madeleine, and she *knew.* "Logan," she whispered.

"His death bought the city another ten years of stability," Reese continued. "But everyone knew the tremors would start up again. Well—everyone who was privy to this terrible secret. The heads of the Council families and the elite members of the priesthood."

"My father and Heloise. Of course," Madeleine said tonelessly. Oh, if there was any malevolent scheming to be done over the course of decades, she would count on the two of them to conduct it without shirking. But then her heart faltered. "Harlo?" she said in a small voice. "He knew?"

"Harlo," said Reese, "oversees the whole operation."

Madeleine nodded twice, the motion jerky and uncertain. She tried to say something, but suddenly she felt her balance give out, so she sat down abruptly in the window seat. Her fingers curled around the edge of the embrasure as she attempted to hold herself upright. "Yes, of course," she said. "If this ritual is designed to appease the god, naturally the high divine would be involved. It's just that he—I've always loved him more than I loved my father. He's been so good to me."

"He's had reason to be good to you," Reese said. "The safety of the world rests on your shoulders."

She looked up at him. She felt, suddenly, so lost and frail and tiny and alone. "So then he—they—all of them. They plan to—to—kill me? To feed my body to the god?"

He crossed the room in three strides and knelt in front of her, taking her hands in his once more. Impossible that anything could be reassuring in a moment like this, and yet his touch was just the tiniest bit comforting. "Oh no. No no no. They need you alive. You have to produce the *next* generation of children who will be sacrificed to Cordelan."

In her head she heard what her father had said when she warned him that a hasty marriage would make everyone think she was pregnant. *I wish you were.*

He *wanted* her to produce sons and daughters who would be slaughtered in the name of religion. He had known what fate awaited his own children before they were even born.

What kind of monster can plan to bring a child into this world merely to send it deliberately to its death? she wondered. *No wonder he never loved me. How could he bear to? And even knowing what lies in store, he wants me to have children with Tivol—*

Tivol—

The pain was so sudden and so real that she doubled over. Reese was still gripping her hands and so she folded over his arms as well as her own while her heart stopped and her lungs emptied and her ribs seemed to pierce every internal organ.

"Madeleine," Reese said urgently, creeping closer on his knees. "Maddie, what is it? I'm sorry, I'm sorry, I cannot believe I had to tell you all this—"

"Tivol," she gasped, still bent in half. "He knows. Doesn't he?"

Reese was silent a moment. "I can't be sure. But my guess is that he does."

"He wants to marry me and father my children and then send them off to die—"

"He believes—he must believe—that it is a good thing. The right thing. The only way to save the world. He must believe he has been given a terrible and solemn duty."

She rested her forehead on their clasped knuckles and tried to breathe without panting. She thought Reese might be right. Tivol had probably known this dreadful truth since they were quite young. To some extent it explained why he seemed so frivolous now, so determined to pursue light pleasures. His future would be grim enough. She briefly felt a surge of pity for him—but it was almost instantly obliterated by rage.

"I hate him," she said, pulling herself upright, her back absolutely straight. "I hate all of them."

Not letting go of her hands, Reese scrambled up from the floor and perched next to her. "I don't blame you," he said. "I hate them all myself."

"What I don't understand," she said, "is why they haven't been breeding me like a prize bitch for the past seven or eight years. I could have produced a whole *litter* of children by now. Why wait?"

"If I understood correctly, there's some chemical that has to form in your body before you will bear children whose blood is of the right composition."

"Well, I suppose I must thank Cordelan for that particular grace," she said with heavy irony. "But how do they know that I—*oh.*"

His hands tightened anxiously. "What?"

"They've been testing my blood. For the past five years at least. Every time I would have the slightest illness, my father would send for a physician, who always took a sample. And then, these past few weeks—all these little accidents—" She shook her head, reviewing the events that had seemed so small and unimportant. The day the glass had shattered in her hands when she was serving wine to Harlo. He had stanched the wound with a napkin—which he no doubt took back to the temple. The day Tivol had cut her thumb with a knife while serving cardu bread. Red droplets had stained one of the white chairs and Heloise had made her curious comment. *Nothing is more important than your blood.* More droplets on the table, on the brown bread, on the cloth Tivol magically produced . . .

"Tivol definitely knows," she said in a constricted voice.

Reese didn't ask her why she was so certain. He just said, "What are you going to do?"

She shook her head. "I can't even begin to answer that."

"I'll take you away," he offered. "We can go to Chibain, or anywhere else you want to go. I'll protect you to the limits of my life."

She focused on him for a moment. That dear face. Those blue eyes. That expression, so full of horror and fear and determination. How could she have ever thought she didn't love him? "What?" she said in gentle mockery. "You aren't prepared to sacrifice me to save the world?"

"I'm prepared to sacrifice the world to save you."

She leaned forward, and he did the same. Their foreheads touched. For a moment, she thought that the contrary pressure of his body was all that kept her from falling over flat again. "There has to be a way to save us both."

"I don't care," he whispered. "All I care about is you."

She hadn't wanted Reese to leave, but she hadn't wanted him to stay, either. Her head was full of thunderstorms and carrion crows, and she couldn't hear her own thoughts over the din. She had eventually sent him away so she could curl up in the window seat and think, but it turned out she still couldn't concentrate. So she just rested her cheek on her updrawn knees and listened to the wordless howling in her mind.

It was almost a relief when Jayla announced herself. Madeleine climbed stiffly to her feet as Jayla stepped in and closed the door. For a moment they regarded each other in the fading afternoon light.

"I learned something terrible today," Jayla said. "But by the look on your face, I'm thinking you might already have heard the story."

"If it concerns the plans that have been made for me by my father and Tivol and Harlo, then yes. I've heard the story. Reese told me this afternoon. How did *you* find out?"

"I know a man. An ex-priest. It's complicated, but I had a reason to ask him and he had a reason to tell me."

Madeleine nodded, too weary to inquire into additional secrets. "I am still trying to think through how my life has changed in every possible way. And what I have to do about it."

"It seems pretty obvious. You have to leave Corcannon."

"Reese offered to take me to Chibain."

Jayla regarded her steadily. "If Reese told you, does that mean he has always known this terrible thing?"

"I don't think so. He said his father just told him, to prepare him for his role as head of the Curval family. He looked even more shocked than I feel right now."

"I'm glad to hear it. I didn't want to think badly of him."

Madeleine surprised herself by laughing. "Oh, I'm sorry, but it pleases me so much to hear you say that! You have always seemed to favor Reese over Tivol, even though you never said a word—"

"It is not my place to have opinions about your friends." A beat. "Though I *did.*"

"And it bothered me that you might not think highly of Tivol." Madeleine sighed. "Well, of course, *now* it doesn't bother me."

Jayla grinned as if she couldn't help herself, but instantly grew serious. "So Reese is on your side. He could be a powerful ally. Would you be safe in his father's house in Chibain?"

"Would I be safe anywhere? If the world comes apart along the god's hand-sewn borders, will any of us be safe?"

"It's a serious question," Jayla admitted. "And I don't know how to answer. I just know that I will help you any way I can."

Madeleine surveyed her a moment. "I think the task of guarding me is about to get more complicated," she said at last. "And my father will certainly not pay you to help me rebel against him. This might be your best opportunity to walk away."

Jayla studied her in return. As always, Madeleine thought, the guard's pale face and serious eyes gave very little away. "I am going to have to keep Aussen's safety as one of my priorities," she said at last. "And if I think she will only be safe outside of this house and outside of this city, I will have to take her away. But for me, this is no longer about the job. This is about protecting you—and you need protection now more than ever."

"I think what I need most now is information," Madeleine said. "And then maybe I will have a better idea of what I need to do next."

"All right."

"But I also need—" She took a deep breath. "I also need to defy my father. And that will make him angry. And I'm not sure how I will handle that."

Jayla nodded. "I have a few ideas. Let's talk them over."

It took all of the next day for Madeleine and Jayla to finalize their plan, but Madeleine was pleased with how the pieces came together. She wished she could get Reese's opinion before putting it in motion, but he had business in Chibain and would be gone for the next few nights. But she was fairly certain he would approve.

The following morning, she rose from bed still nursing a headache, but nonetheless feeling a cold resolve that replaced some of the formless anxiety of the previous days. She had a faint idea of what to do next, and from this point on she would be feeling her way forward.

She dressed carefully, pinched some color into her cheeks, and threaded a ribbon through her dark hair. Not that her father would notice how she looked. He had never actually considered her a *person;* she understood that now. So she made the effort for herself.

She had timed it so she would arrive in the small dining room just as he was about to leave for the day. Indeed, he was on his feet and gathering up a handful of papers when she walked in. "I need to talk to you," she said.

He finished off his juice and set the glass down. "It'll have to wait until tonight."

"It has to be now," she said.

"Oh, for—what is it, Madeleine? I'm late already."

"I'm not going to let you marry me off to Tivol so I can produce children who will be sacrificed to Cordelan."

For a moment, she had the satisfaction of knowing she had caught him completely off-guard. His face showed a complex series of emotions—astonishment, something that might be fear, and something that was definitely calculation—before it shut down again. "I'm sorry you feel that way," he said coolly. "I admit, it is a great deal to ask of someone."

"I'm glad you're being so reasonable about it. I will send for Tivol and tell him our engagement is off."

"You won't," he said. "You will marry Tivol—very soon—and you will bear his children. You have a role to play and no choice but to play it."

"I am refusing to play it."

He took a step closer, his big body radiating menace. He had never struck Madeleine or her brother—never, as far as she knew, lifted a hand to their mother—but she had always believed he was capable of extreme violence. "You have no choice," he repeated. "If I must confine you to your quarters by force, I'll do it."

"People will miss me."

"People will hear the tragic story of your terrible illness. Who knows, you might even die."

"It will be awfully hard for Tivol to marry me and set up a household with me if I'm dead."

Her father shrugged. "The marriage is an attempt to give you some kind of normal life. It is not strictly necessary to meet the requirements of the god. Tivol could suitably mourn you and marry some other girl and move on with his own life."

Madeleine had never felt so cold, as if her bones had turned to icicles inside the snowbanks of her body. "While he visited me from time to time in order to get me with child?"

"Tivol—or anyone else who might play a similar part."

"You would turn me into Cordelan's whore," she said, deliberately vulgar.

"Only if you give us no other option. So think very carefully before you start telling me what you will and will not do."

She stepped deeper into the room. She was pleased that—despite her glacial chill, despite her escalating rage—she remained so steady. So calm. "Who do you think knows the true story?" she asked. "All the heads of the Council families, I suppose. And Harlo. But do all the devout young priests know? The bankers and the businessmen? The workers in the warehouses? Are they aware of this very delicate arrangement between the city and the god? How do you think they would react to that news?"

He grunted. "They would panic in the streets. Some would revolt against the priesthood for their centuries of lies, and some would tear down the houses of the Council families, calling us barbarians. But most would riot in terror, burning and looting and trampling each other to death in their haste to abandon the city, afraid of the destruction the god might rain down. We have always known this was a secret we had to keep or risk a completely different kind of ruination."

"What about my cousins and my aunts and uncles? How many of them are in possession of the secret?"

She could tell he was getting tired of her interrogation, but he had decided he needed to handle her carefully, so he answered. "My brother Archer knows, as he would take my place if something happened to me. None of the rest have been informed. The truth is too complex for ordinary men and women to be expected to understand."

So he didn't consider himself ordinary. Well, that wasn't a surprise. "I suppose you wouldn't like it if I told my cousins and my friends. If I shared the secret with your trading partners. And your bankers. And your servants."

Now he was angry again, and his eyes bored into hers. "No, Madeleine, I wouldn't like it, and you will do no such thing. I am starting to think I will need to cancel my appointments for the day and begin the unpleasant task of confining you to the house—perhaps for the rest of your life."

"I think you will be sorry if you do that," she said.

His eyes narrowed. "Can you possibly think you have something to threaten me with?"

"Information," she said. "It's always the best leverage."

"Be more specific."

"If I'm imprisoned. If I disappear. People will find out about this scheme of yours."

"It's not my scheme. And how do you think they'll find out?"

"There are letters. In the hands of someone who is watching the house. They'll be sent to people all over the city." She smiled. "I actually enjoyed putting that list together."

For the first time he looked uneasy. Even appalled. "You haven't done such a thing."

"I have. Explained the situation. Played up the arrogance of the Council families in maintaining this secret for so long—"

"You could—knowledge like that could bring the whole city down—even before the next quake hits!"

"That's what I thought," she agreed. "So I think it would serve you better if I maintained my freedom."

His expression turned grim. She could tell his mind was working furiously, trying to determine if she was bluffing, trying to figure out how to outmaneuver her if she wasn't. But she was pretty sure he couldn't follow this trail to its conclusion. Jayla's friend Cody had the letters. If Jayla didn't communicate regularly with Cody, the letters would be delivered. Even once her father pinpointed Jayla as an accomplice, he wouldn't know who else was in the chain.

"For the moment," he said, "you have your liberty. What do you intend to do with it?"

"I'm still determining that."

His gaze was intense. "Once you think about it, Madeleine, you will see that there are no other choices. You will pay a terrible price—you must realize I have paid the same price—but your actions will save the world. It is a noble cause, if a heavy one."

"I'm having a hard time seeing it that way."

"You're a silly, selfish girl who has never thought of anything but herself!"

"And you're a murderer."

He was on her before she had time to react. He slapped her across the face so hard that she staggered against a table, sending two plates crashing to the tile. Before she could do more than cry out, a blur burst through the door, and Jayla flung herself across the room. The force of her attack brought both of them to the floor, Jayla with a knife at her father's throat.

"The world might need Madeleine, but it doesn't need you," she said.

For a moment they were all frozen in place, Jayla and her father staring pitilessly at each other, Madeleine gaping at both of them. Her father was the first to recover.

"Let me up," he said.

For an answer, Jayla ground her knee into his stomach, causing him to grunt in pain. Her blade never wavered.

Madeleine gathered her wits and crossed the room, stepping daintily past the broken china. "I can tell what you're thinking," she said, peering down at him. "And it would be just as foolish for you to try to do away with Jayla. Because if *she* disappears, those letters are also going out to all your associates and all your relatives."

His eyes still on Jayla, he repeated, "Let me up."

"Very well. Jayla, you can release him."

Jayla came smoothly to her feet, but didn't put away her knife. Her father more slowly clambered up. He was trying to keep his expression neutral, but she could see a storm of emotions scudding across his face. Rage. Frustration. Uneasiness. An edge of panic. Each one gave her a sense of bitter satisfaction.

"We'll talk again tonight," he said.

"We won't," she answered. "I want you gone from here. I don't think I can manage another civil conversation with you—and I can't bear to look at you."

"You're barring me from my own house? Where do you expect me to go?"

"You have enough money to buy ten houses. Go wherever you like."

He eyed her a long moment, as if he still thought he could come up with some argument that might move her, and then he nodded. "Give me an hour to collect my things. Do you want me to send you word of my new address?"

"Certainly. It would be useful to have if I ever find myself with the desire to speak to you again."

He shouldered past the two of them and paused at the door for a parting shot. "I'm sure you will," he said. "I expect it will be at your wedding."

She and Jayla waited in the dining room for the entire hour it took him to pack a few bags and gather his necessary papers. Between her headache and a rising nausea, Madeleine couldn't bring herself to eat, but she nibbled on a piece of toast just to have something to do. Two of the servants crept to the door as if they wanted to clear the table or sweep the floor, but she just shook her head and they backed away. She wondered how much of the argument they'd heard. The door had been cracked open just enough to allow Jayla to monitor their conversation—because Jayla had predicted her father would try to hurt her—and Jayla had been standing guard that whole time. Madeline didn't think anyone else could have caught the incendiary accusations about the priesthood and the god. She didn't think any of the servants had heard her call her father a murderer.

But everyone would know she had kicked him out of the house.

This story would be all over Corcannon before noon. She would have to invent some way to explain it to her own circle, since she obviously couldn't tell the truth.

She caught the sound of her father's footsteps descending the stairwell, heard him give an instruction to the footman. The door opened—he spoke again—and the door closed.

That was when Madeleine sank bonelessly to the floor in a puff of fabric and buried her head in her hands.

Chapter Twenty-five: Madeleine

Tivol was the first to arrive, not two hours after her father's departure. Madeleine briefly entertained the thought that he was dropping by for a casual visit, and she was tempted to have Ella tell him she was too unwell to see him. But that would just make him suspicious, and Tivol could be as persistent as Reese. He might actually run upstairs and barge into her room—and if she asked Jayla to throw him out, Madeleine would give away the whole game. She had to come up with an explanation that he would believe. And that would preoccupy him so much he wouldn't probe deeper for the truth.

So she agreed to receive him in the downstairs gilt room, but she presented herself as sick and suffering. When he strode through the door, she was lounging on a sofa, resting her aching head against a pillow and letting all her weariness show on her face.

"Madeleine! My darling!" Tivol exclaimed. He came over to give her a quick kiss on the cheek, then pulled up a footstool to sit on. He took both her hands in his and said, "You are always beautiful, of course, but you look as dreadful as a beautiful woman possibly could."

She wanted to wrench her hands away; she wanted to scrub his kiss from her face. Instead, she lay there quiescent, allowing her lips to tremble. "I have such a headache," she said.

"I am so sorry to hear it! I won't stay long. But Madeleine—I have heard the most extraordinary tale—"

She turned her face away. "I've quarreled with my father."

"And demanded that he leave the house? What could possibly have brought you to such a pass?"

It wasn't hard to make her voice wavering and woebegone. "I told him—I told him I'm not going to marry you next month."

There was a short silence, then Tivol rubbed his thumbs along the backs of her hands in what he seemed to think was a comforting manner. "It's been a lot, I know," he said. "To have this decision so suddenly thrust upon us! Trying to plan the wedding, and looking for a house, and thinking about how everything will change—but, darling, don't be overwhelmed by all the details." He kissed her knuckles. "Just think about finally starting our lives together. Something we've both wanted for longer than I can even remember."

Still staring at the back of the sofa, she said, "I told him I wanted to marry Reese instead."

Now the silence in the room was profound. Tivol's hands all of a sudden seemed stiff and bony; he released her. "I see," he said.

She covered her face. "I'm so confused!" she wailed. "Reese makes me so angry—and yet I can't stop thinking about him—and he tells me he loves me. And I think I love him, but I'm not sure, but I think I do." Now she pulled herself into a smaller shape and presented herself as one wretched ball of misery. "And I don't want to hurt you, but I don't see how I can marry you if I want to be with another man."

It was a long time before he answered. She had to imagine that he was furious but trying hard not to show it. She was too valuable a prize to lose; he would have to placate and cajole her, aim to keep her friendship even as she spurned his love. He had to try to win her back. The thought was sickening.

"Well, this is a blow," he said in the unconvincing tones of a man trying to use bravery to cover an almost fatal wound. "Give me a moment to absorb it."

"It's not like I meant it to happen," she whispered.

"No. I don't suppose you did. Love is like that sometimes."

It was such a generous thing to say that for a moment she was pierced with doubt. Maybe he didn't know. Maybe he wanted to marry her simply because he loved her. But then she remembered the cardu bread and the knife and the blood, and anger filled her again with cold certainty.

"And I told my father and we had a terrible fight and he said the most awful things to me—and so I asked him to leave. And he did."

"You will reconcile with him soon enough, I'm sure."

"I don't think so. He's a terrible man."

"Madeleine!"

"Well, he is." *And so are you.* She managed not to say it out loud.

"What do you plan to do next?" he asked. "You can tell me that while I try to adjust my mind to the idea that you are no longer in my life."

"I will marry Reese. I think."

"Ah. Well, then—I hope—I hope you and I will still be friends."

She rubbed her hands across her face, inhaled deeply, and finally turned to look at him. "I hope so, too," she said. "But it might be hard."

"Almost impossible," he agreed. "But truly impossible would be losing you altogether."

She rearranged her lips, but she was sure her expression did not resemble a smile. "Don't be angry with Reese," she begged. "It's not his fault."

"Isn't it?" he said. "I'd rather blame him than you. I'm not sure I'll be able to avoid punching him in the face next time I see him."

Her expression of alarm was only half false. "Then you must avoid him!"

"I will as much as possible. But I assume he will be at the next Council meeting, as I understand his father is too frail to travel."

"I hope the next meeting is a long time from now, so that you will have gotten used to all this by then."

He sighed. "Sadly, no, it is the day after tomorrow. We will all be meeting at Harlo's apartment. You would know this, of course, if your father was still in the house."

"No, I wouldn't. My father rarely told me anything."

He gave her a serious look. "Your father always underestimated you, I think," he said. "I believe people often make that mistake with you."

She held her breath as she stared back. That didn't sound like a rejected lover speaking. That sounded like a man acknowledging a skilled opponent. She wondered if he had not been fooled, after all, by this afternoon's charade. "I think my father never bothered to get to know me," she said softly. "And maybe I never tried hard enough to understand him."

"Maybe that will change in the coming days."

"I don't think so," she said. "But lately I've found that I've been wrong about almost everything."

Tivol lingered much longer than she would have expected, still playing the part of the wounded suitor determined to accept his dismissal with grace. She finally had to ask him plaintively to leave so that she could try to sleep away her headache. He kissed her cheek, gave her one more sorrowful look, and departed.

But before she could even leave the room, the next visitors were at the door. Two of her friends, who had also heard the news and were agog to learn the details. And once they left, her cousin arrived; and the whole afternoon went like that.

Eventually her headache was bad enough and the gossip had been spread far enough that she decided she could just tell the servants to stop admitting any other visitors. Massaging the back of her head where the pain was worst, she went looking for Jayla, and found her in the kitchen with Aussen and Norrah. Madeleine beckoned, and Jayla followed her out into the hall.

"The day after tomorrow," Madeleine said in a low voice. "The Council is meeting at Harlo's. I have to attend."

Madeleine chose her favorite dress, a simple scarlet sheath that made her skin and hair looked radiant, and topped it with a scarf shot through with orange and yellow and red. "You look like a walking bonfire," Jayla said.

"Exactly the impression I'd like to give," Madeleine replied.

They took a public chugger to the Quatrefoil, something Madeleine had only done a few times in her adult life, though when she was younger, she and Logan had hopped off and on the big transports all the time. Jayla seemed perfectly at ease navigating the route, despite having lived in the city for a relatively short time. But then, casual competence was Jayla's defining characteristic.

They stepped off at the stop nearest the temple and walked the three blocks to Harlo's residence. The streets, as usual, were packed with attractive young people dressed for a night out. They were greeting each other with warm hugs and chattering excitedly about the theater or the restaurant they planned to patronize that night. Madeleine was surprised at the strength of her conflicting reactions. Jealousy, because their lives were so simple and joyous in a way that hers would never be again. And scorn, because they wasted their days in such meaningless pursuits.

Five days ago, she had been one of them.

What would have to happen to make all of them as angry and desperate and afraid as she was?

Unlike the last time she had visited it, Harlo's residence was not gaudy with lights and crowded with partygoers. Instead, a few soft lamps threw the white walls into inviting relief, and only two guards watched the entrance.

"I'm here for the meeting," she said in an imperious voice. She wouldn't be on the invitation list, but any temple guard in Corcannon would recognize her face. "I believe my father is inside."

The two men exchanged swift glances, and the one who appeared to be the ranking officer briefly nodded. "He is, dona," said the younger one, pulling open the door. "They are upstairs in the patri's private rooms."

She nodded regally and swept inside, Jayla at her heels. "Thank you. I know the way."

Harlo's suite was on the third story, up a grand staircase broad enough to accommodate a marching troop. To the left were his personal quarters, which Madeleine had never been inside; to the right were his office, a library, and a dining hall that could hold about twenty people. Madeleine could hear the low hum of voices as she approached the room, could smell the rich scents of expensive food. She glanced back just to make *sure* Jayla was with her, then she stepped through the open door.

In the moments it took for anyone to realize she was in the room, she took a swift look around, noting where all the Council members sat. They tended to be grouped by the lands they represented. Heloise and Tivol sat near Cherse Bandelo and his daughter, all of them owning property in Marata. Lara Dargenten and her son, who were from Chibain, had taken seats by Reese. She focused briefly on Reese, because just the sight of him made her steadier, even though he hadn't seen her yet.

Then she surveyed the rest of the table. Harlo and her father, representing the interests of the city, had been joined by Madeleine's uncle Archer. She had always considered Archer a cold and dispassionate man, though her cousins were extremely fond of him; now she supposed his knowledge of her eventual fate had made it hard for him to show her any affection. She noted that Harlo had come alone. Did he not have a successor who knew the whole story? Surely the secretary of the sanctuary must know the truth. She even wondered if he had shared the details with Benito.

She also noticed something she should have realized a long time ago. No one on the Council represented the islands or Oraki, which apparently didn't deserve votes in government. She wondered how the goddess Zessaya felt about that.

As she was trying to decide how to announce herself, there was the sound of a glass falling over and Lara Dargenten muffling a curse. Everyone looked Lara's way—and then turned to see what she was staring at with such dismay. The room grew absolutely still.

"Good evening," Madeleine said, pleased to find her voice did not tremble. "Have you all been discussing me?"

Her father came to his feet. "Madeleine," he said sharply. "You shouldn't be here."

She stepped deeper in the room. "I think I should."

Now Harlo was standing, reaching his hand out and offering his usual benevolent smile. To think that she had always gone to Harlo when she needed solace! To remember that he was the one who had comforted her after Logan died! "Madeleine," he said in his sweet way. "Has something happened? We are always happy to see you, but we are in the middle of Council business. It's not the best time for you to be here."

"It is the perfect time for me to be here, as *I* am the Council's business."

Her father came striding around the table, his face red with fury. She thought he might try to grab her arm and fling her out of the room, so she moved quickly to put a serving table between them. He would look ridiculous trying to chase her around a piece of furniture, and he knew it, because he came to an abrupt stop. "This is not the time," he said in a low, frustrated voice.

"I'm no longer interested in your opinion," she said.

Tivol had also jumped to his feet. He called out her name, but it was lost in the general swell of questions from everyone else at the table. Most of the others had also risen, but they stood uneasily by their chairs, not sure what to do next. Harlo was the only one brave enough to approach her, his arm still outstretched.

"What's happened, my dear?" Harlo asked. She twitched away when he tried to take her hand, but he maintained his expression of concern. "Tell me."

She focused on his face when she answered. "What's happened is that I've learned I—and my children—have been chosen as sacrifices to Cordelan. I thought we should talk about that."

Harlo's face showed such shocked alarm that Madeleine felt a rush of savage triumph. He staggered back, but her father stepped closer and Tivol came hurrying around the dining room table. She flung out a hand and ordered, "Stay away from me."

Tivol halted beside her father and stared at her, his face stricken. "Madeleine—is this why you—oh, Madeleine, if you only knew how many times I wanted to tell you—"

She spoke directly to him. "If you had wanted me to know, you would have told me." She glanced from her father to Harlo. "And you. And you. All pretending to love me, and all scheming behind my back."

Harlo had a hand to his heart, as if it was breaking and he thought he might hold the shattered pieces together with his fingers. "Never pretending," he said, his beautiful voice broken. "Child, I have loved you so much and grieved every day at what lay in store for you—"

"Even if that were true," she said, "I hate you."

Lara Dargenten spoke up over the resulting hubbub. "Fine, you know the truth, you're furious," she said in her strident voice. "Nothing changes, except that maybe we move ahead with less secrecy. Which is what I've always favored anyway." When Madeleine looked her way, Lara gave her a brief, brisk nod. "It's a tragedy, but we might as well enlist your willing cooperation. Easier on all of us."

"Oh, you are too optimistic if you think I am endorsing your plans," Madeleine said. "Willing does even remotely describe my state of mind."

"You have no choice," Lara said shortly.

"Madeleine," Tivol begged. "Don't you see? They will *compel* you. Your only hope for any kind of life is to agree to their terms—"

She glanced at her father, her eyebrows raised. He said shortly, "She has shared the information with confederates who will publish it widely if she is mistreated in any fashion."

There was a collective gasp at that news, then a few moments of furious arguing. Harlo touched her arm again, and again she shook him off. "Madeleine," he said, his face creased with distress. "That is terrible, dangerous information to set loose in the world."

"So don't mistreat me," she said. "It seems simple enough."

"None of this is simple!" he exclaimed. "How do you think I feel, presiding over the deaths of the wholly innocent? But what else can I do? Who would not choose one life over millions of lives? Are *you* so selfish and depraved that you would condemn all those people to death?"

"And are you so omniscient that you know what will happen?" she shot back. "If the blood is withheld. If the lever doesn't move. You don't know the consequences."

"The world is already shaking at its seams!" her father shouted. "We know what comes next!"

"You *think* you know."

"The continent will come apart," Harlo said. "The mountains will shear away from the midlands, and the islands will break off and return to the sea."

"That doesn't sound so terrible to me," she said.

For the first time, Heloise spoke up. "Then you lack a brain as well as a heart," she said. "Almost all the water in Marata comes from the Darrish River, which springs from the mountains and crosses the god's divide. If the continent comes apart, the river rushes to the sea, and Marata becomes a desert."

Reese answered, his voice so welcome to Madeleine's ears that she almost wept. "It was a desert before, and people survived."

"Do you think so? From the records I have seen, very few people populated the midlands until the god turned those barren fields into farms. And now? Hundreds of thousands live upon that land. What happens if it suddenly turns infertile? How many will die of thirst or starvation within a year?"

Madeleine felt her heart twist at that question—how many, indeed?—but Reese answered without hesitation. "If one of them is you, Heloise, I might be willing to make that bargain."

Tivol turned on him. "Shut up!" he shouted. "Don't say such things to her!"

Heloise shrugged. "I don't care what Reese Curval says to me, but he needs to think about his own situation."

"I *have* a river to water my lands," he said outrageously.

"Do you?" Heloise answered. "How many crops do you grow in the mountains of Chibain? Don't you import at least half of your food from Marata? What will you eat if that whole prairie turns to dust?"

He stared at her with no attempt to disguise his disgust. "I'm not killing Madeleine just because I'm afraid to find out."

"No, and I don't want to kill her either!" Heloise exclaimed.

"You just want me to bear a dozen children so you can kill *them.*"

Heloise stared at Madeleine across the room, her dark eyes so cold Madeline could feel the ice. "If the blood of my son could work that device, I would sacrifice him," she said. "If *my* blood would be enough, I would sacrifice myself."

"How do you know it wouldn't be?" Madeleine retorted. "Maybe we should try that first."

Tivol uttered her name again, horrified, but she was watching Harlo, who was shaking his head. "You think we haven't tried that?" he said sadly. "We had willing volunteers—priests and Council members who knew the truth and had no fear of death. But their blood was too mortal. It was not enough to appease the god."

"So you were back to slaughtering children."

"There was no choice," Harlo insisted, his voice barely above a whisper. "The consequences were too dire."

"The consequences? The world breaks into the patterns it held before Cordelan intervened," Reese said. "Heloise is right—there will be monumental adjustments. But to continue this barbaric practice—"

Harlo whirled around to face him. "*Adjustments!* Do you think the land will ease apart gradually, a little at a time, each region drifting peacefully from the others? I tell you, it will roil with avalanche and explode in flame! It will be a parting so violent that it's possible no one will survive!"

Madeleine felt herself blanch again, but Reese remained cool. "You have no way of knowing that."

"Of course I do! The ruined lands to the east—*they* were first assembled by the god's hands, and *they* came apart when the proper sacrifices were not made. You wonder why I am so afraid? I have seen that place for myself, and there is almost nothing left but landscapes of melted rock and beaches of salt and ash."

Reese held Harlo's gaze. "How do you know that destruction was caused by the god? Maybe the ground shifted of its own accord and had nothing to do with Cordelan's displeasure."

Harlo's voice was weary. "We have papers in the archives. Accounts from hundreds and hundreds of years ago. The god assembled the eastern continent when he assembled ours. But the people of the eastern lands did not take the proper measures, and the continent tore itself to pieces." Harlo's hand made an arc in the air. "The eruption was so loud it could be heard in Corcannon. The smoke and cinders were so thick in the air that the sun could barely break through for months. Summer was chilly and the harvest was poor. There was plenty of death in our lands, too, from the resulting famine. But there was annihilation to the east."

Every word was a dagger in Madeleine's heart, but Reese remained stubbornly unconvinced. "The god may have assembled the eastern lands, and those lands may have shattered, but my original question remains. How can you be sure of the catalyst for that destruction? It might have had nothing to do with the blood sacrifice you think the god demands."

Harlo gazed at him somberly. "I know that every decade or so, our land is rocked by powerful quakes. I know that when we appease the god with blood from his descendants, the quakes stop. Can I be sure the devastation will be absolute if we fail to move the lever? No. But can you be sure it won't be if we don't?"

Lara stirred and spoke up again. "And yet, even if this is all true, we have very limited options. If we were to sacrifice Madeleine today—"

"*You will not sacrifice Madeleine!*" Reese roared.

"We still would not have solved our problem. If she is the god's last surviving heir, we will face exactly the same dreadful dilemma in another ten years."

"That's why she must marry me instantly and bear children as soon as possible," Tivol broke in.

Reese turned on him. "Whatever else happens, she will not be marrying *you.*"

Her father made a brushing motion. "Fine. You can marry her and sire her children. But are *you* prepared to see them surrendered at the temple? At least Tivol can be counted on to see his duty through."

Lara raised her voice to be heard above the squabbling. "But we still have solved nothing. It would be another ten years before a child was large enough to be useful. Do we even have that kind of time?"

Madeleine wanted to shriek from revulsion at this cold calculation. She had never been the kind of person who yearned for babies, who pictured herself cuddling a cooing infant in her arms. But Lara was talking about children, *Madeleine's* children, as if they were livestock being bred for the slaughterhouse.

Harlo shook his head. "I don't know. I don't think so. The quakes are getting stronger. But—we have no choice but to try." He turned back to Madeleine, and his expression was pleading. "We beg you to help us. To marry and conceive—and to be willing, when the time comes, to give up your most precious gift to save us all."

She tried to preserve her calm, but she still wanted to shriek and rage and strike every single Council member across the face—and then run from the room, curl up in a corner, and sob. She took a slow breath. "I don't know that I am willing," she said, her voice as steady as she could make it. "I just know that you have presented me with a terrible dilemma, and the fact that you have lied to me for my entire life does not make me trust you or wish to accommodate you."

Harlo bowed his head. "Keeping you in ignorance seemed like the kindest course, but perhaps we were wrong. Do not let your anger at us blind you to the terrible price everyone else in the world will pay."

She gestured toward the table. "As Lara says, even if I cooperate, it will be years before—before anything can be done. Would there be any value in me giving you *some* of my blood? As much as I can stand to lose?"

She heard Reese's voice say "*Maddie,*" but she didn't look his way, just kept her eyes on Harlo.

"I don't know. It might be enough to move the wheel an inch or two. It might buy us a couple of months." He shook his head. "It might not."

"That is a donation I am willing to make," she said. "So that we—you—I can think through what else we might do to avert catastrophe."

"We *know* what we must do," Heloise said.

Madeleine looked at her. "No," she said simply, "we don't."

Tivol stepped closer, his face eager. "Madeleine, if we could just talk—"

She jerked back, even though he wasn't close enough to touch her. "I don't *want* to talk to you."

Reese practically leapt across the room to come to her side and put an arm around her shoulders. She knew it was cowardly, but she leaned against him just because she needed the support so badly. "You stay away from her," Reese said fiercely. "You don't deserve to ever talk to her again."

Tivol started forward angrily. "If you think—"

Madeleine's father grabbed him in a hard hold. "Let it go," he said. "At least for now."

"But—"

"There is much we still have to determine," Harlo said, intervening smoothly. "But when can you come to the temple to give your gift?"

"Tomorrow, if you like. Unless you want to traipse over there now, in the dark."

"Tomorrow will be excellent."

Reese said, "I'll come with you."

She glanced around the room and then up at him. "Are you done here? You could leave with me now."

He didn't look back at her father or Harlo or anyone. "Of course."

"Before you go," Harlo said.

Reese was shepherding her toward the door. "You can tell her in the morning."

"She needs to hear this."

Madeleine didn't quite pull free of Reese's hold, but she did stop and look back. "What is it?"

"The attempts on your life," Harlo began.

Now she and Reese both spun around to face him, wearing matching expressions of apprehension. "What?" she demanded.

"I'm afraid they might continue. For almost as long as this continent has existed, there have been fanatical groups who suspected the truth about the god's requirement. And who made it their mission to try to—eliminate—the sacrifice."

"I thought those were myths," Heloise said.

"Sadly, no. I thought—we all thought—the group had been eradicated years ago. But it seems someone has revived it. These fanatics call themselves Reversionists. They have some fevered notion of returning the world to the way it was before the god reshaped it. And they think to do that by killing you." Harlo gave her a long, troubled stare. "You must be very careful."

"I have my guard."

"I doubt a solitary person will be enough to protect you. As each of their attempts fail, they grow more emboldened. You need a cadre of soldiers. I can have a detail of temple guards sent home with you tonight."

"Thank you," she said, but Reese spoke over her.

"No," he said. "I don't trust Harlo's men."

Harlo gave a twisted smile. "I understand why your opinion of me has fallen so low, but I assure you, Madeleine's safety is as important to me as it is to you."

"Oh, I don't think *you* want her dead. But I'm guessing some of these zealots come from within the temple ranks."

A low murmur of uneasiness went through the dinner guests, and Madeleine felt a chill along her spine. "Why do you think that?" she asked.

Reese nodded at Harlo. "Who else knows about you? The priests—"

"Only a few of the priests," Harlo interrupted.

"And this lot." He gestured toward the Council members. "It might be one of your cousins or your closest friends scheming to do away with you, but I'm betting fanatics are more likely to be bred in the temple. *And,*" he added, raising his voice when Harlo attempted to speak, "the patri knows it." He glanced down at Madeleine. "That woman who attacked you the night of the party? Harlo told you she died by her own hand, but I heard she was killed by someone in the temple." Now he looked at Harlo again. "Because someone in the priesthood didn't want her interrogated."

"Harlo, is this true?" her father demanded.

"It is true she died while in custody," Harlo said. "And we're not sure how."

Her father swore loudly and violently enough to earn disgusted looks from Lara and Heloise, but Reese ignored him. "So you see why I don't trust the patri's guard," Reese concluded. "I have hand-picked soldiers in my employ. I'll put them at Madeleine's disposal."

"Thank you," she said in a strangled voice. She really wasn't sure she could handle one more revelation today. "Can we go home now?"

Reese's arm tightened. "Of course."

She ignored both her father and Tivol as they called her name again, and she looked straight at Harlo. "I will come to you in the morning and give you what I can," she said. "And after that—after that, I will decide what I owe you and what I owe the world."

She thought it was as good an exit line as she would be able to devise. Without another word, she headed toward the door, Reese beside her and Jayla falling in step behind them.

She had no idea what she had just bargained for. She had no idea what she would do next. She thought it hardly mattered if the god turned his blind wrath on her. As far as she was concerned, the world had already fallen apart.

Chapter Twenty-six: Pietro

Pietro was lying in Stollo's arms when he said, "I need to visit the ruined lands."

Stollo rolled to his back and laughed. "Now that's a first," he said, his voice full of good-natured mockery. "I've had lovers praise my skill, and I've had lovers carefully explain to me why our night of carnal bliss meant absolutely nothing. But I've never had one tell me, after only one night of passion, that he wanted to go journeying to the far ends of the world."

Pietro managed a crooked smile. "It is not to escape *you* that I need to make the trip."

"I don't suppose you'll tell me the reason, though."

Pietro sighed silently, because Stollo was right. Pietro had become a distrustful, secretive man who never told anyone anything. "Maybe once I get back." Because by that point, it might not matter.

"When do you plan to leave?"

"As soon as I can find a boat to hire."

Still lying on his back, Stollo turned his head to look at Pietro, who lay propped up on his elbow, gazing down at the other man. *My lover,* Pietro thought, savoring the simple syllables. He had resigned himself to never having reason to speak the words again.

Stollo said, "Should I ask my cousin?"

"Who?"

"My cousin Danner. I mentioned him a couple months back. He runs a boat out of Corcannon harbor."

Pietro remembered. "Do you think he'd take me?"

"If he doesn't have another job lined up, I can't see why he wouldn't."

"Would you introduce me to him? Vouch for my character?"

Stollo poked him playfully in the ribs. "I don't know how I could do that, since I've never known a man who was *less* forthcoming than you. I scarcely know a thing about you."

"Then you've shown remarkable lack of judgment by climbing into my bed."

"I'm impulsive," Stollo agreed. "Careless. Someday I'll reap the consequences."

Pietro flattened his hand over Stollo's chest, which was pleasingly muscular and covered with sleek dark hair. "Don't say that," he replied, troubled. "I hate to think of anything bad happening to you."

Stollo placed his own hand over Pietro's. "I was joking," he said. "I'm not as rash as all that. And I'm certainly not afraid that *you* will be the one to harm me."

"I hope not." Pietro dropped down so the back of his head hit the pillow, and stared up through the darkness. It must be close to midnight, but they had left the curtains open, and faint lights from the street played through the window. He could almost make out the spot where the vertical walls joined the flat horizontal plane of the ceiling. But mostly everything in the room was in murky shadow.

Just like everything in his life.

"I never *want* to do harm," Pietro said slowly. "But I think I've inflicted my share nevertheless."

"We all have," Stollo said. "If a man walks through a meadow, he crushes flowers underfoot, but that doesn't mean he is cruel. Just by moving through life, you crash into other people. As they crash into you."

"So intent is all that matters?"

"Intent is half of it. The other half is what you do to make reparation."

"Well, there I'm not so sure I'm absolved, either."

"You're in a bleak humor tonight," Stollo observed.

"I've been in a bleak humor for ten years," Pietro said. "Sometimes I'm able to hide it better."

"And you think a visit to the ruined lands will lift your spirits? I'm inclined to think the opposite is true." Now Stollo lifted his head. "Unless you consider that the perfect place to seek your own destruction. In which case, I will *not* introduce you to my cousin after all."

Pietro's smile was small and bitter. "No. I'd have done it years ago if that was my plan. I'm going with a probably doomed hope of discovering—something. I don't even know what."

"Is it a journey you have to make alone?"

"What? No. I need the ship's captain, of course."

"I meant—would you want me to come with you?"

This was an entirely new thought. Pietro turned to look at him. Stollo had shifted again and was lying on his side, watching him. "Would you be *willing* to join me?"

"If I wouldn't be in the way. If you wanted my company."

"What about your priestly duties? You can't just walk away."

Stollo grinned. "I can get a leave of absence. Say I have an urgent family matter. Which will be the truth, if my cousin takes us." Stollo scanned Pietro's face. "I don't mean to pressure you. I won't ask to come if you'd rather travel alone."

"I feel like I have traveled the whole world by myself," Pietro said. "I can't remember the last time I had the grace of a companion at my side. What worries me is the fact that you would begin your association with me by lying to your superiors. How can I be good for you if I set you off on a course of deceit?"

Stollo leaned forward and pressed his mouth against Pietro's—to reassure him or to simply stop him from talking, Pietro could not be certain. "Since I have become a priest, I have lived by a creed that I will go where I can do the greatest good," Stollo said in a husky voice. "And that belief has taken me to the docks and the slums more often than it has taken me to the temple or the mansions. It has put me in the path of people who need me. And I can't shake the idea that you need me."

Pietro tried to keep his voice steady. "So I'm a charity case."

Stollo produced a muffled laugh. "You're a puzzle I want to solve. You're a fascination I can't look away from. You're a child I want to comfort and a man I want to embrace. I will talk to my cousin in the morning. And if you want me to accompany you, I shall pack my bags in the evening. But I won't beg you to take me on this mysterious quest, so I'm not going to offer again. If you want me, you have to say so."

Pietro rolled forward, covering Stollo's mouth with his own. "Yes, I want you with me," he murmured. "I don't know how I thought I could manage this without you."

Three days later, they were on their way. It turned out that Stollo's cousin had been unenthusiastically contemplating the idea of taking his small craft down the rough eastern edge of the continent to the southernmost harbor tucked into the Marata coastline. But it was a familiar route and he was a man who liked the occasional adventure, and he had been hoping that a better opportunity would present itself.

"He says you have to pay the wages for himself and two crewmen, but if he picks up any cargo, you won't have to pay travel expenses," Stollo said.

"Does he *expect* to find cargo?"

"Says it's a good possibility. People live in the ruined lands, you know—

just not very many of them—and they do a little mining and farming. They have goods to trade, but not in enough volume for most captains to be willing to make the voyage."

"Tell me how much I need to pay in advance, and I'm ready to go."

The Corcannon harbor was inconveniently situated for anyone not absolutely determined to get onto the ocean in the quickest manner possible. It lay off the southeast edge of the city, accessible only via a narrow, two-lane bridge that descended abruptly from the mountain plateau to sea level. Traffic in both directions was steady, as shipments were constantly being delivered to warehouses in the dock district and empty wagons were returning to pick up the next load, but it wasn't particularly heavy. The city harbor was too small and its waters were too shallow to permit large vessels to drop anchor, so the majority of the goods that flowed into Corcannon came overland across the Maratan bridges. But anyone who just wanted to slip out of the city and hop aboard a small seaworthy craft could take the mountain route and be out on the open water within a few hours.

Stollo's cousin Danner was about average height, thick-bodied, with a guarded expression and intelligent eyes. On his left wrist, he wore a sailor's bracelet, stamped with stylized fish and set with an assortment of ocean-colored jewels. On his right was a gold bracelet edged with silver, a slim silver circlet, and two gold bands. Pietro interpreted this to mean that he was a widower with a pair of sons. Judging by the features of the strapping young men who helped them load their luggage, Danner's boys doubled as his crew.

"Welcome aboard," Danner said, ducking down a narrow stairwell to lead them to a cramped space belowdecks. "These will be your quarters." He glanced at Pietro. "I was led to believe you'd share a room, but if my cousin was misleading me, I'll throw him overboard and you can have the place to yourself."

This was said so seriously that it took Pietro a moment to realize the man was joking. "No, indeed, he told you the truth," he answered. "But thank you for looking out for my interests."

"Paying guest is always favored over freeloading relatives," Danner said, still without cracking a smile. "Let me know if he becomes a nuisance."

Stollo was grinning as if this was familiar raillery. "Never any respect from my family," he groused.

"Well, if you'd take a job befitting a real man," said Danner.

"Careful. Your paying guest was once a priest, too."

Danner appraised Pietro. "Seems he's thought better of it, though. Makes him a wiser man than you."

"Is it the profession or the deity you dislike?" Pietro inquired.

Danner grunted. "Don't have much use for Cordelan." He pulled out a leather cord, hung with a cherloshe charm. Pietro leaned close enough to decipher the pose. In one tiny hand, the goddess was holding a fish, the symbol most closely affiliated with her; in the other, a sheaf of wheat. This was goddess as provider. "A man who sails the ocean knows who deserves his fealty," Danner said.

Pietro smiled and drew out his own chazissa, hung with the goddess in her pose of knowledge. "Even a landbound man has cause to honor Zessaya," he said.

Danner examined the charm with an impassive face, then glanced over at Stollo. "I approve," he said, and departed without another word.

"That seemed to go well," Pietro said, but Stollo had already collapsed on the narrow bunk. He was laughing too hard to keep to his feet.

Danner had estimated that the outbound journey would take a week. At the news, Pietro had stifled a silent protest, because he couldn't imagine how he could fill so many empty days. However, within a few hours of casting off from the small harbor, Pietro was far more preoccupied with nausea than boredom. Stollo hustled him over to the window, so he could vomit directly into the water, though the sight of the lashing waves did nothing to calm his stomach. He could hardly blame Stollo for exiting the room with all speed. He threw up two more times, then sunk to the floor in abject misery, thinking how pleasant it must be to die.

Stollo bustled back in, looking offensively healthy and unimaginably cheerful. "Well, you look as wretched as a man might be!" he exclaimed. "Here, I've brought you something to drink."

The very thought made Pietro's stomach rebel. "I couldn't possibly."

"This will make you feel better. I promise," Stollo said, sinking to his knees and holding out a mug of some herbal concoction. "Come on. Just have a few sips."

Reluctantly, Pietro took the mug from his hand and lifted it to his face. In the rising steam, he thought he recognized the scent of ginger mixed with unfamiliar ingredients that made him think of woodlands or garden dirt. "If I throw up all over you, you have only yourself to blame."

He managed a few cautious swallows. The liquid was hot enough to burn his tongue, but its salutary effect on his stomach was almost instantaneous. He took another sip.

"And stick out your hand. Palm up. This should help too."

Obediently, Pietro extended his left arm. Stollo balanced a small, thick metal disk on Pietro's wrist and bound it in place with a tightly wrapped strip of cloth. "Now your other hand."

Pietro transferred his drink and held out his right arm. "What are you doing?"

"Old sailor's trick. Putting pressure on certain spots helps with the queasiness."

When Stollo was done, Pietro finished off the concoction, then leaned back against the curved wooden wall with his eyes closed. "I feel a little less like dying," he admitted. "But what a very romantic journey this is proving to be."

Stollo laughed. "It gives me an opportunity to prove my devotion."

"I have to think you had hoped for different opportunities."

"Well, it'll be a long trip. There might still be some of those opportunities after all."

The first two days were rough, but after that Pietro found himself feeling remarkably well and ravenously hungry. By this time, he could stand at any spot on the ship's deck and stare out at a limitless and absolutely empty landscape of water. No point of land was visible in any direction. No other ships gave a sense of scale to the horizon. They were entirely alone on the rocking blue waves under a cloudless and infinite sky.

This was the moment, Pietro thought, when a devout man might find himself most acutely aware of the might and presence of the god. When the distractions of mortal demands dropped away—when the world offered up nothing but the primal materials of existence. But Pietro had never felt farther away from Cordelan, less convinced of his divinity.

Yet the ocean itself seemed imbued with sentience; even the air he breathed had a weight and consciousness to it that he had never noticed when he was on solid land. He couldn't have said that the elements were benign, but they were present, they were real, and they were powerful. He closed his hand around his cherloshe charm. The Zessin people believed Zessaya ruled the oceans, had carved the islands from her bones. Maybe hers was the hand that roiled the waves, or stilled them; maybe she would listen if he prayed.

He bowed his head and touched the amulet to his forehead. His lips moved, but he made no sound. If the goddess heard, she gave no sign.

Once his appetite returned, Pietro made himself useful by taking over the cooking duties from Danner's younger son, who was only too happy to relinquish them. There wasn't much to choose from in the galley, but the crew seemed appreciative anyway.

"You ever need a job, I could recommend you to half a dozen captains," Danner told him.

"I'll keep that in mind. I've been casting about for what profession I should pursue next." *Assuming the world doesn't end. Assuming I have anything left to live for.*

By late afternoon of the sixth day, they could spot widely spaced smudges on the eastern horizon, gradually taking on more size and substance as the ship moved closer. Stollo joined Pietro at the bow as the shapes were slowly lost to the gathering darkness.

"The ruined lands," Stollo said. "And what will we find here?"

In the morning, they were close enough to make out details of some of the closest land masses. Two were so small that Pietro could trace almost the entire perimeter, so flat that he could see over them with a glance. Both of them were nothing but irregular black surfaces, stretches of uneven rock intercut at intervals by gullies as smooth as glass. Here and there, patches of weeds clung to shallow crevices, defiant stalks of faded green, but for the most part, each island looked empty and uninhabitable. Ruined, indeed.

"It's not all like this," Danner informed them late in the afternoon. "All the flat lands, they're just barren stone, but some of the bigger islands, the ones with hills and high land, they're just as fertile as Marata."

Not until the next morning did they reach one of those larger islands, divided down the middle by a formidable array of tall, notched peaks. Everything on the western edge was the same dreary expanse of unrelieved black stone—but then they sailed past the demarcation line of the mountains.

And it was a different world. It was as if every surface had been claimed by a different shade of green as moss, grass, shrubbery, and low tropical trees competed for space in the soil. Pietro gazed in amazement at great masses of flowers in brilliant reds and purples, and fancied that he could catch perfumed puffs of air drifting through the salty breeze. It was ridiculous, but the air felt warmer, thicker, heavier against his skin.

"Do many of the ruined lands have this same configuration?" he asked Danner, who stood with Pietro and Stollo at the railing. "Black on one side, green on the other?"

"Some of them," Danner answered. "And people live on the green side."

Stollo split a look between the other two. "And we're planning to talk to some of these people?"

"I've never stopped at this particular island," Danner said. "Water's not deep enough to get close. But there's a place about a day from here that I've been to a few times." He glanced at Pietro. "If that's good enough for you."

Pietro nodded. "I don't even know who or what I'm looking for. So that seems like a fine place to start."

They spent the day gliding along an invisible channel through the ruined lands. Pietro was so fascinated he delayed going belowdecks to begin his cooking chores. Sometimes their way seemed to be nothing but water, and any islands that were nearby were barely blots to the north or south. Other times, their ship passed close enough to the variable clumps of land that Pietro could see the nests the seabirds built along the sand. Now and then they spotted figures standing on the beaches or along the terraced slopes of the higher hills, watching them; here and there they passed smaller crafts riding the waves, hugging the shore or darting across the narrower channels. Sometimes the men in the other boats shouted and waved, but other times they just stared.

"We'll be there by morning," Danner predicted after dinner, so Pietro made himself seek out his bunk instead of standing at the railing through the whole night, trying to make out ghostly shapes. By now, he had come to find the rocking of the boat comforting, and it lulled him to sleep just as surely as the sound of Stollo's even breathing.

He was awakened by a series of gentle bumps and splashes, then an unnerving feeling that the world had come to a halt. *We must have dropped anchor,* he thought. The boat still tipped and righted with the incessant waves, but there was no sense of continual motion. Pietro wondered what it would be like to stand again on obdurate ground.

He woke Stollo with a kiss. "I think we're here," he said, "whatever that means."

Chapter Twenty-seven: Pietro

One of Danner's sons stayed with the boat, but the rest of them crammed into a dinghy that had hung off the starboard side until they dropped it into the water. During the fifteen minutes it took for Danner and his son to maneuver the craft to the beach, Pietro studied the prospect before them. They had arrived at a small natural harbor, a deep curve in the coastline sheltered by an overhanging cliff that might have been thirty feet high. To the left, the plateau above the cove stretched out in acres of rough black rock; to the right, fronds of greenery dripped down from the lush stretches of the higher ground. A narrow but well-trodden path wound its way up from the beach to the fertile land on the right. A few small rafts and skiffs dotted the sand, pulled up close enough to the walls of the cliff to be safe from the hungry pull of high water.

A group of people stood at the edge of the path, watching the dinghy come ashore. They looked poised to run in either direction, as the situation dictated—down to the water to offer help, or up the hill to seek safety. They were simply dressed, in loose tunics of light-colored fabric. Pietro supposed there must be some kind of plant life here that yielded fibers that could be beaten or woven into cloth. As they got closer, he could tell that most of the tunics had been ornamented with dyes or beads or shells or braided fringe. For some reason, that detail heartened him. Whether they lived in a fancy mansion on Council Row or camped on an island in the middle of an ocean, people couldn't resist the urge for self-decoration. They were driven always by the desire to distinguish themselves from their neighbors by color or shape or pattern. They invariably sought to make themselves unique.

The dinghy scraped against sand, and the four of them jumped out. Danner and his son grabbed a pair of ropes and hauled the craft up to the beach, Stollo and Pietro following, all of them splashing mightily. The water was cold and Pietro was shivering when they made it to land.

Danner dropped his rope and held his hands before him, palms up, clearly a gesture designed to show he offered no threat. The other three copied his movements. Then, moving slowly, Danner pulled a knapsack off his back and let it drop to the damp ground. Whatever its contents were, they clinked merrily when they landed. Pietro guessed Danner had brought tools or knives, things it would be hard for someone in this part of the world to mine or smelt. High-value items for barter.

The gesture seemed to reassure the onlookers, for the waiting group moved closer. Danner stepped forward, still keeping his hands out, and said something in a language Pietro didn't know. One of the others came close enough to respond—a woman who looked to be about middle age. She had freckled skin and ginger hair that reminded him of Aussen, and the small, trim build he associated with islanders.

That was interesting, he thought. Maybe before Cordelan started moving bits of the world around, all the islands had clustered closer together; maybe they had been peopled by a single race. He listened more closely to Danner's halting conversation with the native woman, wondering if he could pick out any words he recognized. If he'd had a better grasp of Zessin, he might have been able to do so.

He studied the woman talking to Danner. She had festooned herself with ropes of beads—around her throat, around her wrists, around her ankles. They were small and irregularly shaped, mostly white but streaked with gradations of color from citrine to snow.

Cherloshe, Pietro thought, wondering if these people worshipped some incarnation of Zessaya. It seemed likely.

The tenor of the conversation changed—now the woman was pointing at Danner's companions, clearly asking who they were and why they should be trusted. Danner introduced them one by one, then the woman called over her own entourage and did the same.

"Does this mean we're all friends now?" Stollo murmured.

"I think so," Danner's son said.

"This is Cossi," Danner told them. "She's the head of the families who live here. She's willing to do business with us, but doesn't want us to venture any farther than the beach. She'll send her sons back to their village for items to trade."

Pietro was disappointed. If he never saw more than this small sliver of land, he wouldn't be able to find what he was looking for—whatever it was. But maybe after a successful exchange of merchandise, Cossi would be more welcoming.

Two of the islanders ran lightly up the hill; two others produced thin blankets and spread them over the sand. The city folk knelt on one blanket, the islanders on the other, and Danner opened his bag.

Pietro's guess had been right—Danner's bounty consisted of a dozen knives of assorted sizes and uses, a hammer, nails, an awl, needles, a length of chain, and other items that he produced ceremoniously one by one. Cossi and her companions picked up each piece to examine it, then whispered amongst themselves. They seemed pleased, not astonished, so Pietro assumed they had seen similar tools in the past.

It wasn't long before her sons returned carrying heavy cloth bags that they placed on the blanket before Cossi. She began pulling out an assortment of rocks that looked a great deal like cherloshe studded with coin-sized deposits of some blue material. Pietro guessed these might be rare minerals that could be cut and polished into exquisite jewels. Worth the trade.

Danner had gone through about twenty good-sized rocks when Stollo leaned over to whisper in Pietro's ear. "Who's this?"

Pietro looked up to see another stranger carefully negotiating the sloped right-hand path. A man, maybe Pietro's age—and not an islander. So dark-haired and dark-skinned he might almost be a pureblood Cordelano. He was dressed in the simple tunic of the island folk, but gold bracelets gleamed on both of his wrists.

A Corcannon man. How unexpected.

Cossi glanced over her shoulder at the Cordelano's approach, then said something to Danner, who translated for the others. "This is Jino, he lives here, he wanted to meet the strangers. I can't tell what his status is," Danner added. "She spoke his name with respect, but not fear."

"Jino," Stollo said, and looked at Pietro.

Pietro nodded, and he and Stollo came to their feet. Many people bore names that ended in o, but *every* priest had such a name—and this man bore himself with the authority and serenity that clerics cultivated from an early age.

"I don't recognize him," Pietro said.

"I don't either."

Neither Cossi nor Danner seemed too interested in Jino's arrival, so Pietro and Stollo strolled over to intercept the newcomer. For a moment the three of them just sized each other up, confirming their swift suspicions. Pietro made no attempt to hide the fact that he was glancing at Jino's hands, and the other man obligingly extended his arms.

On his left wrist, a gold circlet stamped with simple quatrefoils, Cordelan's most common symbol. On his right, a gold band with the edges bent up and over themselves to make thin channels on both rims. Celibate.

Stollo and Pietro spoke their names and offered their own arms for inspection. Jino nodded. "You're from Corcannon, then," he said. His voice was low and pleasant, and he didn't seem like he was having any trouble remembering the Cordish language.

Stollo hung back, letting Pietro do the talking. "We are. It seems you must have lived there at some point as well."

"On the continent, at least," Jino said. "I wasn't in the city much, though I was an ordained priest. I spent more time as a missionary, visiting the islands and the desert to spread the word of Cordelan."

Which explained why he wasn't familiar. Pietro smiled slightly. "The people of those regions tend to prefer their own gods, from what I've observed," he said.

"They do," Jino agreed. "And after many years of living among them, I found myself in some sympathy with their views."

"Zessaya has a seductive pull," Pietro admitted. "Perhaps it is the fact that she seems so unimpressed with Cordelan's power."

"That," Jino said, "and the fact that she has power of her own."

"I am curious," Pietro said, "to learn how you moved from those postings to this one."

Jino motioned behind him toward an arrangement of small logs drawn together around a firepit in the sand. Pietro assumed that this was where islanders gathered to await their sailors when they'd been out on the ocean for a worrisome period of time. The three of them took seats on the logs so they could all watch each other.

"When I was a young man, I was in some favor with the priest who was then high divine," Jino began.

Pietro thought about it a moment. Harlo had held the post for decades, so this would be his direct predecessor. "Morado?"

Jino nodded. "Yes. He thought I wasted my talents by living among the islanders and the Oraki tribes, and he often tried to lure me back to the city. Promised me an elevation in rank and access to all the secrets of the temple."

Stollo perked up at that. "Secrets?"

Jino glanced between them. "He doesn't know? But you are both priests, are you not?"

"He is," Pietro said. "I used to be. And he doesn't know the secrets, but I do."

Jino studied him. "Which is why you are no longer a priest."

"Yes."

Jino nodded. "So Morado showed me the lever and taught me how to move it, and I was horrified. And he explained that unless the wheel was turned, the continent would be destroyed and become just like the ruined lands."

"It must be a speech every high divine has to memorize," Pietro said. "I heard one very like it."

"Who has the office now?"

"Harlo. You might have known him."

Jino nodded. “Another of Morado’s favorites. A good man, I always thought. Devout. Passionate. Unflinching.”

“Those aren’t always good traits,” Stollo observed.

“Yes, they can also describe zealots and martyrs,” Jino agreed. “At any rate, when Morado delivered the speech, I said, ‘Very well, I want to see the ruined lands.’ So we crossed the ocean and cruised between the blasted islands.”

Jino linked his hands and stared down at the sand between his feet. “I did not react as Morado expected. I thought those burned, blackened lands had an austere and terrible beauty, and I was struck with the rich, bounteous flourishing of the areas that had recovered. When the harbors were shallow enough, I insisted that we disembark and attempt to talk with the inhabitants. I was pretty conversant in Zessin, and the language these people speak is not terribly different, so we were able to communicate in limited ways. I was impressed with their strength and resilience and generally sanguine outlook on life. Their oral histories and their few written records contained graphic descriptions of the catastrophic events that had broken their continent apart, but many generations removed from that event, they were quite recovered. Yes, they were confined to small spheres of hospitable land, and yes, they had lost the great mysterious engine that used to power their society—but in their small, interconnected pockets of life, they had created a thriving, successful community.”

Jino lifted his head and looked directly at Pietro, and then Stollo. “And there were no more quakes,” he said. “Once the continent came apart, all that turmoil simply stopped. The land was content.”

Pietro took a sharp breath, but exhaled it without speaking.

Jino glanced around. “I was intrigued. I was entranced. I told Morado I was not returning with him to Corcannon. He argued with me for three days. Eventually I got tired of the quarreling, and I slipped away with one of my new friends in the middle of the night. I learned later that it was a week before Morado pulled anchor and went home.” Jino looked over his shoulder, toward the lush green lands behind them. “I have never regretted it.”

“What do you do here?” Stollo asked. “Since I assume you do not serve in a religious capacity.”

“It is generally women who act as guardians of Zessaya’s temples,” Jino said. “But I still feel called to similar service. I act as a teacher and a counselor, and I have learned the rituals for conducting weddings and consecrating the dead. I have no authority, but the guardians make use of me, and I am convinced the goddess is pleased at my devotion.”

“It’s a remarkable tale,” Pietro said. “It gives me some faith that even if the worst happens, there is some hope in the far future.”

Stollo looked at him. “What worst? What do you anticipate?”

But Jino knew. "The quakes are back, aren't they? It's time for another sacrifice?"

"*Sacrifice?*" Stollo repeated.

"It's time," said Pietro. "But all that's left is one young woman who is so far childless. And once she's gone—" He spread his hands.

"Wait," Stollo said. "What are you talking about?"

Jino glanced at Stollo, then turned his gaze somewhat accusingly to Pietro. As if to demand why Pietro hadn't shared this terrible, incriminating information. As if Jino believed all men should know it. Pietro sighed and answered. "When Cordelan gathered the scattered lands into one great mass, he linked them in some fashion to his own body. Every so often the lands begin to shift and push against each other, and all that calms them down is a libation of blood."

"*Blood?*"

"It must come from the body of one of Cordelan's descendants. And the world is fast running out of those."

"But—how much blood? How often? What happens to—"

"And that is why this is such a terrible story," Pietro interrupted him. "Because of the answers to those questions."

Stollo simply stared at him.

Pietro turned back to Jino. "We are in dire circumstances, as you might imagine. Millions live on the continent, and the quakes are increasing in ferocity. Our options are limited and appalling." He shrugged. "I thought if I came here, I might learn something. But I don't know what there is to learn."

"I could show you the cave where the lever for the eastern continent was located," Jino offered. "If you think it might offer you any clues."

Pietro arched his brows. "Probably not," he said. "But I would like to see it, anyway. Is it nearby? Could we sail to it within a day?"

Jino gestured toward the ruined half of the island. "It's here. Maybe a two-hour's walk away."

Pietro felt his face light up, and he jumped to his feet. "Then yes, I would like to see it."

It required about thirty minutes of preparation before they could set off on their expedition. Cossi was not inclined to let strangers roam her land at will, so she wanted two of her own people to accompany them. And no one wanted to set off without provisions, so a few of Cossi's companions hurried back up the hill to fetch food and water. Danner's successful bargaining session had left him mellow, and he agreed to wait the half-day it would take them to return.

"Even if we don't cast off until tomorrow morning, no harm done," he said.

"You won't leave without us," Stollo said. "How would you explain that to my mother?"

Danner's face didn't relax from its usual stolid expression. "I can't help it if you're clumsy enough to fall overboard on high water."

Stollo grinned at Pietro. "We've always been close."

Eventually, their guides returned—a young woman named Dessa and an older man named Brin. Pietro thought they might be father and daughter, but no one explained their relationship. Like the others, they wore loose, light-colored clothing that allowed for easy movement. Brin's tunic was completely plain, but Dessa's featured bright splotches of red and green in what Pietro took to be a floral motif. She was small and wiry, with a wide grin and a curious expression. Brin seemed more taciturn, though not unfriendly. He handed everyone sacks of provisions with a few words of instruction.

"Everyone's responsible for their own supplies," Jino translated, hoisting his over his shoulder. "Let's go."

Dessa led the way up the left-hand path. The loose black rock made the climb hazardous, so they moved slowly and carefully in a single file. Pietro noted that large swaths of the path were choked by hardy weeds, indicating that few people came this way on a regular basis—and that the island was gradually reclaiming even its most devastated acres.

Once they crested the hill, what lay before them was an eerie landscape of almost uniform black and gray. But it had an odd, irresistible rhythm to it, of flat lands interrupted by fields of jagged, broken rocks and undulating rivulets as slick as ice. They stepped forward carefully, finding the smooth patches as treacherous as the sinks of loose gravel. On their right-hand side, the land canted downward from the peak of the mountain range, sometimes sharply, sometimes on a gentle grade, but Pietro always felt that his right leg was a few inches higher than his left. It added to the arduousness of the trek, the unreality of the whole outing.

The sun was high and the day, which had started out cool, grew quickly warmer. As they hiked along the black surface, Pietro began to feel unpleasantly hot. He hoped the stone beneath their feet didn't heat up so much it burned through the soles of his shoes. They were only about twenty minutes from the beach when he reached into his sack to pull out a waterskin. He was glad to see there were several in the bag.

Brin had taken the lead and never once looked back to see if the others were following. Stollo fell in next to Dessa, and the two of them seemed to be having a grand time attempting to communicate. Pietro thought they were trying to teach each other words like *sky, rock, black,* and *mountain*, but they were laughing so much it was hard to tell. He had never seen anyone to compare with Stollo for putting people instantly at ease. He'd like to see him make the attempt with Jayla; if anyone could win her over in five minutes, it would be Stollo.

That left Pietro paired up with Jino. As the oldest two members of the party—and the two that were clearly in the worst physical shape—they didn't have much breath left for conversation, but whenever they reached relatively level land, Jino began questioning Pietro about life back in Corcannon. They had a few acquaintances in common, so Pietro could supply updates on their lives, and he described some of the new buildings that had been constructed in the last three decades.

"But I wouldn't say the changes have been sweeping in the past thirty years," Pietro said. He sighed. "Nothing like the changes that may come."

Brin stopped the group once, and briefly, for a refreshment break, then set off again without a word. Pietro was generally good at judging the passage of time, but between the heat and the unrelentingly monochromatic landscape, he was beginning to lose his bearings. The trip had seemed to last far longer than two hours by the time Brin slowed and came to a halt. He pointed up the steep mountainside to a narrow slit in the sleek black wall.

"Here we are," said Jino.

Stollo glanced back at Pietro, grinning. "Looks like a bit of a climb."

Jino pushed ahead of the others and set his foot carefully on the narrowest imaginable path. "It's not so bad," he said. "Just go slowly."

Brin said something that Pietro guessed meant *We'll wait here*, because the two islanders seated themselves on boulders that didn't look quite as spiky as some of the others. Pietro took a deep breath and followed after Jino. Over his shoulder, he said to Stollo, "You can catch me if I fall."

"You won't fall," Stollo said confidently and started after him.

They climbed cautiously up the slope, finding handholds when they could, suspending their breathing when loose stones rolled out from under their feet. But all three of them made it without mishap to the small door in the side of the mountain. From this vantage point, it was clear that it had once been a grander opening, perhaps three times as wide and fronted by a modest plaza of fired bricks laid in a complex pattern. But an avalanche had covered half of the door and most of the decorative entrance, and all that remained was a slim slot that could only be reached by clambering over a pile of stones.

"Be careful here," Jino said. "Sometimes the rocks shift underfoot."

Pietro glanced back expressively at Stollo, who grinned. But they had come this far. They would find the broken lever or die in a glorious tumble of black stone.

Jino picked his way up the layered rocks and disappeared inside. Pietro nerved himself before reaching for the first handhold and pulling himself up.

He made sure he had both feet firmly on one stone before attempting to climb to the next one. Once or twice, his landing spot shuddered beneath his feet, but everything stayed solidly in place.

Jino helped him down the other side into a space that was blessedly cool and dark. Pietro dropped his bag of provisions next to Jino's and let his vision adjust while they waited for Stollo. Like the formal entrance, the interior was a mix of ancient artefacts and obliterating rockfall. In the faint sunlight that drifted through the narrow opening, Pietro could make out mosaics and murals climbing up the walls, carved pillars lying on the floor. Everything was obscured by layers of dust and ash.

"Well, this is a treasure trove," he said in a hushed voice. "What could we learn about our past if we had a few days to spend here?"

"I wonder sometimes if Cossi's people would help me excavate the place," Jino said. "There are three corridors that branch off this first room. Two are completely blocked by debris, and I always want to know—what lies beyond those impasses? Was this a temple? Would we find rooms where the priests lived? Archives with their writings? Would anything be salvageable? I would love to know."

Stollo's form briefly blocked the sunlight, then he dropped easily to his feet on the other side. "Incredible," he said, gazing around.

Jino gestured toward the back of the cave, which disappeared into darkness. "Brin is a patient enough man, but I don't think he's disposed to linger. Let's find what we came for before we waste time exploring."

Pietro felt a stab of dismay. "It's too dark to see anything."

Jino began rummaging in his bag. "Perhaps Cossi thought to tell her people to supply us with candles."

Stollo reached into his pocket to pull out a short stick. "I've got a chemlight," he said. "I usually carry one."

"A what?" Jino said.

Pietro was grinning. "I forgot to mention that particular innovation when I was recounting stories of the city," he said. "Very useful."

Stollo scraped the stick along a rough wall, and an orb of milky illumination sprang up along one end. "This direction?" he asked, and led the way forward.

They found themselves in a narrow corridor whose walls were mostly intact, though bare of any decoration. At intervals, they came across small glasslike disks that had been set into the walls—lights, Pietro guessed, that had once been animated by the same kind of engine that powered Corcannon. In the near-dark, it was difficult to judge distance, but they had gone unnervingly deep into the mountainside before the corridor abruptly opened up into a small cavern that seemed to be about twenty feet in each dimension.

Well, "opened up" was the wrong phrase, Pietro thought, as the three of them crowded at the entrance and looked around by Stollo's handy light. Pietro could still make out the walls and part of the ceiling, but the chamber was about half filled with a clutter of stones, ranging from pebbles to boulders, that appeared to have gushed down from some shaft overhead and buried a central feature of the room. Time and inevitable settling had rearranged the rockfall so that it made a waist-high mound around that middle point, and it was possible to make out only glimpses of what lay beneath the rubble.

A gleam of metal, twisted and blackened. Maybe a basin of gold, designed to catch a body's worth of blood. A stone pedestal, no doubt with a hollow core that fed to some collection point thousands of feet below the surface.

Pietro cast his gaze upward, seeking to pierce the shadows overhead, but he could not see to the top of the open shaft. "A little different from the arrangement in the city," he murmured. "Instead of walls closing in, there must have been—what? A pile or column overhead? And when the mechanism was oiled, the pile remained suspended. And when it was not—the rock came crashing down."

"That's how I interpret it," Jino said.

"This does not give me any clues," Pietro said, "on how to stop it from happening again."

"No," Jino said. "Were you really hoping to find any?"

Pietro didn't answer, but he was aware of a heavy weight in his chest, as if disappointment had created its own rockfall over his heart. He stepped cautiously into the room, wading through a fine sift of grit and gravel. Jino stayed at the door, but Stollo followed him in.

"Look at this," Stollo said, his light wavering wildly as he bent to pick up something lying the floor. "It's stamped with a quatrefoil. Just like all the temple doors in Corcannon."

"No doubt," Pietro said. "This place was built by the same people."

Stollo scooped up another rock, this one long and flat. "And here. That's a portrait of Dar, do you see?"

Pietro examined it. "You're right. Identical features."

"I'd be careful about just picking up bits and pieces," Jino called nervously from the doorway. "You don't want things to start shifting around."

"Just stuff from the edges," Stollo promised, and snagged another scrap from the floor. He studied it for a moment. "That's an odd thing," he said, handing it to Pietro.

It was a slab of stone, maybe ten inches square and two inches thick, with heavy bolts extruding through the back. Clearly a decorative piece designed to be affixed to the wall. Pietro flipped it over and found himself staring at the simple imprint of a hand. It was carved into the tablet with such precision and skill that it actually looked as if the stone had formed itself around the palm and fingers.

"That's remarkable," he said.

"What? What is it?" Jino asked

Stollo crowded nearer to make a closer inspection, holding the chem-light directly over Pietro's wrist. "It's a hand," Stollo said, trying to fit his own over the indentation and covering it completely. "A small one, though. Maybe a child's."

"A woman's," Pietro corrected him.

"How do you know?"

"Because there's a casting just like this in the temple in the city. Legend has it that Dar and Cordelan were having an argument. In a fit of rage, she slapped her hand against the wall and left this mark behind." Pietro angled the slab to try to get a better look. Except for the imprint, there was no decoration on the tablet at all. "But that can't be the right story. Obviously, these castings were hung in these chambers on purpose."

Jino overcame his unease and scuffed through the ash to join them. "Not Dar," he said. "Zessaya."

"Why do you think that?"

Jino shrugged. "That's the story that's been handed down by Cossi's people. Cordelan wooed Dar and took her as his wife, and together they rearranged the scattered lands. They created the mechanism and decreed that it had to be kept oiled with the blood of their descendants. But Zessaya was furious at their arrogance. She reminded them that the islands were made up of her bones and still responded to her will. She threatened to tear the continent apart unless Cordelan and Dar in some fashion acknowledged her power."

"And then she slammed her hand into the wall and left this mark behind," Stollo said in an admiring voice.

"Wait," Pietro said.

"The legend claims that, when the eastern continent began to tremble, Zessaya could have stopped the destruction if she'd wanted to," Jino went on. "If she'd put her hand on the wall and *pushed,* the lever would have turned. The lands would have settled. That was the bargain she made with Cordelan and Dar."

"Then why didn't she do it?" Stollo asked.

"All the gods had stopped walking the world by that time," Pietro said in a choked voice. "If you believe they were even gods. They might have been men—and women—with extraordinary abilities."

"That's blasphemy, of course," Jino said, in a tone that indicated he subscribed to the same theory.

"Gods or humans, it doesn't really matter," Stollo said impatiently. "You've been going on and on about the blood of their offspring. Didn't Zessaya have any heirs lying around? Couldn't *they* have run up here and pushed the lever in place?"

Pietro glanced mutely at Jino. A thought was forming at the back of his mind, but he couldn't quite grasp it. Or couldn't quite believe it . . .

Jino nodded. "Oh, certainly. The islanders will tell you they're all descended from Zessaya. That's true here, and it's true back on the mainland."

"So?"

"They have to be descended from Cordelan as well," Pietro guessed.

Jino nodded again. "Cordelan was vainglorious and conceited—or, if you prefer the interpretation of the sacred texts, too wise to completely cede any power to the lesser deities. It's not enough to carry blood from Dar—that won't turn the key. It's not enough to be the daughter of the daughter of the daughter of Zessaya—your hand won't be strong enough to move the mountain."

"You must be bred from Cordelan and Zessaya both," Pietro whispered.

Stollo was frowning. "But—*is* there anyone with such a lineage? I mean, if Dar was his wife—"

"The tales vary," Jino said. "Some say Zessaya agreed to lie with Cordelan once and bear him one child, as long as she could take the child back with her to the islands. Other versions say that Dar flew into a jealous rage at the very notion, and insisted that Zessaya be banished altogether."

Pietro was staring down at the tablet in his hands. Could it *be*? "I tend to believe the first set of stories," he said. "Cordelan always seemed determined to leave behind his mark in as many ways as he could."

"I agree," Jino said. "Not only did he reshape the world to better suit his fancy, he had such a colossal sense of self-worth that he required it to be fed over and over again with remnants of his own body. A man like that—or a god like that—would never allow someone else her own undiluted power."

"But the question remains," Stollo said. "*Is* there anyone alive who can claim both Cordelan and Zessaya as ancestors?" He gestured around the destroyed cavern, and the light from his chemstick bounced over the tumbled walls. "It doesn't seem that anyone like that was living in the ruined lands when their quakes started."

"No, and if any of their joint descendants ever lived in Corcannon, the priests lost track of them a long time ago," Jino said.

Pietro turned the tablet over and over in his hands, feeling first the smooth indentation of the palm print, then the rough, rusty protrusions of the bolts. It had to weigh a good ten pounds; it was a miracle it hadn't shattered when it was thrown to the heaving floor. "I can hardly believe it," he said. "But I think there's one. A little girl."

Chapter Twenty-eight: Brandon

Brandon and Villette spent almost a month plotting their escape, trying to anticipate every disastrous eventuality and plan a way around it.

"We have to leave at night," Brandon said, "when the other guards are asleep. I can't defeat two of them and—I don't want to kill either one. And that's what it would come down to if they caught us."

"Please, no, don't kill anyone on my behalf!" Villette exclaimed. "That would be unbearable."

"And we should pick a night when the servants are gone," Brandon added. "I don't think they'd fight me, but they'd sound the alarm if they saw us leaving. The fewer people in the house when we go, the better."

"I agree."

He had thought finances might be one of their biggest concerns, but Villette waved away that consideration. "I have enough money to fund *five* escapes and keep us in food and housing for a hundred years," she said. "How do you think I bribed all those other guards who tried to help me?"

"I thought you seduced them with your charm and beauty."

"Charm and beauty only go so far when people are about to give up everything for someone else. Most conspirators require a cash deposit along the way." She peered up at him in the darkness. It was very late and unexpectedly cool, and they were sitting outside on the patio, sharing a metal bench and a large knitted blanket. "I would happily give you money, you know. As much as you asked for. You could—"

He silenced her with a kiss, closing his arms around her so tightly that she wouldn't have breath to argue. It was still astonishing to him that she would allow him to take such liberties—incredible to him that she would cling to him, kiss him back. Oh, he knew she didn't actually love him. He was a tool, a means to an end. And she needed his services so badly she would give him anything she thought he wanted. Her money. Her body. The rest of her life, maybe, if he was able to secure her freedom.

He should be too proud to accept that bargain. He should only love a woman who would love him in return, *truly* love him, light up when she saw his face at the end of the day, worry about him when he was gone from her sight.

But it didn't even matter to him. He didn't care that she didn't love him. He just wanted her out of this place. He wanted her free. Safe. He wanted to build her life from the bones of his own.

"I don't care about your money," he whispered against her mouth. "Except to use it to get you out of the city."

She nodded. "So we'll leave at night."

"But all the bridges close at sunset," he said, still thinking it through. "We'll need a place to stay till morning."

"It will look suspicious if we arrive at some inn in the middle of the night, clearly fleeing disaster."

"I know. Maybe I should rent a room in a quiet part of town. Pay a month's rent in advance, and visit it on my days off so the neighbors think I'm furnishing it. Then we'll just be able to unlock the door and walk in, no matter what time we arrive. Stay there one night, and leave in the morning."

He thought about it a little more, and frowned. Villette read his expression and demanded, "What's wrong?"

"Unless I can buy horses, we'll be on foot, which means any search party will catch up with us within a day. But that means I'd have to buy horses in advance—which means we can't just capitalize on a lucky chance to escape one night when everyone else is, say, laid low with a fever."

"So buy horses."

"But any stablemaster will think it's odd for me to buy horses and then leave them idle until I suddenly demand them one day at dawn. He would certainly describe me to any temple guards who came looking."

"If we're far enough out of the city by then, maybe it won't matter."

He nodded. "Something else worries me."

She responded with a laugh that was more frustration than mirth. "I can't decide if I should be vexed or grateful that you are looking ahead to perceive so many obstacles," she said. "What concerns you now?"

"Your bracelet."

She freed her left hand from the folds of the blanket and held her arm so that the filigree glinted in the surly moonlight. "Ah. It identifies me."

"Even the guards who won't recognize *you* will be told what your bracelet looks like. I don't have the tools to saw through it."

"This time, *I* am the one who has been thinking ahead," she murmured, lifting her other hand. She touched the bracelet—and snapped it open.

Brandon gasped. "I thought they were always welded on," he said. "Mine are."

"They're supposed to be," she said. "A year or two before I was imprisoned, I had a friend who was a jeweler. Even then it had occurred to me that I might—sometime—want to leave this identity behind. He cut it from my body and remade it with a hidden clasp. No one else has ever known about it."

"That's exceptionally useful," Brandon said. "Of course, if we're stopped, and you're not wearing any bracelet on your left hand—"

She fastened the band around her wrist again, and he heard the small click as it locked in place. "Oh, but I was still thinking ahead," she said gaily. "He made me a second bracelet, just a plain band, the kind that would be worn by any ordinary laborer."

Brandon drew back to study her face. As if he didn't already know it by heart. It hardly even mattered that there wasn't enough moonlight to make it out clearly. "Though you look nothing like any laborer I've ever seen. And your clothes—I don't suppose you laid in some plain gowns or trousers while you were plotting?"

"I did! I bought two new dresses for my maid and told her I'd dispose of her old ones, but I kept them in the bottom of a drawer."

"That was clever."

"So that's another problem taken care of. Anything else?"

"Your face and your hair mark you as Cordelano," he said. "You're dark enough that I don't think there's much you can do to alter your appearance. But maybe if you don't have the bracelet, they won't realize it's you."

She sighed and leaned her cheek against his jacket, tucking her hands back under the blanket.

"And if they catch up with us, and recognize me, and take us into custody?" she whispered. "What happens then?"

He was pretty sure she could hear the sudden acceleration of his heart. "I suppose they bring you back here and your incarceration begins again."

"I know what happens to *me,*" she said. "I was inquiring after *you.*"

He was silent a moment. "I don't know what happens to temple guards who try to help prisoners escape," he lied. "I think it's likely I might be incarcerated myself, at least for a time."

She lifted her head again, and her dark eyes were liquid with apprehension. "They wouldn't—they wouldn't *hurt* you, would they?"

He imagined hanging *did* hurt, but only for a short time. "I don't think so. I've never heard stories like that."

She kept her eyes on his face, as if she wasn't sure he was telling the truth. "I wouldn't want any harm to come to you," she said, "not because of me."

He kissed her, then drew her head back against his chest. "Neither of us will come to harm," he said. "Because we won't get caught."

During his afternoons off, Brandon went exploring. The closest bridge was the northern span, but it also had the most drawbacks, in his estimation. First, it was the logical place the temple guards would look for them. Second, it was the narrowest of the three main bridges, so on days when traffic was heavy, travelers might line up for more than an hour before they were able to cross.

Third, it had one foot in the elite neighborhood of the city, where there were no affordable housing options nearby. It would take Brandon and Villette longer to get to the next nearest bridge, but that one was so close to the warehouse district that cheap lodgings were plentiful—and it was so wide that it permitted hundreds of travelers to cross every hour.

So Brandon spent a few days prowling through the working-class neighborhood, looking for just the right kind of accommodations. He wanted a building that was large enough to suggest the neighbors didn't all know each other, shabby enough to indicate that no one was keeping close track of the property, but decent enough that Villette wouldn't be alarmed.

Fortunately, that description applied to a lot of the buildings in this part of town, so Brandon added a fourth qualification: close enough to the bridge to allow them to cover the distance quickly. Finally, one afternoon, he came across the perfect spot, a long, three-story complex bare of any ornamentation, with all its windows intact but all of its doors in need of paint. When he sought out the landlady, she led him to a cramped and dingy set of rooms while he grumbled about the trouble he was having getting out of his current lease.

"I keep arguing with my brother, because he doesn't want me to leave, so I think it will be a week or two before I have all my things transferred," he said. "But I want to have my new place ready so I can just pick up and *go,* you know? I'm tired of the quarreling."

The landlady nodded politely, but he could tell she didn't care. Still, he hoped she'd keep this story in the back of her mind if anyone asked why the new tenant hadn't moved in. "Did you want to pay one month in advance, or two?"

Brandon pretended to debate. "Well, if I don't move in right away, it seems like a waste to—but, you know what? I'm a man who likes some certainty in his life. I'll pay the two months in advance."

"Excellent," she said. "Let's go down to my office and I'll give you a key."

So Brandon was in a cheerful mood when he made his way back to the mansion that evening. He'd hung the key on a cord around his neck, and it lay against his chest, just below his chazissa. Which seemed fitting, as he had to think Zessaya was overseeing this mad venture.

Had to *hope* she was.

He tried not to look too pleased with himself as he strolled through the door. That was the sort of thing Finley always noticed, and then she'd pester him with questions about how he'd spent his day. He didn't have any convincing lies ready.

But although Finley was in the atrium when he stepped inside, she didn't appear to have any attention to spare for Brandon. She was sitting at the wrought iron table, closely interrogating a temple guard whom Brandon had never seen before. Both of them looked over when he walked in.

"And this is Brandon," Finley said, as if she was in the middle of listing all the inhabitants of the house. "Brandon, this is Linnet. She's replacing Nadder as of today."

Brandon had completely forgotten Nadder's tenure was almost up, and he felt a clutch of terror. Nadder was efficient and watchful, so Brandon had always known they would have to move carefully to avoid catching his attention—but at least he understood how Nadder's mind worked. Brandon had no idea how smart, how curious, how observant this new person was. How might her arrival derail their escape plans?

"Hello," he said, coming over to join them. He hoped his face looked friendly instead of stricken. "When did you get here?"

Linnet didn't bother to stand to greet him, but she tipped her face up to look at him. From her hair and skin, he guessed that she had a fair amount of bastard Cordelano blood in her. "Hello," she replied coolly. "About an hour ago."

"Nadder was already packed," Finley said with a laugh. "I think he was gone five minutes after Linnet walked in."

"I never had the feeling this was his favorite posting," Brandon said.

Finley snorted. "It's not mine, either. But I don't have that much longer to go."

That was something else Brandon kept forgetting. He didn't have limitless amounts of time to get Villette out of here. If he didn't free her before his assignment was over, he'd never see her again.

He couldn't think about that right now. He kept his attention on Linnet, still trying to make a quick assessment. Her face was impassive, her eyes guarded. Either she was the kind of person who didn't like to give away what she was thinking, or she was trying to hide nervousness behind an aloof mask. "So what kinds of assignments have you been on before?" he asked.

"I just spent a year as part of the guard for the high divine," she said.

Brandon raised his eyebrows. That was an elite appointment, usually a mark of favor. Had she committed some infraction that had brought her to this lower post? She must have read his expression, because she added in a cool voice, "All the guards in his detail are rotated out every year or so. Just to keep them fresh."

"She probably has the best stories," Finley said enviously.

Linnet glanced at her. "Most of them I can't repeat."

Finley always ignored any attempt to put her in her place. "But some of them you can. You can tell us over dinner."

Linnet abruptly rose to her feet. She was shorter than Brandon by about an inch, with a solid, muscular build. He had to guess she had strength and stamina in her wiry arms. "I'm going to sleep for a couple of hours so I'm fresh for my shift tonight."

"Oh, I'll work overnight," Brandon said. "I prefer to."

But Finley was shaking her head. "New guard always pulls night watch. You know the rule."

"It's not like anyone cares if we rearrange the schedule to suit ourselves."

"I understood that the night shift was my duty, and I'm prepared to serve it," Linnet said. And without another word, she headed down the hallway toward the room that used to be Nadder's.

Brandon stared after her, filled with a complex mix of irritation, indecision, and worry. She was a complication. He didn't know how to factor her in. "Well, *she's* not very friendly," he observed.

"The women never are, not at first," Finley said. "Always so intent on proving to everyone that they're as tough as the men."

He looked back at her. "You're not like that."

She grinned. "That's because I *know* I'm good. I don't have to prove anything."

"I think I'd rather have Nadder back."

Finley yawned. "It's just a few more months. You can take anything for that long."

A few more months. A few more months. Brandon lay in bed, staring at the ceiling, unable to sleep, even though he had to be alert in the morning, when his own watch would start. He wasn't used to being in bed at this hour. He was used to meeting with Villette in the garden while the whole house slept around them.

Now they would have to carry out their plotting in broad daylight, constantly aware that anyone might overhear them or notice them in conversation. They would not be able to speak openly or touch freely—the gods knew they would be unable to kiss—

Brandon stifled a groan and rolled to his side. He could bear the physical separation. But it would be agony to be unable to talk with Villette, to share ideas about their escape or warnings about some new obstacle he had perceived.

And then he almost started out of bed. They wouldn't even be *able* to leave if Linnet decided to keep the overnight shift permanently. All of their plans hinged on them being able to sneak out of the house when everyone else was asleep—

Brandon forced himself to lie back down, to relax his muscles, to clear his mind. Linnet would have time off eventually and someone else would have to take her place. Finley hated the night shift and would gladly let Brandon claim it. He and Villette would just have to make meticulous plans during their rare interludes of solitude. They wouldn't be able to rely on chance and error—

He brought his forearm up to cover his eyes. *So many things could go wrong,* he thought. *We will have to be so careful.*

Brandon felt heavy-lidded and heavy-limbed as he took up his duties the next morning. He wasn't sure he'd slept at all the night before; he'd finally just given up and gotten out of bed when dawn sidled up to the window. He could only pray that no determined assassins came bursting onto the property, because he could tell his reflexes were slow and his mind was foggy. He wouldn't be much use in a real fight.

Linnet had passed him in the hallway without a word, heading back to her bed. Villette had not yet made an appearance, but Finley was at breakfast. "I'm heading down to the Quatrefoil," she said. "Want anything?"

He yawned. "A better night's sleep."

She laughed. "You'll get used to being on normal hours again. You'll like it better."

He was sure she was wrong.

Villette finally left her room around noon, floating down the stairwell so soundlessly and mournfully she could have been a ghost. She paused for a scant breakfast and headed out to the back garden to enjoy the flimsy sunlight of late summer. Finley was still gone, Linnet was still sleeping, and Abe was on the front lawn planting a line of new shrubbery. As long as the cook stayed in the kitchen and the maid busied herself upstairs, Brandon thought, he might be able to manage a few minutes of conversation with Villette.

He dawdled a bit so it didn't look like he was rushing right out after her; he even completed a circuit of the upper stories just to prove he wasn't in a hurry. Then he made his way down the back corridor like a man with one more task to complete.

Villette was sitting on one of the benches overlooking the fish pond, staring at the water with so much despair she might have been watching a funeral. She didn't even lift her head when Brandon stepped out of the house. He stopped near the edge of the patio, not too far from the door, a position that gave him a good view of the entire garden. It was the spot he would normally hold if he was just standing here, keeping watch.

For the next hour, they stayed that way, Villette keeping all her attention on the pond, Brandon allowing his eyes to sweep across the small enclosure as if he was constantly looking for trouble. He kept his head cocked back slightly toward the kitchen, hoping he would detect any sounds indicating that someone else was about to come outside. But all the other inhabitants of the house seemed to be absent, sleeping, or occupied.

Finally, Villette stirred and glanced his way. "Hello—Brandon, is it?" she called. "Can you come here a moment? I have a question about the fish pond."

"Yes, dona," he said, and marched across the lawn to her side. She was pointing at some invisible defect in the stone border at her feet.

"Do you think the mortar has loosened? Do you think the water is leaking?" she asked.

He was trying not to grin. It wasn't a very convincing ploy, but it would do for their purposes. He knelt in front of her and ran his hand over the inlaid stones. "It's hard to tell," he said. "Maybe there's a problem."

"So we have a new guard," Villette said in an undervoice. "How does that affect our scheme?"

"It gives us less leeway," he admitted. "We can't just wait for an opportune moment—we'll have to make a plan and stick with it."

"Will she *always* be on the night watch?"

"Until she earns a day off. Which will be in a couple of weeks."

Villette caught her breath. "Does that mean we should be prepared to leave that very day?"

"I think so."

"I'll be ready."

"Good." He stood up and brushed the dirt off his knees. "I think that should take care of the problem," he said in a slightly raised voice, in case anyone was listening. "That's the best I can do."

Chapter Twenty-nine: Brandon

The next two weeks passed in a similar fashion, though Brandon slept better after that first day, and consequently had a clearer head in the mornings. Linnet didn't exactly warm up to them, but she did join them for dinner most nights and managed to be civil if not cordial during their conversations.

One afternoon at the end of that second week, Brandon was standing indecisively in the atrium, wondering if he could manufacture an excuse for talking to Villette if he went out into the garden, when Finley rammed through the front door. He was startled enough that he put a hand on his sword, but he could see her face was excited, not alarmed.

"Michalo's just arrived at the gate," she announced. "I didn't even know he was coming today. Should we wake Linnet up?"

Brandon automatically started straightening his collar and his sleeves, checking his navy uniform for any signs of dust. "*I* wouldn't want to be yanked out of bed two minutes before the secretary of the sanctuary strolled in," he said.

"Next time, then," Finley decided, coming to stand shoulder to shoulder with him so they looked like a respectable fighting force.

Just then Abe opened the door, and the temple delegation swept in. Finley and Brandon bowed in tandem as smoothly as if they'd been practicing for weeks.

"Villette?" Michalo demanded.

"In the garden, patri," Finley answered. "Would you like me to escort you out?"

"I know the way," Michalo said, brushing past them without another word.

His guards lingered in the atrium, so Brandon and Finley did as well, all of them trying to look stiff and formal and completely incurious about their counterparts. The cook carried a tray of refreshments out to the garden. Brandon tried to imagine how Villette had received Michalo this time—gaily, sullenly, mockingly, morosely. He had seen her show all those moods to the secretary of the sanctuary. Michalo himself was always the same—cool, determined, unyielding. A man who knew he had the power in the relationship and was willing to bide his time.

A man who *thought* he had power. Who *thought* he had time.

It was probably an hour before Michalo strolled back into the house, unruffled as always. He paused to inspect Finley and Brandon where they stood with their spines straight and their heads high.

"I know I've met both of you before," he said. "But hasn't a new guard arrived recently?"

As the senior member of their group, Finley answered. "Yes. But she's been taking the night watch and sleeping during the day."

"Ah. Perhaps next time I'm here I can be introduced."

Finley didn't make the obvious answer. *If you'd told us you were coming, you could have met her today.* Instead she asked, "Would you like us to wake her?"

"No, no. I'll return soon enough. Besides the arrival of the new guard, is there anything of importance to report?"

"Nothing at all, patri. Everything continues to go smoothly."

"Excellent. Just what I like to hear." Michalo nodded and strode to the door, his soldiers falling in step behind him. Finley followed them out to lock the gate.

She was back inside a couple of minutes later, rolling her eyes. "Never saw a man with such a *big* red-hot poker up his ass," she said.

"Is the high divine just as bad? I've never met him, only seen him from a distance."

"No! He seems like a sweet old man—like he'd be everybody's favorite uncle. Though I have to think he's probably not really that nice." She shook her head. "Nobody who's got any power ever is."

"Can't argue with that," Brandon said.

The visit had ruffled them both, so Finley didn't retreat to her room for the rest of Brandon's shift. Instead, she chatted with him while he was in the foyer and followed him when he made his rounds. Ordinarily, he wouldn't have minded—he rather liked Finley—but he wanted to talk to Villette. Michalo's visits always unsettled her, and he wanted to make sure she was calm. And soothe her if she wasn't.

He didn't get a chance till well past dinner. Linnet had emerged from her room to join them for a couple of hours before her watch began at nine. Brandon excused himself while they were still eating, saying he would take one final walk around the grounds. He headed out to the gardens, because

Villette had never come back inside after Michalo left. The whole enclosure was full of shadows, but he could make out her denser shape, once again sitting on a bench by the pond.

They didn't have time to be cautious, so he just went straight over to her, hoping no one was watching from the house. But he came to a halt just behind her, the position of a servant who was responding to a summons from an employer.

"Are you all right?" he asked in a low voice.

She was wrapped in a light cloak, leaning forward as if fascinated by the ripples of water glinting faintly in the moonlight. He could see the slight motion as she shook her head. "No," she whispered.

He had to fight the urge to step closer, to take her in a protective embrace. "Why? What did he say to you?"

"Brandon—I'm so stupid. I forgot. I was so happy I got careless."

"Forgot what? Careless about what?"

"The cherloshe," she whispered.

For a moment, he had no idea what she was talking about.

"My *blood,*" she added. "I forgot to swallow the cherloshe. Michalo came here today, and he took a sample of my blood, and I realized—I'm so afraid he'll find that I'm fertile! I'm so afraid they'll turn me out of this place and force me into marriage—" Her voice broke on a choked sob.

She had finally told him, a week or so ago, why she had been imprisoned, what value she held for the temple. Michalo had been right—it was a fantastical tale, almost impossible to believe. Yet Brandon had chosen to believe it. Even if it wasn't true, Villette was genuinely terrified of *something* the priests would do to her. It hardly mattered to Brandon what it was. He only knew he had to prevent it.

"All right," he said, thinking fast. "All right. How quickly will they get results?"

"I don't know. Maybe a day or two."

"And then how quickly will they remove you from this place?"

"I don't know, but I'd guess immediately. They have waited *years* for this moment. They're not going to waste any time."

"Then we have to leave before the week is up."

"*How?*"

"Three nights from now. That's Linnet's day off. I'll take the night shift. As soon as everyone is asleep, we'll just walk out."

"They'll catch us. They'll never stop hunting for me."

"We'll go so far from Corcannon they'll never find us."

"I want to believe you," she whispered. "But I'm so afraid. I don't want them to take me. I would rather die." She glanced at him over her shoulder. "I would. Brandon, I would rather be dead."

"Don't," he pleaded. "Don't take your own life. Not until we've tried to escape. Maybe—if we don't get out of here. If they catch us. But not until then. Not until there's no hope at all. Promise me, Villette."

She took a long shuddering breath. "I promise," she said. "But Brandon. I am so afraid."

He came close enough to lay a hand on her shoulder and feel her trembling. He wished he could open a vein and pour some of his courage, some of his conviction, into her own body. "I know you are," he said. "But we'll make it. We will."

He heard the faint clatter of the door opening and took a hasty step away. "Is that all you wanted?" he asked in a formal voice.

Villette shook her hair back and came gracefully to her feet. "Yes," she said in a languid tone. "Thank you for your help."

Without another glance at him, she turned and headed toward the house. He heard her murmur a courteous greeting to someone, heard Linnet reply *good night, dona.* He waited until the door opened and shut again before he sauntered back toward the house.

"Everything all right with her?" Linnet asked. "She seemed upset."

"It suddenly occurred to her that the fish might start dying when the weather turns cold," Brandon answered. "I told her that some might, but most of them would be fine as long as the water didn't freeze solid."

Linnet glanced at the pond, then at Brandon. He could barely see the gleam of her eyes in the faint light. "Huh. I hadn't given it any thought. How do you know?"

"Had a pond like this when I was growing up."

"I don't like fish," Linnet said.

"To eat or to look at?"

"Either."

There wasn't much to say to that. He wasn't sure *what* Linnet might like, but he didn't care enough to ask. "Well, Villette seems to enjoy watching them. So I was glad to be able to reassure her."

She nodded, but he could tell she'd lost interest. "Anything happening out here?"

"Nothing to report," he said. "You should have a quiet night."

"See you in the morning."

After breakfast, Brandon offered to run errands for the cook, saying he was getting so restless he had to do something useful or lose his mind. She gratefully accepted his offer and handed him a list of ingredients, so he took off before Linnet had even finished her twelve-hour shift.

He didn't have much time. Everyone would expect him to dawdle over his chores, because anyone who left the house was always gone longer than the errands would seem to justify. But he still only had a window of a few hours. He hopped onto the first chugger headed south, and exited near the bridge nearest his lodgings.

There were four or five stables in the immediate vicinity, and Brandon applied his usual criteria. He wanted one that looked clean enough to be respectable but rundown enough that its owners would be grateful for any business, and not inclined to ask questions. There were two that seemed to perfectly fit that description, and he chose the one closest to his apartment.

"I need a couple of dependable horses and all the gear," he told the stable owner. It wasn't hard to make his voice disgruntled, his expression irritable. "My wife says—well, I don't think her father's *ever* going to die, you know what I'm saying? But she thinks it might happen this time, and she wants to be there."

The stablemaster nodded, trying to fix a sympathetic expression on his face but clearly putting more effort into calculating the charges. He was a broad man with massive arms and powerful legs. The bracelets he wore on both arms were made of braided leather studded with bits of gold and silver. Brandon had seen such a style employed before by blacksmiths, who were understandably wary about wearing metal directly against their skin, and workers who labored in dirty jobs.

"Would you rather rent or buy?" the stablemaster asked. "If you won't need the horses long, you might be better off renting."

Brandon grunted. The chances were very slim that he would ever have the chance to return the beasts. And—despite the fact that he was fast becoming the most adept liar he'd ever met—he couldn't bring himself to swindle an honest workingman. "I'd rather buy just because—well, who knows how long we might have to be staying with him? But if you're open to a re-purchase when we get back—"

"Might just be," the other man answered. "Let me show you what I've got on hand."

Brandon knew enough about horses to be pretty sure when he wasn't being cheated, so he agreed to the first two animals the stablemaster suggested and only haggled a little on the price. "Might be three-four more days before we leave," he said. "You can board them until then? For a fee, I mean."

"Of course."

"Good man."

He made a few other stops to pick up the barest necessities for a brief overnight stay. A couple of blankets. Some dried food that would keep for a few weeks and travel well. A bottle of wine, just because, if they ever actually made it to their desperate refuge, they'd both probably need it.

He carried all his purchases back to the rented rooms and placed them neatly on the floor. Then he stomped around for a few minutes and knocked on the walls, just so the neighbors would realize he was present. That way they'd be less startled when he and Villette showed up in the middle of the night. Or so he hoped.

Finally, he set off for the food markets to pick up the items the cook had requested. He'd been gone longer than he planned, but he felt pretty good about what he'd accomplished. They were ready for a midnight flight. And that midnight was only a few days away.

When Brandon made it back to the house, Finley met him at the door. "Took you long enough," she said.

He grinned. "I got distracted. Anything going on here?"

"Yes," she answered, her voice low and full of excitement.

He raised his eyebrows, but she just shook her head. "Drop this stuff off, then come out and walk the grounds with me."

She was clearly bursting with news, so he didn't waste time asking more questions. He took all the food to the cook, brushed off her thanks, then headed back out the front door. Finley was already halfway down the fence line as if checking the integrity of the posts. He glanced around and located Abe near the far corner of the house, digging up something that might be a rosebush. Too far away to hear anything.

Brandon hustled to catch up with Finley as she continued walking the perimeter. "What's up?"

"Visitors all day long! Well, two."

"So who were they?"

"The first one was from the temple."

Brandon felt his heart thump with anxiety. "Michalo again?"

"No. The high divine this time! He went directly up to Villette's room and walked right in. We could hear both of them yelling."

"Who could hear?"

"The maid and the cook and me. Linnet was asleep and Abe was in the garden. But the three of us were all in the foyer, and we could hear everything."

"What were they arguing about? Could you tell?"

Finley looked disappointed. "No. Well, she kept saying, 'You can't compel me!' and he said, 'I assure you, I can.' And then once he said, 'I would like to make this as civilized as I can. Please make it possible for me to avoid doing you any harm.'" Finley looked over at him, her eyes blazing. "What could that *mean?"*

Brandon knew exactly what it meant, and his heart thumped even harder. Villette's carelessness had cost her dearly; cleared of cherloshe, her blood had proved itself to be clean and fertile. "I don't know, but it sounds big."

"And then she said something about how soon he expected her to move, and he said preparations were being made, and I think—Brandon, I think they're about to take her someplace else. I don't know why, and I don't know where, and I don't think she wants to go."

Why do you care? he wanted to say, shouting the words in her face. *You don't even like her. It doesn't matter to you if she lives or dies!* Instead, he tried for the verbal equivalent of a shrug. "I don't think she likes being *here*, either," he said. "She doesn't seem to have a very happy life in general."

"No," Finley said. "It's hard to feel sorry for a beautiful rich woman, but I'd never want to be her."

Brandon couldn't keep talking about Villette, so he changed the subject. "Well, I suppose we'll be back at the barracks in a few days, waiting for our next assignment," he said. "Linnet will probably be glad of that."

"*Linnet,*" Finley hissed. She glanced over her shoulder, but Abe was still safely kneeling in front of the house, while the two of them had reached the corner of the fence line and come to a halt. "The second caller was for her. A man."

"That's odd." Neither Nadder nor Finley had ever had a friend over the whole time Brandon had been here; he'd assumed such visits were forbidden. "Was it an emergency?"

"Who knows? She's so close-mouthed. She was sleeping, of course, and he wouldn't leave a message, so I had to wake her up."

"Better you than me."

"She just rolled out of bed like she was already awake. The two of them went out into the yard and talked for about five minutes. Then he left, and she went back to her room. She didn't say a thing."

"It could have been news about a family member."

"Probably. But it was still awfully strange."

"Did she look upset?"

"Not really."

"Maybe she'll tell us something over dinner."

Finley made a face. "Maybe. But probably not." Then she rolled her eyes. "Oh, right, dinner. It's the cook's night off. So it will be warmed-over stew and any scraps we can scrounge from the kitchen."

Brandon was sure his dismay was showing in his face. "Tonight? It's the servants' night off? *All* of them?"

"Yes, all of them! Every once in a while they get to leave this place and go off and be normal people for a few hours."

"No, of course, I know that, I just—" *I just wish it had been a couple of days later!* he wanted to wail. How perfect that would have been, to have all the servants out of the house the very night he and Villette needed to sneak away! Clearly Zessaya was not watching over this misadventure as closely as he had hoped. "I just forgot," he ended lamely. "Cold stew it is."

"And then we'll grill Linnet and see if we can get her to tell us about her friend," Finley said. "But I bet she won't say a word."

Indeed, Linnet could hardly have been less forthcoming when the three of them gathered for a meal a couple of hours later. She answered Finley's persistent questions with shrugs, shakes of the head, and terse replies like, "Just someone I know."

"You realize we're not supposed to have visitors here," Finley finally said.

Linnet looked at her a moment. "All right," she said. "That'll be the last one."

Brandon toyed with his food and barely paid attention to the conversation, if that's what it could be called. His mind was too busy going over possibilities, worrying over the details of the escape. The public chuggers ran all night, but rarely more than once an hour. He and Villette would have to start out on foot and hope a transport rattled up before she had raised blisters on her feet from the unaccustomed exercise. Did she even have the right shoes for undertaking such a long journey? It hardly mattered. Her blood had betrayed her. They had to act now.

"So what are you going to do on your day off?" Finley was asking. "Do you have family in town? Friends? You don't talk about them a lot."

Linnet pushed herself away from the table and abruptly stood up. "And you talk *too* much," she said, and marched out.

Finley sneered at her back, then turned to Brandon with a grin. "Well, I guess that's told *me,*" she said.

"Just leave her alone," he advised. "Go to your room as soon as her shift starts and leave her in peace."

Now Finley was openly laughing. "Oh no, I like getting under her skin. I'm going to hang out in the atrium, play some card games, ask her if she'd like to join me for a round. You should stay too. It'll be fun."

"Not my idea of fun," he said, coming to his feet. "All right. I'm done for the night. See you in the morning."

Finley stood up and gestured toward the foyer. "Come on. Just a few hands. Just to annoy Linnet."

He only agreed because he was so jumpy that he wasn't sure he'd be able to stand himself if he was just cooped up in his room, endlessly reviewing his escape plans. Since it was still her shift, Finley made one more round of the house and grounds while Brandon sat at the wrought iron table, shuffling and reshuffling the deck. It was easy to imagine Linnet standing right behind her closed door, hearing the faint whiffle of the cards and fuming with impatience.

I don't know how I'll stand her once Finley's gone and it's just me and some other new guard, he thought. And then he realized that he would be gone even sooner than Finley, and he would never meet another new guard at this house.

Or anywhere in Corcannon. He would be abandoning his post, his career, the beginnings of the life he had started to build from will and tenacity. Throwing everything away for the sake of a woman he barely knew and didn't entirely trust and loved so helplessly that it sometimes frightened him. Maybe he was crazy.

He shuffled the cards again. And maybe they would be caught and Villette would be sacrificed and he would be hanged. All this plotting would lead to nothing but heartbreak and disaster.

He almost shrugged. Nothing could turn him from this course. Better to die than to live with the knowledge that he could not save Villette. That he hadn't even tried. And maybe Zessaya *hadn't* turned her back on him. He dropped the cards to the table and put one hand around the chazissa that lay under his shirt. She loved to defy Cordelan and his acolytes, after all. Maybe she would shepherd the two of them through the dark streets, make smooth the road they traveled as they fled from the priests and their blood rites. Maybe Zessaya would watch over their mad venture.

"Don't look so intense, you'll make me think you're cheating," Finley said as she dropped into the seat across from him.

He had to shake off his fierce mood and force himself to smile at her. "An island man doesn't cheat," he said. "He just plays better than a city girl."

Finley hooted at the challenge and grabbed the cards. "Give me those. I'm dealing. And we're playing for money."

Chapter Thirty: Brandon

In the end, Brandon sat with Finley until nearly eleven as they played cards and gambled for low stakes and argued half-heartedly. Linnet emerged from her room exactly at nine and didn't even glance their way as she made her first pass through the house. Finley and Brandon watched her make the entire circuit around the second-floor balcony, the entire circuit of the third floor, before she descended and headed out the front door to check the grounds.

"I think she tried every doorknob to make sure it was locked," Finley whispered. "Don't you supposed Villette wondered if someone was trying to break into her room?"

"She better not try our doorknobs tonight while we're sleeping," Brandon answered. "I sleep with a knife under my hand. If I hear someone rattling around outside, I'm liable to come out blade first."

"Me, too! Especially now that I know she's prowling the house."

"Well, I prowl around at night, too. But I don't try the doors."

"I wonder if she checks the gate to make sure it's locked."

"I do that," he said.

"So do I."

They played a few more hands, got bored, tried a different game, got bored again. "I'm going to bed," Brandon said, yawning as he stood up. "But feel free to stay out here all night just to make her crazy."

She grinned up at him. "I just might do that. Not much other entertainment around here."

He retired to his room and made himself lie down, but he was wide awake. Squabbling with Finley had taken off some of his restless edge, but his mind was still fretting over details. Maybe he was wrong to plan to take the land route. Maybe it would be smarter to cross the eastern bridge that led to the small city harbor and board the nearest ship. Maybe there would be an islander vessel flying the fish-covered flag of Zessaya—the captain of such a ship might be willing to help out a fellow countryman and not ask any questions. Islanders were more likely to be loyal to each other than to the city or the priests who ran it. Sometimes they'd spite a Cordelano, even if cost them, just because it was such a satisfying thing to do. If Brandon could find a captain like that—

Maybe the harbor was a better bet after all. He'd have to ask Villette in the morning. Right after he asked her what terrible news the high divine had brought when he came to visit.

The decision made Brandon feel more peaceful than he had in days, and he turned on his side. It had to be well past midnight by now; he had better get some sleep. He would have to be certain he was rested before they fled the house. He closed his eyes, squeezing them tightly to make sure they stayed shut. He promised himself he wouldn't stir from his bed until morning.

There was a sound in the corridor.

Brandon's lids flew open and he tensed on his bed, the knife already in his hand. He lay motionless for a few seconds, straining to hear, but the noise didn't come again. It had been a slight rasping sound, like metal dragging along stone. He couldn't think what natural nighttime activity might have caused it.

Impossible to just roll over and go back to sleep. He climbed soundlessly out of bed and pulled on a pair of pants, not bothering with a shirt. The tile floor was cool beneath his bare feet as he stole across the room and stood motionless at his door, still listening intently.

He couldn't hear anything amiss. There was probably nothing wrong. But there was no reason not to creep out and check. Opening the door slowly, so it didn't creak or click, he glided out into the corridor.

The short hallway that served the bedrooms was completely dark except for the faint light that spilled in from the atrium, where wall sconces provided a chalky illumination. Nothing was moving in his immediate line of sight, so he edged forward until he could view the entire open space of the bottom level. It was completely empty except for the wrought iron table, where Finley had apparently played solitary card games until she fell asleep. Brandon smiled to see her forehead resting on the cold table, her face turned toward the wall.

Frowned as he noticed the liquid dripping between the woven metal slats.

His mouth had just gathered to form the syllables of her name when another faint sound drew his attention upward. The balconies of the top two stories were wreathed in shadows, but surely that was a darker shape flitting along the second level. Coming to a halt beside one of the closed doors. Bending over with a sense of purpose. There was no one in the house tonight except

Villette and the three guards, and Brandon was pretty sure Finley was dead.

That meant Linnet was picking the lock on Villette's room.

He flew across the slick tile floor, not bothering with stealth or silence. "Villette!" he shouted. "*Villette!* Watch out!"

Above him, he heard the splintering sound of a doorframe breaking and a faint cry of alarm. He leapt madly up the stairs, galvanized by terror, and raced down the balcony so fast that his feet skidded along the smooth tile. The sounds from Villette's room grew louder—a scream, a thud, another shout. Linnet might have broken in, but Villette was putting up a fight.

He charged through the shattered door, straight toward the tangle of bodies that were barely visible in the curtained room. Villette was wearing a white nightdress, so he concentrated on the darker mass that had to be Linnet in her navy blue uniform. He grabbed her by the shoulders and wrenched her away, trying to kick her feet out from under her at the same time.

She surprised him by releasing Villette and allowing herself to fall backward on him so heavily that she almost brought both of them to the floor. He let go, scrambling sideways, and she twisted around to face him. She lifted a hand in a wild strike, and he felt her blade scrape once against his shoulder, once against his ribs, drawing blood both times. She couldn't see him any more clearly than he could see her or he would probably be dead already.

She swung again and he dropped low, flinging himself at her legs, and this time he brought her crashing down. He heard her grunt as she struck the bedframe, but the collision wasn't enough to deter her. She kicked free of his hold, then shoved her boots violently in his face as he tried to pin her down. He probably only had twenty or thirty pounds on her—not enough to help him win the fight by mass alone. She kicked him again and rolled away, leaping to her feet. He was off the floor just as fast. They circled each other in the dark.

"Villette! Can you get us some light?" he called.

Linnet surprised him by speaking. "If you can see me, I can see you."

He didn't bother answering, just watched her shadow for cues. Villette was behind him now, which meant Linnet would have to kill him before she could attack Villette again. She probably had multiple weapons, but if he could get the knife out of her hand, he could at least improve his odds. He feinted to see if she would strike at him again, and when she did, he grabbed her arm and twisted hard. She yelped and responded with a vicious kick, aiming for his groin but connecting with his thigh. She hadn't dropped the knife, so he clamped his other hand around her forearm and savagely snapped down on the bone. He felt it crack beneath his fingers as she swept her leg out and knocked him off his feet.

He slammed to the floor and rolled to his knees as Linnet leapt across him, trying to reach Villette. He thrust his hand upward, a hard palm against her ribcage, spinning her off course. She crashed against another piece of furniture and he heard chairs and table legs squeal across the floor, but she never lost her balance. He jumped to his feet as she launched herself forward again, and he felt the impact of their bodies across every surface of his own.

Just then the room flared with a thin, cool light, and he could finally see what he was doing. He was chest to chest with Linnet, nose to nose; her normally serene features were contorted with passion. For a moment, he was simply bewildered. "What is *wrong* with you?" he whispered.

"She has to die," she panted, and tried to shove herself away from him.

Brandon swept his arms up and crushed her against him, exploiting his slight size advantage and the brute strength in his arms. She struggled fiercely, but her broken wrist was trapped between their bodies and he could tell that the pain was sapping her strength. He could feel her trying to free her good arm, and he guessed she'd switched her knife to that hand, so he tightened his hold so much he thought his own ribs might fracture. She grunted in pain and butted her head against his forehead with such force that his arms loosened and he stumbled.

With a yell, Linnet sprang past him, knife already extended. Brandon whirled around just in time to see her stagger backward, hit by a copper water pitcher Villette flung straight at her face. It was enough for Brandon. He pounced, his dagger hand arcing through the air, and cut her across the throat with two quick slashes. For a moment, she teetered on her toes, her expression showing surprise and her mouth working soundlessly. Her good hand came up to cover the wounds, then her face smoothed out and she seemed to sigh. A second later, she crumpled gracelessly to the floor.

Brandon stood over her, breathing heavily, his knife still at the ready in case this was a trick. But the blood was flowing so freely and so fast that within a minute he knew it was over.

Not until then did he turn to appraise Villette. She was standing motionless, staring down at the guard, another weapon in her right hand—this time a decorative metal paperweight that looked like it might weigh five pounds. Her expression was part fury and part resolve, and he thought, if he hadn't arrived in time, she might have been able to fight Linnet off all on her own. He wanted to comfort her, to put his arms around her in a much more tender hold than the one he had used on Linnet, but she radiated such menace that he thought she might not be safe to touch.

"She's dead," he said.

Villette lifted her gaze to his face. "She wanted to kill me."

"Yes. I don't know why."

Villette shook her head. "Michalo always said—I didn't believe him—but—"

"She had the look of a fanatic," Brandon said. "She wanted you dead for the very reasons the temple wanted you alive."

Now she wavered; she put her left hand to her face as if she was too weary to think. That was when Brandon noticed that whatever light she had managed to conjure in this dark room seemed to be spilling between her closed fingers. Its chilly glow threw her cheekbones into stark relief. "My blood," she said.

"Yes," he repeated. He came close enough to wrap an arm around her shoulders and she leaned into his embrace. "She must be one of those—what did you call them?—Reversionists. Securing a post here must have been a goal they'd been after for a long time."

She rubbed her cheek against the bare skin of his chest. She didn't seem to mind that she was getting his blood on her face, her clothes. "Why wait until tonight? She's been here for a couple of weeks."

He kissed her hair. "What news did the high divine bring today?"

She lifted her head. "The very worst. Their tests confirmed that I am now fertile, and they plan to marry me off by the end of the week."

Brandon nodded; it was what he had suspected. "Linnet must have gotten the same news, because she had a mysterious visitor this afternoon. As long as you couldn't have a child, you weren't a danger, so they let you live. But once your blood was clean, they wanted to get rid of you before you could produce an heir."

She pulled away from him. Her anger and determination were fading, and she was beginning to look anxious and afraid. "What do we do now? There's a dead body in my room! And the high divine promising to be back in a few days! Brandon, there is no hope left for me!"

He caught her shoulders and drew her closer, making shushing noises and dropping a quick kiss on her mouth. "We leave," he said. "Right now. Tonight. The servants are gone. Finley is dead—"

"What?"

"I know. It's terrible."

"But I liked her!"

"Me too. Linnet killed her before she came upstairs." He shook his head, shaking away the grief. He had no time for it. "But now we have an unexpected opportunity. There is no one in the house but us. It's a few hours until dawn—we have a little time—"

She brought her hands up between their bodies, wringing them together. "A few hours—we cannot get far enough away—and when Michalo realizes that he's been right all this time, that I really am in danger—Brandon, we will never get away!"

Suddenly it was all clear to him. The entire plan. "Get dressed. Grab your things," he said. "We'll be out of here in fifteen minutes."

"But—"

He reached for her left hand and gently unsnapped her ornate gold bracelet. "We'll put this on Linnet. We'll strip off her uniform and dress her in your robe. And when they find her body—"

"We look nothing alike!"

"She's got Cordelano coloring, just like you. And when they find her remains, charred by fire—"

She stared at him. "You want to burn the house down," she whispered.

"If they think you died, they won't look for you."

"Brandon! *Yes!* But will it work?"

"I don't know. But it could. It might. It's our best chance."

She pulled away from him, suddenly full of brisk purpose. "Go. Pack up your own things. I'll get my money and a change of clothes."

He toed Linnet's limp body with his bare foot. He should be more horrified that he had just killed another living human, and more distraught that Finley had been murdered, but mostly what he felt was a profound sense of relief. Such a terrible night, and yet how much worse it might have been. "I have to cut off Linnet's bracelet and gather materials to set a couple of fires. One here in the bedroom, I think, and one or two downstairs. So maybe it will be an hour before we're out of here."

"Maybe an hour," Villette said, almost blithe. "And then we'll be gone."

He headed for the door, then turned back briefly to kiss her one more time. "You're free," he whispered. "I swear to you, as of this night, you're free."

She leaned forward to kiss him in reply. "Let's run away."

Chapter Thirty-one: Madeleine

It wasn't even dawn when Madeleine heard the insistent clatter of heavy vehicles laboring up the street, caught the faint echoes of people shouting from what seemed like a far distance. She stirred in her bed, half tempted to run to the window and peer out, trying to guess what disaster was in the making.

Reese moved beside her, wrapping his arms around her and pulling her closer. "What is it? What's wrong?" he murmured into her neck.

"I hear noises outside."

That brought him all the way awake, and he pushed himself up to an elbow, though he managed to keep one arm around her. "You think someone's attacking the house?"

"No, no—something in the distance. As if a couple of chuggers have collided and people are coming from all over the city to provide assistance."

He yawned, threw the covers back, and climbed out of bed. "Let's see if I can tell anything," he said, opening the window as wide as it would go. He stuck his head out so far she was afraid he might fall to the garden below.

"*Reese!* Be careful!"

He turned back with a grin, closing the window to keep out the chilly morning air. "Ah, if I fall, there'll be someone there in a minute to set my broken bones," he said, crawling back next to her. "You know I've got guards patrolling night and day."

She snuggled against him. Even that brief moment at the window had cooled his skin. "Well, I don't *want* you broken. Could you tell what's going on?"

"Smelled like smoke. Maybe a fire up the street."

"Oh, I hope not."

"Nothing you can do about it. Go back to sleep."

He did, almost on the instant, but Madeleine lay awake for the better part of an hour. It wasn't the commotion in the neighborhood that kept her eyes wide open, but the commotion in her head. The constant churn of worry and fear and indecision. What should she do?

Life had changed dramatically in the two weeks since she had confronted the Council. That very afternoon, Reese had moved into her father's house, bringing his very masculine presence and a cadre of soldiers. He had ostentatiously taken a room on the opposite side of the balcony and made it clear to Madeleine that he was here to protect her, not seduce her. They had slept separately for three days before she went to him in the middle of the night and simply said, "I can't bear to be apart from you." After that, he shared her bed.

It had been a surprise to her, how much she relished lovemaking. She had always enjoyed Tivol's warm affections—his kisses, the feel of his arm around her shoulder, the way she fit so neatly against his body when he took her in a loose embrace. Few of the women in her set were virgins, and she'd been willing to experiment outside the marriage bed, but Tivol had always rather sweetly insisted that they wait. Now, of course, she was certain he was following Harlo's directive to let her body mature to its optimum state, but she had been so charmed that she had never pushed the matter. Nonetheless, she had expected to derive a certain amount of pleasure from their intimate relations.

But she hadn't expected this—this—*craving* she felt for Reese's touch, this sense of starvation she experienced when she had been apart from him for more than a day. She hadn't been prepared for the absolute giddiness of physical delight. It was wrapped up with but somehow separate from the emotional madness of love—an extra dimension—a magnifier of all the things she already felt.

"I love this so much," she whispered to Reese one night. "I'm afraid I'm becoming *wanton.*"

He laughed and gathered her tightly to him. "You could not say anything that pleased me more," he assured her.

So Reese had been the greatest, and the happiest, change in her life. But around the sun-drenched circle of his presence was a ring of pitch-black night, and every day the darkness encroached more and more closely on Madeleine's bewildered heart.

She had fulfilled her promise and presented herself at the temple. Harlo himself had cut a slice in her arm and collected the liquid that fell. Reese had accompanied her, a physician of his choosing beside him, and the instant they thought Madeleine grew weak, they practically snatched her away from the high divine's hold. She didn't stay to watch him pour her blood into his infernal fountain, but it seemed to have some effect. At any rate, the tremors that had rumbled beneath the city for days died away to nothing.

Impossible to know how long the partial offering would satisfy the god.

She shifted position in the bed, trying not to wake Reese. She always came to the same conclusion: If the city erupted—if the continent exploded at the seams—it would be her fault. If people died and mountains crumbled and the entire civilization sank into the sea, Madeleine would be to blame. She could not endure the idea of bearing a child and sending it off to be killed. But she could not live with the guilt of destroying the world.

She had never shared her thoughts with Reese. He knew that she was troubled about the role she had been assigned, he knew that she felt great responsibility and concern, but he didn't know how deep her anguish ran.

"We'll go to my property in Chibain," he told her on the nights he noticed her distress and thought he could soothe her.

"I thought Mount Dar was already spewing ash and cinders?"

"That mountain has stood for a thousand years. It won't come apart now. We'll be safe."

But the world would not be safe.

She flung an arm over her eyes, trying to block out what little light filtered through the room. She didn't want to die. She didn't want to murder her sons and send her daughters off to terrible fates. But she didn't know what to do.

When Madeline woke in the morning, Reese was gone. Truly gone, because he was off to meet with a merchant who ran a mining operation about a day's ride outside of the city. She buried her face in his pillow and breathed in the traces of his scent. She would put this pillow in the closet so the maid wouldn't wash the casing before he returned.

As soon as she was dressed, she made her way down to the kitchen. It was still something of a shock to realize how many people were likely to be in the house at any given point—two or three soldiers always on watch in the great open atrium, two or three more who could be glimpsed through the windows, patrolling the fence. Reese's manservant and secretary had also taken up residence, though she thought the secretary might have lodgings of his own somewhere in the city. If so, he almost never used them. She didn't mind the extra bodies—she rather liked the purposeful bustle of having a large household to care for. Until she remembered why all those new additions were suddenly in her halls and spare bedrooms.

The kitchen was the busiest room in the mansion, since an undercook and two serving girls had been hired to help feed the expanded numbers.

Norrah looked up as Madeleine wandered in.

"Good morning, dona," she said. "Are you looking for breakfast?"

"I'm *starving.*"

"Aussen, why don't you make up a plate of eggs and toast for the dona? And some fruit, too."

Madeleine appropriated a piece of bread from the counter and nibbled it as Aussen began gathering food. "Did anybody else wake up last night, hearing noise in the street?"

The undercook looked up from where she was stirring a pot on the stove. "Yes! And this morning we learned there was a big fire."

"Two streets over. An entire house burned down," Norrah confirmed.

"Was anyone hurt?"

"They say a woman died," a serving girl said in an important voice.

"Oh no!" Madeleine exclaimed. "Do you know who it was?"

"The courier who came this morning told us it was an old woman," said Norrah. "She lived all alone and her neighbors never saw her."

"That's awful."

"It is," Norrah agreed. "Aussen, my dear, what a nice plate you've put together. Now why don't you carry it out to the small dining room?"

"I can't just eat in here?"

Norrah waved at the broad wooden table, covered with bowls and pans and bags of ingredients. "It's baking day, and there's just no room," she said.

"I'll eat with you," Aussen offered.

That made Madeleine laugh. "Well, then. You have to fill your own plate."

As soon as they were seated in the smaller dining room, Aussen began chattering away in a mix of Zessin and Cordish. Madeleine didn't entirely follow her story, but she thought it involved a visit to Cody's house and a footrace with some of his roommates. She just nodded encouragingly and concentrated on her food.

Jayla stepped into the room fifteen minutes later. "I'm sorry," she said. "Norrah just told me she'd sent Aussen in with you."

"To get both of us out of the way, I think."

"I *help* in the kitchen!" Aussen said, offended.

"Of course you do," Madeleine said gravely. "Norrah tells me that all the time."

Jayla hid a smile. "Tokah is the one who will be arriving today, and her code word is eleven," she said.

In the past two weeks, Madeleine had met Jayla's friend Cody, an easygoing young courier, and a whole host of his friends. They had set up a complex schedule of visits to ensure that one of them saw Madeleine every day to receive her assurance that she was safe and under no duress. If the day came that these things weren't true, Cody would hand-carry letters to a designated list of Council families and businesspeople, telling the raw truth of Madeleine's situation. As Madeleine understood it, the couriers all took different routes to the house, arrived at different times of day, and followed circuitous paths home to make it difficult for any spies to track them down.

Sometimes she wondered if Jayla was taking overly dramatic precautions. Other times she wondered if there was any value in threatening to reveal her fate. Maybe no one else in the city would care that the occasional woman or child was surrendered to keep the rest of them safe and happy. But Harlo and her father seemed worried about what might happen if the news leaked out, and she had nothing else to bargain with.

"Tokah," she repeated. "That's Cody's sister, right?"

"Yes."

"I like him so much."

"You've spent all of five minutes with him."

"I still like him."

"Most people do."

"I *love* Cody," Aussen announced. "And I love Tokah, and I love Kammi. I don't love Rovyn."

"Which one is Rovyn? The petite pretty girl?"

"That's her," Jayla said, her voice dry.

Madeleine tilted her head, hearing a hint of dislike. For someone as reserved as Jayla, that spoke volumes. "What makes her so disagreeable?"

"Nothing. She seems nice enough."

"She follows Cody around," Aussen supplied. "All the time! She's always touching him!"

Madeleine smothered a laugh and watched Jayla fight to keep down a blush. "Oh, a *rival,*" she said. "Let's figure out how we can get rid of her."

She expected Jayla to deny her conclusion, but the topic of Rovyn seemed to get under her skin. "No point in fighting over a man," Jayla said. "Either he loves you or he doesn't."

"True," Madeleine said. "But that doesn't mean you can't scheme to get him to yourself."

"I have other things to think about."

Aussen was inspecting Madeleine's plate. "You haven't eaten all your breakfast," she scolded. "Norrah always makes me eat all of *my* breakfast."

Madeleine shoveled a forkful of eggs in her mouth. "I've been too busy talking to *you,*" she said around the food.

Jayla rested her hands on Aussen's shoulders. "Stop being a pest," she said with stern affection. Then, addressing Madeleine, "If you don't need me, I can take her away for the day."

With Reese's men deployed around the grounds, it should have made very little difference if Jayla was in the house or not. There were plenty of people on hand to protect Madeleine. And yet she found herself almost panicky every time she gave Jayla leave to take a few hours off. As if Jayla was the only one she could trust to keep her safe.

"Tomorrow, if that's all right," Madeleine said. "I'm expecting Tivol this morning and Harlo this afternoon. And I know it's irrational but—"

"I don't want to be gone when either one of them is in the house," Jayla interrupted. "Tomorrow is fine."

"Thank you."

Tivol arrived less than an hour later. She received him in the most formal room in the house, where her father used to meet business contacts he wanted to intimidate. It had a high, rounded ceiling, painted an accusing white; three walls tiled in a hostile red; and a collection of black wooden chairs that were hard and unyielding. The tall windows let in a brooding sunlight that didn't even attempt to lighten the mood.

Tivol's mouth quirked as Ella showed him in, because he understood very well why Madeleine had chosen this setting, but he did not complain. "Thank you for seeing me," he said.

She had refused his request the last three times he'd made it, but each time she'd felt a little more wistful. He was the person in her life she had liked the longest; she found herself grieving his absence as if he had died. Could she make a kind of peace with him? Would that, in some small way, heal her lacerated heart?

She gestured at a couple of chairs and they took their seats, both of them squirming in a futile effort to get comfortable. Madeleine folded her hands in her lap. "I am wondering what you think you have to say to me," she said. "Or I to you."

He had clasped his own hands together, and he leaned forward, resting his elbows on his knees. His expression was open and earnest. "I don't know what is more likely to make you forgive me," he said. "An apology or an explanation."

"I don't know that forgiveness is even an option," she said. "But I would like an explanation." As he thought it over, seeming to debate where to begin, she added, "How long have you known?"

"Forever, I think," he said. "I don't remember learning the story, so my mother must have told me some version of it when I was quite young. It's as if, from the time I was born, it was made clear to me that there was a special fate in store for you, and it would be my job to see you through it. I always thought this made me—" He straightened and lifted a hand in a vague gesture. "Heroic, somehow."

"Heroic."

"Your protector. The thing you had to do was so hard, but I could make your life so much easier. That's how I always viewed it." He sighed. "It sounds stupid, said out loud. It's what I believed."

"And you weren't—shocked? Horrified? Repulsed? These are not just *my* children we're talking about, you realize. If you were my husband—"

"I know. I know." He ran a hand through his hair. "My sons would be sacrifices and my daughters would be forced into the very same position you're in now." He leaned forward again. "But their fates would be noble. Tragic but transformative. I always believed it. "

"Did you ever think to *tell* me?"

He nodded. "So many times. You're my closest friend, Madeleine! The woman I love best in the world! And to know I had been lying to you my whole life— But then I thought how such knowledge would break your heart. I couldn't bear to hurt you that way."

"I think I have been hurt in a way that is so much worse."

"I know. And I'm so sorry. I don't know how to undo the harm."

"You can't."

There was silence between them for a moment, and then Tivol spoke again, hesitantly. "What do you think—what do you plan to do now?"

"I don't know."

"You have felt the tremors. You must realize—"

"I *know,*" she said, her voice rising. "The fate of the entire world rests on my shoulders! Do you think I have somehow *overlooked* that fact?"

"Of course I don't. But if you—Madeleine, I know you have been bullied and lied to and coerced, but—"

"But you think I have a clear duty," she said coldly.

He watched her unwaveringly. "I do."

She stared back at him, both furious and terrified, because how could he say such a thing to her? And because she thought he might be right. "I am not the only one who has to agree to such a scheme," she said, almost spitting the words. "And I can tell you now that Reese will never allow a child of his to be used in such a way."

Tivol flinched, but kept his gaze steady. "Then perhaps Reese should not be the father of your children."

She narrowed her eyes. "There is no other candidate for the post."

Tivol laid his hand on his heart, a melodramatic gesture that somehow did not look ridiculous. "Any time you would consider me for that position, I would gladly reclaim it."

Before she could decide if that was the most generous or the most insulting offer she had ever had, there was a polite knock and Aussen entered, carrying a tray of refreshments.

The girl said, "Norrah thought you would want—" followed by a handful of incomprehensible islander words.

"Thank you," Madeleine said. "You can set the tray on that little table."

"*What* did she say?" Tivol asked.

"I'm not sure. She's from the islands, and she speaks Zessin half the time."

Aussen settled the tray on the table with great delicacy. "I'll come back for your dishes later," she assured them solemnly, and slipped out the door.

"She doesn't seem like your usual well-trained staff," Tivol said. "And a bit on the young side."

"She's Jayla's ward."

"Jayla?"

"My guard. The one who was with us that night at Harlo's."

His face tightened in sympathy as he remembered that evening, and then he nodded. "Of course. But why is she delivering food? And looking perilously like she might break the china."

"She helps out in the kitchen, mostly to keep her occupied. While Jayla is occupied protecting *me*."

"You seem fond of her."

She looked at him a long moment. "I am. I think I would grow fond of any child who came into my life."

He returned her gaze. "That's why it would be best," he said. "If you gave up your children the minute they were born."

She felt a sharp pain beneath her ribs; she almost glanced down to check for an injury. "Is that what you planned to do?" she whispered. "Take them from me while I still lay in the birthing bed, then tell me they had died?"

He didn't answer, and she knew she was right. The wound in her chest seemed to grow larger with every heartbeat. She abruptly came to her feet, and Tivol scrambled up beside her.

"Madeleine," he began, but she shook her head. He stepped closer, and she flung up a hand to keep him away. She stumbled toward the door, so blinded with tears that she almost could not find her way.

He didn't follow. He didn't say her name again. She fled across the floor, staggered up the stairs and burst into her room, sobbing the whole way.

How could she ever have loved him?

What was she going to do?

Madeleine had mostly recovered her equanimity by mid-afternoon, when Harlo was supposed to arrive. She had not seen him since the day she accompanied him to the temple to offer up her blood, because she was so hurt and angry at his level of betrayal. No doubt Harlo, like Tivol, had cast himself as a tragic but noble figure. She did not want to hear his justifications, and she was weary of spouting her own recriminations. But she knew that, eventually, they would have to come to an understanding, and so she had agreed to let him visit.

She had no intention of ever seeing her father again. That decision left her feeling so free that sometimes she forgot how trapped she was.

She washed her face and straightened her clothes and studied herself in the mirror. She wanted to look wise and thoughtful, not nervous and sad. She wasn't sure she had come close to succeeding.

Two people were in the atrium as she descended the stairway—Jayla and the lanky young woman who was Cody's sister. Madeleine paused long enough to present her daily code word to the courier, then headed again to the unfriendly formal receiving room. She was too restless to sit, and the chairs were too uncomfortable anyway, so she spent the next fifteen minutes just standing at the window watching traffic rattle down the gridway. Her back was still to the door when she heard it open and the footman announced, "Dona, someone from the temple is here."

"Thank you, yes, show him in."

There was the tap of footsteps, but not the click of a latch engaging. Jayla had insisted that there should never be a closed door between Madeleine and the guards any time there were visitors in the house.

"Good afternoon, Madeleine," someone said, and she whirled around, because that wasn't Harlo's voice.

"Benito," she said, making no attempt to hide her surprise. "I wasn't expecting you."

"The patri was so sorry he was unable to keep his engagement," Benito answered. "He sent me to make his apologies in person and to beg you to receive him tomorrow at around this time."

She could hardly imagine any commitment Harlo could have that would be more important than this one, but in truth she was relieved that she would not have to face him today. "Yes, of course," she said. "I hope nothing terrible has happened."

Benito made a graceful gesture with one hand. His dark, serious face was so handsome that it was distracting. She had always believed the rumors about him and Harlo were true. "Many terrible things are happening all the time," he replied. "The patri's role is to try to make them a little less dire."

She found herself wanting to ask this question of everyone she met. "Did you know?" she said. "About me?"

He watched her solemnly from those deep, liquid eyes. "I did. I thought it was a heavy burden for the patri to bear."

"For the patri!" she said indignantly. "What about *me?*"

"As long as you did not know, it was no burden to you at all."

She came a few steps closer, feeling suddenly combative. "So you agreed. You thought it was best I did not know."

"From what I understand," he said, "in the past there were women who knew the truth and women who did not. Those who were aware of their fates were angry and desperate and afraid. Those who were unaware led gentler lives, though marked by mysterious tragedies." He shrugged. "I can understand why the decision was made to keep you in the dark."

"What happened to those women? The ones who knew the truth?"

"Sadly, they are all dead."

"Killed in childbirth, I suppose," Madeleine said spitefully.

"The last one was murdered by Reversionists."

Madeleine caught her breath. "I didn't realize—I thought the fanatics had never been successful in their attempts—" She wrapped her arms around her shoulders, feeling a sudden chill.

"They have been responsible for quite a few deaths," Benito said, "including that of the last remaining woman who knew what her destiny was supposed to be."

"What was her name? What happened to her?"

"Villette Rowan. Her throat was cut and her house set on fire. At least one of her guards was also found dead in the house."

She almost gasped. "There was a fire last night—"

He shook his head. "Oh, no. This happened fifty years ago."

Madeleine spared a moment to wonder about that woman—Villette, he had called her—who had died at the hands of fanatics. Had that other woman railed against the terrible destiny that had been laid out for her, only to meet another end that was even worse? She must have been related to Madeleine in some fashion. Maybe they even looked alike. Would their fates be similar?

She tried to keep her voice cool. "So the Reversionists have been around for decades," she said. "Did they ever seek to harm my mother or my grandmother?"

"Not as far as I know. Harlo says everyone believed the cult had died out after Villette's death."

"I wonder what caused them to rise up again."

Benito casually strolled across the room, casually pushed the door shut as he passed it. "New members reading old texts. Wondering about the will of the god. Realizing the world was never meant to hold this shape."

Madeleine felt suddenly, unaccountably nervous. Why had he closed the door? Why was he still approaching her, eying her so intently? "It's the shape the god chose."

"Cordelan called himself a deity. But there were goddesses here long before he arrived, and they were never happy with this patched-together land."

He was closing in on her. She backed away, but the grim furniture was badly placed to offer her any protection. "Stay away from me," she ordered, trying to make her tone peremptory. "No—get out of here."

Something gleamed in his hand. "Everything will go back to the way it is supposed to be," he said, "once you're dead."

Madeleine screamed. Benito lunged. She managed to put one of the black chairs between them, then thought to snatch it up in her hands as a weapon to hold him off. Benito dodged her wild thrusts, wrapped his free hand around one of the chair legs, and tried to wrench it out of her hands. She hung on, but the motion propelled her forward, her shoulder practically next to his, the chair canted off uselessly to the side.

She screamed again, rearing back as his knife hand came down, slicing along her upper arm with a line of brutal fire. She flung the chair down and tried to twist away, but her ankles caught in the stiff wooden legs and she tripped, falling awkwardly to the floor. Benito had to leap backward as the chair skidded in his direction, but a second later he was diving over it, falling on her from above. She shrieked and rolled to one side as the blade came down, biting heavily into her shoulder.

There was a loud crash and shouts and hard booted footfalls. Madeleine was curled in a protective ball, her arms over her face, so she didn't see who hurtled through the room, bringing Benito down with a horrific sound of rending wood and snapping bone. She heard a terrible gurgling sound of pain and fury, then a repeated wet thudding, then a gasp, then stillness.

"Dona! Dona! Are you all right? Dona!"

An insistent voice at her ear, urgent hands on her arm, and she recognized the deep bass tones of Reese's senior guard. She felt light-headed and dizzy, but she allowed him to help her rise shakily to her feet. She could sense brisk activity in the room, people moving, calling out to each other, asking sharp questions, but she could only focus on one spot, one unmoving form.

Benito sprawled faceup on the floor, red blotches staining his ivory robe, his mouth slack, his sightless eyes trained on the harsh white ceiling.

Jayla kneeling beside him, watching him, clearly ready to kill him again if he even thought about coming back to life. Her hands were covered in blood; there was blood on her trousers and tunic, on the wicked silver blade she still held at the ready.

"Jayla," Madeleine whispered.

Jayla's eyes never wavered from the priest's face. "How badly are you hurt?"

"Cuts in both arms, one pretty deep, but no worse damage," Reese's captain answered for her.

Jayla nodded. "Do you think the high divine sent him?"

"No," Madeleine burst out, the word almost a wail. "I am absolutely certain Harlo wants me alive."

Jayla nodded again. "Then he was one of those—whatever that fancy name was."

"Sit down, dona, and let me bind your wounds until we can get a physician here," the captain said, urging her to a chair.

Madeleine would have resisted, but she thought she might fall over at any minute. She dropped onto the stiff seat and said, "I wonder if that was always his goal. If he became Harlo's lover just to have a chance at me."

Jayla gave her the briefest glance and returned her attention to Benito. "Maybe. Or maybe someone recruited him once he was close to the source of power."

Madeleine momentarily closed her eyes. She wondered how much blood she'd lost. She didn't have that much to spare after her recent offering. "Then I'm still not safe."

"Maybe not," Jayla said in a hard voice, "but Benito's death will make any other fanatic think twice about attempting assassination."

Someone rushed into the room, and Madeleine heard a woman say, "Let me see her. Ella, go fetch my medical kit." The housekeeper, sounding calmer than Madeleine thought *she* would have if she'd walked in on such a scene. The woman bustled over, all authority and purpose, and even Reese's captain stepped out of her way.

"The physician's been sent for, but we'll wrap these cuts till he arrives. Can you make it up to your room or should I have someone carry you?"

"Someone might have to carry me."

The captain stepped forward again. "I can do it."

Madeleine nodded and he took her in a careful lift. The movement jostled her arms and she couldn't bite back a cry of pain. "I'm sorry, dona," he said, and turned for the door.

"Wait," she said, twisting in his hold to look behind her. "Jayla."

Jayla looked up. Her face was so still, her pose so calm, that it took Madeleine this long to realize she was blazingly furious. "Thank you."

"I shouldn't have allowed him to get that close. I should have been in the room with you."

"I would have had you wait outside. I wasn't afraid of him."

"As soon as he shut the door, I knew."

"You saved me."

Jayla's mouth shaped a word, and Madeleine was sure she was going to say, *That's my job.* But instead she answered, "I'm glad."

Chapter Thirty-two: Jayla

Jayla was still smoldering with rage and self-recrimination when she went to her room to clean up. The stained clothes she left in a pile to be dealt with later; she wanted to throw them in a heap on the back lawn and set a match to them, but that was wasteful. The housekeeper, she knew, would consider it a sacred honor to wash away the blood that had been spilled to save Madeleine's life. The clothing would be returned to her in a near-pristine state.

She stripped naked and scrubbed herself clean, giving special attention to her hands. As far as she knew, this was the first time she'd killed a man, though she'd been in some pretty intense skirmishes before and didn't know how some of her opponents had fared once they disengaged. And she'd meant to kill Benito—she'd kicked down that door intending to take his life. The soft snap of the latch engaging had caught her attention, but she'd hesitated. Possibly Madeleine had agreed that theirs was a conference no other ears should overhear, and she wouldn't appreciate a clumsy intrusion. But Jayla had crept close enough to lay her hand on the knob, to catch the faint interplay of voices. As long as they were simply talking, no reason to interrupt—

Jayla toweled her hair dry and slipped into fresh clothes, then washed her hands one more time. Her skin felt hot and her blood was moving too quickly through her veins; her peripheral vision seemed to have narrowed down so much she had to turn her head if she wanted to see anything that wasn't straight in front of her. This was combat adrenaline, she knew, and it might not fade for hours. It could keep pain at bay so long soldiers didn't realize they'd been dealt a mortal wound until the battle high suddenly faded and they collapsed.

It was similarly useful for keeping horror at bay, at least temporarily. *I killed a man.* She felt awful enough now. She could hardly imagine how she would feel when realization rushed in upon her in the middle of the night.

The room was too small, and curiously airless. Norrah would surely keep Aussen with her for the rest of the afternoon, maybe into the evening; everyone would realize that Jayla needed space to recover. She stepped into the hall and followed the stairs down two flights, automatically noting which of Reese's men were on guard. The captain saw her and started her way, but stopped short when she shook her head. No one spoke to her as she pushed through the door and out into the chilly afternoon.

She wanted to run somewhere, to an alley maybe, a dark place with no windows and no one to stare at her. It was, she knew, safe for her to leave the grounds. Every single one of Reese's soldiers would be on high alert; this would be the one night of the year no one would be able to break in. Still, Jayla couldn't bring herself to abandon her post. It was as if her act of violence had chained her to this place, made her its eternal guardian. Without her presence, the house would not be safe.

Ridiculous, of course. She pressed her body up against the high fence, her face between a pair of cool bars, her hands wrapped loosely around the metal. She peered out wistfully at the street just past the semicircular drive. If she stepped beyond the gate—if she always stayed within sight of the house, within easy call—

Two private sprinters rattled past, headed south, and a chugger lumbered more slowly north. As soon as the street was clear, she gazed across it, her eyes automatically sweeping the scene for signs of trouble. Her attention caught on a dark, compact shape crouched in front of the fencing on the other side of the gridway. A man, clearly waiting. Her eyes narrowed and her hands tightened on the bars. Then he came easily to his feet, a flash of diamond at his wrist, and she was out the front gate before she had even decided to move.

Fortunately, there were no cars bearing down from either direction, because Jayla didn't even pause to check before she dashed across the tracks and flung herself at Cody. He caught her with his usual lithe grace, drawing her so close she could smell the soap on his skin. She realized he was murmuring comforting phrases into her ear before she realized she was crying into his shirt.

She couldn't remember the last time she had wept in someone's arms, and she knew she shouldn't be doing it now, and she couldn't stop herself. He drew her a little farther down the street—not too far, just to the shade of a large tree planted in a neighbor's yard—and then wrapped his arms even more tightly around her. He was still speaking nonsense phrases. She was still weeping.

But she managed to force out a few words. "How did you know?"

"Tokah was here."

Jayla frowned, trying to remember. "I thought she left before Benito arrived."

"You know Tokah. She stayed a few minutes to flirt with the housemaid. Heard all the commotion. Hung around long enough to learn what happened, then ran back to tell me. I've been here for the past ten minutes. Wasn't sure if I should come in. Wasn't sure if you'd want to see me."

"I would have said no," she said into his shirt. "If you came to the door. But then—when I saw you sitting there—you were the only person I could think of. In the world. That I could bear to talk to."

His arms still around her, he pulled her to the ground, and they simply sat there a long time in silence. The ground was chilly beneath her body, and rocky besides, and when a big transport trundled south a few minutes later, Jayla could see a few travelers peering curiously out at them. But she didn't care about any of it. For a moment—for the first time in longer than she cared to remember—she felt like she had come to rest.

"I killed him," she said. "I meant to do it and I'm glad he's dead. But I don't know if I'll ever be able to get over it."

His hold briefly tightened. "I wish," he said, "I knew something profound to say. To make it all right for you. But I don't think anything I say would help. I think you're just going to have to wrestle with it until it makes sense."

She tilted her head back to look up at him. "It doesn't change how you think of me?"

He kissed her, which was the reassurance she'd been looking for, of course. "For bringing him down or for agonizing over it?"

She could tell her brows quirked down as she puzzled that over, and he kissed her again. "I'm so proud of you for being able to save her," he said. "But I love you because you let it hurt you."

She sighed and rested her cheek against his chest. "I think I'll get past it. Eventually. But tonight will be hard. I don't know if I'll sleep."

"Come stay with me," he invited. "I'll be there any time you wake up."

"I think Madeleine would be uneasy if I was out of the house. *I'd* be uneasy if I was out of the house." A pause. "You could stay here."

He shifted next to her and she knew he was looking down at her in surprise, but she kept her eyes trained on the ground. He had coaxed her toward the center of his life, but she had steadfastly kept him on the fringes of hers. "That doesn't seem like the sort of thing dona Madeleine would approve of," he said.

Jayla snorted. "*Her* lover has moved into the house—and everyone knows they're sharing a bedroom. She wouldn't have any moral qualms."

"Yes, but it's her house. She can do what she likes."

Unexpectedly, Jayla felt a smile play around her lips. It was so rare that *she* was the one trying to persuade *Cody* to participate. "She has a vested interest in keeping me happy. And steady. If I tell her that I need you with me, she'll write you an invitation in her own hand."

"Don't you share a room with Aussen?"

Now she was laughing. "I do. We would have to lie there very chastely, just sleeping."

He bent in to press his lips against her cheek. "Well, then what's the point?"

She turned her head just enough so that they were forehead to forehead, nose to nose, his eyes so close to hers she couldn't entirely focus. "Really? You wouldn't stay with me just to soothe my soul?"

"I would," he said. "I will. I'd sleep on the floor at the foot of your bed. I'm just enjoying the novelty of having you beg me to be with you."

She tried to hold back the smile. "I wouldn't deign to beg."

"Would you implore? I like imploring."

"I was trying to *tempt* you."

"By telling me there will be a child in the room with us? You have a lot to learn about seduction."

And now she was laughing. She almost felt giddy. It was so odd. "There's an empty room next to mine. It's as small as a closet, but Aussen uses it to play in. I think she'd like to sleep there."

He pretended to consider. "We'd have to ask her, of course."

"Of course."

"And receive Madeleine's permission."

Jayla thought of the conversation that morning—an hour that seemed so long ago now!—when Madeleine recommended that Jayla fight Rovyn for Cody's affections. She was pretty sure Madeleine would be delighted by this particular development. Delighted to have something else to think about except danger and duty and death. "We'll ask both of them," she said. "But I think you'll be going home to pack a bag."

So, after all, it turned out the night wasn't as bad as Jayla had feared. Madeleine had welcomed Cody with a flash of gaiety, saying, "It has become my goal to fill the house with a *hundred* people, so please make yourself at home!"

Aussen was pleased by the notion of having her own room, though she seemed to think it would be jollier if they all shared a space. "We could talk and sing and play games until we fell asleep," she suggested.

"I'll play a game with you in your own bedroom," Cody countered. "And then you'll go straight to sleep."

And he did. And she did. And then he joined Jayla in their own room, and they did not go straight to sleep. But once Jayla closed her eyes, she fell instantly into dreaming, and didn't wake till morning.

Madeleine was alone in the breakfast room when Jayla tracked her down. "How are you this morning?" Jayla asked.

Madeleine looked up from a mostly untouched plate of food. "Nervous," she admitted. "On edge. My thoughts—" She made a circular motion beside her head. "They keep spinning."

Jayla nodded. She could understand completely. "When does Reese get back?"

"This afternoon, I think. I hope."

"What do you have planned for the day? Any visitors?"

"Nothing! No one! Three of my friends have sent notes asking to come by—because of course they want to hear all about yesterday's dreadful ordeal—but I told them I wasn't up to company. And Harlo was supposed to come by this afternoon, but I sent him a message and postponed. All I want to do today is sit quietly in my house, and think about my life, and not have anyone drop by and try to murder me."

"That sounds like a good plan."

"What about you? Wasn't there something you wanted to do today?"

"It can wait until you feel safe again."

"Don't be ridiculous. There are ten guards littering the house and the lawn. I feel safe."

"Still. After yesterday—"

Madeleine pointed a finger at her. "After yesterday, you *deserve* a day off. I insist. I order you. Go do something fun—and take that darling Cody with you."

Jayla laughed. "I'll tell him you called him that."

"I really do like him."

"But he's already gone. He has work to do."

"He'll be back tonight?"

Jayla felt her cheeks prickle with heat. It was annoying; she never used to blush. "He'll be back."

"So it's settled. You'll take the day off. I'll hide in my house."

"Thank you, dona."

"Everything will be fine."

It had been too long since Jayla had headed east to the islander district and checked with the guardian of Zessaya's temple. In her defense, life had been complicated. But Madeleine wasn't the only person under Jayla's personal protection, and her obligation to Aussen weighed on her almost as heavily.

Accordingly, she spent the morning playing with Aussen before heading out to the Zessin temple shortly after lunch. During the whole long chugger ride across town, she stared unseeingly out the window. In her mind, she replayed yesterday's events over and over—the closed latch, the nervous wait, the scream, the fight, the broken door, the remorseless dagger strike. It always ended the same way. She reviewed it again.

It was a relief to climb off in the Zessin district and force herself to focus on something else. As always, there were people everywhere, and some of them might not be friendly. She needed to keep her keep her wits about her. Be ready for anything.

She headed directly to the temple. Stepping inside the small, plain space, she found the candles lit and the fountain splashing, but no guardian in sight. This was not uncommon, but she had to hold back a sigh anyway. She took a seat on one of the worn wooden benches and studied the embroidered wall hangings one by one, just to pass the time. She was deep in contemplation of the fourth tapestry when the guardian stepped in and headed for the fountain to speak the words of her regular ritual. Jayla managed to sit patiently until the guardian stepped back from the fountain and shook the water off her hands.

The woman came straight over to Jayla and spoke without preamble. "I have news about Tezzel. Aussen's mother."

Jayla practically catapulted to her feet. "You do? Is she here?"

"She has been in the city ten days, and hoping for news of her daughter that entire time," the guardian said severely.

"I'm sorry—there have been so many demands on my time. But she's *here?* Can I see her?" Jayla felt a ballooning sense of lightness in her chest; it was so powerful she thought it might tug her off her feet and send her bouncing gently along the ceiling trusses.

"I will send someone for her. She has started a job in the warehouse district, so it might take a little time to find her."

Jayla weighed her choices. She would prefer to return to the house as soon as possible, but she didn't know if she would be able to get away tomorrow. And how wonderful if she could reunite Aussen with her family before nightfall! "I'll wait," she said. "It seems best for everyone."

The guardian nodded. "There is a room in back if you would like someplace to stay."

"Thank you. But I'll stroll around for a bit and come back in an hour."

She returned to the main road and browsed the market and the small shops. She should buy Aussen a present, something to remember her by. It would be so odd not to have the little girl chattering in her ear at night, dancing around her during breakfast, making herself at home in Cody's ramshackle house. But maybe Tezzel would let her know where they were living in the city. Jayla could visit from time to time. She was sure Cody would come with her.

She was in a shop, tossing through a pile of colorful knitted gloves, when she felt the first faint tremor under her feet. She looked up, wondering if it might just be the effect of a massive transport rumbling by, but then it came again, more of a jolt than a roll. Someone in the back of the building cried out in alarm; an older Zessin woman staggered and fell to the floor. Jayla raced over to help her up and guided her outside while the ground continued to shake beneath them.

In the street, the whole community had gathered in anxious clusters, groaning and shouting each time a new wave sent them careening back and forth. Behind her, Jayla heard flimsy market booths come crashing down; flower pots and metal stands flew across the walkways. Not five yards from where she stood, the road seemed to briefly fold in half, and a narrow crack opened up right down its center. She pulled the old woman back, but in truth there was no way of knowing where the most danger lay.

Suddenly the motion stopped; the world seemed solid again. The people standing in the street looked cautiously around, wondering if it was safe to breathe. Several took a few steps forward, testing the ground with one foot before lifting the other one. A few laughed. The crowd dispersed a little more. A middle-aged man came rushing up to pull the old woman from Jayla's hands. She thought he said *thank you* in Zessin before he hurried them both away.

Jayla took a deep breath. She had been hoping for a calmer day than yesterday. So far, the gods were not cooperating.

She headed back to the temple and was relieved to see it had suffered no damage. Stepping inside, she seated herself on the bench again, resolved to stay until Tezzel arrived. Maybe there would be less drama if she just planted herself in one place and didn't move.

Over the next thirty minutes, a handful of people drifted in and out of the temple, staying just long enough to say a silent prayer or exchange a few words with the guardian. Then suddenly, the outer door opened with so much force that it was clear someone was rushing to get inside. Jayla rose to her feet as a compact Zessin woman hurtled in and headed straight to the guardian, asking questions in a sharp, eager voice. It was no surprise when they pivoted toward Jayla.

"Aussen?" the woman demanded, laying a hand on Jayla's arm. "You have my daughter?"

Tezzel spoke Cordish; that was a small mercy. "Yes, she has been with me about three months now," Jayla answered. "The woman traveling with her died on the way. I'm sorry."

Tezzel put her hands to her cheeks, then pulled them away, as if she didn't have time to grieve. "She had been ill, but I thought—but Aussen? She is safe? Can you take me to her?"

"Of course. Can you come now?"

"Yes, yes!"

"Thank you," Jayla said to the guardian, then turned toward the door, Tezzel at her heels. "I'm Jayla, by the way."

"Thank you, Jayla. Can we hurry?"

They strode swiftly down the side street to the main road, then broke into a run to catch a transport that was rumbling down the gridway. Jayla and Tezzel collapsed onto an unoccupied bench, and Jayla found that she was smiling again. Tezzel's mother arrived! One of her burdens about to be lifted!

Tezzel still looked anxious and a touch suspicious. "I don't understand," she said, "why you didn't leave my daughter with the temple guardian. Where I would find her instantly."

Which was when Jayla realized her burden might not be transferred after all. No reason Pietro couldn't come looking for Aussen just because Tezzel had arrived. In fact, wouldn't he be more likely to find Aussen if she was living in the Zessin district? Jayla felt her heart rapidly regain all the weight she thought she had shed. She answered steadily. "It's complicated, but I wanted to protect her. Someone in the city believes Aussen is a descendant of the god Cordelan, and such descendants are prized for the miracles in their blood. And that puts her in danger."

Tezzel frowned as the car jounced over a particularly rough patch, and for a moment Jayla wondered if the woman didn't know Cordish well enough to understand the complex explanation. "I always thought those were just stories," she said at last.

Jayla felt her pulse quicken. "Which part?"

"My grandmother Villette told us that she was descended from Cordelan. Yes, and she claimed that the priests would kill her if she ever returned to the city."

"Well, it might be true," Jayla said. She took a moment to study Tezzel. She had the delicate bones, freckled face, and crinkly hair of the typical islander, but her skin was darker than most and her hair was more brown than ginger. "If you carry Cordelano blood, you're in danger as well."

"How did anyone even guess that?" Tezzel burst out impatiently. "I've never told Aussen those tales!"

"There's a trick she can do—with a clump of dirt—"

Tezzel nodded. "I can do it too. It's a handy ability, though an odd one."

"A gift from the god, apparently," Jayla answered. "Or a curse."

Tezzel took a deep breath. "I despise what I know of Cordelan. The only deity I honor is Zessaya."

"I have learned to prefer her myself," Jayla said with a flash of humor. "But I'm not sure she can protect you from Cordelan's zealots."

"But then—"

The chugger rocked violently, and everyone on board screamed. The instant it righted itself, all the passengers shoved and clawed their way to the exits, then stood miserably in the street, wondering what to do next. Which way lay safety?

"How far now?" Tezzel panted. "Can we get there on foot?"

"We can. It might take us more than an hour of hard walking. And if the quakes start up again—"

Tezzel's face was set. "Let's get going."

They strode down streets clogged with residents too nervous to reenter their homes and workers guarding broken wagons and sagging doorways. Most people were just milling around, but some, like the two of them, were clearly on purposeful journeys toward critical destinations, and they pushed past the bystanders with an impatience that bordered on hostility. The ground shifted under them a few times, but grudgingly, as if it was tired of this pastime and merely wanted to settle. The sun edged toward late afternoon and the air cooled considerably, but they walked with such dogged energy that they were warm enough to sweat. At least, Jayla was. Tezzel, pacing along determinedly beside her, didn't bother to complain. She didn't speak at all except to say "look out" or "how much farther?"

Finally, they attained the wide, gracious avenues of Council Row. Finally, Jayla could tell her, "Just a few more minutes. Just the next street over."

But when they turned the last corner and the Alayne house came into view, Jayla could tell at once that something was wrong. There was a tangle of crumpled metal right in front of the house where a handful of gridcars must have been upended during a tremor. And there was a group of soldiers milling before the front gate, agitated and confused.

Jayla broke into a run, Tezzel easily keeping up. In the knot of people outside the gate, Jayla recognized first Norrah, then Reese's captain, then Reese—then, unexpectedly, the priest Pietro. Even more unexpectedly, Cody. All of them were shouting. All of them whirled to face her as she came jogging up.

"What happened?" she demanded. "Where's Madeleine?"

Everyone answered at once, so she turned to Cody for clarity. He took her arm to steady her. "Tivol took her," he said, his voice low and grim. "And Aussen, too."

Chapter Thirty-three: Pietro

Pietro had been in a fever of impatience ever since they had sighted land that morning. By the god's own *face,* how long could it take to sail into a harbor, and dock, and disembark?

Hours, apparently, but at last he was on solid land, having made the sketchiest of farewells to Danner and his sons. The ground seemed curiously uneven beneath his feet, but he didn't let his unsteadiness slow him down. He merely hitched his pack over his shoulder and headed for the narrow uphill bridge that led from the harbor to the city. The gridway didn't run down this route, and there were no horse-drawn wagons immediately available, so he set out on foot.

Stollo fell in step beside him. "Where to now? To find that girl?"

"Yes."

"Do you have any idea where she is?"

"No, but I know someone who does." He glanced over at Stollo. "It might take me some time to track her down. You don't have to come with me—I'm sure you've been missed at the temple."

"I'm sure I have," Stollo said cheerfully. "But I need to hear the end of this story."

Pietro was breathless by the time they made it off the bridge at the top of the hill; there was no way he could race all the way to his lodgings, even though his instincts were screaming for him to *hurry, hurry, hurry.* But it would accomplish nothing for him to exhaust himself in one ill-advised sprint. "There's a chugger," he exclaimed as one heaved into view, and they ran for it.

It took a maddeningly long time to get to Pietro's rooms, where he'd written Cody's address on a scrap of paper. While they were there, he grudgingly acted on Stollo's suggestion that he change his clothes, wash his face, and shave. "You look like an old sailor just washed ashore," Stollo observed. "If I was a little girl, I'd be terrified."

"Aussen knows me. She won't be afraid," Pietro muttered, but he freshened up anyway.

Finally, they were back on the street, catching another chugger to Cody's neighborhood. They were almost at their destination when the car lurched violently to the side, its wheels making a horrific screech across the pavement and sparks raining down from the cable overhead. Passengers screamed in panic and stampeded out of the doors and windows before the vehicle even stopped moving.

"A quake," Pietro murmured. "The day wanted only that."

Stollo was tugging him toward the door. "Come on. If another one hits—"

One did, of course, almost on the words, but they managed to exit safely with the last of the riders. The driver was already outside, trying to assess the damage, recruiting the brawnier passengers to try to shove the transport back into alignment. He looked hopefully in Stollo's direction, but Pietro grabbed his arm and said, "I think we're close now. Let's go."

The pavement stuttered beneath their feet a few more times, but they didn't lose their balance and nothing fell on them from overhead, so Pietro thought that counted as success. He found Cody's street easily enough, but he had to cast around to find the right place, as nothing was numbered and Cody's description of the exterior matched about half the buildings in the neighborhood. Finally he spotted a red vest propped in the window of one of the old warehouses, a signal that couriers lived on the premises. He strode up and knocked furiously.

A moment later, someone flung the door open, clearly expecting disaster on the other side. "What is it? What's wrong?" the young man exclaimed. Or maybe young woman. Pietro wasn't sure and didn't have time to study personal jewelry.

"I need to speak with Cody right away. Is he here?"

For an answer, the person turned and bellowed into the house. *"Cody!* Someone's here to see you!"

Over the doorkeeper's head, Pietro could spot a few other figures hovering inside the front room. Clearly his urgent summons had roused the whole house. He wasn't sure he wanted an audience for this conversation—then again, he didn't care. He just had to find Aussen. He thought the ground shifted slightly beneath him, but maybe that was his body still trying to anticipate the roll of the ocean.

There were running footsteps, then Cody brushed past his housemates to push out the door. His open, friendly face looked concerned. "Pietro. What's wrong?"

"I need you to take me to Aussen. Right now."

Cody took a quick step backward, and his friendliness disappeared. "No. I can't."

"You don't understand! I won't hurt her. I swear it, Cody. This is so important—"

Cody was shaking his head. "No. No. I promised Jayla. I'm sorry."

"Cody, *she can save the city!* Don't you feel the tremors running under the street?" As if to prove his point, the ground rocked with another restless wave. "The whole place is going to come apart!"

Cody crossed his arms and backed away, as if he would retreat into the house and slam the door shut. "No. I won't. You can't sacrifice Aussen."

"I don't want to sacrifice her! I can't explain—but I think she has a special ability—"

"*I'm not taking you to Aussen!*"

Pietro stared. He had not factored this in. Jayla distrusted him so much that Cody wouldn't even listen to him. "Then—will you go to Jayla and tell her what I said—*beg* her, Cody—tell her from me—"

A slim Cordelano girl pushed past the roommate who still guarded the door. "You want to find Aussen and Jayla?" she said. "I'll take you to them."

Cody whirled on her. "Rovyn! You can't!"

She shrugged. At any other time, Pietro might pause to analyze the malice in her expression, but today he didn't care about anything except finding Aussen. "Thank you. I'll pay you whatever your courier rate is—"

She flounced out of the doorway, not even looking at Cody. "Then let's go."

They formed an odd, uneasy procession as they hurried down the crowded streets, watching for the next chugger to come along. Cody and Rovyn were in the lead, arguing, while Pietro and Stollo lagged behind. Pietro was still keyed up with excitement, but he could feel weariness eating at the edges of his energy. When this day was over, he might simply disintegrate.

"I wonder what their story is," Stollo murmured, watching the other two quarrel.

"She's spiteful and he's furious, but I don't even care," Pietro said.

"He's furious, but he hasn't physically restrained her," Stollo said, a note of admiration in his voice.

Pietro glanced at the two couriers again. "Not Cody," he said. "I don't think he has it in him. Even when violence would solve his problems." He flashed a look at Stollo. "And don't say violence never solves problems."

Pietro hadn't been sure the gridway would still be functional with all the tremors still dancing underfoot, but they'd been following a cable line for half a mile when one of the big chuggers came rumbling up. It was empty except for a few nervous riders who looked ready to fling themselves out the windows at the first uneasy rattle. "We'll get as far as we can," the driver said. "If the way's blocked, I'll have to let you out."

Rovyn flashed a smile at Pietro and Stollo as they clambered aboard, and Stollo smiled back. "I thought you couriers just ran all over the city on foot," Stollo said to her.

She laughed. "We do whatever's quickest. For short routes, especially through the Quatrefoil, it's always faster to run. But long trips from one end of the city to the other, nothing beats a transport."

"Rovyn. Don't take them there," Cody said, still not looking at Pietro.

She gave him one burning glance and turned her back on him. "In case we get separated," she said, "do you know where Madeleine Alayne lives?"

Cody groaned and turned away. Pietro nodded. "Aussen lives with Madeleine?" he asked in some surprise.

"She lives with a guard named Jayla, who works for Madeleine," Rovyn corrected.

Pietro's eyes sharpened. He remembered now. Jayla had mentioned Madeleine's name, claimed to have met her at some function. A lie, obviously. "Thank you," he said. "That's useful to know."

Cody tilted his head just enough to address Rovyn. "I will never forgive you."

The other courier a hunched a shoulder. "You don't care about me, anyway."

Beside him, Pietro heard Stollo say *ah* under his breath. A love triangle, probably. Rovyn must have had her heart set on Cody. But he'd only had eyes for Jayla from the minute they met. That had been obvious even from the first campfire by the ruined Chibani bridge.

"He will *kill* Aussen because of you!" Cody whispered furiously.

"I won't. Cody, I swear I won't," Pietro said.

"I'm not talking to you!"

There was a long moment of silence except for the hum of the chugger and the occasional deep rumble of the ground. Pietro became aware that Stollo was watching him thoughtfully.

"You won't, will you?" he asked presently. "Kill that little girl?"

"If you even have to ask me that, I'm astonished that you've spent five minutes in my company."

"Because I'm of the opinion that sometimes violence *is* justified," Stollo said. "So I'd stop you if it came down to it."

Pietro stifled a sound and dropped his head into his hands. He couldn't tell if he wanted to laugh or moan or shout aloud with pure undifferentiated emotion. "I wouldn't," he said. "But I confess there are days I can understand why some people think there isn't a choice. And that terrifies me as much as any realization I've ever had."

The car came to a shuddering stop and all the riders looked up uneasily. "The track's blocked," the driver called out. "Everybody has to get out."

The passengers muttered among themselves as they climbed off and looked around, trying to figure out where they were and how to get where they wanted to be. The road ahead was a tangle of downed cables and three of the tall poles that supported them. But up ahead, Pietro thought, the way looked clear and the wires were still solidly in place.

"What now?" Stollo asked.

"We walk," Rovyn said. "It's not that far."

They set out after their guide. Cody, who had given up arguing with her, dropped behind their little procession, but stuck with them doggedly. Pietro could tell his own energy was ebbing; he had allowed himself to relax while they rode the transport, and now he could feel his muscles protesting as he forced them to work again. But if they found Aussen—if he could explain everything to Jayla—explain everything to Harlo—

He frowned. No. He couldn't tell Harlo anything, not until he was certain he was right. If Harlo knew of Aussen's existence, and Aussen couldn't perform as Pietro expected, she would never be safe again.

Once they were clear of the twisted wires, Rovyn picked up the pace, and the rest of them hurried to keep up. Pietro glanced around, recognizing more and more of the houses they passed. This was Council Row, where the political families and the wealthy merchants and the successful bankers lived. He'd spent many evenings here with Harlo, back in a different life altogether.

Over a small rise, down a short cross street, onto another one of those wide, beautiful promenades. Pietro was concentrating on his feet, not the vista ahead, but he looked up when Cody cried out with alarm and took off past them at a run. Flooded with fresh anxiety, Pietro watched him dash to the open gate of the Alayne property, where a disorganized group of people formed a knot of agitation.

"What's wrong?" Stollo asked.

Pietro shook his head and forced himself forward at a jog. He couldn't even begin to guess what the news might be, except he knew that it would be terrible.

Chapter Thirty-four: Madeleine

True to her word, Madeleine kept to her room for the whole of the morning. But it turned out silence and solitude were the wrong conditions for keeping her mind from endlessly replaying the sounds and images from the day before. Benito's solemn face, his slow advance, his swift attack. Then a blur and a jumble, then chaos, then suddenly blood. Blood everywhere.

Someone had tried to kill her.

Someone had been killed on her behalf.

She could not entirely comprehend either of those truths.

She was not sure she would ever get the pictures out of her head.

By lunchtime, her own thoughts had put her in such a state that she had to go downstairs just to be around other living creatures. She consulted with the housekeeper on trivial matters, checked with Reese's secretary to make sure he had everything he needed, and dropped into the kitchen pretending she wanted a snack.

"It looks like a fine sunny day outside," Norrah said, when Madeleine had consumed a plateful of muffins and still didn't budge from the table. "Why don't you and Aussen go outside and play a game?"

Aussen was already on her feet. "I have a ball," she offered. "Oh! And a little net! You catch the ball with it."

Madeleine managed a smile for the cook. "Am I really so much in the way?"

Norrah smiled back. "A little exercise will be good for both of you."

A few minutes later, Madeleine and Aussen were out on the wide green lawn, laughing and chasing after each other as they threw the ball around. Madeleine noticed that a few of Reese's guards had drifted outside and were watching them—more out of amusement than a strict observance of duty—

but she didn't even care. Norrah was right. She already felt better.

"I'm going to catch you!" she called, putting on a menacing expression as she advanced on the little girl. "I'm going to get that ball!"

Aussen shrieked and hared off, running so hard that she tripped over her feet and somersaulted to the grass. Or—no—Madeleine felt her own legs tremble and give out, and she flung out an arm to break her fall as she came crashing down. The land roiled beneath her, as if some giant underground creature was reaching up with a massive claw, trying to scrape through to open air. It felt like the world was spinning out of control.

"Aussen!" she cried and crawled over to wrap herself around Aussen's trembling body. Prone on the ground, they clung to each other through another set of tremors. Madeleine kept whispering, "It will be all right," though she didn't entirely believe it.

Aussen whispered back something unintelligible, and then repeated it in Cordish. "Zessaya is angry and she's shaking the land."

Zessaya—or Cordelan. And how did you placate a god? With blood . . . "It will be all right," Madeleine repeated. She didn't have anything else to offer.

When the ground finally steadied, they pushed themselves into sitting positions and looked around. Most of the house had emptied, soldiers and servants alike gathered in pockets on the lawn, everyone clearly planning to stay outside until they were sure the quake was over. It seemed like the wisest course.

"Let's just stay right here for a while," Madeleine said. "I'll tell you stories about when I was a little girl and I used to play games with my brother Logan."

Just thinking about Logan made Madeleine's heart spasm with grief, but she was determined to talk about him. Her father and Harlo had conspired to erase him from the world. Maybe she could, in some small way, bring him back.

She was on her third tale about her brother's exploits when she heard noise from the front gate. At first she thought it must be Reese, who should be arriving at any minute, but she soon realized that the newcomer was arguing with a guard. "But I need to talk to Madeleine! Let me in!"

She recognized Tivol's voice. For a cowardly moment, she wanted to lie back down in the grass, so flat and so still that he would never notice her. But they had parted on such bad terms the day before. And eventually she was going to have to come to some sort of truce with him. She swallowed a sigh and came to her feet, pulling Aussen up by the hand. "That's Tivol," she said. "Shall we go talk to him?"

Hand-in-hand they crossed the lawn to the tall front gate. Tivol was still arguing with the guard when he spotted them. His face showed first surprise, and then relief. She nodded at the guard, and the man slipped away to allow them privacy.

Tivol's fingers were wrapped around the bars as if he wanted to pry them apart with brute strength. "There you are! Madeleine, I heard about what happened yesterday with Benito—"

Madeleine nodded wearily. "It was too awful. I can't bear to talk about it."

"But are you all right?" he asked urgently. "He didn't hurt you?"

It was all she could do not to glare at him. *Do you think he's the only one who has tried to hurt me lately?* she wanted to ask, but she managed to refrain. "Jayla was there," she said. "But thank you for thinking of me."

"I would have come by anyway to check on you," he said. "But just now, when I felt the quake—"

She couldn't keep the bitterness from her voice. "You thought, 'What a good thing that Madeleine survived Benito's attack! Now she will realize how important it is that she do these terrible things.'"

"That's not what I thought! I was worried about you! Your *safety!*"

Aussen glanced up at her. "What terrible things are you going to do?"

She squeezed the girl's hand. "Nothing. It doesn't matter." And then, to Tivol, "We were fine. We were outside when the quake hit." That sounded a little bare, so she added, "And you? Are you all right?"

"There are downed wires and wrecked gridcars along the main routes, but I didn't have any trouble. But I wanted to come see you." He gestured behind him where his sprinter was parked on the drive. "And I brought a present for the little girl."

"For me?" Aussen squealed before Madeleine could reply *Don't try to buy my forgiveness by giving gifts to a child.*

So instead she had to say, "That was kind of you."

He gestured at the car again. "I'll just go get it."

He was back in a moment, carrying a large unwieldy box. "It's carvings, mostly. Fish and flowers and little goddess statues. We used to have a Zessin gardener, and he made these all the time. We found a whole room full of them after he left. And I remembered Aussen was from the islands, and so I thought—"

Aussen was on her tiptoes, trying to peer through the railings. She said something in Zessin, then added, "I can't see them."

"Here, let me open the gate and Tivol can hand them to us."

She threw the lock and pushed open the metal gate, and Tivol set the box on the grass just inside the fence line. Almost cooing, Aussen bent over to look inside.

Tivol grabbed her around the waist and yanked her into his arms, crushing her against his chest. Aussen made a small sound of distress and gazed at Madeleine in fright, but she didn't scream for help. Madeleine was too stunned to do anything but stare.

"Tivol! What in—put her down!"

He shook his head. "I didn't plan this but—come with me, Madeleine, it's the only way."

"Come with you *where?* And *why?*"

"You can't marry Reese. You know it. He'll never let—he'll never do the things that have to be done. And there's no *choice,* Madeleine. You have to come with me."

"I *don't* have to! I won't!"

He backed up toward his little sprinter, still holding Aussen tightly against him. Now she was squirming in his arms, kicking against his shins. Her face looked stark with fear. "Then I'll kill her," he said calmly.

"You wouldn't do that."

"You already know that I'm prepared to sacrifice children. If you don't come with me right now—"

He did something—maybe he squeezed Aussen in his arms to prove the power in his hands—and the little girl wailed in terror. Loud enough to rouse the guards? Did Madeleine even want the guards involved? Would he really hurt Aussen?

You already know I'm prepared to sacrifice children.

"All right," she said hastily, slipping out the gate. "I'll come with you. Put Aussen down. Leave her here."

He was already at his car, slinging Aussen into the cramped back seat and securing her hands with something. A scrap of rope. A belt, maybe. Madeleine followed helplessly. "I can't leave her anywhere until I'm sure of you," he said.

There was a shout behind him and they both jerked around to see guards pouring out of the house, the captain in the lead. "Stop them," Tivol hissed, his hands suddenly around Aussen's throat. "Or her life is forfeit."

She waved her arms wildly at the guards. "*Stay back! Stay back!* Or he'll hurt her!"

The guards came to a messy halt, looking furious and uncertain. "Dona! Where are you going?" the captain shouted.

"Don't answer. Get in the car," Tivol ordered. He still had his fingers wrapped around Aussen's neck.

Madeleine just gestured at the guards again and climbed in. "Let go of her," she said coldly.

Tivol cast a last glance at the soldiers, vaulted into the gridcar, and sent it spinning around the drive and out onto the road. She clutched the side of the door to keep herself from pitching out the open window as they careened too fast down the deserted gridway. She was surprised when he headed north.

"You're taking me to your *mother's* house?" she said, trying to infuse her voice with scornful amusement. "I suppose an abduction would be just the sort of thing to meet with Heloise's approval."

He shook his head. "No, no. She wouldn't—well, maybe she would, but that's not where we're going."

"Your rooms are the other way."

He glanced at her and then looked away. And that was the moment—above all the other moments, when she realized how long he had lied to her, when she realized what he was capable of—that she understood that she had never known Tivol at all. "There's another place," he said.

Madeleine felt a stab of despair. She knew the guards would rally—knew that Reese and Jayla would return soon—knew that they would make a plan and come rescue her before nightfall. But they would be looking for her in Tivol's rented rooms or his mother's cold and elegant mansion.

But if he was taking her to some sequestered hiding space, no one would know where to find her.

"What are you planning to do with me?" she said, raising her voice so he could hear her over the rattle of the road, but hoping it was too noisy for Aussen to catch her words.

He shook his head. He was going so fast that he had to keep all his attention on the route. Twice they passed vehicles in the southbound lane that had been twisted sideways because of the quake. Once Madeleine heard an entire building collapse behind them, seconds after they rushed by. But their own passageway was damnably clear.

"I told you. I didn't plan this. But—I mean—there's only one thing to do." He risked a swift look in her direction, then returned his eyes to the road. "You have to marry me, and we have to produce a child instantly."

"As convenient as that would be for you and Harlo," she said icily, "there is nothing *instant* about bearing a baby."

"No. But I mean—we have to instantly start trying."

"I'm not going to marry you."

"Maybe not. But you'll still have my child." He glanced at her. "I don't want it to be this way, Madeleine. All I have ever wanted was to cherish you and protect you. But you have made everything impossible."

Would he really do it? Take her to some secret hideaway and rape her, the whole time believing himself a hero? In his own way, that made him as much of a fanatic as Benito. Made him just as cruel.

She turned awkwardly in her seat and stretched her arm out, trying to reach Aussen. She could just barely lay her hand on the child's ankle. The little girl was curled up on the back bench, her hands tied to a railing, her eyes streaming with tears. "I'm so sorry, love," she said, trying to make her voice soothing even though she had to shout. "Don't be afraid. Everything will be all right. Don't be afraid."

Nothing would be all right. There was every reason to be terrified. It was clear Aussen didn't believe her anyway, because she just gulped down a sob and didn't say a word.

Their mad flight continued for another thirty minutes, maybe longer. They had soon left Council Row behind, and now they were traveling along the elevated road that ran along the base of the mountain. She thought they had passed the cross street that would take them to the Quatrefoil and were headed farther east, toward the more unsavory parts of town.

The sporty gridcar was constantly striking debris and jouncing over cracks in the road, but miraculously, their way remained open. It was enough to make Madeleine think Cordelan was smoothing their way, signaling his approval of this terrible turn of events. Madeleine had never been particularly devout, but she'd always had a casual respect for an abstract divinity. Now he seemed real, and malevolent, and she hated him.

The sun was hovering over the horizon and the air had grown noticeably colder when Tivol abruptly wrenched off the road and onto a narrow parallel track. Madeleine looked around, fear gurgling up at the back of her throat. Was this their destination? They were coming to a halt along a row of featureless buildings, long and low and somehow slovenly looking. Most of the windows appeared to be covered with dark, heavy curtains; at any rate, not one of them admitted the faintest spill of light. Madeleine strained, but couldn't hear much noise—no laughter, no loud voices, no music. Everything that happened in this district occurred in secrecy.

"Where are we?" she whispered.

"Just—a place I go sometimes when I want to be alone."

He had stopped the car and hopped out, instantly retrieving Aussen from the back. Aussen wailed in fear and he muffled her mouth against his shirt.

"Give her to me," Madeleine said.

He shook his head. "Up that way. The second door. Go on in."

A broken walkway led to the designated spot, which opened into a shadowy hallway marked by half a dozen other doors. Tivol headed to the first one on the left, fished a key from his pocket, and let them in, flicking on a wall sconce as they entered.

Inside was not the chamber of horrors Madeleine had half-expected, though it was bleak enough. A few pieces of tumbledown furniture, heavy draperies on the window. No rugs or artwork or anything to soften the bare outlines of chair and table and scarred wooden floor. There was another door, half-open, that probably led to a bedroom. There was a small space consisting of cabinets and a sink, which she guessed was supposed to be a kitchen. There was a faint smell of forgotten garbage or rotted food or unwashed clothes.

This was where Tivol came not just when he wanted to be alone, but when he wanted to be unmoored from civilized conventions. When he wanted to forget his obligations to his mother, his betrothed, his city, and his god.

"Do you bring your friends here and drink all night?" she asked. She could tell that her composed voice made him relax a little.

"Sometimes."

"And women? Do you bring them here, too?"

He eyed her. "Sometimes. Not once we're married, though."

She had to swallow a laugh of hysteria. As if, after all his other betrayals, she would care about his fidelity. "Is there a place you can put Aussen so she can sleep? I'm worried about her."

He hesitated, then stepped past her and through the other door. Madeleine followed. It was a bedroom, as spare and uninviting as the rest of the place, furnished only with a dresser, a chair, and a half-made bed. She decided not to wonder whether he had ever had the sheets washed.

Tivol lay Aussen clumsily on the mattress, and the girl immediately cried out and lifted her arms toward Madeleine. "Don't—" he said, but she brushed past him.

"Let me get her settled," she said. "Then I'll come out and talk to you."

She turned her back to Tivol and sat beside Aussen, leaning in and taking her into an embrace. "I'm so sorry, baby, I'm so sorry, everything will be all right."

Aussen whispered unfamiliar words into her neck, but Madeleine didn't have to know Zessin to guess what she'd said. She just made hushing sounds and repeated her empty reassurances, smoothing back Aussen's hair and kissing her forehead.

Behind her, she heard Tivol shift uncertainly, then quietly exit the room. He left the door open, though, and she thought he was probably on high alert, waiting to see if she would try to lock the door between them. She had glanced at it as she stepped through, and she hadn't been impressed. It looked like he could break it down with a couple of hard kicks.

No, she would need a better plan.

She stayed with Aussen as long as she dared, knowing that Tivol was getting restless in the other room. She could hear him pacing, then growing still to listen, then pacing again. When Aussen finally fell asleep, Madeleine stiffened her spine, smoothed down her hair, and came to her feet. Time to face her captor.

Tivol instantly swiveled to face her as she stepped out of the room. "How is she?"

"Well enough, I suppose, for someone who's been kidnapped and terrorized."

"I *didn't—*"

She just shook her head and walked past him, straight into the little kitchen. "Do you have food here? I'm hungry, and I'm sure Aussen will be when she wakes up."

He seemed caught unaware by her prosaic concerns. "A little. Crackers and dried meat. I stock up when I think I'll be here a while, but I wasn't planning—"

"So you keep saying." She rummaged around in a couple of drawers and cabinets, coming across plenty of glassware and bottles of wine, a shelf full of plates, but not what she was looking for. She tried another cabinet.

"I could go get food, but you wouldn't like it," he said.

She kept her back to him. "I wouldn't like the food you fetched for me? Right now I'd be happy with bread and cheese."

"No, I mean—I couldn't just leave you here. I'd have to—" He hesitated, as if hoping she'd fill in the blank for herself, but when she said nothing, he blew out his breath. "Tie you up."

"Everything you say just inclines me to love you more."

"Madeleine! This is not my fault! If you—"

"Don't you dare try to blame me," she said. On these shelves, a couple of empty jars and a bag of old beans. She couldn't imagine how he ever made a meal here. Maybe when Tivol and his friends gathered here, all they did was drink liquor. And carouse.

"I'm not *blaming* you."

"But I don't think you've thought it through," she said, moving on to the next cupboard. Empty. "You know that my disappearance will trigger a series of events. Letters will be delivered across the city. By morning, everyone will know—everything. My role. Harlo's role. And the fact that Corcannon is on the verge of destruction."

"I know," he said, his voice ragged. "But maybe—Harlo and your father are terrified of exposure, but I'm not so sure. Maybe it's for the best. Once people get past their initial horror, they won't be afraid. They'll understand why the sacrifices have to be made, and they'll honor the ritual."

"You think they'll rise up *against* me instead of *for* me. Well, maybe." Ah, here it was. The drawer that held everything she needed. She sorted silently through the possibilities, trying to decide which one was best.

"They all want to live," he said. "They want the city to survive. They'll choose the greater good."

She slipped the knife into her sleeve and turned to face him. "I've been thinking, Tivol. Ever since I learned the truth, thinking about what I should do. And I've come to my decision." She took a deep breath. "I'll have this baby. But I won't allow it to be put to death."

"You *have* to, Madeleine."

"No. I'll have a child and then, when the god demands more blood, *I'll* go. He can drain *me.*"

It was almost comical the way shock reshaped his face. "*What?*" he whispered.

"It's the only way I'll agree to any of this. This way, I'll have a good life, just a short one. I can protect my children *and* protect the city. It's the only answer."

"I don't think I can agree. I can't watch you die."

Now her voice turned steely. "We all have to give up something we don't want to lose. I do. You do. All of us."

He shook his head. "You know Reese will never agree to such a plan. He'd spirit you out of the city so fast—no. You have to marry me. There's no other choice."

"People keep saying that to me," she replied, "and it's just not true."

She whipped the knife out and held its sharp edge to the tender skin under her jaw. She thought she could feel her pulse, rapid but steady, fluttering against the lethal edge. "If you don't take me home, I'll end my own life, right now," she said, her voice utterly calm. "I won't bear *anyone's* child. My blood will flow out here on your dirty floor and you won't even be able to pour it down your god's greedy throat. You'll lose *everything,* Tivol. And it will be your fault."

Now he looked stricken, panicked, aghast, every satisfyingly devastating emotion she could have wished for. "No! No—no—Madeleine, I'm begging you—"

"I know I'm going to die, Tivol, one way or the other," she said, still calmly. "So *you* decide. Will my death mean something? Or will it condemn the city to annihilation?"

He took a hasty step forward and she pressed the blade deeper, feeling it bite. Tivol gasped and froze. A droplet burned down the cool column of her neck.

"Madeleine—"

He wasn't going to back down. He wasn't going to release her. She closed her eyes and willed herself the strength to make good her threat.

There was a violent commotion at the door.

Chapter Thirty-five: Jayla

They formed a small, desperate group in front of the gate, Jayla and Reese and Pietro and Cody. Bracing themselves impatiently against the occasional sullen rocking of the street. Speaking rapidly, interjecting what bits of information they had, trying to understand, trying to plan.

"He took her," Reese said furiously. "He's going to force her—"

"We'll find him," Jayla said, though she had no idea how.

"Where would he go?" Pietro asked.

"He has lodgings south of here," Reese said. "But my captain says he drove north."

"His mother's house is just up the street," Jayla said. "Maybe he went there?"

Reese spit out an expletive. "I'd believe it of Heloise," he said, "to connive at a scheme like this."

But Cody was shaking his head. "No—no—there's another place."

They all stared at him. "Who are you?" Reese demanded.

"I'm Cody. I'm a courier. And I've made deliveries to Tivol Wellenden on the northeast edge of the city."

Reese loosed another oath. "Oh, yes, all the fashionable young wastrels have quarters there," he bit out. "Where they meet to gamble and whore—" He glanced at Jayla. "Sorry."

Jayla ignored him. "Can you find it again?" she asked Cody.

He nodded. "Of course I can."

Reese wheeled for the driveway. "We can take my car."

Tezzel pushed past him to Jayla's side. "What about my daughter?" she demanded.

"She's with them," Jayla said. "We'll find them both."

Pietro's attention was suddenly riveted on Tezzel. "You're Aussen's mother?"

Jayla shoved him so hard he staggered backward. "Not *now,* you wretched man! We have to find them!"

He recovered his balance and glared at her. "Yes, now! The city is tearing itself apart! Aussen could save us all!"

She moved so fast she had him by the neck before anyone else could react. "Do I have to kill you before we leave?" she growled. "Because I killed one man yesterday, and I think I'm about to kill another one today."

Behind her she heard Reese say, "What? Who?" She heard Cody answer and Reese exclaim "*What?*" again. But she was focused on Pietro, on the feel of her hands around his throat. His ragged heartbeat pattered against her palm. He was afraid of her, but she thought he was afraid of something else even more.

"I don't want to hurt her," he managed, speaking hoarsely against the pressure of her grip. "I think she can save the city with her hands—Jayla, let me go!" He clawed at her fingers.

She felt someone grab her shoulder and haul her back. "Let him explain," Reese ordered. "But *hurry,* man. We have no time."

She relaxed her hold but kept her hands loosely around his neck, just in case she didn't like what he had to say. He stood before her, motionless, his eyes fixed on hers. "I went to the ruined lands," he said, speaking rapidly. He gestured behind him. "Stollo will corroborate everything I say. We found the old temple. We realized—we *think* we realized—no one's blood has to be spilled. If someone is descended from both Cordelan and Zessaya, all they have to do is push a lever. But that person must carry the blood of both of the gods."

She stared back at him. "That's ridiculous."

He pointed in Tezzel's general direction. "Ask her. Ask her heritage."

But Tezzel had already explained it to Jayla as they rode the chugger north. Slowly, almost reluctantly, she dropped her hands and motioned Tezzel forward. "Tell him," she said.

"My grandmother was Cordelano," Tezzel said. "She claimed she had the blood of the god in her veins. And every islander is descended from Zessaya. But what this has to do with Aussen—"

Pietro's face blazed with excitement. "Then *you* could do it! *You* could turn the key!"

"I want to find my daughter!"

"If we don't engage the lever, it won't matter if we find Aussen or not," he replied bluntly. "This whole city will implode."

As if to underscore his warning, the ground shifted under their feet again. Tezzel cried out and would have fallen if Reese hadn't caught her arm. Jayla abruptly came to a decision.

"All right," she said. "Reese and Cody and I will find Madeleine and Aussen. Pietro and Tezzel will go find this stupid lever—do you even know where it *is?*"

"Yes," Pietro and Cody said in unison.

She returned her fierce glare to Pietro. "But if you harm Tezzel—" She swiveled around to locate Reese's captain and motioned him forward. He joined them with alacrity. "Go with them. If he tries to harm this woman, kill him."

The captain looked horrified, and both Reese and Cody dissented loudly. "Disable him," Reese said. "Don't kill him."

The captain nodded. "All right. Where are we going?"

"The main temple," Pietro said. He glanced over his shoulder. "But—with all the roads blocked—I don't know the best way to get there. Cody—"

"He's coming with us," Reese interjected.

"All right. We'll find our way."

Rovyn pushed forward. "I can take you," she said.

Good. Make yourself useful, Jayla wanted to say, but she restrained herself. She was trying to figure out why Rovyn was here to begin with. Actually, she still didn't understand why Cody was here, or Pietro. Reese had apparently arrived just moments before she and Tezzel showed up, miraculously managing to navigate the disrupted gridway on his journey from the northern bridge.

"Then that's settled," Jayla said.

"No, wait!" Pietro exclaimed. "We need the key to get to the bottom levels. Cody, do you have it with you?"

Cody shook his head. "I've got my big keyring, but the temple key is in my room. You'll have to stop there first."

"I've got one." The soft words came from the stranger who appeared to be Pietro's companion, a good-looking man wearing the bracelet of a priest but bearing the physique of a fighter. "Harlo gave it to me right before we left on our trip. I can get us in."

"Good," Jayla said. "Let's go."

Reese was driving a mid-sized sprinter that wasn't designed to hold four people, but they squeezed in anyway. Jayla and one of Reese's guards crammed themselves in the tiny back seat while Cody sat in front to give directions. Reese tore out of the drive at a pace that rivaled Tivol's at his most reckless, but within five minutes he had to screech to a halt because of hazards in the road. A pair of gridcars—one going north and one going south—had apparently been spun around by a recent tremor and smashed against each other. Several people were already laboring to move the southbound vehicle off the road.

All four of them jumped out of Reese's sprinter and ran over to help, though they convinced the whole group to shift their attention to the northbound lane instead. It took maybe ten minutes before they were able to push the car far enough to the side that Reese would be able to squeak by. They flung themselves back in the car, and Reese took off with a jerk. There was a sound of rending metal as they scraped the derelict, but they made it past.

Two more roadblocks were dispatched in similar fashion. Jayla felt her fear and tension rising. Every minute they delayed was another minute Tivol could do violent harm to either of his captives. It didn't help that the sun was rapidly sinking, making the whole world seem like a darker and scarier place.

The fourth obstacle was a chest-high pile of bricks that used to be a building that must have practically hugged the gridway before a tremor brought it down. The four of them climbed out of the sprinter, Reese's bitter, hopeless cursing serving to express what they were all feeling. Ahead, in the failing light, Jayla could see another rockpile sprawled across the road.

"We'll just have to go on foot," Cody said. "We're only a few miles away now."

Jayla took his arm. "Would it be faster to run the cable?"

He glanced down at her. "Maybe. We wouldn't have to detour around fallen debris."

Reese glanced up at the gently swaying netting overhead. "Is it safe?"

As if in answer, a spark shimmered along one of the wires and blinked out. Cody actually grinned. "Maybe," he said.

"All right," said Reese. "Let's do it."

"Not you," said Cody. "It takes skill and practice, and you don't have time to learn."

"If it gets me there sooner—"

"Cody and I will run the cable," Jayla said. "You two follow on foot. We'll only beat you by a few minutes." *If we aren't electrocuted,* she thought.

"All right, just go!" Reese exclaimed. "But tell me the address."

Cody shook his head. "I don't know street numbers. It's on Kalmien Road, if you know it."

Reese looked unsure. "I know the general vicinity."

The guard spoke up. "I can find it," he said with quiet confidence. "I used to patrol that district. But how will we know which building?"

Reese ripped a sleeve off his blue silk shirt and handed it to Jayla. "Tie this to the outside," he said grimly.

"Probably multiple units inside," the guard cautioned. "How will we know which one?"

Jayla knotted the sleeve loosely around her neck so she wouldn't lose it. She said, "You'll hear the screaming."

Reese nodded. "Go! Go!"

Without another word, Cody headed for the nearest utility pole and shimmied up. Jayla waited till he was at the top, then followed. Below her, she saw Reese and the guard skirting the fallen brick, trying to find their way past it.

"Pay attention," Cody said sharply, taking her hand as she stepped out onto the webbing. "Follow me, but watch your feet. And if I drop down to the street, you drop down. Don't try to go ahead if I say it's too dangerous."

She nodded. "All right. Let's go."

Cody plunged forward, moving with swiftness and grace. His sure feet moved nimbly from rope to rope; his lean body swayed effortlessly from side to side as his balance transferred. She made certain her own feet were securely placed, then released her hold on the pole and followed him.

The trick was to keep moving. There was the constant sense of tumbling forward, of an unreliable base giving way beneath her shoes, but if she never paused, she could translate that falling feeling into forward motion. Her arms were stretched as wide as they would go, counterbalancing her shifting weight.

They had practiced this; there was a rhythm to it. Race forward on the thick cable until she felt herself start to careen, then widen her stance and slow her pace by placing her feet on the great loops of the supportive webbing. The cable was stronger, less springy, a swifter track; the ropes of the netting had too much give, forced her to take slower steps, lift her legs higher to reach the next foothold. But the cable was dangerous and dizzying, and she couldn't follow it for long. She alternated.

Ahead of her, Cody danced from cable to netting, cable to netting, running so smoothly he seemed to skim above the street, supported by nothing but air. Below them they passed another set of crashed gridcars, two more mounds of bricks, groups of people shouting, a child wailing, a pile of splintered wood that had somehow caught fire. Above them, the sky hardened from tired turquoise to obdurate indigo; an unforgiving onyx was traveling in from the west. Jayla felt an irritable wind scratch at her face.

Suddenly, the cable beneath her feet loosened, then snapped taut; she felt herself flung to the netting and grabbed frantically for a hold. "Down! Get down!" Cody shouted, and she swung herself over the side of the webbing and dropped to the street below. She landed in a hard crouch, feeling the impact all the way to her hips, and slapped her hand to the pavement to hold herself steady. The ground bucked beneath them; somewhere nearby, glass shattered explosively. Not ten yards ahead of them, one of the utility poles sizzled, then erupted into flame, falling sideways and taking down a whole line of cable with it. Cody grabbed her and pulled her back before the sparking wire could fall on her head.

"On foot the rest of the way!" he called over the sounds that came from all directions—more glass falling, more cars crashing, more stones hailing down from collapsing buildings. Somewhere, someone was screaming. "We're almost there!"

She just nodded, and he set off again. They were in a part of town she didn't think she'd recognize even in daylight, all low buildings and empty windows, trash in the shallow ditches, grime on the stone foundations. She knew they were in the northern part of the city, because the mountain face reared up so close and so solid that she could almost touch it.

There were fewer rockfalls in their way, no more crumpled gridcars. This wasn't a part of town that saw much traffic, and the buildings that made up this neighborhood lurked as far from the main street as possible. The ground steadied beneath their feet and they were able to race forward with nothing to slow them down.

A short, narrow drive looped off from the main road, and Cody veered down it without hesitation. The street was lined with more of those anonymous, shuttered buildings, all of them ominously quiet, and a handful of private vehicles.

"That's Tivol's sprinter," she said.

Cody nodded. "And that's the house."

They approached the door from a sideways angle, just in case Tivol happened to be peering out of the curtained windows. Jayla slipped Reese's blue sleeve from around her neck and tied it to the curved metal handle of the door. Cody had already ducked inside. When she entered, she found a short, smelly corridor lined with six doors. Cody had his hand on the nearest one. From the other side, Jayla could catch the faint sound of voices, but she couldn't make out any words.

"Locked," he mouthed.

She lifted a foot and mimed a hard kick. He shook his head and reached into his pocket for a ring of spectacularly assorted keys.

"One of these should fit," he breathed.

She raised her eyebrows, wondering—but not particularly caring—if it was even legal to own such things. He picked through the array, tried one without success, then tried another. She felt a jolt of triumph as his hand turned the key through its full revolution. The door fell ajar by half an inch.

Inside, the voices had risen enough that Jayla could tell a man and a woman were arguing. She thought there might be some value in making a violent entrance, so she motioned Cody to stand aside. Loosing a combat yell, she kicked the door open and leapt inside.

One quick glance gave her the scene—a small space, drab furnishings, and two figures struggling in a far corner of the room. She yelled again and charged forward just as the larger figure whirled around with a cry of his own. It was Tivol, and he had blood on his hands. He shouted in rage or alarm and rushed toward her, his fingers curled like claws before him. It was easy to take him down, smash his head against the hard floor, flip him to his stomach to neutralize his flailing arms, lay her dagger against the side of his neck.

Tivol tried to wrench himself free. She slammed his head against the floor again, then dropped heavily onto his back, feeling his body spasm as her weight bowed his spine. Through that whole exercise, she hadn't once lifted the blade.

"Jayla, no. No! Don't kill him!"

That was Madeleine's voice, and it jerked Jayla's head up. Madeleine was standing a few feet away, swaying with exhaustion, her hands at her throat. There was blood trickling between her fingers and staining her jacket.

"He hurt you!"

"He didn't. I was threatening to kill myself—and I found a knife—"

Cody moved closer. "Let me see those cuts. If they're deep—"

"I don't think there's a single thing in this house that would be clean enough to serve as a dressing. How did you *find* me?"

Tivol thrashed under Jayla's body. "Let me go! I have to explain to Madeleine—"

Jayla made sure the dagger was nice and tight before she leaned forward to murmur in his ear. "Madeleine doesn't want you to die. But there's no reason you have to be conscious, so if you don't lie still, I will beat you senseless."

"Jayla!" Madeleine exclaimed, but Tivol stopped struggling.

Jayla looked back up at her. "Where's Aussen? Is she all right?"

"In the other room. Sleeping, I hope."

Cody was still fussing over Madeleine's wounds. "These have to be cleaned and treated."

"There's water here in the kitchen—"

"Wait, this is better. Whiskey. Sit down."

Jayla felt more than saw the two of them circle around her and take seats on the dilapidated furniture. "Here, you can use my jacket to make bandages," Madeleine said. "Just rip it up."

There were tearing sounds and then a soft warning from Cody. "This is going to hurt a little."

A short silence, a choked whimper, and then soft breathing. "Ow," Madeleine said. "That hurt a *lot*."

"Sorry."

"When you're done with her," Jayla said, "see if you can find some rope."

"There has to be some in the house," Madeleine said with mordant humor, "because he was threatening to tie me up."

"I didn't—" Tivol started. Jayla kneed him in the kidney and he shut up.

"How did you *find* me?" Madeleine asked again.

Jayla was too preoccupied to answer, so Cody explained, adding details about Pietro and Rovyn and Reese as Madeleine kept asking questions.

"Reese is back?" she said. "Where is he?"

"He should be here any minute."

It was as if the words conjured him, because a second later Jayla heard the front door crash open and footsteps charge down the hall. The cries of *Reese!* and *Madeleine!* were so heartfelt and so numerous that for a moment there didn't seem to be any other words in the human language.

A shape dropped to the floor next to Jayla, and she glanced over to find Reese's soldier uncoiling a serviceable bit of cord from his belt. "Good job," he commended her. "I can handle him if you want."

She nodded and rose to her feet. A quick look showed her that Reese and Madeleine had collapsed together on the sofa, and she was looking weary but safe within his protective arms. Madeleine's throat had been swathed so thickly in a gaily patterned cloth that she probably couldn't lower her chin, but other than that she didn't seem to be in particular distress. Well, she was crying. But smiling at the same time.

Now to find Aussen, praying that she was just as safe, just as whole. Jayla hurried into the bedroom to find Cody before her, kneeling on the floor, his arms crossed on the bed, his chin resting on his wrists. Aussen lay on her side, her eyes closed, her breathing steady.

"She's still sleeping," Cody said. "She doesn't look like she's been hurt."

Jayla nodded and crawled onto the mattress, curling her body around the small, clenched form. "Aussen," she whispered. "It's Jayla. I'm here. You're safe."

Aussen startled awake, and Jayla felt her small frame clench and relax. "Cody!" she whispered. Then, turning her head, "Jayla! You *found* me!"

Jayla kissed her ear. "Cody found you," she said.

"But Tivol! He's here and he—"

"Jayla took care of Tivol," Cody interrupted. "She punched him and he fell down, and he's not getting back up."

"Good," said Aussen. "He's a terrible man."

"He is," said Jayla.

"Where's Madeleine?"

"She's in the other room. With Reese. Everything's going to be fine," Jayla said. She squeezed the little body tighter. "Everything's going to be *better* than fine," she whispered. "Aussen! I found your mother!"

Aussen rolled over in her arms. "She's here? She's here? Does she know where to find me?"

"We'll take you to her as soon as we can get out of here."

And then Aussen started crying—Aussen, who had gone days and weeks and months without shedding a tear, was now sobbing against Jayla's chest. Cody climbed onto the bed and put his arms around both of them, Aussen a small shape between them. Jayla thought he might be crying, too, but she couldn't tell, because her own eyes were so full of tears.

There was too much terror and madness and hope and danger and love. It was impossible to manage it all. Who wouldn't be weeping?

It didn't help that the house started juddering around them.

Chapter Thirty-six: Pietro

He was too old. He didn't have the stamina to run all the way across Corcannon and then halfway back again. Pietro staggered and paused for breath, bent forward, his hands braced against his knees. The others clustered around him.

"We can stop somewhere—rest," Stollo suggested.

Pietro shook his head, gasping for air. They had been hurrying through the city for the past half hour, winding through alleys and down side roads that he had never known existed. Everywhere there were fallen poles, tumbled buildings, blocked passages. Everywhere there were people crowding in the streets, putting out fires, crying out for help, trying to find missing loved ones. Maybe he was imagining it, but he sensed a rising tide of alarm and hysteria sweeping through the city. He sensed an insistent menace coiling and uncoiling deep under the surface of the streets.

"There isn't time," he said. "Can't you feel the tremors?"

"There are always tremors."

"Not like this." He pushed himself upright again. "Let's get going."

Rovyn pointed. "The guard is trying to find us a ride."

Looking in the direction she indicated, Pietro saw Reese's captain arguing with an old man who stood beside a small horsedrawn wagon. It was a brilliant notion, Pietro thought, since a horse wasn't confined to the gridway, which appeared to be increasingly impassable. The old man didn't look eager to risk his animal on this chancy night, however, and Pietro didn't feel too hopeful when the guard returned to them.

"He says he'll take us, but his asking price is ludicrous. And he'll stop the minute he thinks it's too dangerous."

Pietro pulled out a bag of coins. Cordelan himself knew there was no better use for the money. "Will this cover it?"

The guard's eyes grew big. He shook out a few gold pieces and returned the bag to Pietro. "Yes. Let's go."

The cart wasn't large enough to easily accommodate six people. The guard and Rovyn crammed themselves onto the bench with the old man, while Tezzel and Stollo and Pietro tried to fit themselves into the back. The rough jouncing over broken pavement made the trip even more uncomfortable, but even so, the conveyance was a vast improvement over the desperate half-walk half-run of the last thirty minutes. Pietro closed his eyes, trying to calm his breath and still his soul. When he opened them again, he found Tezzel staring at him fixedly.

"Who are you?" she demanded. "Why does Jayla think you're going to hurt Aussen?"

How quickly could he make her understand—and believe—this unlikeliest of stories? "I used to be a priest in Cordelan's temple," he said. "One of the few privy to the knowledge that the city is built on a terrible secret. The whole continent will be subject to quakes and destruction—" He swept an arm out to indicate the smoldering city. "Unless, every few years, a blood sacrifice is made to the god."

Tezzel's face showed a sudden ferocity. "You want to kill my daughter!" He thought she might dive across Stollo and strangle him. Unlike Jayla, she probably wouldn't let go until he was dead.

He lifted a hand to fend her off. "I don't. I left the priesthood once I found out the truth. But the victims had to be direct descendants of Cordelan. And those descendants have been in mighty short supply in recent years." His eyes bored into hers. "But it's not just Aussen who's descended from Cordelan. *You* are, apparently."

"Oh, so you want to kill *me!*"

"No! I don't want to kill anyone! I believe—with all my heart, I believe—that no blood has to be spilled if a different kind of descendant can be found. One who mixes the heritage of Cordelan and Zessaya. Someone like you." He was still staring at her. "How is it possible? How did you even come to *be?*"

"My grandmother was Cordelano. Lived in Corcannon until she fell in love with an island boy, and they ran away together fifty years ago. She never talked much about the city, she just said it was a dangerous place." Tezzel frowned. "And when she was older—when she was dying—she started to claim that she was descended from the god. Yes, and she insisted that the priests would have killed her if she'd ever returned to the city. We thought she was just raving."

Pietro was trying to guess who her grandmother had been. Harlo had sworn that there were no women left who knew the truth of their doomed heritage. That branch of Cordelan's family, he'd said, had died out decades ago. Of course, Pietro had come to assume that Harlo lied as often as he told the truth. "What was she called? Your grandmother?"

"Villette Rowan."

That was it, that was the name Harlo had spoken the night ten years ago when he told Pietro the terrible story. "Huh," he said. "The high divine of that era believed that she perished in a fire. The priests never went looking for her because they thought she was dead. I wonder how she managed that." He smiled at Tezzel. "Maybe your grandfather helped her escape."

"Apparently, he used to be a temple guard, but I always thought he was a mild old man. I can't see him doing anything heroic."

"Well, people will surprise you," Stollo said.

"Would they really have killed her?" Tezzel asked.

"Eventually," Pietro said. "They thought it was the only way to save the world."

"And you think there's another way?"

"I do. And I believe you and Aussen both have the power in your hands."

She thought that over for a moment. The cart bounced over a particularly rough stretch of road, and the guard on the front bench cursed and grabbed for a handhold.

Tezzel said, "Would *all* of us have that power?"

If he hadn't been thrown against the side of the cart by another nasty jolt, Pietro would have felt himself grow very still. "All of whom?" he asked carefully.

"My aunts. My sisters. My cousins."

He heard Stollo suck in his breath. It hadn't even occurred to him—they had lived so long with only a single tenuous lifeline— "How many of you are there?"

"I have three aunts and four sisters and fourteen cousins. Oh, and five nieces so far, and my cousins have more children than I can keep track of."

He felt Stollo glance at him, but he was so stunned he could do nothing but stare at Tezzel. Stollo asked, "Do they have to be women? To manipulate the device?"

"I—I don't know. The handprint is small, but maybe the hand of an island man is daintier than that of a Cordelano man—"

Tezzel laughed. "Well, it hardly matters. Only three of my cousins are male and so far there's only been one boy born in Aussen's generation. We joke that Zessaya hates our Cordelano blood so much she can't bear to make a child in his image."

Pietro managed a ghostly laugh of his own. "It might not be a joke."

"So then you think—if I can move this lever—any of us could do it?"

"If Zessaya is merciful, that would be true," Pietro said fervently. "If she is powerful. If selfish, spiteful Cordelan was willing to do one generous thing—"

"Pietro," Stollo admonished.

"I don't like your god, either," Tezzel said.

The cart came to a rough, disorganized stop and they were all banged against the sides again. Rovyn would have fallen out except the captain grabbed her. "Can't get any farther," the driver spit out. "It's all blocked. And I'm not laming my horse on one of these bad roads."

Rovyn freed herself from the captain's hands—though she gave him a sideways grin of thanks—and slipped smoothly from the cart. "We can walk the rest of the way," she said.

The "walk" was more of a skid and a slide and a hike and a hustle as they navigated cracked pavement, rock-strewn sidewalks, and ill-lit back streets. But suddenly they burst through a narrow alley and Pietro was shocked to realize they had arrived in the Quatrefoil. He'd had no idea they were this close. He could not have retraced their steps if Stollo's life depended on it.

"And now the temple?" Rovyn asked.

Pietro nodded and led the way forward. Like the major roads, the main plaza was full of people standing in groups and wandering around restlessly, too excited to go home, too frightened to step back indoors. Pietro tried to be polite as he pushed his way between them.

They were almost at the sanctuary door when another quake came, this one hard enough to send Pietro to his knees. The wail of the crowd was followed by a string of loud crashes as architectural accents ripped from buildings and shattered on the ground. Pietro stayed low while the tremor roiled beneath him, choppier and longer than any tremor he could remember from the past.

They were almost out of time.

The earth had steadied, though it hadn't quite stilled, when Stollo reached out and hauled him to his feet. "Well, there's one good thing," Stollo said. "That last quake sent everyone out of the temple. I don't think there's going to be anyone in there but us. No one will stop us."

"Then let's go."

They hurried up the steps and through the massive doors, and Pietro took a hasty look around. Some of the oval wall sconces were still glowing a ghostly white, but a few flickered oddly and at least half seemed to have failed completely. In the uncertain light, the usual gaudy assault of color was muted; overhead, the stained glass skylights looked flat and black. Pietro didn't feel his usual joyous uprush of emotion at walking into the sacred space. Maybe he didn't have time to be dazzled by divinity, or maybe he was more preoccupied with gauging their degree of danger. Half of the statues lay smashed on the floor, which crunched with broken mosaic tiles and other debris. The great pillars were still intact, though Pietro thought a few of them had developed vertical cracks. Not a reassuring sign.

"Do you have one of those chemlights with you?" he asked Stollo.

"Unfortunately, I used the last one on the island."

He glanced at Rovyn and the captain, but they both shook their heads. He turned to Tezzel. "Your daughter has the ability to take a clump of dirt and turn it into a source of light," he said. "I very much fear that as we descend to the lower levels of this building, the illumination may fail us completely. Is there a chance—"

She was already glancing around. "Yes."

Stollo led her to a waist-high ornamental vase holding a flowering red bush. Miraculously, the vase had not overturned in all the chaos. "This was potted not a month ago. The high divine is very fond of the plant, which I believe came from Chibain."

"She can make a light out of *dirt?*" Rovyn demanded, watching as Tezzel scooped up a couple of handfuls of soil and did just that.

"A useful skill. Unless the high divine sees you do it, and then a suicidal one," Pietro answered. Rovyn flicked him a look that made it clear she thought he was insane.

The floor shifted beneath them, and he felt his panic rise again. "We have no time—no time!" he called, and spun around, looking for the hidden door. Yes—there—tucked behind the pillar with the thin fracture—

He headed that way and the others fell in line behind him, the strangest parade he could ever have imagined leading. Stollo edged past him to unlock the hidden door, and the four of them filed after him into the long hallway with the insufficient lighting. Pietro pushed ahead again to take the lead. He remembered this journey from the trip he had made two months ago with Cody—and ten years ago with Harlo. The first task was to find the door that led to the next level down. It was this one—no, this one—

His second guess was correct. They cautiously descended the steep, ill-lit stairwell and exited onto the level that held a series of meditation spaces for the priests. All the doors were wide open and every room was empty, as anyone who had come down here for a reflective retreat had clearly run for the exits when the walls started shaking. The five of them quickly traversed the corridor, navigated the second stairwell, and hurried through the open storeroom with its piles of discarded furnishings and linens.

The next door resisted opening, and Stollo had to jiggle the key in the lock to convince it to turn. They all held their breath until they heard a faint, welcome click.

But no one was eager to step into the shadows of the narrow ramp that led down to the bottom level. It was all too easy to imagine one powerful quake bringing these stone walls crashing down, crushing everything beneath them. Pietro's mind replayed images of the ruined temple on the eastern islands, which must have been destroyed by an event very similar to this one. He found it hard to draw a breath.

"I'm not going down there," Rovyn declared.

"You don't have to," Pietro said. "Only Tezzel does. And me."

"And me," the captain said quietly.

"I'll go," Stollo said, but his voice was shaky.

Pietro glanced at Tezzel, to find her eyes wide with fear and her face pale in the dusky light. But she nodded and stepped forward, one clenched hand held above her head to light the way, the other running along the rough wall to steady her as she descended. The others followed, moving so gingerly Pietro could hardly hear their feet against the uneven stone.

At last—the thick wooden door that marked the end of their journey. "It's not locked," Pietro said, and Tezzel pushed her way through.

Pietro, close on her heels, froze with shock as he entered the final chamber. Stollo and the guard bumped into him, apologizing and backing off, but Pietro could not stop staring. The last time he had been here, the walls had closely ringed the stone altar with the curved metal basin. But the room had still been the size of a small bedroom, and even a tall man could stand upright.

But now the place was a cramped, tiny closet, its ceiling so low Pietro and the guard had to stoop to enter. Two of the walls were so close to each other he could spread his arms and touch them both. Only one of the opalescent disks still functioned, throwing an illumination so faint it could have been mist.

The metal pitcher lay on its side, resting against one of the encroaching walls. The great spoked wheel that covered the basin was canted up on one side, as if a shift in its stone support had shoved its alignment out of true.

Stollo, Tezzel, and the guard glanced around, curious and uneasy. "It's so small in here," the guard said.

"Too small," said Pietro, his heart hammering with fear. "The walls are moving in. They'll crush the instrument. And then—and then—"

Tezzel's voice was steadier than his own. "What is it you want me to do?"

It was so dark Pietro couldn't see the marks and incisions on the walls. He began running his hands nervously over the jagged surfaces, hoping to find what he needed by feel. What if it had already been covered up by the inexorable advance of stone? "There should be a casting of a hand print—maybe shoulder height—set within a smooth block. We need to find that."

They all crowded into the tiny space, blindly tracing the edges and contours of the walls. "Here! Here! I found it!" Stollo exclaimed.

They shifted awkwardly around each other so Tezzel could stand beside him and he could guide her hand to the right spot.

"I feel it," she said. "Now what?"

"Now—" Pietro said, and the floor started shaking. There was a terrible, unearthly groaning, as if the very world was wailing out its grief and desperation, and the walls crept forward by an inch. The ceiling dropped hard enough to make Pietro and the captain grunt. Sand sifted down into their hair.

"Now!" Pietro shouted, slamming his hand over Tezzel's where it rested against the stone. "Push it with all your strength!"

He was pressed so close against her that he could feel her shoulders cord with effort; he felt the tendons rise in the back of her hand. The floor beneath them continued a slow, incessant shuddering. More dust sprinkled down.

The walls didn't budge.

Tezzel gasped and fell back against Pietro, panting. "I can't—it's too heavy—"

"Tezzel," he said, "you have to."

"I'm not strong enough!"

"Or Cordelan is too strong," Stollo said. "He never wanted Zessaya's interference."

It was the only thing Pietro could think of. He yanked out his chazissa, depicting the goddess with her head bent over a book. Oh, why hadn't he purchased a figurine of Zessaya in her warrior pose, ready to do battle with her longtime enemy? "Take this," he said. "Hold it in one hand and push with the other. I'll help you. We all will."

She dropped her glowing clump of dirt in Stollo's outstretched palm, and instantly the room went dark except for the glancing light cast by the single remaining lamp. She closed the fingers of one hand around the small charm and laid her other hand in the imprint on the wall. Again, Pietro placed his hand over hers, covering it completely. Stollo positioned himself behind Pietro, his hand against Pietro's shoulder, and the guard moved behind Stollo. Pietro could feel every ounce of their weight bearing down on him.

He leaned into Tezzel with his whole body, pressed her hand into the wall with all the strength he could summon. She muffled a cry, and he wondered if he had snapped her finger bones. He pressed harder. Against his back, Stollo felt so heavy, heavier than the earth itself, crushing the air from Pietro's lungs and compacting him into a single driving pylon of intent.

The room shifted around them and they all stumbled forward a pace. "The ceiling is coming down!" the guard yelled.

Pietro couldn't believe it. "No!" he shouted back, shot through with a brutal euphoria. "We pushed the wall back!"

Only an inch or two, but he had *felt* it give way under their combined assault. Tezzel sucked in a great lungful of air, braced her arm, and waited for the rest of them to reposition themselves. When Pietro increased the pressure of his hand over hers, she shoved herself forward again with a low growl.

The wall slipped back about a foot. The ceiling creaked alarmingly as it winched itself up.

Stollo loosed a cry of delight. “We did it! We’re doing it!”

Tezzel was panting. “How far?” she asked.

“As far as we can make it go,” Pietro answered.

She nodded grimly and once again fitted her hand into the narrow casting. In the impossible light, Pietro couldn’t be sure, but he thought he saw blood trickle between her fingers.

This time they propelled the wall back about a yard. The ceiling retreated enough that Pietro felt himself grow giddy with an internal sense of expansion.

“Aren’t we done yet?” Stollo demanded. “How big is the room *supposed* to be?”

Pietro glanced over his shoulder. “I don’t know exactly. Maybe twice this size?”

“I’m worried about Tezzel,” Stollo said. “Maybe this is good enough to hold the city for a while, and she can come back some day when she’s stronger.”

Tezzel shook her head. “I’m not coming back,” she said. “Someone else can do it next time.”

“Do you have one more try in you?” Pietro asked, as gently as he could.

She nodded and braced herself again, waiting for them to line up behind her. Once more, she took a deep breath, but this time she let it out in a sort of battle cry, ramming herself forward as if her arm was a lance and the rough stone surface was a bitter enemy.

The walls fell back and fell back and fell back, seeming to move along rails suddenly oiled smooth. Then abruptly, with a *clunk* so loud it echoed around the chamber, they locked in place. Carried forward by momentum, the four of them tumbled against each other and skidded to the floor. Stollo started laughing. Pietro landed on his side and rolled to his back, gazing around him in wonder.

The ghostlight of the single lamp showed them a chamber the size of a nobleman’s atrium, with a ceiling so high it was lost in the shadows. Except for a grimy patch around the basin in the middle of the room, the floor and walls looked scraped and new, as if they had just this morning been hacked out of the bedrock. The air felt fresh and abundant.

The foundation lay motionless beneath them. The whole world was still.

Chapter Thirty-seven:
Madeleine

Later, Madeleine could barely remember how they made it home. She knew that part of the time she walked, stumbling along with a drunkard's erratic gait, and part of the time Reese carried her. At some point, Reese was helping her into a vehicle, but she had no idea if it was his or he had just commandeered it from some hapless passer-by. She didn't care. She collapsed gratefully on the front seat and immediately twisted around to peer at the people riding in the back.

"*Tell* me," she demanded. "Tell me what happened."

Holding a sleeping Aussen in her arms, Jayla filled her in on Tezzel's arrival and Pietro's mad theory. Cody added a few helpful details, while Madeleine gasped in disbelief. She was so exhausted and so dizzy that she had to wonder if she was hearing them correctly or if she might be dreaming the whole thing. She was in the middle of asking a question when she fell asleep.

She woke up as Reese was carrying her into her house, where it seemed like fifty people were awaiting her, all crowding close and calling out her name. Choking back a sound, she buried her face in Reese's jacket. She heard him reassure everyone—"*She's all right, she'll be fine*"—and felt him run upstairs, taking two steps at a time.

Not until he laid her carefully on her bed did she nerve herself to ask about the final actor in this wretched drama. "What did you do with Tivol?"

"I left him in his house with the guard. Two more of my men are on their way to help watch over him."

"What will happen to him?"

He gazed down at her soberly. Jayla had been the one to subdue Tivol, but Reese looked like he'd been in a fight. His face was flushed with remembered fury and his shirt was ripped to shreds. One of his sleeves was completely missing. "I don't know. I imagine the Council will determine an appropriate punishment."

"I told him," she whispered, her low voice breaking into a sob. "I told him I'd have a baby—but I wouldn't let it be killed. I said *I* would be the sacrifice when the time came."

Reese caught his breath, then leaned in and enveloped her in a fierce hug. Too tight; her ribs protested. But she didn't want him to let her go. "You won't have to," he said. "Can't you feel it? The quakes have stopped. The world stopped shaking while we were making our way back."

"Pietro did it?" she asked in a wondering voice. "Are you sure?"

"Pietro did—or Aussen's mother. They put the world back together."

The reprieve was so profound that it felt like a blow, like a bolt of electrical current that left her momentarily senseless. "Then I—" she said. "Then we—"

He bent down and kissed her tenderly. "Then you get to live," he said very gently. "And we get to be happy."

She fell asleep in his arms, too tired to savor her joy, but woke up maybe an hour later at the sounds of a muted celebration downstairs. She was alone; Reese must have left her to take care of some of the hundreds of details this night would have left undone. Her entire body ached and her head was still spinning, but her chest felt curiously weightless, as if someone had pulled out half of her ribs and replaced them with sparkling chemlights. It was so easy to breathe. So easy to smile.

She pushed herself out of bed, determined to see what all the noise was about. A glance in her mirror left her horrified, but she was too impatient to spend more than a few minutes freshening up, though she did wind a scarf around her throat to cover the clumsy bandages. She stepped out of her room and paused on the balcony, looking down at the scene in the atrium below.

There appeared to be dozens of people deployed in concentric rings. Reese's soldiers formed the outer circle, staying out of the way. The household servants made up the middle circle, smiling and clasping their hands and, in Norrah's case, wiping away tears. Cody and Jayla stood beside the cook, their arms looped around each other's waists, leaning against each other as if only the angle of the other's body was keeping them upright. Jayla's face looked as open and peaceful as Madeleine had ever seen it.

In the center were two small figures, so tightly entwined they might not ever be able to loosen their grips and let go. Madeleine could see very little except a wild knot of curly hair, a pale flash of a freckled cheek, but their emotion was so raw and dense it seemed to paint the very air. Madeleine felt her heart flutter in her chest with something too powerful to be pain. She gripped the bannister with both hands as if to keep herself from falling.

Reese was the only who saw her, and he came leaping up the stairs. "Are you all right?" he asked, standing behind her and placing his hands over hers where she clutched the bannister. "Your face is so pale."

She laughed and leaned back against him, lifting her mouth to kiss the underside of his chin. "I'd forgotten what it feels like," she said. "Or maybe I never really knew."

"What what feels like?" he said.

She didn't think she could list all the ingredients. Some were subtractions from what had become her daily life—jittering terror, gnawing guilt, limitless despair—all gone, all wiped away. Some were additions that seemed just within her grasp—the promise of love, the possibility of joy—threaded through with an iridescent counterpoint she thought must be hope. Some were emotions she took for herself, laying them into the contours of her heart like tiles in a mosaic. Some were reflections from the people around her, glancing through her own bones like refracted light. She shook her head and tried to distill it into one word. "Happiness."

Chapter Thirty-eight: Jayla

Never in her life had Jayla experienced the level of exquisite pain she felt when Tezzel rushed into the atrium of the Alayne mansion and folded her daughter in her arms. Jayla knew the emotion was joy, but it hurt so much it was almost devastation. Maybe because some other, barely averted confluence of events could have led to tragedy instead of elation. Maybe because Jayla was so unfamiliar with euphoria that she still had to learn how to breathe in its sharp and hallucinatory scent.

She swayed on her feet, finding her balance unreliable, and Cody instantly put his arm around her to steady her. "I'm usually not much of one for crying," he said. "But that's a sight that would break anyone, I think."

She shook her head by way of answer and leaned into his embrace. All around them, she could feel the other residents of the house draw nearer, forming a loose circle around Tezzel and Aussen. Everyone else was smiling or sniffling, surreptitiously brushing their cheeks to flick away tears. No one else spoke, and no one seemed able to break away from the dense magnetic pull of that powerful emotion.

A flicker at the doorway caught Jayla's attention and she felt her body revert to readiness before she had even gauged whether or not the motion constituted a threat. It was a moment before she recognized the man on the threshold, whom she had only seen once before—the muscular priest who had accompanied Pietro here earlier today. Then he had seemed confident and hopeful; now he looked worried.

"What do you suppose he wants?" she asked Cody.

"Who?" He followed her gaze. "Oh—that's Stollo. I wonder if something's happened to Pietro."

She freed herself from Cody's hold, and the two of them threaded their way through the tangle of people to meet the newcomer at the door. No one else seemed to notice his arrival.

Stollo greeted them with relief. “Cody. Maybe you can help.”

“What’s wrong? Where’s Pietro?”

Stollo shook his head. “He *insisted* on coming all the way back here with Tezzel, because he wanted to be *sure* that Aussen was all right and safely reunited with her mother. But he’s utterly exhausted, and he basically just collapsed in the street.”

Jayla pushed past him and headed out into the cool darkness, trotting down the path toward the circular drive. Stollo had exaggerated slightly. Pietro was on the ground, but not actually in the street; he was leaning against the outer edge of the wrought-iron fence, his body looking frail and crumpled. She stepped through the gate and dropped to her knees beside him. “Are you all right?” she asked.

In the chancy streetlights, his face was pale and worn, but he tried to smile. “I am trying to make that determination,” he said. “It seems I am too old to be running back and forth across the city for hours, trying to save the world.”

Stollo and Cody had gathered behind her. “I told him *I* would return here and check on Aussen, and then I’d report back to him, but he insisted on coming,” Stollo said. “We’ve been traveling all day. Even I am weary, and I’m thirty years younger than he is.”

Pietro rested his head against the fence and closed his eyes. “Stop reminding me that I’m too old for you.”

She heard Cody snort with laughter, and she had to hold back a smile. Pietro couldn’t be at death’s door if he was making jokes, however slight. “Pretty heroic, for an old man,” she said. “Since it seems you really *did* save the city.”

He didn’t open his eyes. “Tezzel did,” he said. “Remind me to tell you about it someday when I have the energy to speak.”

Stollo crouched down beside them. “I’d hire a wagon to take him home, but I don’t know if I can find any at this hour. And with so much debris littering the streets—”

“He can spend the night here,” she said. “You both can. There will be an empty room somewhere.”

Pietro opened one eye. “I’m not sure that’s an invitation a hired guard is authorized to issue to an unexpected guest.”

Now she was grinning outright. “I think Madeleine would grant me any request I made right now.”

Pietro opened his other eye. “So does this mean you and I might be friends after all?” he asked. “No more threatening to kill me every time you see me?”

"*You're* the one who told me you couldn't be trusted," she pointed out. "I would think you would be pleased that I just did what you asked."

He sighed and closed his eyes again. "I will be pleased—with the whole lot of us—after I've slept for about five days. I think."

Jayla rose to her feet. "Come on," she said to the other two. "Help me get him inside."

It was another twenty minutes before Pietro and Stollo were settled into a small cluttered room that was mostly used for storage but still offered a bed and some welcome privacy. Madeleine herself had flown down the steps to offer Pietro assistance, and Jayla remembered that the two of them had known each other back in an earlier time. She didn't know what their relationship was or how it might have been altered by recent events, but clearly Madeleine was ready to provide succor to anyone who had played a part in tonight's tumultuous events.

Jayla herself was so tired that just the sight of Pietro's bed made her long for her own, but she didn't want to overlook anyone else who might need her attention. "Where's Aussen?" she asked Madeleine as they stepped onto the balcony and shut the door. "Where's Tezzel?"

"In my room," Madeleine said. "I think they're both already asleep. I'll stay in Reese's room tonight."

Jayla nodded. "Is that everybody?"

Madeleine laughed softly. "Everyone you're responsible for, you mean?" she said. "Yes, Jayla. You've taken care of every single one of them. Everyone is safe. You can rest now."

Jayla managed a crooked smile. "Maybe. Not sure I can ever relax."

Madeleine hesitated, as if not certain the gesture would be welcome, then flung herself across the small distance between them to give Jayla a tight hug. "Thank you," she said. "I don't know which of the gods brought you into my life, but I will be grateful to you forever."

Jayla was just as surprised as Madeleine probably was when she lifted her arms to return the embrace. "The day was just as lucky for me," she said. "And I will be grateful for just as long."

Cody was waiting for her in her room. She took hold of his shoulder and pulled him down next to her on the bed. "I'm too tired to take off my clothes," she murmured into his throat. "You'll have to undress me and tuck me in."

"I can do that," he said. "Just lie still."

But when they lay together under the cool sheets, her back to her chest, his arms folded around her and her hands clasped on top of his, she found she couldn't sleep. Too many of the day's images kept replaying in her mind, too many of the night's emotions hammered against her heart. After about thirty minutes, she sighed and turned onto her back. Cody kissed her cheek and snuggled up against her.

"Want to talk instead?" he asked.

"Maybe."

He lifted a hand to play with her hair. "I've been thinking," he said.

"About what?"

"If the city's safe, you don't have to leave, taking Aussen and running to the islands."

"I don't," she agreed.

"Does that mean you'll stay in Corcannon? I know you're always thinking about moving on."

For a moment, she tried to imagine that. Collecting her final paycheck, packing up her things, heading back across one of the bridges to Chibain or southern Marata or Oraki. She'd never been to the western islands. Maybe she should book passage on a merchant ship and travel as far as it would take her.

"It seems impossible," she said.

His hand stilled. "That you'd stay?"

"That I'd ever leave. That I'd *want* to."

His fingers started moving again, traveling down the contour of her cheek, the line of her jaw. "So what will you do? If you're living in Corcannon for the rest of your life."

She smiled in the dark. "Well, I don't want to sound overconfident, but I feel pretty certain that Madeleine will be happy to keep me on for as long as I want a job."

"She might want to live in Chibain on the Curval estates."

Jayla considered that. "She might. At least part of the time. But her heart is in the city. She'll always come back." She shifted to her side so she was facing him. "What about you?"

"I never want to leave the city."

"You said you would," she reminded him. "Before. You said you would come with me if I needed to run away."

"And I still would," he said. "If you needed to run away again." He took a deep breath. "If I would leave for you, would you stay for me?"

She was not used to giving promises. She was accustomed to concluding transactions, honoring commitments, and holding up her end of a bargain, but she liked to have the terms defined and the parameters clear. She preferred a timeline and an end point. She wanted clarity.

Love was messy and unpredictable, chaotic and mutable. How could she be sure she had the required skills, when it was a job she had never attempted before? How could she be certain she wouldn't fail, wouldn't simply walk away, the work unfinished, the contract broken?

“I want to,” she said. “But I’m so afraid I won’t get it right.”

He kissed her, gently and with infinite sweetness. “I’m afraid, too,” he said. “But I’m more afraid of not trying.”

“Then maybe that’s what we do.”

“What?”

She leaned in and kissed him. “We try.”

“Then you’ll stay?”

“I’ll stay. With you.”

Chapter Thirty-nine: Brandon

It was early winter in the islands, which meant day after day of sullen sky, raw wind, and spitting rain. As was the custom, everyone in the village grumbled good-naturedly about the weather any time an opportunity for conversation arose.

"Outside for five minutes to dig in the yard, and I thought my fingers would freeze off."

"Woke up this morning, looked out the window, and just went back to bed."

"If you're taking the path down to the road, be careful—big muddy patch just sprang up overnight, what with all the rain."

But Brandon never heard Villette utter a single word of complaint.

It had been two months since they arrived at the settlement that stretched along a thin border of arable land between the steep border of the coastline and the hills that hulked in the center of the island. They had been exhausted and anxious after more than two weeks of hard travel down roads that grew narrower and less hospitable with every fifty miles they made it from the city.

Despite the dramatic events of their final night in Corcannon, they could not be entirely certain that the high divine would believe Villette was dead. They could not be sure that the temple guards were not in close pursuit. Every two or three days, they switched up their mode of travel, selling horses, buying new ones, hiring a carriage, taking a public coach. Every time they stopped at an inn for the night, they registered under different names. If the town was big enough, they slept in separate establishments. They wore unremarkable clothing, only used coins of small denominations, made no special requests.

It still would be possible to trace them, Brandon knew, but only with a great deal of effort. And only if the high divine believed they were alive.

Not until they arrived in the village where he had grown up did they draw any attention, and then they made quite a stir. But that was only because Brandon's parents and brothers and cousins and friends were so happy to see him home, two years after he'd gone off to seek his fortune in the wide, mysterious world.

"You finally realized there's nothing so special about Corcannon after all," his father said. "Everything you need is right here."

"Got tired of being the island boy that all the city folks made fun of," his older brother teased him. "Did they always tell you that you smelled like fish and brine? Because you *do.*"

"Being a soldier is too much hard work, I suppose," one of his cousins said. "You'd rather lie in a boat all day and hope the fish bite."

Everyone had been agog with curiosity about the Cordelano he'd brought home with him, a woman who reeked of wealth and privilege despite her worn clothing and tired face. Islanders had a strong respect for privacy, so Brandon knew that no one would pester Villette with questions, and he figured that very few would come right out and ask him for details. Clearly, all the villagers assumed the two of them had eloped because Villette's family didn't consider a Zessin boy to be good enough for their daughter.

But his mother looked from Brandon to Villette and back to Brandon, and seemed to guess the whole story. Oh, not the part where Villette carried the blood of the god in her veins. Not the part where Villette had been imprisoned by powerful enemies and assigned to play a great and terrible role in the fate of the world. But she looked at this beautiful, proud, strong, fragile, haunted, hopeful creature, and she looked at her son, and she seemed to *know.* That the woman had needed rescuing and that the man had rescued her and that, even now, they feared they were not entirely safe.

"Villette will stay with us for a while," his mother had said. His mother had a decent command of Cordish and Brandon had taught Villette some rudimentary Zessin, so the two women had already been able to hold a halting conversation. "You will sleep at your brother's. We'll talk about more permanent arrangements later."

She sent Villette directly to bed that first afternoon, and spent the next few days fussing over her, feeding her, and assembling for her an entire wardrobe of loose trousers and embroidered smocks. The first time Brandon saw Villette in a simple handmade island outfit, with her dark hair pulled back and her face at peace, he thought he might not have recognized her if he passed her on the streets of Corcannon.

"Thank you for taking such good care of her," he said to his mother as she walked him halfway back to his brother's house one evening a week after their arrival. It was a cold, wet fall day, a hint of the miserable season to come, but they were taking their time with the stroll. His mother always preferred to speak the hard words outdoors, whether she was asking for a favor or relating the news of an uncle's fatal illness.

"I like her," said his mother. "Her troubles have made her kind, not cruel. That's not always the way it goes."

"Has she told you about her troubles?"

"No, and I don't ask her to. But I can tell she's had them." She put a hand on his arm. "I'm proud of you for helping her."

"You don't know that I did."

"I know."

They walked on a few more yards in silence. "So do you think to marry her?" she asked.

Brandon's breath huffed out in a sound that might have been a laugh or might have been a sigh. "I would," he said. "But I don't want to ask her."

"You don't think she'd accept you?"

"Oh, I think she would. But not for the right reasons."

"You think gratitude is a poor substitute for love."

He glanced at her sharply. That was it exactly. "She feels like she owes me her life. I don't want to make her spend the rest of her years paying off that debt."

"So you'd send her out somewhere in the world to make her own way, just because you're too proud to accept a gift?"

He came to a halt in the middle of the path. They were passing a long open stretch of land that supported a range of crops in milder weather; the setting sun cast molten light over dead cornstalks, muddy furrows, and his mother's calm, stern face. "What do you mean?"

"I think she feels gratitude toward you, yes. And that's a different emotion from love—true again. But I don't think that's all there is to it. You're her safe harbor. You're the one she can lean against when all other supports are gone. I see it in her face. She is always gracious, always sweet, but she's edgy. She's uneasy. Until you come to the house. And then she relaxes. Then she smiles. You're the one person she trusts, the one person she believes in. It would be an unkindness to rip that stability away from her."

He gestured around at the empty land, each house so far from the other the lights were barely visible from one front door to the other. At this time of night, with everything else so quiet, it was possible to hear the ceaseless slap and drag of the ocean against the rocks below. "I can't ask her to stay someplace like this the rest of her life!"

"Where do you think she wants to go?"

"I don't know! Somewhere! Where she can find music—and people—and all the things she deserves—"

"And will she feel safe there?"

He stared down at his mother, at the small, clear features so similar to his own. He had never seen her agonize over a dilemma, never seen her walk away from a difficult decision or hide from a bitter truth. He had always wished he could see the world half as clearly. "I love her," he said. "More than anything."

"Then you'd better take care of her."

His father owned a small property on the far edge of town, a place he'd bought from his sister when her youngest son moved to the southernmost island to marry. The tiny house had been taken over by spiders and mice, while the gardens had surrendered to weeds, nettles, and creeping vines. But the roof was solid and the well water was fresh, and three days of concerted effort by Brandon's entire family had cleared the place both inside and out. Everyone had some piece of castoff furniture to donate—a bedframe that needed just a minor repair, a chair that could be rethatched, a set of dishes with only a few missing pieces. Brandon's sister-in-law made a set of scarlet curtains and his cousin's wife presented them with a quilt of countless colors.

"I cannot imagine ever living someplace that I would love more," Villette told him when he showed her around the day before they were married.

"It's small—"

She kissed him. "It feels so much bigger than my prison in the city."

"And plain—"

She kissed him again. "Every stitch of fabric is beautiful. Every scrap of wood gleams."

"It's just that I want to give you everything," he said.

She put her arms around him and leaned back so she could see his face. "Brandon," she said, "that's exactly what you've done."

The wedding had been a month ago, and since that day, the islands had shown them nothing but rain and wind and dreary skies. Then one morning they woke up to sunshine streaming so brightly through the window that it turned the red curtains a hazy pink.

"It won't last long," Brandon said, as they rose and dressed with alacrity, packing a basket of food and folding up a couple of blankets. "We need to get out there now."

They took a steep, narrow path that led from the back edge of their field straight to the edge of the cliff that overlooked the ocean. There was a rocky and perilous track that descended all the way to the stony beach below, but Villette hadn't yet had the courage to try it, and Brandon wanted to wait until spring weather to shore it up with footholds and railings. But shortly after they'd moved in, they'd found a natural windbreak carved into the hill, a low, curved cup of land where two people could hunker down with their backs against a boulder and their faces turned toward the sea. On the few pretty days that had been granted to them since their wedding, they had hurried down to this spot to enjoy the sun on their faces and the salt wind in their hair.

Now they spread out one blanket to sit on, and curled up under the second one, their arms around each other and their heads touching. The sunlight shone so fiercely on the water that Brandon had to squint against the glare; it was as if the whole ocean was a mosaic of moving mirrored tiles. The breeze was brisk but not unfriendly. Under the blanket, pressed against Villette, he almost felt warm.

"I never get tired of the view," she murmured. "I don't know how you ever convinced yourself to move away."

"I thought I was looking for something else," he said.

She smiled at him. "And did you find it?"

"It seems I did."

She snuggled against him, quiet for a moment, but he knew her well enough by now to realize she had something on her mind and was trying to decide how to say it. He waited, lifting his head just enough to feel the sunlight slide along his cheekbone, his chin.

"For so long," she said, "there was one thing I was afraid of more than anything else."

"The high divine."

"No. Well, yes, I was afraid of him, but afraid of what he would make me do. I thought the worst thing that could happen to me, the thing that would break my heart, would be to get pregnant. To bring a child into the world."

"I can understand that."

"But now—that's the one thing I want most in the world."

He thought his heart might stop. "You want—"

She turned in his arms, raised a hand to his face. "Brandon," she whispered, "I'm going to have your baby."

He couldn't breathe, he couldn't think, and for a moment all he could do was stare into that hopeful, watchful, fearful, beloved face. Then he shouted with delight and snatched her closer, and they laughed and cried and hugged each other so hard they dislodged half a dozen stones and almost kicked the picnic basket over the edge of the cliff. But Brandon whooped and rescued it, and Villette reached in to pull out the bottle of seagrass wine she had packed along with the cheese and biscuits. They toasted each other and the baby to come and the glorious life ahead of them. And then they wrapped their arms around each other again and burrowed under the blankets and gave no more thought to the miraculous sun or the resplendent view.

They never turned their eyes back to the ocean, so they never saw the slim shape that sliced up from the depths and burst into the bright air in a clean golden arc. Once, twice, a dozen times, performing an elaborate dance across the dazzling waters. Later that night, they would hear other villagers claim to have spotted Keshalosha along the shoreline, tell each other excitedly that this meant Zessaya would shower them with good fortune for the coming year, maybe the rest of their lives. They didn't see, but it hardly mattered. The fish flashed through the air one more time, so high it reached the level of the cliff top, and seemed to pause for just a moment midair. Maybe its jewel-green eyes turned toward the two people sheltering in the rocky outcrop, so engrossed in each other they had no time to notice favors handed out by the goddess. Maybe it flipped its tail and cast off droplets of water in a spray of watery diamonds before diving back into the icy ocean and disappearing under the glittering surface.

Brandon didn't notice. The goddess had reached out a hand and reordered his life, mapping out a destiny he would never have dreamed of. He didn't require omens. He already had all the proof he would ever need.

ABOUT THE AUTHOR

Sharon Shinn has published 30 novels, three short fiction collections, and one graphic novel since she joined the science fiction and fantasy world in 1995. She has written about angels, shape-shifters, elemental powers, magical portals, and echoes. She has won the William C. Crawford Award for Outstanding New Fantasy Writer, a Reviewer's Choice Award from the *Romantic Times*, and the 2010 RT Book Reviews Career Achievement Award in the Science Fiction/ Fantasy category. Follow her at SharonShinnBooks on Facebook or visit her website at sharonshinn.net.

OTHER TITLES FROM FAIRWOOD PRESS

No Enemy but Time
by Michael Bishop
trade paper $19.99
ISBN: 978-1-933846-19-4

Dark Dreaming
by Jack Cady & Carol Orlock
trade paper $17.99
ISBN: 978-1-933846-20-0

A Slice of the Dark
by Karen Heuler
trade paper $18.99
ISBN: 978-1-933846-22-4

Geometries of Belonging
by R.B. Lemberg
trade paper $18.99
ISBN: 978-1-958880-01-2

Hellhounds
by David Sandner &
Jacob Weisman
small paperback $9.00
ISBN: 978-1-958880-02-9

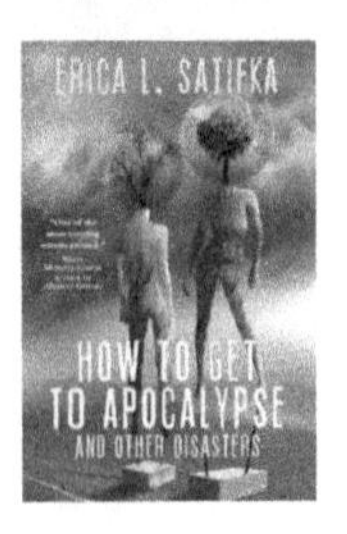

How to Get to Apocalypse
and Other Disasters
by Erica L. Satifka
trade paper $17.99
ISBN: 978-1-933846-95-8

Rain Music
by Patrick Swenson
Ltd hardcover $28; trade $17.99
ISBN: 978-1-933846-14-9
978-1-933846-13-2

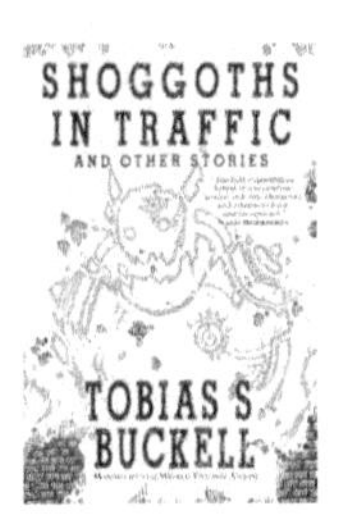

Shoggoths in Traffic
and Other Stories
by Tobias S. Buckell
trade paper $17.99
ISBN: 978-1-933846-18-7

Find us at:
www.fairwoodpress.com
Bonney Lake, Washington

CPSIA information can be obtained
at www.ICGtesting.com
Printed in the USA
BVHW080010011222
653122BV00009B/44

9 781958 880005